MADNESS
OF THE
FALLEN

THE GODLING CHRONICLES

MADNESS OF THE FALLEN

BRIAN D. ANDERSON

4 Horsemen
Publications, Inc.

Published By: 4 Horsemen Publications, Inc.

4 Horsemen Publications, Inc.
PO Box 417
Sylva, NC 28779
4horsemenpublications.com
info@4horsemenpublications.com

Cover & Typesetting by Autumn Skye
Edited by Joseph Mistretta

Paperback ISBN-13: 979-8-8232-0539-9

Hardcover ISBN-13: 979-8-8232-0540-5

DEDICATION

For Kyle DiBattista. May your future hold a life of magic and wonders. I have no doubt that all your dreams will come true.

CONTENTS

PROLOGUE

Basanti kneeled at the edge of the tree line, watching with tear-filled eyes as a farmer tilled the soft, rich soil of his field, his horse tossing its head up and down in protest at the crack of the reins and weight of the plowshare. In the far distance, a woman and two young children—no older than three and four—were busy feeding the chickens running free in front of a dilapidated dwelling.

"Why do you do this to yourself?" asked a hushed voice from behind her. "Why do you still come here?"

"It's gone, Yanti," she replied through stifled sobs. "It's gone."

"It's been more than fifty years," he said, kneeling beside her. His voice was tender and understanding as he placed his arm around her and pulled her close. "People were already settling in this area even then."

Basanti laid her head on her brother's shoulder. "I know. I should have moved them years ago. It's my fault."

"There was nothing to move," he said, brushing her hair from her face. "Only stone markers. Their bodies wasted away a long time ago."

"I know," she repeated. "But it comforted me to know that this place was undisturbed. And now that the end is coming..." She looked into Yanti's eyes, a sad smile on her lips. "I just wanted to see it one last time."

"The end is *not* coming," he told her sternly. "They won't find us."

"We're the last." Her voice trembled. "How can you think we'll escape?" She looked a final time over the field where once, long ago, she had buried their parents and siblings. Then, with effortless grace, she rose to her feet and turned to the forest. "They hate us too much to allow us to live. They're monsters."

Yanti moved in front of her and took her hands. "They're fools and brutes. And I will not allow them or anyone else to harm you. I swear it."

"Don't you see?" said Basanti. "They have enslaved the humans and hunted us to the brink of extinction. There is nothing that can stop them. Not even the gods."

Yanti's lip curled, and he sniffed with contempt. "The gods don't care about us ... or anything else. It's the gods who allowed the elves to slaughter us. It's the gods who allowed the humans to be turned into a race of slaves ... and I hate them."

"Don't say that," she scolded. "It was the gods who gave us a new life."

Yanti glared. "And now we are fighting desperately to keep it."

Basanti looked deeply into her brother's eyes for a moment and smiled. "Whatever happens, I'm glad you are with me."

He returned the smile and embraced her. "As am I. Had you not convinced Pósix to change me, I would be dust in the field as well. For that, at least, I am grateful."

They made their way through the forest and around the small farm. Yanti stopped from time to time to listen for signs of elf patrols. They were heading north to the mountains, where they hoped the rough terrain and harsh climate would discourage those who still pursued them. By nightfall, both of them felt it was best to continue, their endurance not having reached its limits. The moon was full in the cloudless sky, but a cool breeze from the north caused Basanti to retrieve a wool blanket from her pack and wrap it tightly around herself.

Yanti looked at his sister with concern. "We can stop and build a fire if you would like."

Basanti gave a slight shiver and then laughed. "I'm fine. But I never did like the cold, even when I was a girl."

Yanti chuckled. "I remember."

Childhood memories of crawling into bed with Yanti on cold winter nights flashed through her mind. He was the eldest and the first to have his own bed. She had always felt safe with him. She loved her other three brothers and older sister, but Yanti understood her far better than anyone. He was always kind and gentle, even when she was being annoying. That was why she had begged Pósix to change him. The thought of immortality without Yanti had been unbearable.

They paused beneath a thick oak to take a short meal of honeyed flatbread and dried apricots. Suddenly, Yanti's back went stiff, and he leaped to his feet. Basanti quickly moved to his side and listened carefully.

"Elves," whispered Yanti almost inaudibly.

Basanti heard it too. A group of six elves was moving stealthily through the brush a quarter mile to the north. She prayed they would pass them by, but in less than a minute, it was clear her prayer would go unheeded. The elves split into three groups and began to circle around their position. Her heart sank. Even with their immense speed, she and her brother would not be able to escape. Though brutes, elves were expert trackers, and their speed in the forests was unparalleled.

Yanti reached in his belt and drew a small dagger.

Basanti looked at him in shock. "You mustn't. It's forbidden."

"What would you have me do?" he shot back. "I will not allow them to harm you."

"I don't know, but I would rather die than have you do this." Her voice was soft, but filled with resolve. She reached out and took the blade from his hand, tossing it quickly onto the ground as if it had burned her skin. Her lip curled in disgust. "We will not become what they accuse us of being."

Grumbling in frustration, Yanti took hold of Basanti's hand. "Then we must run."

The words had barely passed his lips when the elves rushed toward them. Although still several hundred yards away, they were covering the distance with blinding speed. Yanti grabbed his sister, shoving her ahead of him. They ran left in an attempt to pass between the elves before they were able to close in. The trees whizzed by as they deftly threaded the dense forest, and for a moment he thought they might make it. Then, from another quarter mile away, he heard the nimble footfalls of eight more elves drawing near.

Yanti let out a primal scream and ran even harder, passing Basanti and dragging her behind him. They managed to slip between the first six pursuers, but the elves ahead spread out while those behind regrouped and gave chase. Fear gripped their hearts. It was rapidly becoming clear that escape was impossible.

An arrow struck Basanti's shoulder, sending her crashing to the ground. In a single motion, Yanti jerked out the arrow and lifted his sister to her feet. She screamed as the shaft ripped free. But her cry had barely faded when another deadly missile struck, this time into her left thigh. She dropped to her knees.

The song of steel sliding from scabbards echoed through the forest as the elves came into view, their fierce gazes fixed resolutely on their prey while spreading out to encircle the pair. Basanti looked desperately at Yanti. The sight of fear in her eyes sent him into a rage unlike anything he had ever experienced. The sinews of his legs tightened, and he sprang forward just as the first attacker reached them.

Yanti's fist smashed into his jaw, bones cracking under the impact. The elf's head twisted and his body was sent flying several feet before crashing onto the forest floor. The other elves slid to a halt, stunned expressions on their faces.

Reaching down, Yanti picked up the short blade dropped by the unconscious elf. He took a step back, placing himself between the remaining elves and his sister. He could hear her weeping and begging for him to stop. But it was far too late for that.

"You shall hunt us no longer!" Yanti shouted defiantly. This was the first time he had held such a weapon. It felt strangely awkward in his hand.

"This one fights!" yelled one of the elves.

Yanti did not wait for them to recover their senses. He charged at his closest adversary, hacking wildly. The strength of his blow made up for his lack of skill, and for the first time, he caused blood to flow. His blade cut his foe nearly in half, from the shoulder to hip. In a single motion, he jerked it free and ran headlong at the next elf. Warm spots of his enemy's blood splattered across his face, stirring in his heart a wild lust to spill more. He could feel himself growing stronger as seconds passed like minutes and smiled inwardly at the sensation.

Two elves closed in, but his newfound power made them appear as fumbling children. He gutted them both with lethal grace and unbridled fury. He searched for another opponent, but the rest had backed away, hurrying to remove the bows from their backs. Yanti wasn't about to give them that chance. He spanned the distance in a flash, taking the arm off one elf and the head off another. Then he heard Basanti scream out in terror. Spinning around, he saw another of the enemy holding a blade across her throat.

"Lay down your sword, Vrykol!" commanded the elf. "Or I will take her head."

Hearing the ancient language of his people spoken from elf lips made his mouth curl in disgust. "Harm her and I will cut you to pieces." He could see the fear in Basanti's eyes, but there was something else as well. Her mind was begging him to obey.

No more, she pleaded.

Behind him, Yanti could hear bowstrings being drawn.

Better to die, her inner voice cried out.

The elf pressed the blade to Basanti's flesh, causing a thin trickle of blood to run down her neck. Blocking out his sister's voice, Yanti covered the distance between them with unearthly speed and drove his sword hard into the elf's chest. No sooner had he done this than the thwack of bows being loosed was followed by the hiss of arrows. He twisted and dove hard down, but three deadly missiles had already buried themselves deep into his back. He let out a tormented roar as his body slid across the ground. Pain was raging through him, but he still somehow managed to rise to his knees and turn. The remaining elves had dropped their bows and were drawing their swords, vengeance flaming in their eyes.

Yanti glanced at Basanti, who gave him a sad, forgiving smile. A sudden wave of regret washed over him. He found himself unable to look at her any longer. Closing his eyes, he drew a deep breath and waited for the elf blades to release his spirit.

It was then that he heard a sharp thud. His eyes snapped open. One of the advancing elves had fallen. Then another dropped, and another, until only two remained standing. Gripped by a sudden panic, they turned and ran, disappearing into the forest.

Stunned, Yanti stared after them for a moment before crawling over to Basanti, the arrows spitefully digging themselves deeper with every small movement.

She had already pulled the arrow from her body. "Turn around." Her voice was soothing and filled with pity.

Yanti obeyed, never once taking his eyes off their surroundings even as the cruel arrows were pulled free, the tips taking with them a measure of ruined flesh. Whatever had struck down the elves could very well now be coming for them. The snap of a twig from behind a nearby pine tree forced him to his feet, the pain ignored. Basanti reached up and grabbed his sleeve, clinging desperately.

"No more bloodshed," she cried.

"There is nothing to fear," called a voice. It was rich and deep and spoke in the ancient tongue.

"Show yourself," commanded Yanti. His muscles tensed as he realized that he had dropped his sword several feet away.

"Of course." From behind a tree, though far to the left of where Yanti had first heard the voice, stepped a young human male. He looked to be no older than twenty, with shoulder-length flaxen hair and a golden brown complexion. His ice-blue eyes twinkled, and his bright smile was friendly and warm. A white cotton, open-necked shirt, and blue trousers were well fitted to his athletic frame, and though not exceptionally tall, his broad shoulders and thin waist gave him the illusion of greater height. He moved with nimble, effortless ease, quickly spanning the distance between them.

Basanti gasped. "You ... you're beautiful."

Yanti looked at her, his brow furrowed. "What are you talking about? It's just a human."

Basanti cocked her head, looking confused. "A human? Are you blind? No human looks like that."

The newcomer laughed. "He can no longer see. The taint that now inhabits his spirit has blinded him."

Yanti was not amused. "Who are you?"

The man bowed low, his gaze fixed on Basanti. "I am Felsafell."

"I have heard the name," she said. "Though the stories that surround it are ... well ... unbelievable."

Felsafell smiled. "And many are not to be believed. The lies of rumor can blacken a good name."

"It is said that you are the oldest being that walks in the world," said Yanti, doubt in his voice. "Yet you look little more than a boy."

"And how old were you when the gods changed you?" Felsafell countered. "Twenty-five? You look young, yet you have lived for many lifetimes."

"How can you doubt him, Yanti?" asked Basanti. "Can you not see that he is something ... different?" She struggled to her feet and took a step forward.

"He cannot," said Felsafell, with a hint of sadness. "His crimes have taken his sight." He looked at Yanti. "Can you not feel it?"

Yanti sneered. "And what is it that you think you know about me—or my sister?"

"I know that you were created by the gods to shepherd human and elf through this world," he replied.

"Then you know nothing," shot Yanti. "Elves are our enemy. They have hunted us, and all like us, until we are all that remains."

Felsafell shook his head slowly and sighed. "I know it may seem so. But I assure you that Pósix never intended for you to abandon elf kind. That the Vrykol, as they have named you, ignored them is why their hatred for you has festered."

Yanti fumed. "So all of this is *our* fault?"

Felsafell shrugged. "In a way, yes. You became obsessed with freedom for humans—guiding them against their masters—rather than influencing the elves to change their hearts."

Yanti glared. "It is not you that they hunt, and it is not you they have enslaved."

"True," said Felsafell. "But it is not me who violated the laws of my maker. Your actions have justified those of your enemy. They feared your immortality and your power. Now you have shown them they were right to fear."

"And what should I have done?" shouted Yanti. "Allow them to slaughter us?"

Basanti touched Yanti's hand. "Yes, dear brother. You should have."

He turned to his sister, an incredulous look on his face. "What are you saying? You would have me permit them to cut off your head?"

She cupped his face in her hands. "I'm saying that I would rather die than have you spill blood in my name. Felsafell is right. What you have done has changed you. I can see it now."

"Tell your brother what you see when you look at me," said Felsafell.

She didn't take her eyes off Yanti. "I see a being with ebony skin, long silver hair, and striking features: elegant, almost elf-like ears and piercing gray eyes. But I also see the human that he chooses to appear."

Yanti struggled to break his sister's gaze and looked at Felsafell. "Why can't I...?"

"Your actions wounded you," explained Felsafell. His tone was like a father speaking to a confused child. "It has left you vulnerable."

Yanti clenched his fists, his knuckles turning white. "Vulnerable to what?"

"Look at you now," said Felsafell. "Can you not feel the anger in your heart? The blackness?"

A tear ran down Yanti's face. Catching it with the tip of his finger, he smeared it between his thumb and forefinger, staring at the dampness with a mixture of sorrow and fury. "What would you have me do? I cannot change what has happened."

"You must leave," said Felsafell. "You must stay away from your sister. If you do not, you will certainly bring violence with you."

Basanti stepped in front of Yanti, her gaze defiant. "I will not be parted from him. No matter what he has done, he is my brother."

Felsafell smiled. "You must." His eyes shifted across to settle on Yanti. "And in his heart, he knows it, too."

He reached out and placed a hand on Yanti's shoulder. "I will protect her. I will weave a legend and spread it throughout the land so that she will be kept safe."

"What legend?" asked Yanti.

"Better that you do not know," he replied. "But rest assured that the protection of Felsafell, last of the *firstborn*, is not a thing to be taken lightly. While I live, no harm will come to her."

The elves began to moan and stir.

"But you must decide quickly," continued Felsafell. "I have only incapacitated those you did not kill. Soon they will wake, and we must be gone."

"And what of my brother?" asked Basanti, gripping Yanti's hand, tears streaming down her cheeks.

There was a long moment of silence. Finally, Yanti lowered his head and gave a long sigh. "He's right. You must go with him. My crimes have changed me. I can feel the wound inside." He backed away several paces. "I will always love you, my dear sister."

Basanti immediately rushed back and threw her arms around him, clinging tightly. "No! You cannot. I will not let you."

Taking hold of her shoulders, he gently eased her away from him. "I must. But don't worry. We will see each other again one day. Until then, I must try to heal my wounds." His eyes shifted to Felsafell. "Watch over her and keep her safe."

After a final tearful embrace, without any real knowledge of where he was heading, he quickly turned and ran off through the forest.

Felsafell took Basanti's hand. "Come. We must hurry."

She wiped the tears from her eyes as the figure of her brother disappeared. "Will he be all right?"

"Yanti's path is unclear," he replied. "But I suspect he was right. You shall see each other again."

"Where will we go?" she asked.

Felsafell pointed north. "We go to the mountains. There, we will create your legend."

CHAPTER 1

King Lousis stared despondently over the ruined battle-field. Countless columns of thick, black smoke rose skyward, serving as a reminder of the carnage that the Reborn King's armies had wrought. The smell of burned timbers and charred flesh filled his nostrils, making him want to empty his stomach.

His thoughts turned to High Lady Selena. Each day, he was filled with more and more doubt that he would be able to keep his promise to her and return alive.

The cries of the wounded and dying raked at his ears and seemed to surround him. The hilly and broken terrain had forced them to set up dozens of small healing areas rather than create just one in a single location. The healers were doing their best to tend to the overwhelming numbers put in their care, but they had not the tents nor pavilions to accommodate everyone.

Lousis's guard stood a few feet away, their faces showing increasing signs of despair and fatigue. Since they had joined the southern armies, these men had saved his life on three separate occasions. But the cost was high. Six of them had so far paid with their own lives in order to ensure his survival. Angrääl's new weapon had made every inch of the battlefield a deadly place to be.

A rider approached from the north, his face smeared with grime and blood. One of the king's guards leapt in front of the horse, while the rest surrounded their lord. Lousis waved them off and allowed the man to come near.

The rider dismounted and bowed on unsteady legs. "I bear ill news, Your Highness."

Lousis sighed heavily. It seemed as if he had received nothing but ill news ever since leaving Althetas.

"The royal caravan was attacked on the road north," said the messenger, his voice wavering. "All but King Victis were either captured or killed."

The words hit Lousis like a blacksmith's hammer. "Are you certain?"

"I am," he replied. "King Victis is an hour behind me. He sent me ahead to bring you the news. He would have rode harder, but he has captured one of the enemy weapons and fears what may happen if it's treated roughly."

"What of his army?" asked Lousis.

"They flee north, led by Lord Chiron," he replied. "Angrääl is giving chase, but Lord Chiron has been able to stay ahead of them ... for now."

Lousis's jaw tightened. "Is there anything else?"

The man shook his head.

Lousis dismissed the messenger, then made his way to his horse. The ride to his tent was short, yet hard to bear. Anguish showed clearly on his face as he passed the ever-increasing number of makeshift hospitals.

Eftichis awaited him just outside the tent, his armor stained with dried blood and much damaged from enemy blades. "Angrääl has retreated south for the time being," the elf said. "But driving them back has cost us dearly."

The king grunted. "I do not need you to point out the obvious." He pushed his way past and entered the tent with Eftichis close behind.

"Forgive me, Your Highness," Eftichis said, lowering his eyes.

Lousis sat down heavily in a chair that had been placed beside his cot. He rubbed the bridge of his nose and shook his head. "No. Forgive me, my friend. I should not be harsh with you. But the past several weeks have not gone as I had hoped." He told the elf about the fate of the southern rulers.

Eftichis listened grimly. "At least it is good that King Victis escaped, and that he has obtained one of the enemy's weapons. Perhaps we can learn its secrets."

"I pray we can," agreed Lousis.

The sight of his lines being blasted apart by the fiery bolts was still fresh in his mind. After the first explosion, he imagined that Angräal had somehow gained the same ability as Darshan. But that quickly changed when he spotted the enemy catapults sending white balls streaking across the sky—one after another. Almost as soon as they struck the ground, a fireball burst forth, ripping apart flesh and bone and scattering his lines like leaves in the wind. Without Darshan, he knew there was little hope for victory. Nehrutu and Aaliyah had still not arrived from the south, so Lousis could only assume they were still engaged with Angräal, or worse…

He pushed the thought from his mind and reached under his cot to retrieve a bottle of wine.

"Join me," he said to Eftichis.

The elf nodded and took a chair from the corner. For an hour they sat quietly, passing the bottle back and forth while Lousis tried hard to block out the sounds of the battle's aftermath that continued to drift relentlessly into the tent.

He was still sitting wearily when King Victis entered. The slumped shoulders and dark circles under the new arrival's eyes caused Lousis to spring up and help his friend into the vacated chair.

Victis was unable to protest and groaned as he leaned back. "Thank you. This old body is ill-suited to such hardships." He eyed the wine in Eftichis's hand, who immediately handed the bottle to the king. After a long drink, he closed his eyes and sighed with relief. "It's strange how such simple pleasures become infinitely more important in dark times." He handed Lousis the bottle. "I assume you received my message."

Lousis nodded slowly. "Do you know how many survived?"

Victis grimaced and shook his head. "I had just departed to bring you the enemy weapon we had found when I heard the battle erupt behind me. If I had stayed behind just one minute longer, I too would have suffered the same fate. All I could do was watch from the tree line as Angrääl soldiers swarmed over the caravan." He held his head in his hands. "It's my fault. I told them we should flee north. My cowardice doomed them all."

"You did the only thing you could," said Lousis. "There was no way for you to know what would happen." He placed his hand on Victis' shoulder. "And this is no time to despair. What is the state of your forces?"

Victis took a deep breath. "Nearly destroyed; fewer than fifteen thousand swords. What remains is fighting its way east to join you here—but I doubt they will make it. Angrääl moves to cut us in half and surround us. They level every city and burn every village as they march, their infernal weapon causing the bravest to flee. There is no refuge." His eyes were pleading. "How do we fight such an enemy without Darshan to aid us?"

"With heart and courage," interjected Eftichis. "Nehrutu and Aaliyah will come, and Theopolou will not fail us in the north. Besides, Darshan *will* return."

Victis shook his head. "I wish I had your spirit. There has been no word from Nehrutu or Theopolou. For all we know, we are alone. And as for Darshan ... he has his own battles to fight."

There was a long silence. Then Lousis held out his hand. "Come," he said. "Show me the enemy weapon."

The old king gratefully took hold of Lousis's hand and heaved himself up. He led them outside to where five soldiers stood facing outward in a tight circle. All around them, the camp was beginning to buzz with renewed activity as the commanders made plans for the next assault.

"Where is the enemy now?" asked Victis.

"The elves are driving them south about five miles from here while we recover," Louis replied. "But they will return soon. I've ordered scouts posted to inform me of their movements."

Victis looked around disapprovingly. "It seems you are scattered. Can you even withstand another assault?"

"Not if it came at this very moment," admitted Lousis. "They blasted our lines and decimated our heavy horse. It will take until nightfall to regroup—if not longer."

A runner approached and bowed to King Lousis. "The elves are returning, Your Highness. They wish me to inform you that the enemy is in retreat for now, though it has been at a tremendous cost."

Lousis sighed heavily. "Let us hope they have bought us the time we need."

The circle of guards surrounding the captured weapon parted to make way for the two monarchs and Eftichis.

"And let us also hope that we can learn something from this," added Victis, pointing to a small wicker basket resting on the ground.

Inside the basket was a white ball about the size of a man's head. It looked to be made from cloth, though of a weave Lousis had never seen before. From the top protruded a thin black cord, with tar surrounding where it entered the ball.

Lousis bent down to run a finger over the surface. It was hard and smooth, almost as if made from steel. "We need to see what is inside of this," he said.

After a long moment of thought, he stood. "But we must be cautious. From what we have learned, they appear to light the black cord before hurling it at us. Whatever is within, I believe fire is what causes it to erupt."

Eftichis drew his dagger. "Then let us reveal its secrets." He motioned for the guards and the kings to move back.

Lousis opened his mouth to object, but the elf smiled and shook his head.

"If this is to be my end, so be it," he said. "Neither you nor King Victis can afford to be as careless with your lives as I can."

Bending down, Eftichis slowly dragged his blade across the weapon. The cloth snapped apart, causing the assembly to flinch. He pulled these folds back but found only another layer of the same material. Again and again, he repeated this cutting process until, finally, the center of the ball opened up. A cloud of black dust immediately spewed out. An unfamiliar scent filled the air.

"What is it?" asked Victis.

Eftichis dipped his dagger and scooped out a tiny bit of the black powder. Carefully, he stood up and showed it to the kings.

"Bring me a torch," ordered Lousis. A guard sped off, returning a minute later. Lousis took the torch and laid it on the ground. He nodded to Eftichis.

The elf tossed the powder onto the small flame. Instantly, a ball of fire flared up and then disappeared.

"By the gods," whispered Victis. "Have you ever seen such a thing?"

His words were met with stunned silence.

"If only a pinch can do that..." Eftichis shook his head. "With enough, the enemy could level mountains."

"They already have enough to raze a city," spat Victis. "They leave nothing untouched. Not a wall stands from here to the peninsula."

"We should give this to the elders," suggested Eftichis. "Perhaps they can unravel its mysteries."

Lousis rubbed his chin in thought. "Find Lady Bellisia. She is healing the wounded just north of here."

Eftichis nodded sharply before hurrying off with quick, determined steps.

"Have you any prisoners?" asked Victis. "Perhaps they would know something."

"We have a few," Lousis replied. "But even when tortured, they tell us nothing of value. Either they have superior will or, more likely, sensitive information is closely guarded. We have yet to capture anyone of sufficient rank or position who might know something useful."

"Then we can only trust that the wise among us can provide hope," said Victis solemnly, unable to take his eyes off the weapon. "One thing is certain—we cannot continue to sustain such massive losses."

Trumpets blared and orders were shouted as the army began to regroup half a mile to the south. The stench of sweat, steel, and scorched earth mingled to foul effect with the decay of ruined flesh. Nearly an hour passed before Eftichis returned with Bellisia. Her clothes were stained with blood and her eyes showed immeasurable fatigue. As she slowly drew closer, it was plain to see that the staff Gewey had given to her had now become a crutch.

She nodded to Lousis and Victis, and, without a word, kneeled down to examine the weapon. Stirring the powder with her fingertip, she put it to her tongue and then quickly spat it out in disgust. Letting out a soft groan, she stood up.

"Do you know what it is?" asked Lousis, desperation creeping into his voice.

"No," she replied weakly. "But there are scholars among my people who might. I shall send for them at once." Her legs wobbled. Eftichis was at her side in an instant.

"You must rest," said Lousis. "Give Eftichis the names and we will seek them out."

Bellisia nodded. "Yes. I should rest ... but I cannot. Too many lay dying, and even if my power is spent, I still have skill with herbs and salves." She glanced at the staff and shook her head. "Such a foul way to use this marvelous gift."

Once she had provided Eftichis with the names of the elf scholars, Lousis led Victis back to his tent. "You can share my accommodations," he said. "The other tents are being used by the healers."

Victis smiled and bowed his head. "I thank you, my old friend. I do need to rest. Perhaps my dreams will reveal what my waking mind cannot grasp."

The two kings sat in silence for a few minutes, sipping on a bottle of wine while contemplating events. Lousis then helped his friend into the bed. He watched over him until Victis' eyes closed and his breathing was deep and steady.

Satisfied, Lousis heaved himself up and left the tent. Mounting a waiting horse, he and his guard made their way a half mile south to where the army was regrouping. No longer was elf separate from human. The two peoples were now as one in their formed ranks. Had their plight not been so desperate, Lousis would have been gratified to see such camaraderie exist.

For hours he watched, with commanders and runners bearing reports on the progress being his only interruption. As the shadow of dusk crept over the land, Lousis felt a small sense of relief. Even Angrääl would not be so foolish as to attack elves in the dark. And being that the field was clear and the soldiers as ready as they could be, he almost wished that they would try. At least the battle would have hope of falling in their favor. However, elf seekers had reported that the enemy was not moving, seeming content to wait until daybreak to continue the slaughter.

By the time he returned to his tent, it was fully dark and Victis was still fast asleep. The enemy weapon had been taken away, presumably by the elf scholars.

He called for another bedroll to be brought and was just about to climb into it when a young, dirty-faced youth peeked his head through the tent flap. His eyes denoted urgency, so Lousis motioned for him to enter. The king sighed at the prospect of receiving yet more ill news.

"What is it?" he asked, trying not to sound irritated.

"Elves march from the north, Your Highness," said the boy. "They'll be here before dawn."

Lousis's jaw tightened. He knew this could be either a blessing or a curse. If Theopolou had succeeded in his mission, then this could be the reinforcements he so desperately needed. If not, it was surely the end. Before he could ask how the news came, the boy held out a small piece of parchment. Only with effort was he able to steady his hand before taking it. But as he read the words, a smile crept over his lips. At once, he leaped up and shook Victis awake.

Victis instinctively reached for the dagger in his belt but stopped as he realized who had woken him. Rubbing his eyes, he sat up, joints cracking in protest.

"The elves come!" Lousis told him excitedly. "Thirty thousand of them."

Victis looked confused. "The elves? From where?"

"From the north," he replied. "And they fly the banner of Darshan. It would seem Lord Theopolou has succeeded."

Victis sighed. "Thank the gods."

Lousis could see that Victis was still in no condition to do anything other than rest. "I will leave you and spread the word," he said.

Victis nodded and smiled before lying back down. "Wake me before they arrive."

Lousis leaned over to give his friend's arm a fond squeeze. "Of course."

With renewed vigor, he left the tent and ordered that the news be spread throughout the camp, and to the front lines.

Hope had returned to his heart, and for the first time in weeks, despair did not rule him.

CHAPTER 2

Nehrutu stumbled through the hard-packed sands of the beach, his vision blurred by exhaustion. The stench spreading out from the burned timbers of his once proud fleet attacked his nostrils, threatening to drive him mad with rage and sorrow.

He felt a firm tap on his shoulder.

"Lord Nehrutu," said a young human soldier. "The seekers have returned."

"I have not the strength to speak to them now," he replied. The small fire a few yards away was inviting, and the bedroll Aaliyah had set up for him looked soft and comforting.

"What should I tell them?" the soldier asked.

Nehrutu paused, then sighed. "Tell them to join me by the fire." He knew he must speak with them, regardless of his mood or condition.

He sat motionless by the fire, gazing blankly into the dancing flames. They were an awful reminder of his beloved ship's fate. He had watched in utter disbelief as, flaming from end to end, it sank into the deep waters. He now felt totally defeated. Even with Aaliyah by his side, he still couldn't help but fall into despair.

Never could he have imagined the devastation the enemy was able to unleash. Angrääl had waited until they were ashore before attacking. Then their ships sailed in and launched balls of infernal hell, one after another, onto their decks. The explosions were unbelievable to behold. He could feel his fellow elves trying desperately to use the *flow* to repel the attack, but Vrykol had gathered on the deck of every enemy ship, rendering their powers useless. Only a very few of their vessels had escaped the carnage.

Elf sailors who had spent a lifetime at sea now wandered along the shore, confused and despondent. Most of them had not set foot on dry land in hundreds of years. The navigators did their best to comfort their comrades, but it did little good.

There had barely been time to haul in the few survivors onto the beach before they were attacked from the north. Only the speed of the elves and the determination of their human allies prevented a total slaughter. It had taken two days to drive the enemy back, and the loss of life was beyond imagining.

The Angrääl ships had sailed away, but it mattered little. Their backs were to the sea, and an army that outnumbered them three-to-one was massed to their front.

Nehrutu could hear the nimble footfalls of the elf seekers approaching. He looked up to see three of them, all clad in soft leathers and wearing long knives. Following close behind was an elderly elf woman, her deep olive complexion unable to disguise her many years.

"Greetings, Lord Nehrutu," said the lead seeker.

It took a moment for Nehrutu to recall his name. "Greetings, Jahra. What news?"

"The enemy waits," he replied. "They seem content to allow us to remain here."

"They prevent us from aiding King Lousis," said Nehrutu. "They will defeat him in the north, then turn and crush us like worms."

"Where is Lady Aaliyah?" Jahra asked.

"Still tending the wounded." He rubbed his temple. "Her strength is far greater than mine."

Jahra motioned to the elf woman. "This is Kionia. She has come from the eastern elf lands."

The woman stepped forward and bowed. "I have brought healers with me to give further aid to the cause. I wish I could bring swords as well, but there are too few of us to defend our own homes as it is. All who could have already joined you here or with the humans in Althetas."

"I am sad to say that we are in dire need of healers," Nehrutu told her. "Your help is most welcome."

"My brothers and sister are already at work," said Kionia. She cast a sorrowful gaze to the north where the healing pavilions had been erected. "I should join them."

Nehrutu waited until she was out of earshot before turning his attention to the seekers. "Is there any way for us to get around the enemy?"

Jahra shook his head. "Not with so many. And they have Vrykol scattered throughout their ranks. Even if we could find a way around the humans, the foul beasts would detect us."

"I need to send word to King Lousis of our situation," said Nehrutu. "Can this be done?"

The seeker thought for a long moment. "Perhaps. I may well be able to pass unnoticed if I go alone. But if I am caught, you will, of course, have no way of knowing that your message was not delivered."

In spite of his warning, Jahra appeared to be optimistic about his chances. Nonetheless, Nehrutu frowned. "I will not send you unless there is strong hope for success. I cannot afford to lose your talents."

"I will go," called a voice from a few yards away.

Nehrutu recognized Jraleel, a sailor from Aaliyah's destroyed vessel. His face was stone and carried a hint of fury. His strides were long and deliberate.

"I admire your bravery," said Jahra. "But you do not know these lands, and regardless of your powers, you are not trained as a seeker."

Jraleel squatted down beside Nehrutu, his eyes fixed on the seeker. "I have no intention of traveling by land. My kin and I can construct a small raft and follow the coast north."

Nehrutu placed his hand on Jraleel's shoulder. "Are you certain you can-"

"My heart is broken," he snapped, silencing Nehrutu. "My home is destroyed. My feet feel the solid earth for the first time in hundreds of years." His eyes welled with tears. "But I still live. And my duty to my people remains."

"Then I shall accompany you," the seeker said with obvious admiration. "You will need my help once you land."

"I am grateful for your company," said Jraleel. "As for the rest of my brothers and sisters, they are in need of vengeance." His expression grew dark. "They wish to fight."

"That wish will certainly be granted," said Nehrutu. "I have no intention of allowing Angrääl to cage us. One way or another, we *will* break through."

At that moment, he spotted Aaliyah approaching. A young human soldier was walking by her side to steady her as she trod wearily on the sand. Her shoulders drooped and her delicate fingers clutched at the soldier's arm. When only a few feet away from the fire, she dismissed her escort. Without a word, she took a seat beside Nehrutu, allowing herself to lean against his sinewy shoulder.

The seekers and the sailor quickly excused themselves. Aaliyah didn't appear to notice.

"Bond with me," she whispered, closing her eyes.

Nehrutu wrapped his arms around her and pulled her close.

"I know we decided to wait until we returned home so we could share our joy with our families," she continued. "But I fear we will never see our shores again. I would not die without your spirit within me."

"Nor would I," he replied softly. "And I only need to share my joy with *you*, my love." He kissed the top of her head.

Aaliyah sat up and gazed into his eyes. He could feel her spirit drawing near and allowed his will to submit. In just moments, the rush of her heart filled his soul. All at once, he understood true happiness. Renewed strength flowed into his limbs; he pulled her close and kissed her deeply. A tear fell as he fathomed the depths of sorrow that the war enveloping them had caused her. And yet he knew that her profound love for him was as unyielding as his was for her.

The parting of their lips left a lingering sensation of warmth, and the melding of their spirits made his mind reel.

Aaliyah rose. Her strength had returned as well. She gently pulled Nehrutu to his feet. "I have arranged for a wedding tent to be erected down the beach about a mile away."

"When did you do this?" he asked, but her only response was a loving smile.

Nehrutu knew he should be making plans to march his army north, but at that moment, his heart was ruling his actions. The world could burn for all he cared. He would risk the wrath of a thousand demons to have this one night with his beloved.

Their walk to the tent seemed to take a lifetime. His desire had been set aflame by a torrent of emotions and the sensation of being as one with Aaliyah. With each step, he could feel his power growing; not only that, he could now feel Aaliyah's strength as well. He had always known she was by far the most talented among the elves, but only now did he truly understand the extent of her power.

As they approached the small tent, Nehrutu felt an odd sensation through their bond. It was a dark and immeasurably potent presence.

"Is that...?" he began.

"Yes," replied Aaliyah, hearing the question before it was asked. "That is Darshan."

Nehrutu stared at her, stunned. "I never thought his spirit could feel so ... menacing."

"It is not always that way," she said, her voice suddenly distant. "There are times when his spirit is beautiful to behold. But I fear as more evil surrounds him, his heart will become ever more cloaked in shadow."

"And if that happens?" he asked, unsure if he wanted to know the answer.

"I am not certain," she replied in a whisper. Her eyes then brightened, and she smiled impishly. "But tonight is not a night for troubling thoughts—or Darshan."

She took Nehrutu's hand and led him into the wedding tent. Though the sunrise may herald their deaths, the coming night was to be for life and love.

CHAPTER 3

Gewey crept along the banks of the Goodbranch, the moonlit mist hovering inches above the water. The snow-covered ground glowed eerily as he peered at the western shore. Linis was several yards to his back, moving silently in the shadows.

The clumsy footfalls of the Angrääl patrol caused Gewey to grin. *The fools should have fled like the others,* he thought. The journey back through the Eastland had been uneventful. Elf scouts reported that enemy troops were moving south to avoid confrontation, apparently willing to allow them to march west unmolested.

Lee had laughed when hearing of this, suggesting that Angrääl knew they were led by the mighty Darshan and feared his wrath. He was probably right, at least to an extent. The Reborn King had no reason to lose men and supplies in a direct assault. Ultimately, this war would be decided not by armies, but by a final battle between the two gods that now walked the earth. Darshan would face his foe. Then, and only then, would the killing end.

He reached out with his senses. Aside from the tramping of the soldiers and the cold, gentle breeze sifting through the pine needles, nothing stirred. He glanced to the north. Sharpstone was a mere twenty miles away.

Gewey stopped and waited for Linis to catch up. The elf looked at the river and scowled. "I do not enjoy swimming in freezing cold water," he remarked.

Gewey grinned. "Neither do I."

The words had hardly passed his lips when a massive gust of wind wrapped itself around the duo, lifting them skyward. Linis gasped and instinctively clutched hold of Gewey's arm. In seconds, they were high above the river and drifting toward the far side. Gewey struggled not to laugh at Linis's unease.

When they finally returned to solid ground, Linis stiffened his back. His mouth twisted into a frown. "And I enjoyed *that* far less," he said.

Gewey chuckled. "My apologies, my friend. But it was the easiest way to cross."

"Only birds are meant to fly," the elf muttered as he checked his blade.

Gewey gave Linis's arm a fond squeeze, then returned his attention to their task. The soldiers were a quarter mile to the southwest. Gewey could sense that most of them were huddled around a large fire. Four others were keeping watch at the perimeter. They would be dealt with first.

The amusement over the river crossing quickly vanished, and they made their way through the thin forest of pines and leafless oaks. Gewey allowed the *flow* to rage: it felt like a welcome friend. He desired to hold it within all the time, but Kaylia still feared it could drive him mad, as it had so nearly done on their journey to The Chamber of the Maker. He knew it was pointless to argue with her. She was probably right anyway. He had come close to losing himself several times—the closest of all at the fortress of the Vrykol—and though it was ecstasy at first, it was inevitably followed closely by feelings of fear and guilt once he realized what he could become.

As soon as the first soldier came into view, Gewey halted. "Go around and capture the guard to the far west," he whispered, just loud enough for elf ears to hear. "I'll deal with the rest."

Linis flashed a look of protest, but Gewey ignored him and began to creep forward. Clenching his jaw, the elf shifted direction and disappeared into the shadows of the trees.

Gewey's skill at stealth, taught to him by Kaylia, was now beyond that of any elf seeker. He moved to within a yard of the guard without making a sound, invisible to all apart from perhaps Linis or Lee—and even they would struggle to see him.

The snap of bone broke the silence as Gewey twisted the man's neck. He could easily have used the *flow* of air to destroy the entire group in an instant, but his hatred for the Reborn King and all those who followed his banner burned hot. He wanted them to know fear before they died. A quick death for three of their guards was the only mercy he would be displaying.

Linis had already secured his captive as Gewey laid the third guard's body gently onto the virgin snow. He fixed his eyes on the remaining soldiers gathered around the fire. Most were quietly sipping on warm cups of wine. Others whispered quietly in idle conversation.

Slowly, he slid his sword free, the familiar warmth extending his powers beyond reckoning. Using the *flow* of the earth, he caused the ground to tremble. Instantly, loud shouts sounded as the soldiers scrambled to their feet, their frozen fingers fumbling for their weapons.

Faster than a human eye could see, Gewey rushed in, his blade cutting through three men in quick succession. Their blood spewed out, staining the white ground. Before any of the others had fully grasped what had happened, Gewey disappeared back into the darkness.

Cries of fear and panic echoed through the forest as the men pressed their backs to the fire. Again Gewey rushed in, this time with a primal yell that caused some of the soldiers to drop their swords in sheer terror. Four more of them rapidly fell.

This was all the remaining soldiers could stand. In fits of chaos, they bolted in every direction. But Gewey was not about to allow them to escape. A wall of flames erupted, encircling the men before any could make it more than a few feet. The roaring of the fire rapidly muffled their wails of horror and pleas for mercy. By now, every single one of them had dropped his sword and fallen to his knees.

Gewey felt a hand rest gently on his shoulder. It was Linis.

"End this," said the elf.

Gewey turned. "My home is not far from here, and they have invaded it."

"There was no way they could have known this," countered Linis.

Gewey glared. "They chose their side." He faced the flames. "And they chose wrong."

A gap in the blazing wall appeared. Without another word, Gewey walked inside and the opening closed behind him. Screams tore through the air as he finished what he had begun.

In moments, the sounds of the dying ceased, and the fire vanished. Gewey stood over the bodies, his expression blank. With a sniff of satisfaction, he walked over to their bound and unconscious captive.

Linis was unable to hide his revulsion at the carnage and cruel manner in which the soldiers had died. He stared at the ravaged bodies for what seemed like a long time before steadying his nerves and moving to join Gewey.

"You have changed, my friend," he said. "And I am not certain it is for the better."

"I am still the person I have always been," responded Gewey, his voice soft, yet still bearing a power that made him sound inhuman. "But the part of me that is Darshan cannot allow these vermin to go unpunished."

"They were only soldiers," countered Linis. "What crimes did they commit to warrant such a terrible end?"

Gewey met Linis's eyes. "They have murdered the helpless and defiled temples." Steel was in his tone. "And I will not speak of what they did to the priestesses in Gath."

Linis furrowed his brow. "And how is it that you know of these things?"

"I looked into their hearts," he replied. "I could see what they had done—and what they would do in the future." He glared at their captive with intense anger. "This one was part of a patrol that slaughtered a group of refugees fleeing the west. Men, women, and children—they spared none. They left their bodies alongside the road for the scavengers to pick their bones clean. These are not men. They are vermin."

Linis bowed his head. "If this is so, then they do indeed deserve death. But I cannot help but fear for your soul. Such wrath can blacken your heart beyond redemption."

Gewey leveled his gaze, then, after a few moments, forced a thin smile. "You're right, of course. It's a danger I have faced for quite a while now. If it wasn't for Kaylia, there's no telling what I would do—or what I might become."

There was a lengthy pause. Linis eventually returned his attention to the still-unconscious prisoner. "What do you intend to do with him?" he asked.

Gewey closed his eyes. "I'll leave it to you. I already know what I need to know. They were ordered to report if we crossed the river here. There is an army in Baltria and another in Kaltinor, but this soldier doesn't know their strength. All their other forces have fallen back to the north."

"You use the flow of the spirit to know his mind?" asked Linis.

Gewey nodded. "It's dangerous. I have to touch a person's spirit and take their memories. It can be ... damaging."

"And did you damage this one?" asked Linis.

Gewey shook his head. "No. He is still the same wretched creature he was before." He rose to his feet and turned toward the river. "I leave his fate in your hands."

He returned to the riverbank and waited. A few minutes later Linis joined him, the ice in his stare telling Gewey of the captive's fate. At once, he felt a pang of regret. Not for the soldier's death, but for allowing Linis to deliver the final killing stroke. His friend felt deeply, and his compassion was without measure. He killed only when he must and never took joy in the act.

After a few seconds of silence, Linis sighed heavily and looked to the far bank.

Gewey laughed. The *flow* of air burst forth and caressed the surface of the water. In less than a minute, a narrow bridge of ice had formed.

"I thought you would rather walk across this time," he said, smirking.

This helped to lift Linis's dark mood. He smiled and nodded approvingly. "As will the others, I suspect."

While crossing the ice, Gewey allowed himself to feel the life emanating from the Goodbranch. He had found himself doing such things more frequently of late. The rhythm and warmth of the world's essence kept his heart human every bit as much as his love for Kaylia and their unborn child. Each morning since they'd rejoined Linis and the others, he would take a few minutes to listen to the song of life that echoed in every corner of the world around him.

When Lee had first taught him how to listen to the sounds of the earth, he'd been amazed at the sheer beauty of its perfection. Now, he did much more than merely hear the sounds—he was able to become a part of them. The earth took him unto its bosom and made itself one with his own spirit. It was at these times, when the storm raging within his soul was threatening to consume him, that he was able to find peace and calm once again.

It was nearly dawn by the time they reached the encampment. The elves were already preparing the morning meal. Considering the blistering heat of their desert home, Gewey was amazed by the way they managed to handle the cold. The snow was a constant source of wonder for them, and they never seemed to tire of it. Snowballs constantly flew through the air as they played like children—laughing merrily while they traveled.

Linis excused himself and headed off to report what they had discovered to Bevaris and the Sand Masters. Gewey had no interest in such matters, choosing to defer to the judgment of others when it came to planning. The power of Darshan would see them through whatever route they took. He no longer saw their journey as a challenge. He cast a glance north. His challenge was yet to come.

It hadn't really surprised him to find that Angrääl was falling back as they marched. Why engage him? Even a god could not be everywhere at once. It would be a simple matter to retake lost ground once he and the elves had gone.

Helenia was the only city along the Goodbranch River not under the direct control of the Reborn King, and without trade, the city would soon starve. Lee had remarked many times on the brilliance of the enemy campaign. Angrääl had conquered almost all the central kingdoms without a single pitched battle being fought. The East was cowering and fearful of being attacked. Now, only the West stood against them.

Gewey's thoughts turned to Aaliyah and Nehrutu. He could feel that Aaliyah still lived, but that her heart was heavy. He had considered reaching out to her through the bond they shared, but Kaylia warned him against it. She feared that the turmoil in his heart would distress Aaliyah. And if the war had escalated, she would not need such distractions.

As Gewey approached his tent, he cleared his head and focused his attention instead on his bond with Kaylia. She was still asleep and in the midst of a troubling dream. He crept silently inside and changed into a pair of soft cotton trousers and a shirt. Kaylia was lying on their bedroll, a thick wool blanket wrapped tightly around her.

Gewey noticed the foggy mist of his breath and at once warmed the air inside. For a moment, he stood over his *unorem*, watching her sleep. He never tired of her beauty. He lay down and allowed his spirit to drift to her, but before they became as one, Kaylia stirred and threw her arm over his chest.

Gewey pulled her close and kissed her forehead. "Dawn is still an hour away."

"Good," she muttered drowsily. "They will come for us when they need you."

Gewey smiled and allowed his body to relax. His spirit may be that of a god, but his human body still needed rest—and lately, he had gotten very little. Even a couple of hours would do him good. In less than a minute, he was in a deep, peaceful slumber. Kaylia was eagerly awaiting him in the world of dreams.

More than three hours passed before a timid voice called for them to wake. Gewey stretched and yawned. Kaylia scowled, unhappy that they were being forced to leave the shared dream.

"Lee must have returned," she said, once they were dressed.

"Where did he go?" asked Gewey.

"Sharpstone," she replied. "He left not long after you and Linis."

This got his attention. News about home dragged up mixed emotions. Some of his own people had fought on the side of Angrääl near Skalhalis ... fought and likely died. And though he was confident no one there would know anything about his involvement in the war—and they certainly had no idea that he was Darshan—facing the mothers of men and boys whom he had called friends would not be easy.

Kaylia caught his arm just as he was about to leave and motioned to the ground where two bowls of steaming porridge had been left for them.

Gewey grunted but did not argue. He took the repast and shared a few minutes of quiet with Kaylia as they ate. Just as they were finishing, familiar sounds of good cheer drifted inside the tent. These were coming from the desert elves, who treated each new day like a blessing. Taking his last mouthful, Gewey closed his eyes and allowed the laughter to lift his spirits.

The sun nearly blinded them when they first left the tent, its brightness made more intense by the reflection off the fallen snow. Shouts of greeting rang out from numerous directions as they wound their way to the north end of the camp where Lyrial and the Sand Masters had set up their quarters.

Everyone was already gathered around a small cooking fire. Lyrial, Weila, Nahali, Dina, Linis, Millet, Lee, and Jacob were all just finishing their breakfast. Bevaris and Tristan stood a few feet away, each of them holding a bow and carefully examining it as two elves explained its construction.

Dina shot Gewey a troubled glance as he and Kaylia sat down. Her bond with Linis would have made it unnecessary for her *unorem* to tell her what had taken place the night before.

Gewey nodded to the assembled group and smiled. "I take it we're not marching today."

"Normally it would take at least two full days for us all to cross the river," said Lee. "But Linis tells me that you can create a bridge. In that case, I thought you might want to see Sharpstone while you have the chance."

Gewey's mouth twisted into a frown. "You halted the march for *me*?"

"The march continues because of you, Darshan," interjected Lyrial. "And even a god cannot know what the future holds. I would not have you meet your destiny without seeing the place you call home when it is so close by."

"Bevaris and I scouted the town last night," said Lee. "It seems Angrääl did not destroy it as I feared they would. But they didn't leave it untouched, either."

"What do you mean?" asked Gewey. His stomach knotted.

Lee's jaw tightened. "We found Mayor Freidly's body hanging on a post in the market square. How many others have been killed, I don't know. But the body had been up there for quite some time, which means people were afraid to touch it. That ... or there is no one left to bury him."

"Didn't you see or hear anyone?" asked Gewey. His anger was renewed.

"I didn't have time to look for anything other than signs of Angrääl soldiers," replied Lee.

Gewey shot him an accusing stare. With his half-man senses, surely he could have...

Kaylia reached out and squeezed his hand. He relaxed and sighed.

"I wish I could have found out more," Lee continued. "But—"

"I'll find out what has happened," Gewey cut in.

"I had a feeling you'd say that," remarked Lee. "But unless you want the people of Sharpstone to know you as Darshan, you should wait until tonight."

"I'll scout the surrounding area," offered Linis. "If there are enemies about, they may be waiting for you to return."

"If they are fool enough to attack me," growled Gewey. "Then let them come."

"Is that how you want the people of your home to remember you?" scolded Dina. "A vengeful god? How do you think they'll react if they witness the terrible things you can do? Do you want *them* to fear you as well?" Her voice bore unmistakable anger—probably because of what he had done to the soldiers while with Linis, Gewey guessed.

"She's right," added Kaylia. "If you ever intend for us to live there, Darshan must never show his face in Sharpstone."

"We can go to your farm first," said Lee. "That, I *do* know, for sure, has been abandoned. Then we'll enter the town after nightfall."

"I will come as well," said Linis. Dina glared at him angrily, but he ignored her unspoken plea for him to stay behind.

"And what should we do in the meantime?" asked Lyrial.

"Stay here," said Lee. "There are no enemies nearby. We will return by tomorrow morning and make our crossing."

Gewey rose to his feet without another word and returned to his tent. Kaylia followed a few minutes later. While he rummaged through his pack for a black shirt and pants, she sat on the bedroll and scrutinized him for several moments.

"Lee did what he could," she finally said. "He needed to return in time to tell you what he had found."

Gewey didn't bother looking up. "Lee fled out of fear." Disgust seeped into his voice. "He didn't want the enemy to catch him alone and far from aid. He could have easily discovered the fate of the townsfolk and still made it back here before the sun was high."

"And if that is so?" shot back Kaylia. "If he felt fear, does that make him a coward? Does it make him less of the man you once knew and admired?"

Gewey paused, unable to respond. He knew she was right. He knew his anger was undeserved. Lee had always acted with courage and honor. If he had felt fear, he was the type of man who would have pushed it aside.

"You walk the earth without an equal," she continued. "I am the only one who can even fathom the extent of your power. Most think you are invincible. But they are not gods themselves, and they are vulnerable. You cannot judge them by your own standards."

"I know," he said in a whisper. "Sometimes, it's more than I can bear. The idea that I might fail to protect those I love in spite of my strength is agony." He fastened his sword to his belt and sighed. "I suppose I just miss Lee being the strong one. When I first met him, he was a mysterious stranger. Then he became an all-powerful teacher and guardian." He held out his hand to Kaylia. "Now, he is just another person I am charged to protect."

Kaylia allowed Gewey to help her to her feet. "He is much more than that."

Gewey forced a smile. "Yes, he is. And if my heart was not in such constant turmoil, I would never forget it." He put on a black hooded cloak. "Perhaps seeing my home will lift my spirits and remind me of who I really am."

"That the enemy did not destroy the town is promising," said Kaylia.

"And a bit disturbing," he added darkly.

After finishing their preparations, they rejoined Lee and Linis. Millet and Jacob sat nearby, both with sour expressions. Weila and Lyrial were talking with a small group of elves a short distance away.

"I take it Millet will not be coming," said Gewey.

"It's too dangerous," replied Lee. "And as Jacob has taken on the role of Millet's protector, he will be staying behind, too."

"We, on the other hand, will be coming," called Lyrial as she and Weila approached. "I would not miss an opportunity to see the home of Darshan."

Gewey gave her a lopsided smile. "I'm afraid you'll only see the home of a farm boy named Gewey Stedding."

Lyrial grinned. "That will be enough."

The air was bitterly cold as they started out, with the wind reaching its icy fingers beneath their cloaks. But Gewey didn't mind. The familiar landscape was putting a smile on his face and a spring in his step.

The sun was waning as his farm came into view. Gewey reached out with his senses. No one was inside or anywhere nearby. Still, they approached cautiously.

The barn door was flung wide open and Gewey could see that all of his farming equipment was still there. Snow covered the house porch, its surface blemished only by the footprints left by Lee the night before.

"A simple life," remarked Weila approvingly.

Kaylia took hold of Gewey's hand. She could feel his excitement, but it was mixed with anxiety.

Slowly, he pushed open the front door and peeked inside. Only his heightened vision allowed him to see through the darkness. He scanned the main room where the dining table was still in its usual place. On the far side, facing the hearth, was his mother's rocking chair—the very same chair he had seen Kaylia sitting in while holding their infant child during his vision of the future. His father's chair was just beside it, though this was turned toward the door.

While taking a tentative step inside, Gewey felt an odd sensation wash over him. Though nothing was out of place, he could tell that other people had been staying here, and the thought of this was oddly disturbing.

He walked to the hearth and tossed in a cord of wood that had been left behind. Within seconds, it was burning brightly, casting shadows that danced across the wall. Lee set about lighting the lanterns, while the others simply stood quietly near the door.

"I told you there wasn't much to see," said Gewey. As the words came out, he felt suddenly embarrassed for Kaylia to see how poorly he had lived.

"I love it," she whispered into his ear, sensing his feelings. "It's just as I imagined. A good place to raise a family."

Gewey could hear the sincerity in her words. He leaned down and kissed her on the cheek.

After searching the cupboards and finding a wedge of cheese and a bottle of sweet wine, Gewey invited the others to sit at the table. He then went to the rear of the house and examined his bedroom, grunting with disapproval when he saw that the bed had been left unmade by its previous occupant. He opened the chest at the foot of the bed and began rummaging through his old clothing. Exactly why he was doing this was unclear; other than perhaps by touching his old things, this would somehow help him to reclaim his home.

When Gewey returned to the others, Lyrial asked him to tell of his life at the farm. He happily obliged, soaking in the surroundings of a home he'd often wondered if he would ever see again.

"I pity you," said Lyrial after a time. "To leave such peace and contentment behind for war..." She shook her head.

Gewey shrugged. "Let us hope that the war will be over soon."

All nodded in agreement. Just then, the sound of hoofbeats had everyone on their feet and reaching for their weapons.

Lee rushed to the door. A single horse was approaching from the west at full speed, its rider a young man no older than twenty. He was clad, not in the armor of a soldier, but in rough clothing suited to a farmer. Lee motioned for the others to stay inside.

The rider came to a halt just in front of the house and leaped from the saddle.

"State your business," commanded Lee.

"My Lord," said the man with a quick bow, "I was ordered to deliver this message to someone named Gewey Stedding. Is he here?"

"Who sent you?" demanded Lee, his face grim.

The man's eyes were filled with fear. "I don't know who he is. But he travels with the Reborn King's soldiers south of Gath." He held out a piece of parchment. "Please, sir. If he's here, I must deliver this to him. I wouldn't want to cross the fellow who gave it to me. He's not ... not natural ... if you catch my meanin'."

Lee scrutinized the man for a long moment before taking the parchment. "You can tell him it was delivered."

"Beggin' your pardon," he replied nervously. "But I ain't going back there."

Without another word, he jumped back into the saddle and spurred his horse east.

Lee watched until the rider had disappeared before going back inside.

"So they know that I'm here," said Gewey, taking the parchment from Lee.

There was silence as he read it. When he was done, he laid it out on the table and sneered.

Darshan,

By order of my master, your home and village have been left untouched. He hopes this will serve to remind you that this war need not endure. He bids you join him in Angrääl to discuss the future of the peoples of the world. The suffering can come to an end if only you see the wisdom of his words.

This shall be your final opportunity to do so. If you choose to continue your march west, you shall not see your home again. All will burn and none shall live.

I, for one, hope you ignore the generous offer of the Reborn King so that we can meet again. It seems like it has been so very long since we first met in the desert. Word has reached me that you were able to save the elf I poisoned. A wretched waste of power.

I hope this letter reaches you well, and that the scared little rabbit I charged with its delivery hasn't fled before he sees that you have it.

Until we meet again,
–V–

"I would very much like to meet this creature again," seethed Gewey. The vision of Aaliyah's life draining from her body because of the Vrykol's poison was still fresh in his mind.

"It seeks to enrage you and make you act foolishly," said Lyrial.

"If any Vrykol comes near," said Gewey ominously. "I will rip their spirits to shreds. This one is no different than the others, regardless of its appearance."

"We should be on our guard, nonetheless," said Linis. "Until we know its motives, we must assume Angrääl means to prevent our march west."

"Do you think he plans to attack?" asked Weila.

Gewey tightened his jaw. "Whatever his plan is, it will be focused on me. My fall is the key to Angrääl's victory."

"Well, there's nothing we can do about it for now," Lee stated flatly. "We should move on to Sharpstone."

Gewey nodded in agreement. "Yes. Let's find out how *untouched* it is."

They filed out and headed for the road leading into the village. Gewey took a lingering final look at his farm and then focused his mind.

The village was pitch black; not a single lantern shone in any window. Aside from the wind, there was no sound at all. Gewey stopped in the middle of the main avenue and filled himself with the *flow*. Nothing. There was absolutely no one dwelling in Sharpstone. He slid his sword from its scabbard. The others did the same.

They continued to the market and saw Mayor Freidly still hanging from a post, his body bloated and decaying.

"You left him hanging?" shouted Gewey, his eyes burning with fury.

"I thought it best not to leave any signs that I had been here," explained Lee, unmoved by Gewey's anger.

Gewey used the *flow* of the air to lift the body from the post and lay it gently on the ground. A white-hot flame then sprang to life, turning night into day and forcing the party back. In less than a minute, Mayor Freidly's body was reduced to ashes.

"He deserved better than to be left to rot," growled Gewey. "You should have taken him down."

Kaylia touched his shoulder. "That is enough. Lee did what he thought was best."

Gewey snorted and strode off with long methodical steps, sword still in hand. When he reached the main avenue once again, he stopped and closed his eyes. For five minutes, he remained motionless, searching for signs of life.

Finally, he gave a heavy sigh. "They are three miles north of town—all of them." He took Kaylia's hand and looked at Linis, ignoring Lee. "Find out what happened and tell them to return to their homes. I'm going back. They shouldn't see me."

"Whatever drove them there may return," said Linis. "Perhaps they should remain hidden."

Gewey sniffed. "They're not hidden. They only think they are. The Vrykol could find them easily. If they are to be killed, better they should die in their own homes rather than alone and afraid in the cold forest."

Gewey turned and set off east from town, Kaylia at his side. His obviously ill mood kept Weila and Lyrial from following.

"You should not have vented your wrath on Lee," scolded Kaylia as they turned from the road into the forest. "He did not..."

"He left Mayor Freidly hanging like a common criminal," barked Gewey, cutting her off. "I knew that man all my life. When my father died, it was Mayor Freidly who stood beside me as he was buried. Not Lee." Gewey's fists were clenched so tightly that his knuckles cracked. "When the town wanted to take my farm, once again it was Mayor Freidly who came to my aid. Where was the great Lee Starfinder then?"

In a flash, Kaylia's hand struck hard against Gewey's cheek. "Lee is your friend." Her voice was steel. "And he gave up his wife and child for you. He has risked his life, and the life of his own son ... for *you*."

Gewey rubbed his face where the blow had struck. A single tear fell as the truth of her words struck home. "I ... I should never have gone home."

In an instant, Kaylia's features softened, and she took his hands. "I can feel the war waging within you. You struggle to keep the rage from taking control of your spirit."

"And I'm sorry you have to feel it."

"I am grateful," she said, smiling. "I love you, and I would not have you go through such hardship alone. But you have to remember that the others are unaware. They see only your strength. And your anger frightens them."

Gewey thought about what he had said to Lee. He had nearly hit him and probably would have done so if he had stayed around longer. "I will apologize when he returns," he said.

At that moment, the hairs on the back of his neck stood up. He felt a foul, yet familiar presence. Kaylia felt it an instant later.

"Vrykol," she hissed.

Gewey sneered. His blade sang as it slid free. "They must be mindless fools to attack me after what I did to them at their fortress."

He reached out and found twelve Vrykol a quarter mile away, approaching slowly from the northeast. A pang of fear from Kaylia came through their bond. He gave her a reassuring smile and moved forward.

The world burst into life as he drew from the *flow* of the spirit. Bells and laughter filled his ears. The air twinkled with so many lights; they outnumbered the stars.

Why are they attacking? Gewey wondered. Surely they know that it's hopeless.

It was enough to give him pause. He shook his head and pressed on. What did it matter why they were attacking? In a few minutes, he would rip their spirits to shreds and the souls of the *firstborn* would suffer no more. He thought back to the Vrykol he had killed in the Black Oasis. They had endured beyond the death of their corrupted bodies. But that was only due to the nature of the Oasis. In the rest of the world, they remained tainted. Gewey dearly wished that he knew how to cleanse them.

Perhaps soon I'll find a way, he thought.

The instant the first Vrykol came into view, Gewey reached out to destroy the creature. As he did so, the others rushed in with blinding speed, three loosing arrows as they ran. But it was not fast enough to stop the inevitable. Even before Gewey reacted, Kaylia had blasted the arrows with the *flow* of air, sending them falling harmlessly to the ground.

He laughed inwardly, sending loving appreciation through their bond.

The *flow* of spirit touched each Vrykol simultaneously, causing them to flail wildly. Gewey slowed his attack to make them feel every second of their doom. He felt a rush of pleasure as he watched them become more and more disoriented.

He turned to Kaylia. She was staring at the Vrykol with a sinister grin, sharing Gewey's bliss. It was one thing to be cruel to a human or elf, but in her mind, there was nothing more foul and evil than a Vrykol. Only the Reborn King himself deserved a more horrible death.

One by one, the Vrykol fell to their knees, unable to move. It was then that Gewey finished the job and ripped their spirits apart. A metallic scream tore through the air. Then there was silence.

He was about to turn again to Kaylia when a pain shot through his arm.

Kaylia saw the flash of the dart in the corner of her eye and watched in horror as it struck Gewey's right shoulder. Instantly, his body crumbled lifelessly to the ground. A searing pain shot through her entire being as their bond flashed out of existence. With a primal scream of unfathomable suffering, she fell to her knees.

With tears streaming down her cheeks, she pulled Gewey's limp body close to her.

"No! No! No!" she cried to the heavens.

"Yes," came a reply from just a few yards behind her.

In a single motion, Kaylia leaped up, her long knife in her hand. Her body shuddered as the pain of the broken bond increased. She knew that her training with Nehrutu and Aaliyah would keep her from following Gewey into death, but nothing could prevent the agony she now felt. Her eyes fell on a cloaked figure with a long curved blade in its hand.

"I thought your kind perished when a bond is broken by death," the figure said. It pushed back its hood to reveal elf features. "Little matter. You will die in a moment—though I'm afraid you won't be joining your love in spirit. I've sent him to a place where you cannot follow." He laughed cruelly.

His taunts created blind anger in Kaylia. Madness seized her as she charged at the Vrykol with a ferocity that took it completely by surprise. The tip of her blade cut deep into the creature's neck. Only its unnatural reflexes kept its head attached to its shoulders.

Ignoring her pain, Kaylia pressed the attack. Her fury was beyond reckoning. Oblivious to danger, her fist crashed into the Vrykol's jaw, sending it stumbling back. It tried to counter, but could only block the furious onslaught of blows. Soon, several of these found its flesh. Thick, black blood began to ooze, causing the creature's shredded cloak to stick to its thin frame.

Aware that it could not sustain its defense for much longer, the Vrykol lunged desperately, attempting to skewer Kaylia through the heart. Twisting left, Kaylia easily avoided the attack and brought her blade down hard, severing the beast's sword arm at the elbow. The Vrykol stared down in shock at its lost limb on the ground. It was still gripping the sword and twitching violently.

Kaylia paused just long enough to spit in the creature's face before, in a flash of steel, she took its head from its shoulders. The body remained standing grotesquely erect for a moment, then toppled over.

Without a pause, she rushed back to Gewey. His eyes were staring vacantly into nothingness. With all the power she could muster, Kaylia desperately attempted to transfer the flow from her own body into his. But there was no life to receive it.

Gewey was dead.

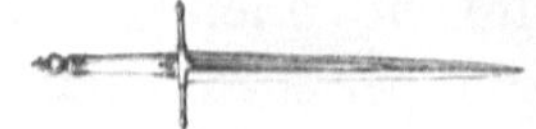

Nehrutu and Aaliyah stood hand in hand on the beach as the elves gathered to march. The previous night had been everything they could have dreamed of.

Several of the elders had suggested that they split their army in two and try to flank the enemy on both sides. Their experience in the Great War told them that the humans would not be able to react in time. If their own army moved fast enough, they should be able to get too close for Angrääl's soldiers to use their deadly weapon.

One of the human commanders offered to charge his soldiers directly at the front as a distraction. Knowing that most of the humans would perish in such an attack, Nehrutu initially refused to allow it. But the commander insisted, and in spite of Nehrutu not wanting to send men on a hopeless mission, he knew that using such a tactic would give them their best chance of success. He couldn't help but admire such selfless courage, nor could he help but be saddened that such sacrifice would likely be necessary.

Aaliyah tightened her grip on his hand, feeling the sorrow creeping into his heart. Though he had been taught long ago what to expect from their bond, it still did not prepare him for the reality of such an intimate union. It was simultaneously unnerving and glorious. It had been less than a full day since the bonding, and already he could not imagine being without it.

"We will see that their bravery is remembered," said Aaliyah. "The songs of every soul that has died will be sung from the Spires of Parylon."

"I long to see those spires once again," mused Nehrutu. "I would survive this war if only to walk the streets of our beloved city with you by my side."

Aaliyah closed her eyes, smiling. "I am well pleased to be with you here and now." She leaned her body close. "Though I admit, I would love to walk the hills and forests of my childhood and share with you the contentment I feel when I gaze upon its beauty and majesty."

Nehrutu wrapped his arm around her, bathing in the unique feelings of shared love that only the spiritually bonded are capable of achieving.

Aaliyah sighed. "We should join the…"

A searing pain shot through her body. Had Nehrutu not had his arm around her, she would have collapsed. He could feel her pain and instinctively saturated her with the *flow*. "What has happened?" he asked.

She squeezed her eyes shut, unable to speak. Her hands trembled and her breathing was quick and shallow.

Finally, she gathered her wits sufficiently to say in a whisper, "Darshan is dead."

CHAPTER 4

Yanti stared nervously at the small rustic house. The wicker chairs scattered indiscriminately on the front porch were rough and not very well made. In fact, the house itself was little more than a shack. There was nothing about it to indicate that the oldest and most powerful being that still breathed air dwelled within.

It had been over one hundred years since he had last seen Felsafell. Yanti still hadn't forgiven him for taking his sister away from him that day, in spite of the fact that he knew it was for the best. Since then, his life had become a never-ending cycle of trials and failures. This latest was by far the worst.

For more than two hours, he had been standing behind a massive oak tree, about fifty yards away from the house. There was no doubt that he feared the encounter. Not that he thought Felsafell would do him harm. But he was afraid of what would come from their conversation. No matter how hard he tried, he could not build up the courage to approach the house. In fact, he was on the point of leaving when the snap of a twig sent him spinning around. His blade was in his hand before he could even see what had caused the sound.

He blinked. Instead of the young man he had met before, standing in front of him now was an old man with a scraggly beard and crooked teeth. In one hand he carried two dead rabbits, in the other a gnarled tree branch he was using as a walking stick.

Yanti knew that he was looking at Felsafell, even though he could not explain his change in appearance. His accusing stare and a disapproving expression were enough to confirm this. He sheathed his sword.

"You have changed," remarked Yanti.

"You have not," said Felsafell, eyeing the blade at his side. "Come. Eat."

Felsafell led Yanti into his home. The simple interior and rough furnishings suited the place well. Yanti took a seat at the crudely built dining table while Felsafell began to prepare the meal.

"Do you still eat?" asked Felsafell.

"Occasionally," he replied. "I still enjoy it. Wine and roasted pheasant in particular, when I can get it."

"I have no pheasant," said Felsafell. "But I do have wine."

Once the meal was ready, they ate in silence. Felsafell did not appear to be interested in conversation and adjourned to the porch as soon as the table had been cleared. Yanti followed.

Felsafell offered him a seat and took out a small flask. The sweet scent of brandy filled the air. By now, the light of day was beginning to fade. The whisper of the wind in the trees was singing in perfect harmony with the chirps of the crickets.

"Why have you come?" asked Felsafell.

"I want to see Basanti," he replied. He was unable to look Felsafell in the eye. Did he know of the many bad things he had done?

"Why come to me?" Felsafell asked. "By now, you know where she is. I will not stop you." He looked sideways at Yanti. "Perhaps you come to ask for my help?"

"I do not need your help."

"No?" He leaned back in the chair and shook his head. "You have killed no less than twenty people, and only a few years ago you were personally responsible for more than fifty thousand elves being exiled to the desert. I'd say you are in desperate need of help."

Yanti didn't bother asking how Felsafell knew these things. "I only killed when forced to do so," he said.

"You were never meant to kill for any reason whatsoever," Felsafell countered. "You lived for hundreds of years, and you were never once *forced* to kill. You faced dangers even before the elves began hunting you. You did not kill then. Before you corrupted your soul with blood, you found ways to live without causing death." His hard gaze softened slightly. "Can you imagine if I had not taken your sister with me? Your sins would have driven her mad. And her love for you would never allow for the possibility that you are beyond redemption."

"Is that what you think?" His voice wavered. "That I cannot be redeemed?

"Do *you* think you can?" Felsafell asked as if he knew that Yanti already had the answer. "You are the one who interfered with the elves and turned them against one another."

In a flash of anger, Yanti jumped to his feet and strode to the edge of the porch. Then, with a great effort, he managed to calm himself. He drew a deep breath. "That's not fair. I only did what you said I should do. I was trying to help them. I was trying to make them see that their treatment of the humans was wrong."

"What you did was inflame their passions," said Felsafell. "You used your knowledge to influence those who already understood the sins their people were committing. They turned on their own kin and named them slavers."

Yanti spun around and faced Felsafell. "And what would you have had me do?"

Felsafell took a long swallow of brandy and offered the flask to Yanti, who received it reluctantly. "I had hoped that you would find a way to cleanse your spirit. I had hoped the gods may take pity on you and show you a path."

Yanti sneered. "The *gods*, bah! They abandoned me and Basanti long ago. They are selfish and vile."

Felsafell raised an eyebrow. "You really believe that? Basanti would say different."

"My sister is a pure soul. She sees only the good—even in me." Yanti held the flask under his nose and savored the sweet scent. "I think I will *not* go to see her. Not until I have found a way to purify myself."

"I feel that is wise," Felsafell told him. He then stared at Yanti for a long moment. "But you think you have already discovered that way, I gather."

"The *jewels* of the gods," said Yanti. His voice was distant and hopeful. "They have the power to undo what I have done."

Felsafell sat up straight. "They are all hidden. And for good reason. The *god stones* cannot help you. Their power cannot be contained. If you find them, you will only find more death."

"You know where they are," said Yanti. "Don't you?"

Felsafell fixed his gaze. "It does not matter. I would not tell you where to find them. Heed my words. Nothing good can come of such a quest. Even were you to locate them, you would *not* accomplish your goals. They should never have been made. The gods knew this, and that is why they have hidden them away."

"If they were such a big mistake, why did the gods not simply destroy them?"

Felsafell shrugged. "I do not claim to know the mind of such beings; nor have I the wisdom to fathom their motives." He scrutinized Yanti for another long period and then sighed. "And yet, I know that you will seek them out, anyway." He turned away and waved his hand dismissively. "Go now. Find your destiny."

Yanti gazed at Felsafell's back for several seconds. Then, with a huff of contempt, he spun sharply around and disappeared into the forest.

Basanti slowly rounded the corner of the house and sank into a seat beside Felsafell. The old man forced a smile and took her hand. "I am sorry. I know how much you wanted to see him."

"You were right to advise against it," she said, forcing a weak smile of her own. "He is lost. He will find the *god stones.* Then, as you said, death will follow." She pulled her hand free. "And there is..."

Her words trailed off.

"What is it?" asked Felsafell, concerned.

A single tear fell down her cheek, and she closed her eyes. "I have looked into his future."

"What did you see?"

"I saw pain, chaos, blood, and betrayal." She began to weep openly. Finally, she managed to speak through her sobs. "He will one day forsake all he loves. He will become ... truly evil."

CHAPTER 5

At first, Gewey couldn't move a muscle. All he could feel was a blast of searing hot air across his back, while the roar of thunder was threatening to split his skull in two. The rough, gritty soil was hot and putrid, filling his nostrils with the stench of ash and sulfur. After a few minutes of struggling, the strength slowly began returning to his limbs. Finally, he managed to raise his head a little.

Thick, black smoke mixed with gray dust swirled and churned, making it impossible for him to see more than a few yards away. As he pushed himself to his feet, he realized that he was clad in the work clothes he used to wear when living on his farm. His sword and other belongings were gone.

Shielding his eyes, he took a step forward. His mind was clouded, and though he knew who he was, he had no idea of how he had come to be in such a terrible place. His last memory was of Kaylia's voice screaming out in terror. It was at that moment that he realized—their bond—it was broken. And yet there was no pain. Before, when Aaliyah had blocked their bond, he had felt the loss of it to his very core. But this time, there was just a total absence of feeling.

"Kaylia!" he cried out.

He knew there could be no response. Wherever he was, she was not with him. He was alone. He reached out for the *flow* but found only a great void. Fear began to creep its way into his mind, but he forced it aside. He was Darshan, he told himself, and Darshan feared nothing.

With no other options, he began to walk blindly into the tempest. The wind howled a hollow cry, and the dust stung his eyes. Through the dark, he caught glimpses of light, but they vanished the moment he turned toward them.

On and on he walked, though the landscape remained the same. The wind continued to whip around him at a constant speed, blasting his face raw and pushing against his forward progress, regardless of which direction he headed.

Hours passed, and still, there was no sign of life. From time to time, the sound of the howling wind seemed to take on a ghostly quality—tormented and angry—and sometimes pleading. Gewey dismissed this as his imagination playing tricks.

The dry, polluted air parched his throat and swelled his tongue.

"To think I'll die of thirst," he said aloud, letting out a defeated laugh.

"Die?" said a strong male voice from behind him.

Gewey spun around, instinctively reaching for his sword, only to realize that it wasn't there. Before him stood a shadowy figure, its features hidden beneath a cloak of swirling darkness. It was as though the light around the figure was somehow being repelled, preventing his vision from focusing on it. Suddenly, the wind lessened, and the smoke began to clear, revealing an endless landscape of black, ruined earth. Towering flames shot to a dull gray sky on the horizon.

"You cannot die," the voice continued. "Not in this place ... brother."

"Who are you?" Gewey demanded. "What is this place?"

The figure laughed. "I asked that very same question when I arrived. But I had no one to answer me. You shall not suffer such a disadvantage." His face became slightly clearer. "My name is Melek." He bowed low.

"I—I am..."

"You are Darshan," interrupted Melek.

"You know me?" asked Gewey, immediately suspicious.

"Not in the way you might think," replied Melek. "But I can see what you have brought with you to this place. And I can see that we are the same."

"I don't understand," said Gewey, his suspicion building. "How are we the same?"

Melek's face and form gradually cleared completely, revealing a human of about forty years old. His salt and pepper hair fell in loose curls just past his shoulders, and in spite of their dull gray surroundings, his deep-set green eyes were bright, friendly, and sparkling. Though not as tall or broad as Gewey, he was clearly strong, and his posture was straight and proud. His tan shirt and black trousers looked to be made from cotton, though as the wind caught the fabric, the cloth appeared to glisten with a slight sheen.

"Come," said Melek. "I promise to tell you all that I know."

For a moment, Gewey did not move. Melek looked at him, smiling like a patient and understanding father. Then, realizing that his choices were to either go with him or stand there alone in the middle of a mysterious wasteland, Gewey followed.

They had walked for only a few minutes, with Gewey just a step behind Melek, when the silhouette of a small house appeared through the gloom. The wind had not yet picked back up to its former strength, much to Gewey's relief.

The house was modest, though it looked to be sturdily built, and the light glowing in its window was a welcoming beacon. Melek opened the door, and with a grand sweeping motion, invited Gewey to step inside.

The interior was sparsely furnished. A small round table and two chairs were in the center of the room, while a small fire burned in the hearth on the far side. There was no bed or stove that Gewey could see. Nor was there a door leading to any other part of the house. It seemed that this was all there was.

Gewey remained by the doorway, taking in his surroundings until he felt Melek's hand on his shoulder.

"Please sit," his host said. "I know that you have questions."

Gewey obeyed and sat at the table. From seemingly nowhere, a bottle of wine appeared in Melek's hand, along with two crystal goblets. Gewey sprang to his feet.

Melek laughed, an apologetic smile on his face. "I forget that you do not yet understand. I have been alone for a very long time and am unaccustomed to the sensitivities of others." He sat opposite Gewey. "Please. Sit back down."

Gewey paused, took a deep breath, and then returned to his seat. "What is this place?"

The smile slowly left Melek's face. "Put simply, it is a prison." He poured the wine and pushed a goblet across the table to Gewey. "One in which I have been kept for a very long time. And one in which you are now trapped as well."

Gewey was unsure what to say.

"I know it is difficult to believe," Melek continued. "When I was first sent here, I had a very hard time understanding what had happened to me. But I soon learned the truth. I was imprisoned in this wretched land—and there is no escape."

Gewey's mind reeled. "What are you saying? That I can never leave here?" At once, his thoughts turned to Kaylia and their unborn child. *I need to get back to them*, he thought desperately.

"And you will," said Melek.

Gewey realized that Melek could hear his thoughts. The intrusion angered him.

"Calm yourself, Darshan," said Melek, sensing Gewey's irritation. "I will leave your thoughts untouched if you wish. I merely wanted to say that now you are here, there is hope."

Gewey sipped his wine. He noticed that his hand trembling, but it was as much from anxiety and fear as it was from anger. "How did I get here?" he asked.

Melek shrugged. "I would guess that you were struck by the Fangs of Yajna, just as I was."

Gewey furrowed his brow. He remembered a sharp pain in his shoulder just before finding himself in this place. He reached around to touch where it had struck, but there was no sign of a wound. "What are the Fangs of Yajna?" he asked.

"A weapon," Melek replied. His lips curled in disgust. "A weapon designed to kill our kind."

"Our kind?" Gewey looked at his companion in disbelief. "Are you saying that you're a—"

"Yes," he replied. "A god. But I am much more than that. I am the first. Born of the Creator. Made perfect by *her* divine grace. Betrayed by my children, and exiled here to Shagharath."

His final few words sparked a memory buried deep within Gewey. "Shagharath," he whispered. "I have heard that name before. It was in some of the stories my father told me as a child. He said it was a place of demons. A land of fire and pain where the wicked were sent to suffer eternal damnation."

"I can only assume you speak of a mortal father," said Melek.

"Yes," replied Gewey. "His name was Harman Stedding. I have never met Gerath. Well—not really."

Melek sneered. "Of course you have met him. But in his cruelty, he robbed you of your memories." He shook his head and cleared his throat. "But we will speak of that soon enough. As for what your mortal father told you—he was wrong. Shagharath does not punish the wicked. It punishes *me*."

The howl of the wind outside rose, carrying with it a succession of ghastly moans and suffering cries. Melek glanced up for a moment, then returned his attention to Gewey.

"Why were you sent here?" asked Gewey. "And how do we get out?"

"I was sent here for doing the will of the Creator," he replied, his head held high. "By your father ... my son ... Gerath."

"Your son?"

"Indeed," he replied. "I am the father of *all* of the gods."

"Then who is the mother?" Gewey was trying hard to wrap his mind around what Melek was telling him.

The man's eyes grew sad and distant. "Her name was Ustrea. She was the love I held most dear—even above the Creator *herself*. She was my wife."

"But ... but..." Questions were racing so rapidly through Gewey's head, he could not seem to focus on a single one.

Melek chuckled, shaking off his melancholy. "And as you were born from the union of the Creator and Gerath, that means I am both your brother and your grandfather."

Gewey tried to put this confusing thought out of his head. "You say Gerath betrayed you?"

Melek sighed. "They all did. But it was Gerath who convinced the others to follow and led them against me."

A deep frown formed on Gewey's face. He was finding it hard to imagine that the being he'd met in the Black Oasis possessed a cruel or vicious nature. Surely Gerath was not capable of sending his own father to perdition. "So why did he turn against you?" he asked.

"Jealousy," Melek replied flatly. "He was always ambitious and strong. Gerath believed that he understood the Creator's plan better than I. He wanted to guide heaven and earth in the manner that best suited his own desires." He stood and walked over to the window. "He also coveted my power."

"But if you are both gods, wouldn't you have equal powers?"

Melek glanced over his shoulder. "I was the first, so I have no godly parents. My power comes directly from the source of all life. You are half-born from the Creator as well. And though Gerath tried to ensure that you would never realize your full potential by erasing your memory of heaven, you do indeed have the same power as I." He turned fully around. "And when we escape this place, I will show it to you. You will be able to create wonders such as you have never imagined."

Melek moved toward Gewey, his footsteps seeming to scarcely touch the floor planks. Holding out his hand, he smiled warmly. Gewey reached out without thinking and allowed Melek to lead him to the window.

"For untold centuries I have been trapped here," said Melek. "Because of the love I held for my children, I allowed myself to be deceived. Within you rests the strength to right the many wrongs done to us both. Together, we will do just that."

"I still don't understand how you know so much about me," said Gewey. He wasn't ready to yield his trust just yet.

Melek draped an arm around Gewey's shoulder. "Tell me what you see."

He sighed and looked out of the window. "Nothing but dust, smoke, and ash."

Melek nodded. "And where are you now?"

"Inside your home?"

"Good." Melek removed his arm and took a step back. "And can you see me?"

Gewey frowned. "What kind of question is that? Of course, I can see you."

Melek chuckled. "What you actually see is a construct of your mind. I have no physical body in this place. And this house is no more real than my body."

The room shook from another powerful blast of wind. Once again, it was accompanied by the ghostly howls.

"And I suppose that wasn't real either?" said Gewey. He understood the concept. It wasn't much different from when he was in the dream or spirit world.

Melek shook his head sadly. "No. I am afraid those sounds are very real."

"What are they?"

His face tightened. "Though this place was made for me, it was not made to keep out mortal souls. Though it is rare, occasionally one finds its way here."

Gewey thought he saw a tear form in Melek's eye, but couldn't be sure.

"It drives them mad," he continued in a half-whisper. "They were never meant to be here. I have tried to help them, but they cannot accept that I exist. In time, they fade into nothing more than the hollow sounds of pain and confusion—their spirits forever lost." He looked up at Gewey and forced a smile. "But you have nothing to fear. You will not dwell here long enough to endure the trials I have. And even if you were to do so, you are a god. It is beyond the power of Shagharath to drive you insane. Only mortal minds succumb to the madness in this place."

"Is there nothing we can do for them?"

Melek shook his head and took a pained breath. "I have tried many times. They are beyond our reach."

"How many are there?"

His face became awash with guilt. "I've forgotten. I am ashamed to say that I no longer pay them mind. When I finally realized it was hopeless, I did what I could to push them from my thoughts. I know I shouldn't have, but it was too heavy a burden for my heart to bear."

"I understand," said Gewey. He could see Melek's pain reflected in his slumped posture. "Perhaps, after we escape, we can find a way to free them, too."

Melek took a long, deep breath. "You have a kind heart. I had forgotten what it is like to hear words of comfort spoken aloud. But before we leave, there are things you must know. Things only I can show you. And they will not be easy for you to see."

"What things?" asked Gewey.

"I will show you what Gerath hoped you would never know."

He took hold of Gewey's hand. "I need your help ... and not just to leave Shagharath."

CHAPTER 6

L ee sat beside a small fire, silently staring at the flames as they swirled and licked in a chaotic dance. The sound of laments forced its way into his ears, bringing a snarl of frustration.

Millet, Jacob, and several others had tried to speak with him, but he was in no mood for conversation. Gewey was dead, and now all hope was lost. More than that, he had sacrificed everything only to fail. His wife was dead—or worse. His son had grown up without a father, and he spent what could have been the best years of his life playing the eccentric noble in a shabby little farming village far from everything he loved.

He glanced up at the nearby pavilion where Gewey's body rested. Through the thin cloth, he could see the silhouette of Kaylia kneeling beside her dead love. Many elves were gathered just outside the pavilion, but none dared to approach her. Kaylia had already attacked three of the desert elves merely for suggesting funeral rites, and only Linis's quick reflexes had prevented her from actually killing them.

By the time Lee and Linis had returned to camp after finding the Sharpstone villagers and convincing them to go back to their homes, Kaylia had already carried Gewey body's back and was standing over him, eyes wild and knife drawn. She scarcely recognized anyone and gave not the slightest reaction when the elves began erecting the pavilion around them.

Linis approached, his eyes still red from weeping. He sat beside Lee and ran his fingers through his hair.

"The desert elves are wondering what we are to do," he muttered, as much to himself as to Lee. "Their spirit is broken."

Lee snorted. "I care nothing for the spirit of the desert elves. Let them do as they will."

"I understand your pain," said Linis. "But now we must -"

"*We* must do nothing." Lee's voice was a deep, rumbling growl. "I will no longer take part in this bloody war."

"What will you do?" he asked, not sounding surprised.

"I will go north," Lee replied. "I will face the Reborn King."

"Then it is as I feared," Linis remarked. "You intend to seek your own death. However, I think your son may object to such foolishness."

"I don't care who objects."

"I see." Linis paused. "Will you at least help us sort out what to do with Kaylia?"

Lee shrugged. "What is there to sort out? The best thing you can do is leave her be. Otherwise, she'll gut you."

"Of that, I am certain," agreed Linis. "But she will not allow anyone near her, or Gewey. She keeps muttering that he is not really dead. I think her mind may be gone."

"And what do you think I can do about it?" Lee snapped. "Her friendship with you is far stronger than it is with me. If she wants to sit here until Gewey's body rots—then so be it."

"Have you no love for her?" Linis's tone was disapproving. "Have you no compassion for—"

Lee's hand shot out and grabbed Linis roughly by the collar. Eyes ablaze, he pulled the elf nose to nose. "Don't you dare speak to me of love and compassion, elf. I was robbed of my love." Pushing Linis back, he returned his gaze to the fire. "And as for compassion—it was compassion that twisted my mind and made me abandon my family. Compassion for a child that now lies dead. Dead, just like the hope he was supposed to bring."

Any anger Linis might have felt over Lee's outburst was well concealed. Instead, he stood slowly up and brushed himself off. "I will leave you to your despair," he said quietly.

Lee did not bother to respond, or even glance in his direction.

Several minutes later, Millet approached and sat down just across from Lee.

"Linis tells me you intend to commit suicide," he said. His voice was hard and accusing.

Lee shot him a hot glance. "I do as I choose."

"You will do as I say, Lee Starfinder," countered Millet. "You are in the service of the House Nal'Thain, and are honor-bound to remain so until I release you."

The fury in Millet's expression and the steel in his voice forced Lee to avert his eyes. His mind reeled, and his heart began beating wildly. He would *not* be spoken to like that. For an instant, a part of him wanted to reach out and throttle his former servant and current lord.

But the anger faded as quickly as it had formed. Like it or not, something in Millet's words had touched him deep within his heart, and all he could feel now was deep and humiliating shame. A tear escaped down his cheek as he struggled to keep himself from weeping openly.

Millet's tone softened considerably. "Your son is waiting for you as we speak. Whatever you may feel right now, I know your love for him has not diminished. Yes, Gewey is dead. And yes, this will likely mean our doom. But until our fate is upon us, Jacob still needs you. He still needs his father."

Try as he might, Lee could no longer hold back the tears. His body jerked repeatedly from his stifled sobs. "My entire life ... a waste. I have failed everyone through my stupidity."

"Nonsense," Millet told him. He shifted, as if thinking to move beside his friend, but then settled back down. He knew this was not quite the moment. "You left Hazrah to protect your wife and child. More than that, you have stood proud against the oncoming darkness. You have stared into the eyes of doom and not lost courage. Where most men, be they human or elf, would have fled for their very lives, you have remained firm."

Millet sighed and smiled. "I have known you since you were nothing more than a child. I may have thought you were stubborn and rash, but never have you been a coward."

"Until now," added Lee.

"Bah!" This time Millet did move beside his old friend. "You despair like the rest of us. Only you have taken it upon yourself to be responsible for Gewey's death." He put his hand on Lee's shoulder. "The Dark Knight caused this. *He* killed Gewey. *He* is the one ravaging the world."

Lee nodded slowly. "I know. And I wish I could banish the shadow that blackens my soul."

"As your friend, I would tell you to look to those who love you. They will bolster your strength." His hand seized Lee's shoulder tightly. "As your lord, I tell you that I swear you will have your chance to let loose your wrath."

Lee looked at Millet, momentarily surprised by his intensely dangerous tone.

Millet forced a smile that quickly disappeared. "I am not unaffected by what has happened. I had hoped that Gewey would avenge Lady Penelope—or perhaps even save her. But that hope is gone. All I can do now is stand against our enemy and make him pay dearly for his arrogance." Getting to his feet, he held out his hand. "And if I am to die, I *will* have you with me."

Lee paused, then took a long, accepting breath. He grasped Millet's hand and stood beside him. "Where is my son?"

"He is speaking with Lyrial and Bevaris," Millet replied, motioning to the far side of the camp. "They are debating on what to do."

"And what of Kaylia?" he asked. "Linis tells me she has completely lost her reason."

"She still will not allow anyone near Gewey's body. She claims that she can still feel him."

"But their bond is broken," Lee pointed out. "She may be insane with grief, but that much she was able to tell us."

Millet's jaw tightened and there was a long pause.

"What is it?" pressed Lee. The look on his friend's face told him there was more to Kaylia's condition than he was being told.

"She claims she can feel him through the bond that connects Gewey and…"

Millet hesitated before adding: "Between Gewey and their unborn child."

This information hit Lee like a hammer. "She's pregnant?"

"Yes," said Millet.

Lee stood silently as he allowed this new revelation to sink in. "Then it is clear what we must do," he said finally.

"What is that?"

"We must protect her at all costs."

"She will not abandon Gewey's body," explained Millet.

"Then we'll bring it with us." Without another word, Lee strode off in the direction that Millet had earlier indicated he would find Jacob.

By the time he reached his son and the others, Dina and Linis had also joined the group. Lee gave Linis an apologetic nod. The elf nodded in return and seized Lee's shoulders fondly.

"It is good you are with us again, my friend," he said.

"I regret..." began Lee, but Linis shook his head, silently telling him that such apologies were unnecessary.

Lee turned to his son and gave him a loving embrace.

"Now don't start apologizing to me as well," joked Jacob with a youthful grin.

Lee was grateful for the moment of levity, but a second later, the mood turned grave.

"Millet has told you about Kaylia?" Dina asked him.

Lee nodded. "He did. Have you been able to get through to her?"

"No," she replied. "She is unable to see beyond her pain."

"I think..." began Weila.

"No!" Linis cut in angrily. "We will not burn Gewey's body. It would destroy her."

"He needs to be given proper rites," Weila countered stubbornly. "Darshan must be laid to rest. Only then will she move on."

Lee shook his head. "If you try, she'll kill you. For now, we must do whatever she wants. And her child must be protected. Gewey has died, and because of that, the world will burn. But perhaps his child can one day redeem us."

"How will we do this?" asked Dina. "Now we are without Gewey. The armies of Angrääl will surely attack us very soon."

"I don't know," admitted Lee.

"We could take her to the desert," offered Lyrial.

"No," said Lee sternly. "Eventually they would find her there." He thought for a moment, then said, "We must get her to Aaliyah. She can take her across the Western Abyss to her lands."

There was a long silence. Gradually, the entire group began nodding in agreement.

Dina cleared her throat. "I should point out that for us to get her to Aaliyah, we must first get her out of the pavilion."

Lee sighed. "I will attend to that." He walked off with renewed purpose.

Despite his determination, Lee could feel the uneasiness in his stomach steadily growing. He knew there was a good chance she would not listen to what he had to say. In fact, she may even try to kill him. The last thing he wanted was for things to turn violent. Kaylia was a deadly foe, even under normal circumstances. How he might be able to subdue her without causing any physical harm was beyond him.

As he neared the entrance to the pavilion, he could hear Kaylia shifting to face in his direction. Clearly, she was aware of someone approaching. He pulled back the tent flaps and cautiously stepped inside.

She was crouched over Gewey's body like a great cat, ready to pounce. The long blade in her hand shimmered in the dim light emanating from a small lantern in the corner. Lee couldn't help but notice that Gewey's body was not pale; in fact, he looked as healthy as one merely sleeping. *She must be using the* flow *to keep his body warm*, he thought.

"What do you want?" she demanded. Her voice was steady and emotionless. But her eyes told a different tale.

"To help," Lee replied, holding up his palm in a gesture of peace.

"If you think for one second that I will allow you to burn him..."

"I have no intention of burning him," Lee quickly assured her. "But we do need to take him away from here."

"He still lives," she said, not seeming to hear what he was telling her. "Our child can still feel him." Her hand passed in front of her belly and she flashed Lee an accusing stare. "I know what you want. You think Gewey is dead. You want to spirit us away so that our child will fight your battles for you when he grows up."

Lee was momentarily stunned by her insight. He could see her muscles tense, preparing to burst forth. He shook his head in denial.

"Do not bother to lie, half-man," she hissed before Lee could respond. "I know your mind. Do you think I would allow my child to be used as you have used Gewey? The child of Gewey Stedding will live a life of peace. And do you know why?" Her voice was becoming increasingly loud and shrill. "Because my *unorem* is *not* dead. He will rise. He will cleanse the world and make it safe again. You will see."

Lee tried to keep his voice soothing and sympathetic. "Kaylia—think. If you are right, then we must move him soon. The enemy will attack before long, and we will not be able to stop them."

"We remain here!" she shouted.

Lee took a step back and crouched down, putting himself at her eye level. He knew this made his situation much more dangerous. If she attacked, he would be off balance.

"Please see reason," he pleaded. "If you remain here, they *will* take Gewey from you. Let us take him away from this place. Let us keep him safe."

"*I* will keep him safe," she shot back. "I do not need you—or anyone else. And when he returns, you will pay for your lack of faith." She let out a maniacal laugh. "You will then truly know the power of Darshan."

Lee could see her madness growing with each passing second. There seemed little doubt that this would have to turn violent. In a final effort, he reached out to her with his thoughts.

The raging turmoil that had become Kaylia's mind threw him back effortlessly, in the process making him momentarily dizzy. In the time it took for Lee to recover, Kaylia had spanned the distance between them and was bringing her blade across in a tight horizontal slash in an attempt to open his throat.

Her speed was astounding. Lee was only just able to rock back out of danger in time. Not that this bought him anything but a moment's respite. Kaylia pressed in, furiously thrusting with the blade. In spite of her insanity, her attack was calculated and controlled. Lee had only a split second to react. A lesser man would have already been slain. But Lee's years of experience and training had taught his muscles to do exactly what was required. Springing forward inside Kaylia's guard, he gripped her wrist firmly. Not wanting to injure either her or, more importantly, her unborn child, he brought her arm back and twisted with just enough force to make her release the knife.

But Kaylia was not to be so easily overcome. Her other hand shot out, striking Lee in the temple. The force of this blow stunned him long enough for her to bring her knee sharply up. With a dull thud, it made contact right in the middle of his groin.

Lee grunted and doubled over, eyes watering and pain shooting through his entire body. Kaylia immediately pulled herself free and sprang over to where her weapon had fallen. Forcing back the pain, he chased after her. Kaylia's hand had barely touched the hilt of her blade when Lee's weight fell on top of her. Once again, he seized hold of her wrist and pulled her arm back. Using his body mass to keep her face down, he quickly trapped her other arm. Still, Kaylia screamed and fought, but Lee's half-man strength was too much—though only just.

"Help me!" Lee yelled out to anyone who might be within earshot. If this went on for too much longer, he had grave fears that she would hurt either herself or the baby.

Gewey's body was only a few feet away from where they lay. Kaylia looked over and began to struggle even harder.

"Do not burn him!" she screamed out over and over again.

"Remove yourself from her at once, Lee Starfinder!" came a commanding female voice.

In the entrance stood Maybell, her hands firmly on her hips, her face red with anger.

"If I let her go, she'll kill us both," he shouted back through several grunts of exertion.

In a move Lee could have never anticipated, Maybell produced a short dagger. With surprising speed, she stepped forward and pressed the cold steel to his throat.

"And if you don't let her go, I will kill you myself," she said, her tone calm and measured.

At first, Lee did not respond. But as Maybell increased the pressure, he felt a trickle of blood running down his neck. There was also a fiercely determined look in her eyes that told him she would most likely carry out her threat.

Reluctantly, he released his hold on Kaylia, who immediately scrambled away to retrieve her knife. Lee expected the elf to renew her attack, but Maybell removed the dagger from his throat and placed herself between the pair of them.

Kaylia stood tensed and ready while Maybell stared silently into Lee's eyes. He could see quite clearly that this was not the same woman he had met and traveled with. She was now burdened with great purpose and filled with unrelenting determination.

"You should leave," she said with imposing authority. "Now! I will speak to Kaylia alone."

Lee was compelled to obey. As he left the tent, he realized that Maybell was no longer wearing her priestess' robes, but a simple blue dress.

Linis, Dina, and Millet were immediately outside. Jacob, Bevaris, and the elves were only a few yards away.

"Where did she come from?" Lee asked, trying to make some sense of what had just happened.

"She just walked straight into the camp and demanded to know where Gewey's body was being kept," Linis replied.

"How the hell did she know about Gewey?"

Lee's question was met with silence.

"What should we do?" asked Dina.

"Wait," replied Lee. "What else can we do?"

CHAPTER 7

Gewey found himself alone alongside a tiny stream. The air was fresh and clean as it blew in from the distant snow-capped mountains, and the deep emerald-colored grass was like walking on feather pillows. The water of the stream, sparkling from the light of the noonday sun, was given an even more delicate beauty by the multicolored pebbles scattered along its bed.

Gewey bent down to touch the water. It was cold, almost to the point of being painful, yet it still brought a smile to his lips. It was at that moment he realized Melek was no longer with him.

Gewey called out his name.

"I am here," Melek said. He was standing beside him as if he had been there the entire time.

"Where are we?"

"Exactly where we were before."

Gewey looked confused, but Melek gave him a reassuring smile.

"This is an image of your memories," he explained. "An image of heaven."

Gewey's eyes widened. "Heaven? This is heaven?" He scanned the landscape. "I have no memory of this place."

"Of course not," said Melek. "Gerath saw to that. But you still have the ... the impression of it, if you like, locked away inside of you." He looked around with approval. "And it is a better image than I expected."

"Image?"

"Your human self could never fathom the majesty of heaven. And even now, it is that part of you that dominates your being. You see heaven in a way you can understand it." Melek waved his arm in a sweeping gesture. "And this is what your mind tells you it looks like."

Gewey creased his brow. "Actually, I've never thought about what heaven would look like. And now that I have, I must admit I'm not impressed."

Melek chuckled. "I am. You transformed Shagharath into a thing of beauty. Even if it is only for a short time."

"So what is it that I'm supposed to see?"

Melek pointed to a small ball of light that had appeared just a few yards away on the other side of the stream.

"What is that?" asked Gewey.

He placed his hand gently on Gewey's shoulder. "Watch and you will see."

The light hovered for a few seconds before drifting gracefully down to the stream's surface. Then, just as it touched the water, it flew skyward for at least twenty feet. On reaching its zenith, the shining ball finally descended slowly back to earth. Gewey started to get the impression that it was playing a game.

A mist formed just behind the light, and from out of this, two figures stepped forth. Gewey recognized them at once. It was Gerath and Ayliazarah. His father was clad in a shimmering silver robe, tied at the waist by a red sash. Ayliazarah wore a blue silken gown that flowed freely around her curves.

Gewey stared in awe, unable to move or speak.

"How long will you let this continue?" asked Ayliazarah. Her voice was as musical as Gewey remembered, even while scolding Gerath. "You cannot keep it in ignorance forever."

Gerath looked intensely at the light and shook his head. "I cannot. I need more time."

The light began to dance and bob. It flew toward Ayliazarah, circling her as if excited. The goddess laughed and held out her delicate hand, allowing the light to brush against her fingers.

"You should not encourage it so," said Gerath, clearly displeased. "It is bad enough that you allow it to see you."

She flashed Gerath a fierce look. "I do as I please. That you cannot reconcile with your own heart is no reason for me to leave the innocent alone and afraid."

"Do not try to shame me, sister." Gerath's voice was low, yet the ground trembled.

Ayliazarah was unmoved by this display. "And you, brother, do not try to cow me. You are not my master. And you do not hold sway over my choices."

Gerath lowered his eyes. "I am sorry. I did not mean to suggest..."

Ayliazarah reached out and took Gerath's hand. "I know why you are so distant. Your heart has always been transparent to me. Though mortals name me the goddess of fertility and love, it was always you who cared too deeply for your own good."

Gerath gave her a sideways smile. He brought her hand to his lips and kissed it gently. "If only the others understood me the way you do." He fixed his gaze on the light. "They would know why I have yet to complete it, and they would not chastise me so."

She pulled her hand away. "I may understand you, Gerath, but I do not condone what you are doing. Make no mistake, I stand with the others. You are abandoning your obligation to us, to the Creator, but most of all, to your child."

Gewey caught his breath. *His child?* The next thought bounced painfully around in his head. *Then the ball of light. It was ... it was me. And...*

"And Gerath could not bear the sight of you," said Melek, finishing Gewey's thought.

The sharp sting of rejection stuck in Gewey's chest. *But surely he didn't continue to feel that way,* he told himself. He remembered the kindness and love coming from the essence of Gerath when they had spoken in the Black Oasis.

"Do not be deceived," warned Melek. "The heart of Gerath is as black as the darkest night. Soon you shall see."

Gewey took a deep breath to steady himself before returning his attention to the vision.

"At least make him aware of you," suggested Ayliazarah.

Gerath took a long look at the light. Finally, he gave an almost imperceptible nod. At once, the light hung motionless. After a few, short seconds, it eased its way closer to its father. At first, Gerath did nothing. Then he raised his hand and touched it with the tip of his finger. The light glowed brighter and brighter until Gewey was forced to shield his eyes and could no longer watch.

"No!" Gerath's voice thundered.

The light withdrew a few feet and dimmed.

Ayliazarah leaned in close to Gerath. "He knows who you are," she whispered.

"He?" scoffed Gerath. "*It* is neither he nor she. At least, not yet."

The goddess flashed a girlish grin. "I have a sense about these things. He has no form as of this moment, but once he reaches the earthly plain ... yes ... definitely a son."

"It makes no difference," he countered angrily. "I will not love this child."

The light began to approach its father a few inches at a time—stopping and hovering, then moving again. Just as it was within arm's reach, Gerath clapped his hands sharply together. The air shattered in a sharp crack and the light was pushed away. After a few moments, it once again tried to move closer, but it was now being held firmly in place by an unseen force.

Gewey looked on in horror. He'd expected Ayliazarah to intervene, but she did not.

"And hurting him is the answer for you, it would seem," she chided. She turned away, shaking her head.

Perhaps in an attempt to escape whatever was holding it, the light began changing color. First it became a shade of green, moments later it became red, and then just as quickly it was back to green again. As it continued to quiver and struggle, Gewey thought he could hear a cry. But he wasn't sure if this was real or imagined. Even his own body was beginning to feel constricted as he watched the fire in Gerath's eyes increase.

"Petty and cruel," said Melek. "That is your father. He is, as he always was."

After a short while longer, Gerath released the light. It immediately fled from him, but only traveled less than one hundred feet before stopping and settling on the grass.

"So, is your intent to make him hate you?" asked Ayliazarah.

Gerath clenched his fists. "I do not know. The Creator forgive me, I do not know what to do. I never wanted this. I never wanted ... *him*." The word "him" passed his lips like a curse.

Ayliazarah threw her head back in laughter. "Since when does the mighty Gerath get to choose the service given to him by the Creator? No, my brother. You cannot delay for much longer. A father you are, and a father you must be."

Gerath made no response to this. Pausing only to glance at his sister for the briefest of moments, he walked off back into the mist.

As soon as he was gone, Ayliazarah moved with graceful strides over to where the light still rested on the grass. She kneeled down beside it and reached out, but withdrew her hand an instant before making contact. "He may be right," she said quietly. "The Creator forgive me, he may be right about you."

The images faded and Gewey found himself back inside Melek's house, staring out of the window. The barren wasteland was even more horrible to behold than before.

"What did she mean: *He may be right about me?*" he demanded. "Right about what? None of this makes sense."

Melek left Gewey's side and sat down at the table. He took a sip of wine and then nodded toward the chair opposite him. After a final lingering look out of the window, Gewey came across.

"What you saw was the real truth about the gods," said Melek. "Their hatred and malice know no bounds. Not even when it concerns their offspring—or their parents."

Gewey saw a flash of rage pass over Melek's face, but it was quickly gone.

"Why would Gerath do this?" he asked. "Why would he reject me—and hurt me?" His fingernails clawed their way into the wooden table. "And why would Ayliazarah not come to my aid?" He laid his head in his hands. "I don't understand any of this."

"These are things you were never supposed to see," Melek told him. "That form—that ball of light—was you before you were given *true* consciousness. You were then simply a being of life and emotion." He shook his head. "How Gerath could have left you that way for so long is beyond my understanding."

He took a deep breath before continuing. "When my beloved wife and I gave birth to the gods, we knew that such an existence would be unbearable. Possessing emotions without the intelligence to govern them is a nightmare.

Gerath had you endure what he never had to. We gave our children a mind the moment they came into this world."

"I still don't understand," said Gewey meekly. His reason was slipping away. "That was me ... and yet it wasn't?"

"It was you," affirmed Melek. "It was your spirit. Your essence. But until Gerath allowed his own spirit to make full contact with yours, you were without a rational mind. You could feel, but you did not have the capacity to make sense of your emotions." He sighed. "It was the same with all of my children. But as I said, we did not leave them to languish in limbo: that would have been cruel. We knew that for every joy, there is also sorrow and fear."

"How long was I left like that?" asked Gewey.

Melek shrugged. "It is impossible to say. Time in heaven is not measured as it is on earth. But even a short time would have seemed like an eternity."

Gewey was grateful he could not remember. This feeling merged with a growing hatred for his father.

"I understand," said Melek. "And in time you will face him and exact your revenge."

Gewey no longer minded that Melek was again reading his thoughts. His words were comforting. *Yes, I would like revenge,* he thought, almost involuntarily.

"But none of this explains why," he said aloud.

"Because of what you are," replied Melek.

"What I am? I'm a god, just like them."

"Like them," said Melek. "But also like me. You have the light of the Creator within you. It is why they fear you. It is why, even if you were able to serve their needs, in the end, they will not suffer you to live. Like me, you will be betrayed." He poured them both another cup of wine. "That is ... unless you heed my words and stand by my side when the time comes."

Gewey found himself nodding without even thinking about it. Then, somewhere in the recesses of his mind, a moment of doubt crept in. There were questions he needed the answers to, but couldn't form the words.

Sensing this, Melek drained his cup and smiled. "But there is more for you to see before you make your decision."

"What happens then?" asked Gewey. He felt anxious to see more, but also afraid of what he might discover.

"Then we will leave this place," he replied. "Together, you and I will right all the many wrongs done to us both."

The house faded, and now they were inside a circular chamber. The floor was made from flawless white marble. In stark contrast, the walls were hewn from a black stone with gold threads running through it that appeared to pulse and flow as blood through veins. Standing in a semi-circle around the edge of the chamber were nine figures clad in the purest white robes. Gewey knew instinctively who they all were.

From left to right stood Saraf—God of the Oceans, Islisema—Goddess of the Moon and Stars, Helenasia—Goddess of Healing and Knowledge, Dantenos—God of the Dead, Gerath—God of the Earth, Althetas Mol—Goddess of Wisdom and Compassion, Pósix—Goddess of the Dawn and Light, Hephisolis—God of Fire, and Ayliazarah—Goddess of Fertility and Love.

All were staring intensely at the small globe of light in the very center of the room.

Gewey could not have averted his eyes, even if he had wanted to. Their sheer beauty and majesty, enriched by a soft golden aura, were irresistible.

"And there they all are," said Melek, not hiding his contempt. "My children. My greatest accomplishment—and my greatest blunder."

Melek's bitter words broke the mesmerizing spell holding Gewey. He shook his head and rubbed his eyes. "What are they doing?"

Before Melek could respond, Althetas Mol stepped forward and faced the assembly.

"Gerath," she said accusingly, pointing her finger. Her voice echoed throughout the chamber, each repetition of her brother's name sounding louder than the previous. Then, all at once, there was silence. "Why is your child still unborn?"

Gerath appeared unaffected—almost bored. "As this is *my* child, I see no reason to explain myself to you." He glanced left and right. "To *any* of you."

"But the child is not yours alone," corrected Hephisolis. "The Creator was directly involved. Defying *her* is not wise and could impact us all."

"I am not defying *her*," he replied, with only a hint of emotion. "I am merely proceeding in my own fashion."

Althetas Mol took a step forward. "Do you think us so easily deceived? You intend to forgo the sacrifice. Do not bother to deny it."

This time Gerath was unable to contain his irritation. His lips twisted into a snarl. "And if I do, that is still my decision to make."

This brought murmurs of disagreement from the others.

"I do not think our brother intends to defy the Creator," interjected Ayliazarah. "He would not risk *her* wrath being brought down upon us all."

Althetas Mol huffed. "Always it is *you* who takes up his banner. Have you no mind of your own?"

Ayliazarah smiled at the comment. "Of course I do, my sweet sister. And, as it happens, I agree that Gerath should complete what he has begun. However, I am not eager to accuse him of endangering us—as you seem to be. In fact, was it not you who screamed like a mortal girl when you were told that the child would be born? Goddess of wisdom indeed. You said in no uncertain terms that this would be the end of us all."

"And I still believe it to be so," she countered. "We all know what will happen once these events are set in motion. Even still, I obey. Though my faith is shaken, I will carry out the will of our Creator. And I am prepared to suffer the consequences I am sure will follow. Are you?"

"I do not know." Ayliazarah lowered her eyes and folded her hands in front of her. "I only know that once the child is truly among us, I must have faith that the Creator will return." A single tear from her eye fell to the marble floor like a silver raindrop, shattering as though made of glass as it landed. "I feel *her* absence as keenly as any of you. As my prayers pass from my lips into oblivion, I suffer—as do you all. But it is like you said: we are commanded to carry out *her* will."

"Then we are in agreement." It was Saraf who spoke. "Gerath should proceed without delay."

"I did not say that," Ayliazarah protested. "I said that Gerath would not endanger us. If he feels he should wait, then I will not try to force him to do otherwise. And if you value peace in heaven, you will follow my example."

As her final words faded, the entire assembly erupted into a heated, unintelligible argument. The volume of angry voices rose to unimaginable levels, forcing Gewey to cover his ears. However, through the tempest of conflicting opinions, he was somehow able to work out how things stood amongst them. Pósix and Hephisolis were in agreement with Ayliazarah that Gerath should do what he considered best. The rest of them were bitterly opposed.

Melek held out his hand and the volume of the voices decreased.

"Look at them," he spat. "Pathetic."

"I didn't understand any of that," said Gewey, the echoes of the debate still bouncing around inside his head.

Melek let out a hearty laugh. "I am not surprised. I am their father, and even I struggle to understand them. Apparently, Gerath refuses to carry out the Creator's edict and bring you fully into the world. He knows your birth heralds their end—something that he is most anxious not to have come to pass. But there is more. It would also seem that the moment you came to be, the Creator abandoned them all." He laughed again, this time for nearly a full minute.

"That much I already know," Gewey said after Melek had settled down. "I learned of it when I discovered who my true mother is. But I was also told that she is to return once my destiny is fulfilled."

Melek cocked his head and raised an eyebrow. "Will *she*? I think Gerath is afraid *she* will not. The rest of them follow blindly, wanting him to complete your birth in order to hasten *her* return. Not that they have any hope, regardless of what happens. The Creator will do them no good, so what would it matter?"

"What are you saying?" asked Gewey, shocked. "Of course, it matters."

"Why? Why would it be so important? What has our beloved Creator done for the world?"

"Well, *she* created it," Gewey pointed out. "Isn't that enough? Without *her*, none of us would even exist."

"True," admitted Melek. "But *she* has also stood idle while millions suffered and died. The *firstborn* drove themselves mad. And, were it not for their immortality, they would have killed each other right down to the very last. Even so, they were able to inflict unbearable suffering. On and on it went until their feeble minds could grasp nothing but blood and destruction."

His eyes met with Gewey's. "Is that the love of the Creator? And when I sought to right the wrongs of my children, *she* allowed them to banish me to this desolate nightmare of a prison." He grunted in a very human way.

"So you don't want the Creator to return?"

Melek shrugged. "I just don't think it would matter, even if *she* did." His eyes returned to the gods. "Ah, I see Gerath is nearly ready to boil over."

As if on cue, Gerath spread his arms. "Enough of this!"

His voice was like rolling thunder. The other gods stepped away, startled.

The group had all but forgotten the ball of light. It was now visibly trembling as Gerath approached, his expression grim. Kneeling down, he placed his hands upon it. In response to his touch, as Gewey had seen before, the light grew brighter and brighter. But this time Gerath did not withdraw, instead allowing it to continue increasing until it had completely surrounded him. After several minutes of this, the brightness gradually dimmed and faded away.

Where the light had once been, a small child of no more than three years old now stood. Its features were fine and delicate, yet strong and proud, giving the impression of being both male and female.

Gerath stood and looked directly into the child's eyes. "I name you Darshan."

This done, he reached out toward Ayliazarah, who rushed to his side and wrapped her arm around him. "I need rest," Gerath told her. "Help me."

A swirling portal of blue light appeared just behind them. Ayliazarah led Gerath through it. Darshan watched as his father disappeared without a word.

One by one, the other gods stepped near to the child, looked at it for a moment, and then also entered the portal. Althetas Mol was the last.

"Where am I?" asked Darshan. His tiny voice was soft and vulnerable.

"You are home," she replied, taking his hand.

"Who are you?"

Althetas Mol smiled but did not reply.

Gewey watched them vanish through the portal. A tear fell down his cheek.

Melek placed a hand on Gewey's shoulder. "Are you all right?"

Gewey noticed that they were back inside Melek's house. He walked over to the table and took a seat. Melek poured him a cup of wine and sat down in the chair opposite.

"I really thought my father loved me," said Gewey. "But clearly he didn't."

The howl of the wind outside rose once again, carrying with it the wild voices of tormented souls.

"There is more," said Melek. "And though I wish it was not so, you must see it. One final time ... then you can decide."

Gewey nodded. "I understand."

CHAPTER 8

Several hours had passed, yet still, there was no news from Maybell about what was happening. Lee had spent most of the time constantly pacing back and forth. It got to the point where Millet was compelled to command him to be still.

Lee and Linis had both tried to hear what was going on inside the pavilion, but even with their heightened senses, they could catch only a few words. Certainly not enough to make out any details of what the two women were talking about.

The camp was buzzing with rumors about who the mysterious woman might be. Some said she was the mother of Darshan—others a priestess came to heal him. A few even went so far as to suggest that the goddess Helenasia had come down to breathe life back into his lungs. This widespread speculation continued apace, even though Weila had been quite free about telling her people who the woman actually was.

"They despair over Darshan's death," said Lyrial sadly. "Their hope is so strong that they would believe anything— even the impossible."

"I would not go so far as to say the impossible," corrected Linis. "Though I doubt that Maybell can raise the dead, she has certainly come for a reason. Perhaps she brings with her the hope your people require."

Dina took his arm and rested her head on his shoulder. "I pray that you're right."

Another hour passed. Eventually, Lee could wait no longer. He set off with rapid strides toward the pavilion, with Dina, Millet, Jacob, and Linis all chasing after him. Flinging back the flap, he pushed his way inside but then stopped short.

"I was about to call for you," said Maybell. "Please sit." She was cross-legged on the ground, with Kaylia's head resting in her lap. The girl was fast asleep.

Gewey's body remained where they had left it; his skin was still pink and looking very much alive. But for the fact that his chest was not moving, he could simply have been resting.

With soft, careful steps, Lee moved closer and sat down a few feet across from Maybell. The others followed a moment later and formed a loose circle.

"You don't need to be quiet," Maybell told them. She smiled tenderly as she looked down at Kaylia and stroked her hair. "She is beyond exhausted and will sleep for some time."

Lee couldn't believe it. The last time he'd seen Kaylia, she had been totally possessed with rage and sorrow. "How did you...? I mean..."

"She is an amazing woman," said Maybell, her gaze still lingering on her charge. "How she endured it, I can't imagine. Were it not for her child, she would have surely tried to follow him in death."

"It is her child that concerns us," said Linis. "They are not safe here."

"And why would you say that?" asked Maybell. "There are no enemies nearby. And soon you will again have the protection of Darshan."

Her words produced a stunned silence.

"You are all a bunch of fools," she scoffed. "You really are. Gewey is a *god*. Do you think him so easily killed?" She began stroking Kaylia's hair again. "Even through her madness, she understood this. She knew he still lived." Maybell glanced up to give the group an accusing look. "After all you have been through and all you have learned, did you not think that perhaps Kaylia might know something you did not? She is his wife and mother of his unborn child. And here you are, ready to drag her away against her will."

"What choice did we have?" snapped Lee. "We have thirty thousand elves exposed and cut off deep inside enemy territory. We are weeks away from Althetas, and our only hope for success has died. Then we find out that, not only has Kaylia gone insane, she's also pregnant. What would you have us do? Sit here and wait for Angräal to figure out what has happened and slaughter us?"

"Of course not," she replied. "But I *would* have you show some faith in Kaylia. She tells you that Gewey still lives. She feels it through her unborn child. Yet you pay her words no mind. You don't even attempt to understand and just want to drag her away from here. I may not be a soldier, but even I know it would take time for Angräal to mount an assault large enough to defeat you."

She wagged her finger at Lee. "And don't you dare tell me you tried to listen to her. I know you, Lee Starfinder. You tried to impose your will. That is why I found you wrestling her to the ground when I arrived. Kaylia will not be dissuaded from what she knows in her heart is the right thing to do. And the moment you all understand this simple fact, the better off you'll be."

"That's not fair," protested Dina. "We had no way of knowing anything other than Gewey had been killed and Kaylia was mad with grief. We have no idea how he died. Only that he did. All she told us was that he had been struck by..."

"A dart," Maybell interrupted. "Yes, I know. But didn't it seem at least a bit odd to you that something so small could end the life of a god?"

"We thought it was likely poison," said Linis. "Though I could not detect any."

"You wouldn't," said Maybell. "Do you have it with you?"

Linis reached into his tunic and pulled out a folded piece of leather, which he carefully opened. Inside lay the tiny dart. The tip gleamed brightly.

Maybell chuckled. "When I tell you what this is, I think you will not be keeping it so close to your flesh again." She picked it up gingerly, holding it with her thumb and forefinger. "What you see here is one of the Fangs of Yajna." This brought no reaction. "The elves have a name for it as well." She looked at Linis and grinned devilishly. "Your people know it as The Needle of Shagharath."

Linis turned pale. "You mean..."

"That you placed the gateway to eternal darkness next to your heart?" Maybell nodded. "Yes. That's exactly what I mean."

She took a long look at the dart before placing it back in the wrappings. Linis got up to place it in the corner, this time holding it as far away from his body as possible.

"What exactly is it?" asked Dina, clearly upset by Linis's reaction.

"It is a weapon created long ago by the gods," Maybell explained. "Created for a single purpose. To banish the spirit of the god Melek."

Again, there was no reaction.

"I have read many volumes," said Lee, after it was clear that no one had any idea who Melek was. "I have spent years within the Trixion Library. I am one of only three people who have a key. But not once have I seen that name mentioned. Nor have I heard of the Fangs of Yajna."

"That's not surprising," said Maybell. "Its ancient knowledge passed on to me by the Oracle of Manisalia. The elves have some legends that mention it. But I doubt even their elders know very much."

Linis pulled Dina close. "It is said that the Needle of Shagharath will send you to a night so black and eternal that you are driven mad the very moment you arrive. The terrors you encounter will make death a sweet release. But you can never die there. You live on, trapped within an endless nightmare."

"I'm afraid your legends are nothing more than stories to frighten children," said Maybell. "Mortal souls were never meant to go to Shagharath. It is a prison with a single purpose. But that is not to say it does not hold peril. It is the dwelling place of Melek, *firstborn* and most powerful of all the gods."

"How is it I have not heard of him?" asked Lee.

"After he was imprisoned there, his memory was then erased from all knowledge and his name forgotten by all but the gods and a few of their servants."

"If that is so," said Dina. "How do you know about him?"

Maybell shrugged slightly. "It would appear the gods feared he might one day manage to escape—or be released. They passed on the knowledge to the Oracle, who wrote this down and gave it to me."

"Why would she pass it on to you?" asked Lee.

"I have asked myself that same question since I was a young novice. It wasn't until I received a letter from the Oracle while in Valshara that it all became clear."

Her expression grew distant. "I was still a wide-eyed girl just two years into my studies when I received a package from Manisalia. I couldn't believe it; it was from the Oracle herself. Not even the high priestess of the temple had met her, and yet here I was—a nobody—receiving parcels from the most famous woman in the world. I was so excited, it was all I could do not to tear the wrapping to shreds. Inside were six leather-bound books and a folded letter."

She let out a half-hearted laugh. "The letter said that I was to learn from the books and keep the knowledge within them close and secret. That one day it would be my destiny to rekindle the light of the world. And when that time came, she would contact me once again. I was so proud that I paid no attention to the ominous tone of the letter. That the Oracle of Manisalia knew who I was and took an interest in me made me the envy of the entire temple. And I must confess ... I loved the attention.

"Over the next few years, I studied and studied until I could practically recite every word from memory. The other sisters and brothers thought I was mad, but being that the request had come from the Oracle herself, not even the high priestess dared to object. She even permitted my other studies to suffer."

Maybell shifted her position, careful not to disturb Kaylia. "Of course, after a few years and having received no further instructions, I eventually hid the books away and moved on with my life."

"What did you learn?" asked Dina.

"They told the story of Melek." The name fell from Maybell's lips like a curse. "He was the *firstborn*, and the father of all the nine gods. In his madness and arrogance, he tried to conquer both heaven and earth. Had it not been for Gerath, who was his eldest son and chief opponent, Melek would certainly have ended up destroying all of creation. Gerath eventually convinced his brothers and sisters to rise up against their father, and so prevented this catastrophe from happening.

"They created Shagharath to imprison his spirit and fashioned a weapon called the Fangs of Yajna that was able to kill Melek's earthly form and send him there." She rubbed the back of her neck. "The story is long, and most of it would mean nothing to you. What's important is that Gewey is in grave danger. Melek is powerful and his heart filled with hatred. Now that Gewey is with him, I must go there and save him."

"How?" asked Lee.

Maybell pulled a letter from the small pocket on the front of her dress. "There is only one way." She handed it to Lee.

Lee studied the words carefully, then read them aloud for the benefit of the others.

"The time has come, sweet Maybell. The hope of the world has been thrown into darkness, and he will be tempted by the father of gods. Now into darkness, you must follow. You know the way and have the courage. The Fangs of Yajna will illuminate your path. But do not fear. You are strong and possess a true and pure heart."

At the bottom of the page was the symbol of the Oracle.

"It could mean only one thing," said Maybell. "And so I came here."

"How will you do this?" asked Linis, though his expression said he already knew the answer.

Maybell only smiled.

Dina gasped as Maybell's intentions became clear. "You mean you are going to... No! You cannot."

"I must."

"If you do this," said Linis. "Will you not also be facing a god?"

"What is the difference between a prisoner and a guard?" asked Maybell.

Her question was met with silence, so she continued. "The guard holds the keys. Melek will have no power over me. I have learned the secrets of Shagharath. If that was not the case, then he would certainly have the advantage. But thankfully, I was an obedient young girl and learned the lessons I needed to fulfill my destiny."

"Can't you return once Gewey has been saved?" asked Dina, tears welling in her eyes.

"I'm afraid not," she replied. "The Fangs of Yajna will destroy my body, making it impossible for my spirit to return." She sighed and looked at her hands. They were wrinkled and calloused from a long life of toil. "I was beautiful once. At least, that's what people told me. I think I'll enjoy being beautiful again."

Dina began to weep openly. Linis pulled her close.

"Are you sure about this?" asked Lee.

Maybell nodded resolutely. "I am. It is time for me to prove my worth."

Lee reached out and placed his hand on hers. "My dear, you have proved your worth long before this day. If all the people had your courage, the Dark Knight would fear to tread even a few yards outside his own fortress."

Maybell couldn't help but laugh. "I wish that were so. But it is kind of you to say." Gently, she removed Kaylia's head from her lap and, wincing as stiff muscles protested, rose to her feet.

The rest stood as well.

Maybell motioned to the near corner of the pavilion, where a small stack of letters tied together with a strip of red silk had been placed. "When I am gone, I would have my correspondence delivered. There are things I would like to have said to people who I will never see again." Her eyes turned to Millet. "Would you attend to this, please? When the war is over, naturally."

Millet nodded and bowed low with deep respect. "It will be done. I swear it."

Maybell touched Millet's cheek and grinned. "Oh, don't be so dramatic," she said playfully. "They're just silly letters from a silly woman to her even sillier friends." She leaned in and kissed his lips with more than simple fondness, allowing the contact to linger for several seconds. "Ah. So that's what it would be like. Please excuse an old woman's one last indulgence."

Millet blushed, not knowing what to say.

She reached again into her pocket, this time removing a folded parchment that she held out to Dina. "This is how I want the rites conducted," she said. Dina recoiled, but Maybell pressed on. "Please, dear. You are the only one who I can trust to do it properly."

After a long moment, Dina reached out and took the parchment.

"Now," said Maybell, with a tone of inevitability. "If you would excuse me, I will speak with Kaylia alone one more time."

Each, in turn, gave her a tearful embrace before departing. Dina's sobs became so uncontrollable that she was no longer able to walk unassisted. Linis was quickly there to hold her tight.

Lee was the last to leave. "You will be remembered," he said, kissing Maybell's hand.

She took a deep breath. "To be truthful, I had hoped to live out my life in obscurity. But now I march headlong into Shagharath to do battle with the most powerful creature to ever set foot on earthly soil."

Lee forced a smile. "I think you will be more than a match for him." His eyes, however, betrayed his doubt.

"It's not Melek that concerns me," she said. "At least, not his power. His prison will make him weak. But his mind will still be keen, and his heart filled with vengeance. I fear that even if I should succeed, Gewey will have fallen prey to his vile nature and lust for retribution."

"In what way?"

"I don't know," she admitted. "But he may need your help when he returns. More than he has ever needed it before."

"I will watch him closely," said Lee.

Maybell rubbed her hands together and took a step back. "And now I must wake Kaylia. So if you please…"

Lee gave her a low, formal bow. It was only with a great effort that he did not weep like the others as he turned and left.

Torches were being lit when Lee emerged. Millet and Jacob were standing near the pavilion entrance. The others were nowhere to be seen.

"What happens now?" asked Jacob.

Lee's grim expression was carved deep into his face. "We allow Sister Maybell to die a hero's death."

Millet bowed his head. "May the gods protect her."

"I think it is Maybell who is protecting the gods," corrected Lee.

The mood in the camp soon became tense. Lee told Weila and Lyrial what had transpired, who immediately spread the news of Maybell's sacrifice.

After an hour or so, a large gathering of elves surrounded the pavilion. Linis and Dina returned, though Dina still had moments when her sorrow completely overwhelmed her. Lee was uncertain if he should enter or simply wait outside for Gewey to emerge. It was just before dawn when the flap finally opened and Kaylia stepped out. Her eyes were red from tears and her posture was bent from exhaustion.

Lee rushed forward, forgetting for a moment that their last encounter had been less than amicable. Kaylia saw him approaching and their eyes met. He quickly saw that the madness had now been replaced by profound sorrow.

"She is gone," whispered Kaylia. "Her body has turned to dust."

Lee was stricken by the thought. "And Gewey?"

"She will not fail," Kaylia replied. She stumbled while taking a step. Lee caught her arm to steady her.

"I am sorry," said Lee. "I should have..."

"My heart has no more room for anger," Kaylia told him. "What you did was not out of hate or malice." She saw Dina and beckoned her over. "Please find an urn for Maybell's remains. She told me that you would know what to do with them."

Dina gasped. "An urn?"

"The Fangs of Yajna have destroyed her body," Kaylia explained. "I will not ask you to collect what is left of her. But I am too weary to find an urn myself."

Dina stood there for a moment, lips trembling. She then turned and hurried away.

"What did Maybell say to you?" asked Lee.

"What I needed to hear," she replied. "But after she awakened me, we did not speak very much. At least, not in words." She lowered her eyes. "Such magnificent courage should never be forgotten."

"It won't be," Lee assured her.

CHAPTER 9

Gewey looked out on a hill-covered countryside. Tiny blue and red wildflowers sprang from the deep emerald turf. The sky was scattered with puffs of cloud that moved swiftly along on a warm and gentle southerly breeze.

In the distance, he caught sight of a small figure skipping playfully toward him, occasionally cartwheeling and spinning around. Gewey very soon recognized the image of himself he had seen just after Gerath gave him full life.

He looked at Melek, who was standing beside him and smiling at the scene.

"See how happy you are?" Melek remarked. "Seldom has there been such joy in heaven."

"Your children never played?" asked Gewey. Seeing himself in a child's form made him wonder if the others were ever like him—infants playing blissfully and without troubles.

"They were never children as you were," said Melek. "They did not have the capacity for carefree play and mirthful games. They grew to adulthood not long after they were born. You, however, carry the spirit of the Creator, as I do."

"So you were a child?"

Melek chuckled. "I was indeed. For longer than you can imagine. Heaven was my playground long before birds flew and beasts walked the earth."

"When did you grow up?" asked Gewey.

"The moment my beloved wife was created," he replied. He closed his eyes and sighed. "She was more beautiful than heaven in all its splendor. I knew in an instant that she was to be my destiny. After that, I no longer needed childish thoughts."

Just as the child was only a few yards away, there was a flash of blue light and Gerath appeared immediately in front of him.

"Father!" exclaimed Darshan happily. He ran to Gerath and threw his arms around him. "Where have you been? I have missed you."

Gerath allowed the embrace but did not return it. "I have been to the world of humans and elves."

Darshan released his father and frowned. "Ayliazarah told me about that. It sounds boring."

Gerath gave him a weak smile. "It is anything but boring. There is much to be discovered there, and much we can learn."

"What are the people like? Are they as strange as Ayliazarah says? Do they really hurt each other for no reason?"

"Not all of them," he replied. "And Ayliazarah should not be telling you these things. They will only upset you."

Darshan laughed. "I am not upset. They cannot hurt us. We are gods, after all. We cannot *be* hurt."

"Why do you say that?" asked Gerath. "What makes you think we cannot be hurt?"

"That's what Dantenos told me. He said that the mortals have no power over us. That the Creator made us to live forever."

Gerath scowled. "He should not have told you that."

"Why? Isn't it true?"

"It is not as simple as that," Gerath said. "We are as the mortals. We have direct knowledge of the Creator. *She* gave us the gift of *her* grace, but this comes at a price." He kneeled to be at Darshan's eye level. "We are servants. It is our duty to carry out the Creator's will. This can be ... difficult at times."

"But, father," his little nose crinkled in a look of confusion, "I have no knowledge of the Creator. I have never seen *her*."

"*She* left us," Gerath explained.

"Then if *she* is gone, there is no one to serve."

Gerath's eyes flashed with instant anger. "*She* left us so that we could carry out *her* will. *She* left us the moment you were born."

Darshan lowered his eyes and folded his arms. "Is that why you never want to play with me? Is it because I made the Creator leave? If I bring *her* back, will you love me then?"

Gerath's jaw tightened, but then his features relaxed. He stood there expressionless for several seconds before taking hold of his son's hand.

"There is something I must tell you, Darshan," he began.

Gewey shook his head. *He couldn't tell me he loved me,* he thought.

Melek sighed. "Because he *doesn't* love you."

Gewey had stopped caring that Melek was inside his mind. In fact, with the absence of Kaylia still fresh, it had become a comfort.

Gerath and Darshan strolled at a leisurely pace. Darshan held tight to his father's hand, swinging it back and forth.

"I am going to take you to the realm of the mortals," said Gerath.

Darshan frowned. "Why?"

"You have a task to perform," he replied. "A very important task."

Darshan's face brightened. "A task?" He sounded much the same as any human child who was eager to please his father. "Whatever it is, I can do it. I know I can."

"It means you must remain there," Gerath continued.

Darshan stopped short. His eyes narrowed with suspicion. "For how long?"

"I don't know," Gerath admitted. "For a long time, I suspect. At least, it will seem like a long time to you."

"Will you be there too?"

Gerath pulled his hand free. "No. You will be alone."

Darshan looked at his father for several seconds before taking a step closer. "And when I'm done? Can I return then?"

Gerath averted his eyes. "I do not know. Perhaps ... if you succeed."

Tears began to fall from Darshan's eyes. "Why are you sending me away? What did I do wrong? Whatever it is, I'm sorry. I swear I am. Please don't make me go. Please!"

Gerath clenched his fists. "Stop this crying at once. You are the son of Gerath, and you will do what is required of you."

"I won't" yelled Darshan, suddenly defiant. "And you can't make me."

In a blinding movement, Gerath grabbed his son by the shoulders and shook him hard. "You will do as you are told. And if you ever hope to return, you must learn to be strong. Otherwise, there will be no hope at all for you."

This stopped the child's tears in an instant. His defiance turned to fear. "What do you want me to do?"

Gerath relaxed his hold. "You will discover your destiny in time. For once you leave heaven, you will have no knowledge that you were ever here, or even that you are a god. You will believe yourself to be human. You will live as one of them. And like them ... you will be vulnerable."

Darshan began to tremble. "Then who will take care of me?"

"Listen to me, son." Gerath's tone took on a fatherly quality that sounded *almost* loving. "Humans and elves are not the monsters you may believe. They have a great capacity for love and kindness. You must look to them for help and guidance. And though you will not remember any of this, my hope is that the impression of what I say will live somewhere deep inside you."

Once again, Gerath's hands gripped his son's shoulders. "I am sending you away because it is your destiny to bring hope to a world that is slipping into darkness. You must become the light."

"But why must I do it alone, father?" he asked, his tears starting afresh. "Why can't you come with me?"

Gerath met his question with silence.

Darshan turned his back. "You've always hated me. You blame me for the Creator leaving. You blame me for everything."

For just a moment, Gewey thought he saw a hint of regret and compassion in his father's eyes. *Maybe he didn't want me to go, after all,* he thought.

"What prevented Gerath from staying with you?" Melek asked him contemptuously. "Why would he leave you alone and unprotected in a savage world? He had the power to defeat your enemy and keep you safe, yet he left it to strangers to raise you and care for you. You need not have suffered the way you did."

His words dug painfully into Gewey's heart, filling it with fury. Suddenly, it all became clear. Melek was right—Gerath wanted him gone. If not, why didn't he simply come down and smite the Dark Knight? Why make his only son bleed and feel mortal pain? The answer was clear. Because he was jealous. He knew that one day Darshan would surpass him, and Gerath feared that. He feared what his son could become.

"That's right," said Melek. "He feared you. He allowed all of this to happen. He betrayed both his father ... and his son."

Gewey nodded sharply in agreement, then returned his attention to the vision.

Gerath was staring down at Darshan, his face no longer revealing his feelings. "You are wrong. I do not blame you. But you are the only one who can do what must be done."

"Why me?" His voice was a quiet lament. "Why am I the one? Why won't you choose someone else?"

"If I could, I would," Gerath replied. "But the choice is not mine. The Creator revealed to me your destiny, and it is through *her* wisdom you have been chosen."

Darshan turned to face him. "When?" His once clear and childlike voice was diminished to a hushed whisper.

"Now," Gerath replied stoically.

Darshan looked directly into his father's eyes, unblinking for several minutes. Finally, defeated and rejected, his shoulders slumped.

"One day you will understand all of this," Gerath promised.

His words had no impact on Darshan. He simply nodded. "Can I say goodbye to the others?"

Gerath took his hand. "No. It is best that you do not see them again."

"If you say so, father."

A portal opened beside them, and Gerath ushered his son through.

Back within the house, Melek poured more wine. "Now, do you understand?" he asked.

Gewey sat down at the table and drained his glass. His eyes burned and his muscles flexed. "How do we get free from this place?"

Melek tilted his head slightly and stared intensely at the brooding Gewey. "The question is: What will you do once you are free?"

Gewey thought about this for a time. "First, I will destroy the Dark Knight."

"Why?" asked Melek. "Are his goals not the same as yours?"

Gewey shook his head. "He's too ambitious. His campaign to destroy the gods is rooted in fear and a desire to rule. Should I bow down to such a man? Because he would have it no other way." Gewey's voice was becoming increasingly powerful; his heart was filling with more and more hatred.

"No," said Melek. "You will never bow to anyone—ever. If you wish him destroyed, I will help you to do so."

Gewey snarled. "I don't need help squashing this ant. He wants to do battle with the gods? He can begin with me."

"I would advise caution. This human has stolen great power and has had many years to learn how to wield it."

Gewey was taken aback. "You don't think I can defeat him?"

Melek held up his hand and smiled. "No, of course you can. But why take any risk? Let me fight by your side. Let me help you make the ant crawl. You say he is driven by fear. Together, we can show him the true meaning of fear. Before he meets his end, he will curse the day he heard your name."

This brought a sinister grin to Gewey's face. "Yes. I would like that."

Melek poured more wine. Gewey took it greedily and drained the glass. Melek smiled with satisfaction and gave him more.

"I would ask for only one thing in return," said Melek.

"Whatever you need from me, you will have it," Gewey assured him.

He leaned forward. "Once your enemy is crushed, you will then help me to crush mine. I alone cannot challenge all nine of my children. But together..."

"Together, we will both have our revenge," interrupted Gewey. "You have opened my eyes. I understand now how gullible I have been, and how I was used by the very beings who now beg for my help. For that, I am in your debt. Gerath may not have taught me anything, but my human father most surely did. He told me: 'Always pay your debts'."

Melek reached out to take hold of Gewey's hand, squeezing it tightly and sending intense heat running through his entire body. "And once our enemies are vanquished, then we can undo the evil that the Creator has allowed to thrive in heaven—and on earth."

His final words gave Gewey pause. He intended to free the world and to save those he loved from the menace of Angrääl. But what did Melek mean by "undo the evil"? Once the Dark Knight and the gods were no more, what evil was there left?

Melek released him and poured another glass of wine. "I only meant that we will bring peace. Do you not think the world has seen enough war? Does your child not deserve to grow up without the threat of annihilation?"

Gewey emptied his glass. The cool liquid turned to fire in his belly, sending more waves of heat rushing through his limbs. "Of course, he agreed." The heat became anger. "Yes. There must be no more war and death."

"Then there is only one way," said Melek. "Only one way to end the madness and never-ending cycle of destruction." There was a long pause. "The Creator must not be allowed to return."

Gewey leaned back, his anger lessening as the magnitude of what Melek was saying sank in. *He means to kill the Creator.*

Again, Melek refilled his glass. And again Gewey drank deeply, his hands almost trembling from the desire to taste the sweet liquid.

Melek eased his chair back from the table. "And if that is so? Would you still fight by my side?"

The growing displeasure on Melek's face pained Gewey, but he had no idea of how to respond. "It's just that I don't understand why you would want to do that. Why would you wish to see the Creator destroyed?"

Melek rose to his feet. His unassuming frame suddenly appeared to grow in stature, becoming menacing and powerful. His voice boomed out, shaking the walls of the small house.

"I served *her* for uncountable centuries. I cared for every one of *her* precious creations. I loved *her* without question. Where was *she* when I needed protection? Where was *she* when my children betrayed me?" His voice rose to a crescendo. "Where is *she* now—now that we are trapped in this flaming pit?"

The house exploded outward, shattering with a force that sent Gewey sprawling. The desolate landscape that had once been beyond the four walls was now a raging inferno. All around them, fire spewed forth from a never-ending succession of hideously misshapen rocks. The heat was so intense that Gewey cried out and covered his face. The howl of the wind was a cacophony of insane screams and pleas for help that raked at his ears, threatening to drag him along with them into sheer madness.

Just behind Melek, the ground fell away into a pit of utter darkness. Even the light from the endless fires was unable to penetrate its depths.

Melek rose high into the air, his arms spread wide. "Now do you see? This is where the Creator thinks I belong—where *we* belong. This is the nightmare *she* allowed my children to trap me within."

Gewey looked at Melek in horror. The absolute fury of what he was witnessing struck his heart with desperation and fear.

Casting his gaze downward to Gewey's huddled form, Melek drew in a deep breath and drifted down to earth. In an instant, the house blinked back into existence, just as if it had been there the entire time.

Melek walked over to Gewey and helped him to his feet. "I am sorry if I frightened you. But I wanted you to know the reality of Shagharath. What you are seeing here—this house, this table, even me—it is all there simply for your benefit."

Gewey allowed Melek to guide him to his chair and pour him another glass of wine. "So that's what this place really looks like?"

Melek shrugged. "To my eyes, at least. It is what I see every waking moment. It takes me great effort to keep it the way you see it now. But I did not want you to be afraid."

"And the screams," Gewey whispered. "Those horrible screams. They were so much worse than before."

"More evidence of the Creator's cruelty," said Melek. "Mortal souls were never meant to be faced with such unspeakable things. *She* could save them. And yet they remain ... forever lost."

"What was that pit?" asked Gewey. The wine was beginning to settle his nerves, and he held out his glass for more. Melek was happy to oblige.

"That is a choice I am faced with," he replied. "Within the pit, there is only oblivion. Should I enter it, I would cease to be. A final *kindness* left by my son. I can choose to end my captivity, but I must pay the ultimate price."

A vision of the pit and the fire entered Gewey's mind. How long could anyone stand to be in such a place? he wondered. Surely death would be a sweet release.

He felt the gentle touch of Melek's spirit listening to his thoughts. He smiled and allowed it to comfort him.

"Many times I nearly took the plunge," Melek told him. "But something always held me back. A faint hope that one day I would rise again—that the implement of my salvation would reveal itself." He smiled warmly and spread out his hands. "And now ... here you are."

Gewey returned Melek's smile. "I will not fail you." His desire to please was rapidly growing. More than anything, he wanted to help Melek escape and exact his revenge. He would not fail, no matter the cost to himself.

"And what will you do when the time comes?" asked Melek. "When we face the Creator. Will you stand with me?"

Gewey nodded. "I will."

CHAPTER 10

King Lousis dismounted his massive steed and raised an arm in greeting. Mohanisi stood at the vanguard of a thirty-thousand-strong army of elves from the Steppes, his expression grave.

The king spanned the distance between them with long, sure strides to embrace the elf enthusiastically. Mohanisi, clearly unaccustomed to such physical displays, stiffened in response. Laughing boisterously, Lousis didn't seem to notice.

"You have no idea how happy I am to see you," he said after finally releasing his hold. He gave the elf's shoulder one final fond slap and then took another look at the army. "You have arrived just in time." He glanced around curiously. "But where is Lord Theopolou? I thought for sure he'd be with you. I would very much like to speak with him as soon as possible. His experience in the Great War is sorely needed."

There was a long pause. The look in Mohanisi's eyes told Lousis that all was not well.

"Out with it," the king commanded.

Mohanisi lowered his eyes. A look of sorrowful reverence washed over his face. "Lord Theopolou fell while freeing the elves of the Steppes from the enemy's curse."

His words struck King Lousis like a massive blow to the gut. He took an unsteady step backward, not wanting to believe what his ears were hearing. The person who had saved his life from an assassin's poison, and who had most likely helped more than anyone else to unite human and elf ... was dead?

"How?" he asked. Words were sticking in his throat. "How ... how did he die?"

"Gather the elders and commanders," said Mohanisi. "I would have them all hear of his sacrifice."

Lousis nodded in agreement. "That would be wise. I would not have rumors spread as we stand at the edge of battle. Theopolou was well-loved among his people. We should all hear of his fate together."

Mohanisi gave instructions for his captains to meet with the commanders of Lousis's army, then followed Lousis to his tent. As he arrived, the king was issuing orders that the elders gather in a small clearing at the western end of the camp. While they waited for this meeting to form, Lousis explained their situation.

"The enemy we face still outnumbers us by two-to-one, even with the addition of your people. But should Lord Chiron manage to break through in time, and with his force intact, I am certain we will prevail."

He went on to tell Mohanisi about the enemy's devastating new weapon they had been facing. The elf listened with keen interest, though he told Lousis he had never heard of such a thing.

"We know of certain minerals that, when combined with each other, will produce colorful sparks and flames. But nothing such as you describe." He rubbed his chin. "Even so, perhaps it is something similar. I will consult with Lady Bellisia once I am finished speaking to the assembly."

"Thank you," said Lousis.

"I visited High Lady Selena before we marched south," added Mohanisi.

Lousis straightened. "Is she well? Did she ask about...?"

Quickly realizing that he was sounding like a lovesick youth, he stopped talking.

The corners of Mohanisi's mouth lifted slightly in a knowing smile. "She asked me to tell you that you must not forget your promise. She also asked that, should you put yourself in danger, I should drag you to the rear ... kicking and screaming if necessary."

Lousis chuckled. "And I assume she made you swear that you would do exactly that?"

"She did," he affirmed. "And I always keep my word."

King Victis soon joined them. Though the news of Theopolou's death did not upset him as much as it did Lousis himself, it still clearly pained him. Lousis offered his friend and fellow monarch his condolences.

Soon, a messenger arrived to escort them to the meeting, where there were now at least sixty humans and elves gathered. After greeting Mohanisi, Bellisia immediately began searching for Theopolou. On failing to find him, she noticed Mohanisi's expression. A harsh understanding immediately rushed over her. She staggered for a moment, then allowed her young elf assistant to help her over to a soft patch of grass just in front of where Mohanisi would speak.

The crowd settled and Mohanisi stepped forward. After giving a respectful bow, he began his speech.

Everyone remained hushed as he told of his journey to the Steppes. But that quiet was not to last for long. The very moment he spoke of Theopolou's demise, sobs and laments erupted throughout the elf ranks. Even some of the humans were clearly distressed. The few who had known Theopolou were well aware of his honor and courage. Those who did not know him still knew of his reputation. It took nearly twenty minutes before everyone had settled down sufficiently for the meeting to continue. Even after that, there was still much whispering of prayers and stifling of tears.

At the completion of things, the crowd fell still and quiet.

"Spread the word of Theopolou's passing," Mohanisi instructed them. "Tell them how he died. Let everyone know of his sacrifice and courage."

Slowly, the gathering dispersed. Only Bellisia and her assistant remained. Her face was racked with grief, with tears flowing in steady streams down both of her cheeks. After King Victis had excused himself, Lousis and Mohanisi sat beside the grieving woman. The guards moved to surround them, but one stern look from the king warned them to keep their distance.

"Tell me the story again," sobbed Bellisia, swallowing hard. "Leave out no detail."

Mohanisi did as asked. When it was over, Bellisia rose to her feet on unsteady legs.

"He never knew how much I truly cared for him," she said. She spoke as much to herself as to everyone else. "Though we had been adversaries in the past, I always respected him. It never occurred to me that he might die. He seemed to me ... eternal. Our eldest and most wise."

"He was indeed," said Mohanisi. "His song will be sung in this land and in my own until the stars fade into oblivion. I will personally write his tale into our books of legend so that the name Theopolou will be known throughout count-less generations."

"Thank you," said Bellisia, drying her eyes. "Then he is indeed eternal." She reached for her assistant. "I think I need to rest for a short while."

She allowed herself to be led away toward her tent. Lousis and Mohanisi watched her until she vanished into a crowd of soldiers. They then made their way to a pavilion where maps had been set up on a large but poorly constructed table.

It seemed that their only hope for victory lay in surprise. The enemy was camped about ten miles away, and that gap needed to be rapidly closed before Angrääl had time to launch its terrible weapon. Only the elves and the cavalry possessed the speed to accomplish this, which meant that elf casualties would be high. This bothered Lousis greatly, but the elves assured him they would not sacrifice others when their duty was clear.

It didn't take long for the elves from the Steppes to integrate themselves into the rest of the army, and before dawn, they were all but prepared. The name of Theopolou could be heard throughout the camp and was quickly becoming a battle cry.

As the sun peeked over the horizon, the plans were in place. Lousis called for his horse and wished all his commanders good luck. He said a silent prayer, though he knew there was no one to hear it. Nevertheless, it gave him comfort. Spurring his horse forward to a quick trot, he made his way to the front line. Both humans and elves cheered as he passed.

Ahead was a vast, hilly landscape. The enemy would be waiting atop the rise just beyond his vision. Lousis closed his eyes and took a long, steady breath. The field fell still.

A moment later, the uneasy silence was broken by the sound of rapid hoofbeats.

A rider approached from over the ridge. It was one of Lousis's scouts. He motioned for his guard to let the man through as soon as he was near.

"They've pulled back, Your Highness," the scout blurted out.

Lousis jerked up straight. "What?"

"The enemy is marching to the coast," he replied. "I just received word from Lord Chiron's seekers. The assault on his force has ceased, and he is on his way. Three of his seekers report that they have spotted the enemy to the south and heading east."

Lousis considered this news for a long moment. *What could it mean? Had they given up?*

A split second after this thought entered his head, he knew that it was just wishful thinking. Whatever the reason behind this retreat, it would only be so that they might gain a greater advantage later on.

Mohanisi, Victis, and several others quickly joined Lousis. He conveyed to them the messenger's news.

Every possibility they could think of was discussed. Suddenly, a flash of realization washed over Victis' face.

"I think I know why they leave," he told them. "Angrääl has burned every city and every port with the exception of one—Dreslin Cove, which is Tarvansia's northernmost port. At first I thought it was merely good fortune, or perhaps they lacked the time. But now I think I can see why they spared it."

The reason suddenly hit Lousis as well, and his heart sank. "They're landing more reinforcements," he said.

Victis nodded. "Why else pull back unless it's to bolster your force? As it stands, they outnumber us. Should they land more men, it will be an utter slaughter."

"How far is Dreslin Cove?" asked Mohanisi.

"Less than a week's march," Victis replied

As he could see his hopes for victory vanishing, Lousis let out a roar of frustration.

"Perhaps this is not so," offered Mohanisi. "There is no way to know their plans for certain. We should send seekers to investigate."

Lousis did not want to dismiss Mohanisi's words, but he knew in his heart that Victis' assessment was right. "Send them," he ordered. "But tell them to be swift."

Without another word, Mohanisi walked away and disappeared behind the lines.

After a moment's thought, Lousis looked at his captains. "Tell everyone to stand down but remain vigilant and at the ready." With a snap of the reins, the king's horse sprang to life. His guard scrambled to follow as he set off rapidly back to camp.

How could Angrääl have raised such a force? Lousis wondered while riding along. Was the world blind? Did no one take notice? Or was his enemy simply far more cunning than he could have fathomed? This final question stuck in his mind, forcing him to think back over every battle they had apparently won.

Had they really been victories? Or was it all a part of some devious grand design formulated by the Reborn King?

Back in his tent, Lousis sat heavily down, staring at the ground. What he chose to do now could very well determine the fate of the world. Darshan was far removed from this battle and could not help him. He could rely only on his own judgment. And should he fail, the young god would have nothing to save anyway, bar ashes and ruin when he returned.

A cup of wine was suddenly shoved in front of his face. Lousis looked up and blinked. He hadn't noticed Victis enter and sit in the chair across from him.

His friend was smiling broadly. This irritated Lousis.

He pushed the cup away. "I see nothing to smile about. It would seem we have run out of luck. If you are correct—and I am almost certain that you are—then we have less than two weeks before our enemy wipes us from the face of the earth."

Victis shrugged and took a drink. "My old friend. It is a miracle that we still live. Through sheer force of will, we have fought an army, the like of which has not been seen for five hundred years. I doubt the Reborn King expected to be so fiercely resisted." He leaned forward, his smile unbroken.

"You know that there is only one course of action you can now take, don't you?"

Lousis's irritation was turning into anger. "If I knew that, would I not already have done it?" He threw up his hands. "If *you* know, please don't keep it to yourself."

"The way I see it," said Victis, "we could stay here and wait to be slaughtered. But where is the honor in that?" His calm tone and bright expression were a far contrast to Lousis's angry scowl. "Or we could retreat to Althetas and wait for them to burn the city down around us. But that would only get more people killed."

"I am aware of all this," yelled Lousis. "Don't you think I have not thought about it already?"

"I know you have," he replied. "And you have seen what I have seen. That there is no way for us to win. We are doomed to die. So why fight for victory if it is out of reach?"

Lousis glared at his friend with growing confusion. "So, what do you propose?"

A menacing glint appeared in Victis' eyes. He raised his cup in a toasting gesture to Lousis.

"We march. If I am to meet my end, I would have it in the manner of my own choosing. The enemy moves slowly. We could catch them before they near the coast and combine with any reinforcements. They will never expect such an attack, and that gives us the advantage of surprise. At minimum, we'll take many of them with us before we fall."

Draining his cup in a single gulp, Victis threw it dramatically into the far corner of the tent. "And you never know. Perhaps we *will* win, after all."

For a moment or two, there was silence. Lousis's scowl gradually became a broad grin. "Guard!" he shouted.

One of his personal guards hurried inside. "Send out orders," the king told him. "We march as soon as we can be ready."

The guard saluted and left.

"You do know we are marching to our ruin?" Lousis said, now in a far more lighthearted tone.

"I know nothing of the sort," Victis replied. "I say we march to our glory."

Both men laughed heartily and quickly finished off what remained of the wine, now disregarding the cups.

Lousis told Mohanisi and his captains of the plan. At first they were shocked, but as the audaciousness of what the king was proposing sank in, their enthusiasm grew. Before long, they were full of the idea.

In less than an hour, the army was prepared and all set to move forward.

Mohanisi walked up to stand beside Lousis's horse. "You do realize that you will make me into a liar," he said. "Lady Selena will not be pleased." His tone was typically serious. Rarely did he smile or show emotion.

"And why is that?" said Lousis. "I intend to live." He paused. "Hell ... I intend to win."

Even though he tried to stop himself, the corners of Mohanisi's mouth began turning up. Higher and higher they lifted until his smile was big and cheerful.

Then, all at once, he threw his head back in unrestrained laughter.

In spite of objections from the human commanders, Nehrutu and Aaliyah decided to inform the army of Gewey's fate. Lord Vasko, a stout, humorless man from Sieren Bay, pointed out that there was nothing to be done, and that knowledge of his death would only demoralize the troops.

Though Nehrutu agreed, Aaliyah would not be dissuaded. Through their bond, he could feel her pain slowly turning inward and becoming wrath. She had come so far and fought so hard, and now the very person they thought was destined to save them all was gone.

At first, the news had exactly the effect that Vasko predicted. Word of Darshan's demise spread like a disease, infecting everyone. Whispers of surrender and rumors of desertion could be heard throughout the camp ... even from some of the elves.

Aaliyah took no notice of this, instead issuing orders for the entire army to be gathered along the shore. Nehrutu wanted to comfort her, but surges of white-hot fury kept him at bay. She had come to a decision and her heart had hardened. Whatever she was going to do, he knew that surrender was out of the question.

The narrow beach could barely hold the entire army, forcing everyone to stand tightly together. Aaliyah was nowhere to be seen, and after a time, the mood began to get restless. Nehrutu could feel that she was near, but when he tried to find her, he was met with stern resistance. He quickly learned that their bond carried with it a responsibility to respect the privacy of the other, even when you were desperate to know the thoughts behind their emotions.

Just as voices were starting to grow loud and irritated, the wind suddenly rose, gaining strength until it was a roar in Nehrutu's ears. He could feel the power raging through his mate as never before. He reached out and offered to add his strength to hers. This time, he was met with gratitude and acceptance.

"Darshan is dead!"

Aaliyah's voice descended from high above. The sheer volume and power of her words caused people to flinch from shock before gazing skyward.

Aaliyah was using the *flow* to carry her more than fifty feet above the water. Clad in armor, her blade in hand, and with hair whipping about like dark flames, she appeared to those below almost like a goddess of war.

All eyes were fixed upon her as she drifted down over the surface of the churning sea. The white caps of the breakers lapped at her feet while the spray from the waves crashing onto the shore formed a mist around her slender frame.

"Darshan is dead!" she repeated. "Because of this, my heart aches ... and I am afraid. Do you not also feel the fear that corrupts your heart now that our savior is no more?"

Nehrutu stared in wonder as tiny flashes of light appeared, swirling and dancing around every soul assembled on the beach. The sound of bells and the laughter of a thousand children drifted on the wind. Just at that moment, the sun was at Aaliyah's back. She held out her arms and the light split, spreading her shadow across the water and centering her silhouette in the setting sun.

He knew that Aaliyah was using the *flow* of the spirit. Through their bond, he could feel it echoing within him like music inside a great stone amphitheater. He had experienced its effects before when with Darshan at the feast in Valshara. That time, it had nearly broken his mind. But this was different. Powerful and limitless, yet gentle and kind. So completely unlike the frenzied might that was Darshan.

"But now," she continued. "It is time to banish our fear and embrace our fate. Elves! Your lands and loved one's need your courage. Will you now abandon them? Will you cast aside bonds of family? For soon our enemy will scorch the earth from the desert to the sea.

"Humans! Your cities burn and your people are ravaged by war. Will you throw down your swords and leave them to the mercy of an enemy who knows not the meaning of the word? Will you allow them to murder your kin and destroy your homes with impunity?"

The *flow* settled on the army, but rather than penetrating them, it washed over everyone like a gentle rain. Their faces became flushed and their eyes filled with the fire of renewed passion—a determination that was more akin to love than fury.

"Darshan is dead!" The words tore through the air. "And now it is left to us to save ourselves. And to save those whom we love."

Her eyes fell on Nehrutu as she floated toward the shore. The army gave way sufficiently for her feet to touch the sand just in front of her husband.

"And it is those we love who will fill our spirits with the strength for victory."

The crowd exploded with cheers and cries of vengeance against Angrääl and its king.

Aaliyah touched Nehrutu's cheek, smiling. "Let us show the Reborn King and his armies what it means to make war on free people."

Without even waiting for orders to do so, both elves and humans immediately began filing from the beach and making ready to march on the enemy. Aaliyah and Nehrutu stood watching them until they were alone. She then took Nehrutu's hand and led him back to camp.

He looked into her eyes as they arrived. "That was..."

He was incapable of finding the right words to finish his thought. Instead, he sent his feelings of awe and joy through their bond.

"It was necessary," Aaliyah said, kissing his cheek. "I would not have a lie become their battle cry. And yet, I would not have them lose hope either."

"So you think we can be victorious without the power of Darshan to aid us?" he asked.

"I think we no longer have a choice." Her voice was resolute. "And I will most surely not wait for the Reborn King to sail across the Abyss and attack the lands I love."

CHAPTER 11

Basanti sat cross-legged on the carpet inside her spacious tent. The marble floor beneath kept it cool and pleasant against the heat of the summer.

She had left her name behind long ago. Only two people now knew her as Basanti, and she missed both of them terribly. These days, she was known as the Oracle of Manisalia. At first, she hated life in the small town. The people had erected a temple for her to live in, but she had never felt comfortable within the opulent marble structure. Its cavernous halls and chambers made her loneliness even more pronounced. And when it was proposed that a statue be erected in her honor, she had come very close to running away.

The only respite from her solitude, other than the people seeking her wisdom, was when Felsafell came to visit. She had grown fond—more than fond—of him. She always thought it was amusing when people would see her walking the streets of Manisalia on the arm of a bent, scraggly old man. Only *she* could see his true form in all its splendor. But his visits were becoming ever more infrequent and short as demands on her time increased.

Pósix had been highly pleased with Felsafell for the creative way he had found to protect her. She strengthened Basanti's ability to foretell the future, and in appreciation of Felsafell's achievement had granted him a boon—though she found his request to be odd.

He asked that the goddess destroy the temple that Basanti so detested. And not only the one currently standing but also any others that the people might try to build in its place. Reluctantly, Pósix complied. It was at that moment that the Oracle's heart belonged to him.

In only twenty years, Felsafell managed to convince people that the foundation was built on the very spot where the gods had first breathed life into humankind, and because of that no structure could ever stand there. After a few more temples collapsed, the story became an established fact passed down through generations and no further attempts were made. Only the immense floor remained. Basanti told her followers that this was where her powers were at their strongest, just in case any thought to build her a temple elsewhere. The only solution after that was the tent where she now dwelled. It allowed her to feel the open air and reminded her of days when life was simple and free. Though she would rather be wandering the world with her brother, it was not such a bad life.

She guided both the mighty and the meek with her visions. And while many of them left her tent more confused than when they arrived, she was satisfied that the gods were revealing their plans through her and was honored by their faith. In spite of all that had happened, she still trusted them.

A comely young woman poked her head inside, smiling brightly. Shilsa had served the Oracle since she was little more than a child and was Basanti's favorite amongst all of her followers. She waved for Shilsa to enter and offered her a seat. The woman complied with the elegant grace of a noble-born. In her arms, she carried a small, plain wooden box. Just as she sat, the fuzzy head of a puppy poked above the rim.

Basanti squealed with delight. "Where did you find it?"

Shilsa carefully lifted the animal out. It was nothing more than a mongrel, but with black patches scattered all over its soft, medium-length white fur, there was no denying that it was truly adorable. The puppy whimpered and whined as it was handed over to the Oracle.

Basanti held the furry bundle close. Within seconds it began licking her face excitedly.

"It was left just outside your tent, My Lady," said Shilsa.

"Left by whom?" she asked. But in that moment, it didn't really matter.

Shilsa held up her palms and shrugged. "We don't know. It appeared from nowhere. One moment it wasn't there, and the next it was. Some of the others think it must be a gift from the gods." She reached inside her sleeve and pulled out a small scrap of parchment. "There was a note with it as well."

"Read it," said Basanti, unwilling to put down her new companion.

"It says: His name is Felsafell—a gift to keep you company and help you remember more carefree days." She folded the note and frowned. "What does it mean?"

Basanti giggled as the puppy continued with its barrage of kisses. Eventually, she placed it on her lap. It struggled and squirmed for a few seconds, then settled down and rested its chin on her thigh. "It means that I have a visitor," she said. "I will see no one else today."

Shilsa stood, smiling with approval. "It's good to see you happy, My Lady." Just as she was about to exit the tent, she paused. "Should I bring food and wine?"

"No, thank you," Basanti replied. The puppy was already beginning to doze, kicking slightly and grunting as it dreamed. "My guest always provides the meal."

"What is your friend's name?" Shilsa asked. "So that I know who to allow in."

"There's no need," she replied. "You won't see him enter."

Pretending to understand, Shilsa nodded and left.

The tent flap was still moving when Basanti heard a movement behind her.

"What did you bring, old hermit?" she said, doing her best to sound serious. "Aside from this mangy animal."

Felsafell moved nimbly to take a seat across from her. In his left hand he held a basket, and in his right, a large jug. "If my gift does not please you, I'll gladly take it away." He set down his load and reached out for the puppy.

Basanti recoiled and glared at him. "You will do no such thing." She maintained her look of anger for as long as she could before finally bursting into gay laughter. "You have stayed away for far too long."

"I will come more often if you wish it," he promised.

"Of course I *wish it,*" she mocked. "You know that you do not need to be so formal with me."

"And you know how I sound when I speak the new tongue," countered Felsafell. "Though it does indeed fit in with my current appearance."

From the basket, he produced a loaf of bread, a wedge of cheese, and a string of summer sausages. Basanti's eyes sparkled at the sight.

When the meal was finished, they talked cheerfully for several hours. Regardless of how long they were apart, after only a few minutes together, it always felt as if he had never left. Just one thing was missing. One thing that gnawed at her heart.

"Have you heard from him?" she asked, trying to sound as if it were merely a passing thought.

"Yanti has become quite adept at avoiding me," he replied. "I do not think he likes that I keep track of him."

"How long has it been?"

Felsafell leaned back and sighed. "More than fifty years. I lost sight of him as he was heading west. He was still searching for the god stones. At least, I think he was. With Yanti it is difficult to know what he is planning." He looked at her with sudden concern. "He has not been here, has he?" But the sorrow behind her eyes already told him the answer.

"All I want is for him to send word," she said. "Just so I can know he is safe, and to show that he still thinks about me sometimes."

"Of that there is no question," he assured her. "Everything he has done—even his blunders, has been to earn his place beside you."

"I asked Pósix to redeem his spirit," she said. "I begged her to repair what he has damaged. I explained that he only did it to protect me."

"And what was her reply?" He moved close enough to allow her to lean against him.

"She said that she was forbidden." As tears began to take form, Basanti buried her head in Felsafell's chest. "She told me it had been decided that Yanti was to be left to his own fate."

"I know it is difficult to understand," he said, stroking her hair. "But the gods do not act without purpose. I will find him for you."

She looked into his eyes. The old man was gone, replaced by his true form. "No. I cannot ask this of you. I must wait for him to seek me out." She forced a smile. "You have been so good and kind to me for all these long years. You have served as my protector and friend. And never have you asked anything for yourself in return. Why?"

He brushed her cheek with the back of his hand. "Because what I desire is far beyond anything I could dare to hope for."

Basanti's heart raced. "If what you desire is me, then I have already been yours for a very long time—in both body and spirit."

Felsafell averted his eyes. "How could you love me? I have driven your brother away, and made you into little more than a prisoner in this place."

She cupped his face in her hands. "You have been the only reason I have not gone mad with loneliness. You saved me from a world that fears what they do not understand." She moved in closer. "And my brother chose his own path. You did what I could not. And for that, I am eternally grateful."

Felsafell simply stared at her, for the moment transfixed and unable to speak.

Basanti's mouth gradually turned upward into a girlish grin. "Of course, if I have misunderstood your inten-"

He leaned in and kissed her. The hundreds of years of waiting suddenly seemed like fleeting moments as he lost himself in the softness of her lips. Basanti wrapped her arms around him and pressed her body close. Within seconds, their hearts were beating in unison.

Their mouths finally parted. The loss of her touch bringing forth a soft moan of sadness from Felsafell. He wanted to say something—to tell her of all the things he was feeling—but she put her finger to his lips and stood up.

He watched as her graceful form glided across the tent to, one by one, put out the lamps.

Felsafell remained in Manisalia for almost a month. Each day was a gift as they laughed and talked, and each night they explored their love—their passion climbing to heights neither could ever have imagined.

But through all of their joy, Felsafell could tell that thoughts of Yanti still weighed heavily on her mind. Eventually, he told her that he wanted to discover what had become of her brother, but promised to return the moment he had news to tell. Their parting nearly broke her heart.

Once he was gone Basanti refused to see anyone for weeks, and very soon the line of supplicants outside her tent was stretching out for more than a mile.

Her attendants worried over her ceaselessly, but she didn't care. Shilsa tried every day to bring her out of her melancholy, though these good intentions only succeeded in provoking a series of angry outbursts. Basanti always felt a pang of guilt immediately afterward, but she was finding it impossible to govern her emotions. Life seemed completely empty and meaningless without Felsafell. And though she understood why he had left, hundreds of years of emotional solitude had been washed away in that magical moment when they had first kissed.

And now she was alone again.

After three weeks, she finally built up the strength to venture outside of her tent. She walked until she was beyond the last of the people still awaiting an audience. That none of these had seen her before allowed her to pass unnoticed, and for this she was grateful. Millions of stars, bright in the cloudless sky, were made even more visible that night by the absence of the moon. The clean, brisk air felt good on her skin. She looked up to take a deep cleansing breath.

"You cannot allow yourself to despair," came a kind, musical voice from the darkness just beyond her sight. "Felsafell will always find his way to you."

Basanti knew at once that it was Pósix. "I know. But his absence leaves such a painful hole in my spirit." Her heart was struck by a terrible thought. "You will not forbid us..."

She could not even finish her sentence.

The goddess remained hidden. "Your love for the *first born* pleases me. Both of you deserve your measure of happiness, and you are well-matched. But I must caution you. You both have tasks ahead that will keep you apart for many years at a time. You must learn to quiet your passion. If you do not, each separation will be unbearable. You will fail in your duty and cause great harm to others."

Basanti closed her eyes and allowed the words to sink in. Pósix was right, of course. While Felsafell had been there, she had scarcely seen a soul. And now that he was gone...

The line of people waiting to see her forced its way into her thoughts.

"Felsafell is good and strong," said Pósix. "He will understand what I say. And should fate unfold as we hope, you shall be together, untroubled, until you decide that this world is done with you both."

The wind began to rise, its wintry breath finding a way beneath Basanti's robes. She hugged herself tightly. When Pósix spoke next, her voice had suddenly taken on an ominous tone. "A dangerous time is coming. Your courage will truly be needed. And your devotion and loyalties will be tested beyond your imaginings."

The sudden chill now touched Basanti's heart. "What do you mean?" she called out into the night. But there was no reply. Pósix was gone.

Basanti returned to her tent using her strength and speed—attributes she had become adept at hiding from others—to enter unseen.

That night she dreamed of Felsafell in his true form. He was running through a dense forest with a bow in his hand. He slid to a halt as a deer bearing a set of proud antlers came into sight. With a single motion he notched an arrow and let it fly. The buck dropped instantly, with only the rustle of the leaves shifting under its fall breaking the eerie silence.

He approached, but just before he reached the animal, it transformed into the body of her brother. As Felsafell reached down to pull the arrow free, Yanti's eyes popped open.

"Why, sister?" Yanti cried accusingly. Blood spilled from both the wound and the corner of his mouth. "Why did you do this to me?"

She tried to call out but had no voice.

"Why did you let him kill me?"

Her brother's anguished words were still echoing in her head when she became aware that Shilsa was gently shaking her awake. She scrambled up into a sitting position.

"What?" She paused and calmed herself. "What is it, dear?"

"King Rätsterfel of Angrääl is here," Shilsa replied, clearly unsettled. "He demands to see you at once."

"King Rätsterfel?" Basanti repeated.

"Yes, My Lady."

She had heard rumors of the man. It was said that his kingdom was mighty beyond the dreams of the elves. His cities boasted towers so tall that they disappeared within the clouds. Not that any of this was important right now. What did disturb her was the widely known knowledge that the king hated the gods with an unrivaled passion, and had publicly sworn that he would see them fall.

He had risen to power over the past ten years, seemingly from nowhere. No one knew who he really was or where he came from, but it *was* well known that he had defeated each tribal leader of the northern barbarians in single combat and then used their might to begin his conquest. After seizing the throne of Angrääl, he then immediately set about uniting all the northland kingdoms under his banner and achieved this in less than a year. After the first three cities fell, the rest simply surrendered as his army approached. Some said that even the *elves* feared him.

Basanti got up and quickly dressed. The puppy Felsafell had given to her whimpered and groveled as if being threatened. She instructed Shilsa to take it away as soon as she was settled down on a cushion in the middle of the carpet.

"He's just a mortal man," she told herself. But she knew that even a mortal man could be dangerous. Particularly if that man loathed the gods and had come to visit one of their most revered servants.

Shilsa called out to her. "He is coming."

Basanti stiffened. A moment later the tent flap flew open, and the king stepped inside. She let out a loud gasp of surprise.

"Yanti!" Basanti's voice was almost inaudible.

Her brother was wearing a resplendent purple satin robe and black boots. Rings of gold adorned his fingers and a gold band encircled his brow.

"It is good to see you, sister," he said, smiling broadly.

Her initial shock was quickly overcome by sheer joy. She leaped up and ran into Yanti's waiting arms. He lifted her from her feet and spun her around.

"I've missed you so much," she said. Tears of happiness began to fall.

After putting her down, he took a pace back and held his arms out wide. "Well, what do you think? Am I not every bit a monarch?"

"*You* are King Rätsterfel?" she asked incredulously. "You can't be."

Yanti raised an eyebrow. "Really? It would seem that I am." He laughed and led Basanti to the center of the room before sitting down.

"But all those horrible things I've heard," she said. "They can't be true."

He held his sister's hand. "People always say horrible things about kings and queens. They need something to be afraid of. Pay such stories no mind."

There was a long pause. Basanti did not want to believe what she had heard. Nor did she want to spoil her moment of elation.

"I see that you have quite the life here," Yanti said, with a hint of sarcasm. "I take it that this is Felsafell's idea of protecting you." His mouth twisted slightly as he spoke the name.

Unwilling to allow the reunion to turn sour, she gave an exaggerated sweeping gesture. "Are you mad? I have all this. A tent *and* a floor. What else could I possibly desire?"

Yanti frowned. "How about to be with your brother? And now you can be. I have come to take you with me."

Basanti's heart sank. "I cannot. You know that. I still serve the gods, and this is where I am needed." She reached out and touched Yanti's face. "Please, brother, let us just talk and enjoy our reunion for a while. Unhappy conversation can wait. Tell me of your travels."

"I am sure Felsafell has told you all about that," he replied with a sneer.

"He only tells me where he has seen you," she replied. "And what he thinks you are doing. Nothing more."

"Because he *knows* nothing more," said Yanti. "He supposes I do not see him lurking in shadows, his watchful eyes ever afraid that I will upset the schemes of the gods." He rose to his feet and turned his back. "I suppose you know that I sought the god stones."

"I do," she admitted. "Did you find them?"

Yanti nodded. "Some. But they were useless to me. Even so, Felsafell was wrong to tell me not to seek them. If I hadn't, they may well have been found by someone else." He glanced over his shoulder. "They are far too dangerous for mortal men."

"What did you do with them?" she asked.

"I hid them away where only I can find them." He faced her and smiled. "You see. Not everything I do ends in disaster."

"I never thought that," Basanti said. She patted the pillow next to her. "Now sit. Tell me what you have been doing."

Yanti waved a hand. "There will be time to talk once you are in Kratis. As I said before, I have come to take you with me."

His words sent a cold chill down Basanti's spine. Several seconds passed before she could compose herself sufficiently to speak. "Then you have wasted a journey," she told him. "I have no intention of leaving. My duty is here."

"A duty to who?" he snapped. "The gods? The very beings who cursed me for protecting you? Is that who you still serve? I know you, Basanti. By now you will have groveled and begged before them. You belittled yourself when you asked them to heal me. Well, I am *not* healed. I can feel the wound in my spirit even now. And it has grown and festered. Pleasures I once relished no longer hold any joy for me. My rage is so great that at times I can barely contain it." His eyes burned with hatred. "But, at long last, I have found a way to end my torment."

Basanti hesitated, afraid to hear what he might say next. "How?" she eventually asked.

He straightened his back and held his head high. "The gods must die. Their reign must come to an end. And I know how this can be done. I have learned their secrets."

Basanti was mortified. Springing up, she seized hold of her brother's arms with a force that surprised even herself. "No. You must abandon such plans. War on the gods is unthinkable. You will end up..."

Her lips trembled. "You will die ... and I could not bear that."

"Let them try," he challenged. "I have openly defied them. I have torn down their temples and desecrated their altars. I have killed their servants and cursed their names. Where is their vengeance? Where is their wrath? I'll tell you. It is nowhere. They do not care enough to bother."

As his fury rose, so did his voice. "They interfere with the world of mortals, leaving nothing but devastation in their wake, then turn their backs and leave it to others to pick up the pieces. And who is here to mend what they have broken?

I am. So it is I—King Rätsterfel—who will free humankind from the blundering and indifference of the gods."

By now, Basanti was weeping openly. "Please stop," she cried. "I cannot hear more." She could not force herself to look at him. "Leave this place ... and me ... now."

"I will leave," said Yanti. "And you *will* come with me. Though it pains me to take you against your wishes, in time you will understand."

Basanti shrank back as her brother moved closer. As he was about to seize hold of her, a blur of gray shot across the tent, slamming into Yanti and sending him skidding across the floor. He shook his head, dazed from the blow, and looked up. Felsafell was standing between him and his sister.

"You will not touch her," Felsafell snarled.

With a roar of anger, Yanti jumped to his feet. In the blink of an eye, a dagger appeared in his hand. Then he charged.

Felsafell waited. An instant before Yanti reached him he spun left, and, as his onrushing opponent drew level, struck him on the back of the head. Yanti stumbled before whipping his dagger around. But fast as he was, Felsafell was much faster. He ducked, easily avoiding the blade, and brought his fist crashing into the side of Yanti's jaw. The impact was immense, twisting Yanti's head so far around that it would easily have killed a mere mortal man.

Before Yanti could recover from this terrible blow, Felsafell ripped the dagger away from his grasp and sank it into his chest. Yanti cried out before falling flat on his back. Felsafell was on top of him in a flash, pinning his opponent and pulling the blade free again. Yanti tried to throw the hermit off, but cold steel pressed firmly against his throat.

"No!" shouted Basanti. "Don't kill him!"

Dark, thick blood poured from the wound in Yanti's chest, and in a trickle from the corner of his mouth. Basanti's dream flashed through her mind. *It's happening*, she thought. *Felsafell really is going to kill him.*

But her plea did not fall on deaf ears. The pressure of the knife slowly eased.

Felsafell stared at Basanti for several moments, then looked down at Yanti. "Leave this place and never return. You may have placed yourself on a mortal throne, but you are not beyond my reach." He jumped up and tossed the dagger toward the entrance. "Do not think that because I have allowed you to live this time, I will ever do so again."

Yanti tore a piece of cloth from his robe and covered his wound. He turned to Basanti, but she averted her eyes. "So be it," he said coldly. "You will not see me again." He strode out, stopping only to retrieve his dagger.

The instant he was gone, Basanti fell to the floor. Wrapping her arms around her knees, she began rocking back and forth, weeping uncontrollably.

Felsafell rushed to her side, but as soon as he touched her she flailed her arms wildly, striking him on the face and chest. Undeterred, he pulled her close. After a while, she stopped struggling and clutched at his sleeves.

Shilsa burst in. "What happened, My Lady? Are you hurt?"

Basanti turned her face away. "I'm fine. Please leave."

After a brief hesitation, the woman obeyed.

"Promise that you will not kill him," Basanti whispered through her tears.

Felsafell brushed her hair away from her eyes. "I will not allow him to harm you. But I will not kill him unless you consent."

"Thank you."

They stayed where they were for more than an hour without saying a further word. Finally, Basanti wiped her eyes and sat up. She gave Felsafell a fragile smile and embraced him tightly.

"You seem destined to keep saving me," she said.

"I will *always* be here to save you."

He paused before continuing. "I am sorry that you were forced to witness me fighting your brother, but had I not, he would most surely have taken you to Kratis by force. And I have no doubt he would never have allowed you to leave." Tenderly, he lifted her chin. "If that had happened, then the result of my actions would have caused you immeasurable pain. For I would have stormed his gates to get you back and undoubtedly slaughtered any who dared to hinder me. As long as I draw breath, no one will ever harm you."

"I know, my love." She leaned in and kissed him gently.

"I was only just able to be here in time," Felsafell told her. "When I discovered that King Rätsterfel is, in fact, Yanti, he was already on his way to see you." He lowered his eyes. "And what else I learned about him is deeply troubling."

Basanti clasped her hands to her heart. "Tell me. What has my brother done?"

Felsafell was unable to look up at her for several seconds. Finally, he sighed with reluctant obedience. "Very well. Not long after I arrived in Angrääl I discovered the king's motives and the full extent of his resolve. The atrocities he has committed against those who serve the gods are too terrible to speak aloud. But more than that, he has designs on heaven itself. He seeks a power that could give him the strength to set the world ablaze."

"He told me he wanted to make war on the gods," Basanti interjected. "Also, that he has found a way to destroy them." She was trying hard not to think about the lives Yanti had taken, nor of the fate of those who served in the temples must have suffered.

"He believes he has," said Felsafell solemnly. "During his travels, he discovered a book containing the secrets of The Sword of Truth. His intention is to find it and use it to murder the gods." Seeing that Basanti was becoming increasingly upset, he placed a reassuring hand on her shoulder. "But his plan is doomed to fail. Amon Dähl will stop him."

"I know of the Sword," said Basanti. "Pósix once spoke of it. She said it contained the power of all nine gods, and that it holds the key to heaven itself. Though I must admit, I have never understood why they would wish to create such a thing. I've also have heard about the Order of Amon Dähl, and how they are the protectors of a great and terrible secret."

She paused as the first hint of fear washed over her. "What if he finds it?"

"He will *never* do that," Felsafell assured her. "You have nothing to fear. The Order of Amon Dähl keeps it safe, and it is well beyond your brother's power to steal it. It is unlikely he could even find *the order*, let alone the Sword itself."

"And if he did?"

"Then nothing could stop him."

After a long silence, Felsafell broke the ominous mood with a silly smile. "But it does not matter. As I said, he will *not* find the Sword, and he will *not* take you to Kratis. So all is well."

Basanti nodded with feigned acceptance. At the same time, she was certain Felsafell knew how afraid she still was that her brother might find a way to succeed. But after what had happened earlier, she considered it best to push her anxiety aside. Her love had returned, and for that at least, she was glad.

She was also reluctant to tell Felsafell of her latest conversation with Pósix. Partly because she wanted him to remain with her without thoughts of parting, but mostly because her heart could take no more. Not for a while.

Just a week, she told herself. *Then I'll send him away.* She kissed him again, this time with urgency.

Just one week of joy. It was now a prayer ... a promise ... a bargain.

Pósix *must* accept it.

CHAPTER 12

Gewey concentrated on the swirling mass of pitch-black smoke. But without the *flow* to help him, he was unable to make any sort of connection. Melek was standing immediately behind him with both hands firmly gripping his shoulders.

"Feel the power inside you," Melek whispered in his ear. "Use your will to overcome what you see."

Gewey gave a sharp nod and redoubled his efforts. They had been at it for weeks. At least, he thought it was weeks. Sometimes it felt like minutes. Other times, he could scarcely remember the world outside of this terrible place. These nonstop attempts to create a portal were taking their toll on his mind. The howls of the human spirits were growing ever louder and more desperate. Several times he thought madness would take him as well, but Melek would produce a cup of wine and a word of encouragement and then he would regain his wits.

"I need to rest," Gewey said. His head was splitting from the exertion. "I can barely think."

Melek's hands tightened their grip to the point of pain. "Do you think your enemy is resting?" His tone was cold and harsh. "Do you think he complains about being tired? No! He thinks his schemes have succeeded and you gone forever. Soon, he will sweep down and slaughter all that you love in your absence."

His voice dropped to the very lowest of whispers. "He will seek out Kaylia. He will take her *and* your child for his own. He will twist her mind and corrupt your child's spirit. They will live out their lives as little more than broken slaves."

His words rapidly became pictures in Gewey's mind. He could see Kaylia sitting beside a golden throne, their infant child in her arms. A crown was atop her brow, and on the wall behind her was a banner with broken scales splashed boldly across it—the sigil of the Reborn King. Her eyes were vacant and her expression of one utterly defeated.

"He covets her," Melek continued. "And if you remain here, he will have her."

Gewey let out an anguished cry. "I will not let that happen! I will kill him first! Do you hear me? I will rip him limb from limb!"

"Yes," Melek coaxed. "You will. *We* will. We will make them all pay." He relaxed his grip. "But first we must escape."

Gewey took a deep breath and renewed his efforts, his desperation to save Kaylia and his desire to please Melek both raging. But even now, he was still unable to make any progress.

This time it was Melek who shouted out in frustration. "Have you not heard me? Is your mind completely addled?"

Startled by the outburst, Gewey lowered his eyes in shame. Melek's discontent pained him. He desperately wanted to make him proud. But no matter how hard he tried, he wasn't able to.

"I ... I'm sorry," he stammered. "I'll try harder."

A strong, self-assured woman's voice carried over the wind. "You've tried hard enough, Gewey Stedding."

Both he and Melek spun around. From out of the choking dust appeared a young woman dressed in the robe of a novice from the temple of Ayliazarah. Her flaxen hair fell carelessly about her shoulders, and her sharp eyes and flawless ivory skin were matched in beauty by her graceful movements. She approached with confident strides.

"Who are you, human?" demanded Melek.

"Does the mighty Melek not know?" the woman replied mockingly. "Is this not *your* domain?"

The howl of the mad spirits rose in intensity. The woman frowned. "And to think those poor souls didn't understand their true power in this place." She shot a fiery gaze at Melek. "For that, you will pay, beast."

"Silence, woman!" roared Melek. The landscape changed in an instant. Towering flames and razor-sharp rocks sprang up from the ground, while surges of searing hot air blasted them from all directions, sending Gewey stumbling back.

The woman laughed. "Is that the extent of your power, Melek?" She waved her hand, and the land transformed once again, this time into a green meadow dotted with multicolored wildflowers. "Much better. Don't you think?"

"H ... How..." Melek stuttered. "What are you?"

"Melek is thinking that I would be a better tool to use than you, Gewey," the woman said. "But whatever he has told you, it is a lie. He means to escape Shagharath and then rule heaven and earth alone. No matter what you think, he is not your ally."

Gewey took a menacing step forward. "Melek is the only one who has ever told me the truth."

The woman was not impressed by his display. "Is that so? I am shocked at you, Gewey Stedding. So easily taken in by this charlatan."

"That is enough!" shouted Melek. He crossed the distance to the woman in only a few steps, his hand reaching out to grab her.

The woman's fist shot out just before he made contact, crashing into Melek's jaw and knocking him flat on his back. He landed with a loud thud. After laying there in shock for a few seconds, he scrambled to his feet, staring at her in stunned disbelief.

"Do not touch him!" Gewey cried out, rushing forward with rage set on his face.

Just as he reached her, the woman's body turned to mist. With nothing solid to grasp hold of, he passed right through, his momentum causing him to stumble and fall to one knee.

"I can see that Melek has been hard at work on you," she remarked with distaste.

Confusion and fear ran through Gewey. Rising, he quickly took a few steps back.

"How is this possible?" hissed Melek. "You are human. You should not be able to-"

"This is *your* prison, Melek," she snapped, cutting him off. "Not mine. Nor that of any other mortal soul. Here, you are the weak and we the strong." She closed her eyes and listened to the cries of insanity. "If they had only known, you would never have been able to drive them mad."

"Melek tried to help them," argued Gewey.

The woman huffed. "Is that what he told you? And you believed him?" She looked closer at Gewey and scowled. "But of course you did. He has poisoned you with his deceit and bile. He hoped to make you his slave, and from the look of it, he has very nearly succeeded." She cast a sideways glance at Melek. "He tortured them out of pure malice, and for his own sick and twisted pleasure—tortured them until they were driven mad. They never knew that in Shagharath they are far more powerful than he. And the irony of it is, Melek had no idea that the humans he so despised and tormented were the very ones holding the key to his freedom."

"You lie!" shouted Melek, his face red with fury. "Mortals are weak and useless. What power could they possess?"

"And yet a mortal knocked you down as if you were nothing more than a small child," the woman jeered. "A mortal turned your nightmarish realm into a place of beauty." She raised her arm in a grand sweeping motion to indicate the landscape she had brought forth. "And a mortal will now undo the evil you have visited upon her friend."

"Your friend?" said Melek. He gave a sarcastic snort. "You are no friend to Darshan."

Gewey could only stand and watch. His mind was clouded, and though he dearly wanted to come to Melek's defense, he did not know how. Whoever this woman was, she could easily overpower him.

The woman gave Gewey a kind smile. "I *am* a friend to him. Though he may not recognize me as I appear now." In a flash of light, the form of the young and beautiful woman transformed into the old and sturdy frame of Maybell.

Gewey gasped, eyes wide.

"Yes," she said in her familiar voice, spreading her arms. "It is me."

"But you ... before ... you were..." struggled Gewey.

She completed his sentence for him. "Beautiful?"

Gewey could only nod.

"I was not always an old woman," she explained. "And here, I am able to look however I choose." In another flash of light, her younger self returned. "And now I choose to be young once again."

"How did you get here?" asked Gewey. He took a nervous step forward.

Melek snarled and spat on the ground.

"The same way that you did," she replied.

"But why?"

Maybell sighed. "To save you, of course. Why else would I come here?"

"Don't listen to her, Darshan," cried Melek. "She is here to trick you. To turn you against me."

"You're half right," admitted Maybell. "I *am* here to turn him against you."

Gewey stepped back again. "I'll not turn on Melek. He has shown me the truth. He is my..."

He wanted to say "friend", but a different word came out. "Master."

Maybell's face tightened. She folded her hands in front of her waist. "We cannot move forward until I undo this." She shut her eyes and lowered her head. "I'm sorry, Gewey. This is going to hurt."

As Gewey stiffened, Maybell vanished, only to reappear behind him an instant later. Before he could move, she wrapped her arms around his torso and held him tightly. At first, he struggled with all of his might, at the same time shouting out every curse he could think of. It was futile. Her strength was far beyond anything he could have anticipated. He quickly realized that he was helpless.

Melek, understanding what she was doing, charged in and lashed out with a barrage of blows. But Maybell was unaffected. It was as if she was made from granite ... and Melek, glass. He withdrew after only a few seconds, his fists bleeding and bruised.

"Release me," Gewey commanded. The sight of the injured Melek fueled his anger.

"As you wish," whispered Maybell.

She opened her arms, allowing Gewey to crumble to the ground. He tried to stand, but a pain instantly shot through his gullet. He doubled over as wave after wave of searing hot spasms caused him to cry out in agony. Then, a final great wave rose, forcing him to begin emptying his stomach. The air was immediately filled with the sickly sweet smell of wine.

But the moment any of this touched the grass, it instantly turned thick and black. Again and again, the poison within him spewed forth until Gewey could no longer hold himself upright. He toppled over, the putrid bile still flowing from his mouth.

Maybell turned to face Melek. "And when he is himself again, I will show him what you really are."

"Know this, mortal," he hissed back at her. "When I am free from this place, I will send your spirit to the depths of oblivion. But not before I strip you of your reason and force you to experience terrors such as your limited mind can scarcely conceive."

Maybell laughed tauntingly. "Were you this boorish and crude before you betrayed your children and your maker?"

Melek sneered. "Again, you speak of things of which you know nothing."

"I know that you showed Gewey his father," she retorted. "But I also know that you showed him only a part of the story. But understand this: I can see everything that you see. You cannot hide what you are from me."

Gewey had at last stopped vomiting and was struggling back to his feet. The thick ooze covered his shirt and trousers and was smeared across his face. Maybell pointed to a spot behind him where a tiny stream had suddenly blinked into existence.

"Clean yourself," she said. "Melek has shown you what he wanted you to see. Now I will show you the rest."

With glazed eyes and skin devoid of color, Gewey did as instructed. Maybell waited patiently while Melek paced back and forth, seething and sulking. When Gewey returned, he looked much recovered and more like himself.

He managed a weary smile and embraced Maybell fondly. "You shouldn't have come here. I don't think I can get us out."

"You needn't worry about that," she replied. "It is I who will get *you* out. But first, there are things to do."

"What things?" he asked.

"Do not listen to her, Darshan," said Melek. "She is not who she says she is."

"Your lies no longer work, Melek," said Maybell, waving her hand dismissively. "Gewey knows who I am."

Gewey scrutinized Maybell for a short time, then turned to Melek. "This is Maybell. I have no doubt of that. But I don't understand. Why would you show me all those things if they weren't true? What was there to gain?"

Maybell cut in before Melek could respond. "He showed you the truth, Gewey. But only a part of it."

"And you can see these things too?" he asked.

"Yes," she affirmed. "And were you to spend enough time here, you would learn to see them as well. All beings carry within them every memory, from the moment of their birth, right through to their final breath. It lives deep inside us, where few can see or touch. But here, these memories are a part of what we are. Over time, your perceptions would change and you would see them as I do now."

"So Gerath really did hate me?" asked Gewey. Without Melek's poison coursing through him, his anger was now mild. "That's what my memories are still telling me."

"Of course not," she replied, smiling.

The meadow faded and Gewey found himself inside a spacious tent. Standing in the center were three people that he recognized at once: Gerath, Ayliazarah, and Basanti. In Gerath's arms was an infant bundled in a soft cotton blanket. He was smiling fondly at the baby, but with a profoundly mournful look in his eyes.

"You *will* see that Darshan is delivered safely," he said, not taking his eyes off his son.

Basanti bowed. "He will come to no harm. I will send for Felsafell and have him escort my maid to Hazrah."

"No," said Ayliazarah. "He must be taken immediately. We cannot wait for the hermit."

"Then I will escort her myself," offered Basanti.

Ayliazarah shook her head. "It would be better if you stayed. There must be as little attention as possible drawn to the child, and your absence would be noticed. Send only a few trusted followers. And only those who will remain silent. No one must know that we were here, or that you ever had contact with this child."

"I will see it done," she replied.

"I should take him myself," said Gerath.

"You know that is not possible," objected Ayliazarah. "You must return right away."

Gerath tore his eyes away from his son and looked hard at Basanti. "The half-man, Lee Starfinder, son of Saraf. He will be my son's protector?"

"As you commanded," replied Basanti, dropping her chin to her chest. "I cannot tell you the details. But know that I have arranged for him to be well-cared for ... and well-loved."

Basanti's words struck Gerath. He squeezed his eyes shut and nodded. "I would speak to Ayliazarah alone."

Basanti bowed low and hurried out.

"I do not trust her," said Gerath. "She speaks to Pósix."

"You should have included Pósix in your plan," said Ayliazarah. "She would have supported you if only you had confided in her."

"No," said Gerath. "Only you can know of my true intentions. My mistreatment of my son has kept the others from becoming suspicious, but I cannot risk betrayal."

His words pierced Gewey. He glared furiously at Melek. "You knew this? You knew that the way he treated me was all an act, yet you still let me believe he hated me?"

Melek met Gewey's anger with a calm silence.

Gewey started to move toward Melek, but Maybell stopped him.

"Be careful," she warned. "He may not be a match for me in this place, but he has been here for a very long time. Do not underestimate him. Leave such things to me."

She gave Gewey a sinister smile.

Gewey nodded and returned his attention to the scene.

"Perhaps *I* will betray you," said Ayliazarah. "You know how I feel about your plan."

Gerath managed a small laugh. "If you were going to betray me, you would have done so already." He looked at his son. "No. I'm afraid that my love for Darshan is rivaled only by your own. And you know this is the only way."

"Yes. I know." She touched Gerath's cheek with the tips of her slender fingers and traced his aspect. "I never thought you capable of such devotion, brother."

"Nor did I. Though I have had mortal children, I never fully understood the bond that mortals share with their offspring," said Gerath. "But then the *Creator* called on me to be a father. To give life to my own kind." He looked at Ayliazarah in obvious agony. "How could *she* do this to me? *She* must have known. How could *she* not? Why would *she* ask of me the one thing that would tear my heart to pieces? Does *she* test me? Or does *she* simply not care?"

Ayliazarah slipped her arm around Gerath's waist. "I understand. For the first time, I, too, have questioned *her* wisdom and compassion. But we must remain steadfast and strong. Though we cannot see *her* design, I must stay true to my maker and believe that *she* loves us."

Gerath nodded. "I know you are right."

In spite of his words, there was a glint of defiance in his eyes as he continued. "But should harm come to my son, I will tear down creation to have my vengeance. Only banishment to Shagharath will stop me."

"And I will be by your side. But we must not dwell on such evil thoughts. Events have been set in motion and we must see this through."

"I am grateful for your friendship," said Gerath. "I have often wondered why you were not chosen to parent this child."

Ayliazarah laughed. "Because you are far stronger than me. I would never have been able to give him up, and all would turn against me."

Gerath stared at Darshan with loving eyes for several more minutes. Finally, he called for Basanti and handed over his son.

"I know you are Pósix's creature," he said. "And I do not expect your loyalty. But if you can find love in your heart for this child, you will not speak of where he has been taken to Pósix, should she ever ask."

"I will not speak of it," she assured him. "If Pósix ever learns of where the child is, it will not be because I have told her. You have my promise."

Gerath scrutinized Basanti for a long moment before nodding his acceptance of her word.

"Come," said Ayliazarah. "There is little time. We must go."

Gerath touched the face of his son, then leaned down and kissed his brow. Darshan cooed and shifted in his blanket. A second later, in a flash of blue light, he and Ayliazarah vanished.

Basanti held Darshan close and sat down on a pillow. "Pósix already knows," she whispered, tickling Darshan's tiny chin. "And she is the reason you will succeed."

Gewey was smiling, his eyes wet with tears ready to flow.

"So now you see," said Maybell. "You have never been unloved or unwanted."

"Yes," said Gewey. "Thank you. Thank you for showing me this."

"You needed to understand that you are not merely a tool of the gods," Maybell told him. "Or a means to an end. And I suspect there is more yet to discover once you have returned."

She took his hand. "Now for the last. To banish any doubt, you shall witness the fall of Melek and the depths of his madness."

"I don't need to see that," said Gewey. "I believe you."

"Yes," said Maybell. "But you will one day be faced with a decision. And you need to know how to decide wisely."

"And this will help?"

Maybell shrugged. "I'm not sure. Perhaps. This was not a part of the plan when I arrived. But my instincts tell me it will be important later." She grinned impishly, her young body contrasting with the wisdom in her eyes. "Call it an old woman's intuition."

The world changed again. This time, Gewey found himself standing at the base of an immense marble statue that he recognized immediately to be of Gerath. A few yards away stood Melek and a breathtakingly beautiful woman with bronze skin and auburn hair. He knew that this must be Melek's wife, Ustrea. Gewey was reminded of Kaylia for a moment and the pain of her absence shot through him.

"A good likeness," Ustrea remarked approvingly.

Melek twisted his mouth in a frown and huffed. "It is a blight on the world. A testament to Gerath's bloated sense of self-worth. What purpose is served from such mindless worship?"

"The people of this world love him," she said. "And he loves them in return. They worship him because he has earned their adoration. He spends a great deal of time amongst them, guiding their future."

"He has placed himself above the Creator," countered Melek. "And now I find out that he is actually *mating* with them." The thought clearly disgusted him.

Ustrea laughed. "And you find that distasteful?"

Melek raised an eyebrow. "Of course. How could I not? And you? Would you have us breed with these animals?"

"I must admit that I find the males to be fair," she replied, smiling playfully.

Melek stared at his wife with a mixture of outrage and jealousy. "So you would—"

"No," she said before he could complete his sentence. "I would never consider such an act. At least, not with them." Her tone took on a distinctly seductive quality. "Though have you not wondered what it would be like for us?"

"Absolutely not!" he replied.

Surprised and displeased by his reaction, Ustrea turned her back. "So, you do not find my physical form pleasing?"

Melek grumbled and shook his head. "I did not say that. But you cannot truly wish for us to engage in..."

He could not bring himself to say the words. Instead, he demanded: "Are you not happy with the love we share in heaven?"

She turned to him and smiled. "Of course I am. But I would share my love with you in all its forms. It seems to bring such joy to the people here. Not to mention to our sons and daughters."

Melek slumped his shoulders in defeat. "If you desire it, I will comply."

Ustrea frowned. "I am not asking you to do so here and now. Only to give the idea consideration. These people bear the spark of the Creator. So perhaps we *should* understand how they express their feelings."

"But what of the offspring?" countered Melek. "Should we explore that as well? Should we make children with these people?"

"Perhaps," she replied. "If it is possible. Would that be so wrong?"

Melek's face turned red and his fist clenched. "I will not allow such abominations to exist. If Gerath desires a child, then he should choose a wife from his own kind."

"But he does not love them in such a way," she pointed out, unmoved by Melek's anger.

"What does love have to do with anything? One does not need love to father offspring." His eyes turned to the statue. "And *this* must stop."

The ground shook violently. In seconds, the marble base of the statue turned to dust. The statue fell, smashing to pieces as it hit the ground.

Ustrea groaned with frustration. "Are you satisfied?"

Melek smiled. "I am."

"This is how it began," said Maybell. "Melek's hatred and jealousy. His unbending nature began to assert itself. Even his wife could see it."

"Ustrea did not understand," snapped Melek. "Such worship was wrong. As was breeding with lesser beings."

"Perhaps," said Maybell. "But it did not end there, did it?"

The scene faded. When Melek and Ustrea returned, they were walking on the shore of a vast ocean. Gewey thought it might be the Western Abyss, but there was no way to be certain.

From out of nowhere, a bolt of lightning struck the ground a few feet in front of the couple. Gerath appeared, his eyes burning with fury. He was brandishing a sword.

"Father!" His voice boomed. "You killed her, didn't you?"

Melek's expression was blank as he nodded.

"What did you do, husband?" asked Ustrea.

"He killed my daughter," roared Gerath.

"Yes," Melek admitted flatly. "I warned you not to mate with the people here. Your defiance caused this. The child should never have been born."

"You killed his child?" said Ustrea in horror. "How could you?"

"Did I not warn him?" he shot back. "Did I not say that there would be consequences?"

"But to kill a child..." Her voice trailed off.

"You are a monster," said Gerath. "A blight on the face of creation." His grip tightened on his sword. "One that I will now erase."

With a primal yell, Gerath charged in, his sword slashing at Melek's exposed neck. Melek made no effort to avoid the blow. The blade struck home but shattered into a thousand tiny shards on impact. Undeterred, Gerath struck his father squarely on the jaw. Once again, Melek made no attempt to move, and once again, the blow had no effect. Melek's palm then shot out and thudded into the center of Gerath's chest. The strike sent him flying through the air for several yards before landing with bone-crunching force on his back. Snarling, Melek moved forward.

"Enough!" shouted Ustrea, seizing her husband's shoulder and jerking him back with surprising ease. "You will not harm him."

"Let him come, mother," thundered Gerath.

"You fool," scoffed Melek. "Do you think you can harm me? I made you. And I can end you as well."

Ustrea moved between the two. "You did not make *me*," she challenged. "And I will tell you only once more. Do not harm our son or I will show you the full meaning of consequences."

Melek and Ustrea stood nose to nose for several seconds. Eventually, Melek stepped back in reluctant submission.

"As you wish, my dear wife," he said. "But I will tolerate no further defiance from him."

Ustrea looked over her shoulder. "Leave, Gerath. We will speak later."

Apparently no more willing to defy his mother than Melek, Gerath vanished.

"I would not have harmed him," Melek said soothingly. "At least, not permanently."

"Why did you kill his daughter?" she demanded, ignoring his attempt to quell her rage. "What gave you the right?"

"She did not suffer," said Melek.

"That does not change what you did."

"I did what needed to be done." His tone bore the certainty of absolute conviction. "I have every right to determine the paths our children take. The Creator gave me that right."

"Then *she* has told this only to you," Ustrea countered. "I have heard no such edict."

"I know the mind of my maker," he said proudly. "*She* has given me the power to guide and protect. And to destroy if needs be."

Melek turned and walked away. His wife could do nothing but stand and watch with dread growing in her eyes.

"You killed your own kin?" said Gewey accusingly. "How could you be so heartless?"

"I do not answer to you, Darshan," said Melek. "I did what I had to do. My children acted recklessly and without concern for anything but their own lustful desires."

"You acted out of envy," said Maybell. "You couldn't understand their love, so you sought to destroy it. And it didn't end with the death of one child, did it? You slaughtered the offspring of every one of your children. And not in the quick, painless way you told Ustrea. You didn't kill them in the womb or the cradle. No. You waited until they were older. Then you tortured them, breaking their bodies and minds until they begged for death. It was for that reason more than any other that your wife turned against you."

"Be quiet!" ordered Melek. But Maybell only shook her head and looked at him in disgust.

"And even with all your power," she continued, "you were still not satisfied. You needed unquestioning obedience. And it was not enough for you to subjugate heaven. You needed to rule all of creation as well."

A city appeared before them, its once-tall spires broken and engulfed in flames. The screams and cries of its inhabitants carried on the wind, leaving a smile on Melek's lips as he watched from a few hundred feet away.

A small group of people began climbing down a rope on the east wall in an attempt to escape. Melek sneered and sent an inferno to consume them. Their agonizing cries and the stench of their burning flesh drifted across the field where he was standing.

"Melek!" Ustrea's voice boomed out. A moment later, she appeared in front of him. Before he had any time to react, she slapped him hard across his cheek. "How dare you do this? What gives you the right?"

Ignoring the blow, Melek laughed. "You are too attached to these pitiful creatures, my love. They have become a disease—a disease which I have deemed unworthy of the Creator's gifts."

"You have no authority to decide this," Ustrea told him. "Only the Creator can choose their fate. Not you."

"And where is the Creator?" he snapped back furiously. "*She* has made no effort to stop me. Have you heard *her* voice? I have not. And yet I am forced to look upon this once pure and tranquil world and watch these beasts desecrate the very ground that provides them with life."

He surveyed the destruction and nodded with satisfaction. "Soon they will be ready to follow the path I set before them."

"So, you mean to rule these people?" Ustrea asked.

"Those that survive, yes."

"And should the Creator make her displeasure known and tell you of your folly?"

Melek laughed. "*She* will not. And soon it will no longer matter."

Ustrea's eye widened. "What are you saying?"

He gave her a loving smile. "My dear wife. If our Creator will not act, then I must set things to rights. Then *I* will become the Creator. I will cast *her* out and do what *she* will not."

His words hung in the air like vapor. Ustrea backed away, tears streaming down her face. She turned and vanished.

"The arrogance," said Maybell. "To think you could raise yourself so high."

"But when was this?" asked Gewey. "I couldn't tell what race those people were. They looked…" He paused. "Well, they somehow just didn't look right."

"It's how Melek sees them," Maybell explained. "You are only seeing things as he does, and to his eyes, all people look the same. But I suspect it was during the time of the *firstborn*. I don't believe he knew what a human was until he met you."

"Then what about the children he killed?" Gewey asked. But he already knew the answer.

"The very first elves," Maybell confirmed. "But his crimes run far deeper. His rampage of death spread like a plague as he destroyed city after city. And all of heaven was powerless to stop him. Well … all but one."

"I will not see this," grumbled Melek, lowering his eyes.

Melek walked the devastated streets of the once magnificent city. Charred bodies littered the avenues and sidewalks, and the foul stench of decay was already beginning to set in.

He had been surprised at how difficult these creatures were to kill. Their spark had been made to never burn out, so it had taken him some time to puzzle out a way of extinguishing it.

"You have been busy, my husband." Ustrea appeared from around a corner a few yards ahead. "Is your appetite for carnage sated yet? Have you killed enough?"

"Before I came here," he replied. "I did not know what it was to kill. Not really."

"And now that you do?"

"It is different from what I expected," Melek mused. "In a way, quite liberating. But it's a pity these creatures were made unable to slay each other. Think how much joy I would be able to experience in that. There are so many ways to inflict pain and suffering. More than I could have ever thought possible. If only they could see as I see."

"And if they could?" asked Ustrea. "What would you do? Incite them to fight one another? Would you have them burn the world to cinders? Would that entertain you?"

Melek scrutinized his wife. "What is it, my love? Why have you come? I know you find this distasteful. Why witness it?" He took a step forward, but Ustrea moved back. "Why do you shy away? You have nothing to fear from me."

He looked at her even more closely. "Something is different. You are ... changed."

"Yes, my love," she confessed. "I am changed. But no more so than you. You have become lost to me. You have blackened your heart and turned your back on everything we hold sacred."

"What have you done?" he asked, suddenly suspicious.

"Only what I had to do."

A tiny object flew from her hand. Melek gasped with surprise and threw himself to his left. The missile missed his neck by a hair's width, instead burying itself into a half-burned wagon a few feet behind him.

A rage that caused the very ground to shake filled Melek as he realized his wife's intent. "You seek to destroy me?" he accused.

Ustrea did not respond. Instead, she ran headlong at her husband, the dagger that had suddenly appeared in her hand slashing furiously at Melek's chest. He instinctively twisted aside, but the tip of the blade still found his earthly flesh. He let out a cry as, for the first time ever, he felt pain.

Ustrea was not about to allow him time to get hold of the situation. She pressed the attack. Melek dodged and spun in desperation, at first uncertain of what to do.

Three more times Ustrea drew blood. But then Melek began to realize that, for some unknown reason, she was in a weakened condition. Compared to how they usually were, her movements that day were relatively slow and clumsy. She thrust the blade at his gullet again, and this time, he was able to catch hold of her arm. He crushed it in his powerful grip. Ustrea cried out as the dagger fell to the ground.

Melek no longer cared why she had changed; rage was blinding him to all but vengeance. His fist smashed against her temple. She fell back, but he pulled her to him, striking her over and over until her legs collapsed beneath her.

In that moment, Melek thrust his hand deep into her chest. Not with his physical being, but with his godly form. Letting out an ear-splitting yell, he ripped Ustrea's spirit from within its earthbound shell. He raised the formless and radiant essence aloft for a moment, the blood lust still coursing wildly through him. Then, with a scowl contorting his features into a mask of pure evil, with a single motion, he tore it apart.

The two pieces of what had once been Ustrea flickered and then vanished.

Melek touched the wounds inflicted upon him by his wife. They were already beginning to close. His hands were covered with her blood, as were his shredded garments. It was then that the awful realization of what he had done struck him.

He fell to his knees and wept.

"You killed her," whispered Gewey. "You killed your own wife."

Melek could not respond. A single tear fell from his eye.

"Ustrea realized that he must be stopped," said Maybell. "And she knew that her children did not possess the power to do this."

"So, how did they defeat him?" asked Gewey.

Maybell nodded toward where Melek still kneeled.

In a flash of light, all nine of Melek's children appeared. Gerath was in front, his eyes searching the area.

"Where is mother?" he demanded.

Melek looked up at his son. In an instant, he knew why Ustrea had been diminished. She had passed on a part of herself to their children.

"I will ask you one last time," said Gerath, this time far more aggressively. "Where is mother?" His eyes took in Melek's bloodstained clothes and hands. Also, to the dart lodged in the wooden wagon behind him. Then he saw his mother's lifeless body lying on the ground a few feet behind his father.

"You forced her to betray me!" Melek shouted. Leaping to his feet, he ran at Gerath, arms outstretched and hands curled into savage claws ready to rip his son apart.

Gerath waited for him to come with clenched fists.

They smashed together with a thud that sent shock waves reverberating through the ground. Even with the added power that his mother had passed to him, Gerath was still not as powerful as Melek. He was thrown violently twenty feet down the cobbled street, two bloody gashes already opened up in his chest. Ignoring the rest of his children, Melek chased after him, spanning the distance before Gerath could regain his feet. He slammed his foot on his son's throat and raised an arm high. His earthly flesh faded into a godly spirit, poised to send Gerath to the same fate as Ustrea.

His hand was already plunging down, and a mere parchment's thickness away from Gerath's chest, when the rest of his children seized hold of him and pulled him away. Melek thrashed and kicked with a madman's ferocity, his immense strength very nearly proving to be a match for their combined efforts. But somehow, they managed to hold on long enough for Gerath to recover and draw a dart from his pocket. It was identical to the one that Ustrea had thrown. With ominous purpose, he moved in.

Gerath grabbed his father's hair and yanked his head straight back. Melek screamed with terror and fury but to no avail.

"This is for all of those you have slain," announced Gerath ceremoniously. "For our children ... and for our *mother*." Having spoken these words, he sank the dart into Melek's neck.

His father's body instantly went limp.

"Now you know what he really is," said Maybell. "And now it is time you returned."

At the sound of this, Melek exploded with rage. "I will not be left here! You will not do this to me!" In a mirror image of his attack on Gerath, he charged at Maybell.

Maybell grinned wickedly and sent a blast of air at the fallen god. Melek was sent sprawling as if struck by an enormous hammer.

He pushed himself up and glared at her. "This is not over, mortal."

Barely were these words out of his mouth when he was surrounded by a swirl of dust and smoke. Within moments, he had completely disappeared.

"Where did he go?" asked Gewey.

"Don't concern yourself with Melek," she replied dismissively. "I will deal with him soon enough."

Gewey frowned. "Aren't you returning with me?"

Maybell touched his face tenderly. "I cannot. My body was destroyed when I came to Shagharath. There is nothing for me to return to." The sound of the mad human souls echoed distantly. "Besides. I have a new purpose. To heal those poor creatures of the wounds inflicted by Melek. Here, I can create a paradise of my own choosing. And I'm safe from the Dark Knight's power."

Gewey was rendered speechless by Maybell's sacrifice.

She pulled his head down and kissed his cheek. "You are a good and kind man, Gewey Stedding. And you will prevail. I know it."

Gewey embraced her tightly. "I have no way to thank you for this. But I will never forget you."

Maybell giggled, the laugh matching her youthful form. "I should hope not. And I hope you will be the one to escort me to heaven when the time comes."

"You have my word," said Gewey. He released Maybell and bowed low. "I will personally hold your hand while you walk through its gates."

She sighed. "What a wonderful dream to hold on to. But you should not delay any longer. Your destiny and, more importantly, your wife, await your return."

A silver light appeared a few feet away. It was oval-shaped and just tall enough for Gewey to walk through.

"All you need do is step inside and you will be returned to your body," explained Maybell.

Gewey started to speak, but she placed her slender, unblemished hand over his mouth.

He chuckled and turned to face the light. After taking a deep breath, he stepped inside.

Maybell watched with a satisfied smile as Gewey vanished from view. But her satisfaction was fleeting.

From seemingly nowhere, the sound of wild howls suddenly assaulted her from all directions at once. Intense heat began blistering her skin and thick choking dust attacked her eyes. It took a moment for Maybell to realize that it was the souls of the mad humans who were responsible for this attack.

"Fool." It was the voice of Melek. "You think me without power or influence?"

The dust lifted just in time for Maybell to see Melek passing through the portal, laughing triumphantly.

She cried out and immediately banished the light.

But it was too late.

Melek was free.

CHAPTER 13

For two days, everyone waited anxiously. Once word spread that Maybell had sacrificed her own life in order to save Darshan, songs praising her courage could be heard ringing out in many quarters of the camp.

Lee and Jacob spent most of their time in quiet conversation; Lee told his son about his many exploits, and Jacob told of his own youthful misadventures. Millet joined them occasionally, but he understood that Lee felt an urgent need to spend more time with his son, so for the most part he left them alone.

Linis, Dina, and her mother used the short respite to get to know each other better. It was clear that Nahali approved of Linis's union with her daughter, and often wept tears of joy at the sight of them together.

No one knew how long they would need to wait. Kaylia had regained her wits completely and was sleeping well, comforted by the knowledge that her *unorem* would soon be back in her arms.

In spite of her reservations regarding Maybell's chances of success, Dina had decided to delay the funeral rites until

Gewey returned. This pleased Kaylia, who took time to learn the significance of the ceremony that Maybell had requested.

Bevaris and Tristan, ever the vigilant warriors, took a group of elves to scout the surrounding area. It was feared that if the enemy thought Darshan was gone forever, this would embolden them and prompt an attack. Lee was hoping that, since Kaylia had slain all of Gewey's attackers, word of his demise would be slow in arriving to agents of Angrääl.

Several villagers from Sharpstone had ventured into the camp to speak with Lee and Millet. Most wanted to go west and join in the fight. Their outrage at the occupation of their town, combined with their utter inability to fight back at the time, made it almost impossible to dissuade them. But Millet, ever the voice of wisdom and reason, eventually convinced them that they were needed far more by the people at home than by the armies fighting in the west.

Before departing, some of the villagers asked to hear tales of Darshan. They had heard rumors of his powers and triumphs and were now desperate to hear more. Given Darshan's true identity, Lee felt this was a bad idea. But Kaylia thought differently. She stepped in and regaled them with tales so fantastic and full of heroism that everyone left the camp in total awe.

"It gives them hope when they hear that such power fights for them," she explained. "And I would see that the people of my *unorem's* home have as much hope as I can provide."

Lee did not dare to argue.

On the morning of the third day, Kaylia rose early and set about educating the sand masters, explaining to them the different landscapes and obstacles they would be facing during their trek west. Weila was far and away the quickest learner. Not only was she soon able to name and describe more than fifty different plants, but she could also state where they could be found, which ones were good to eat, and which had medicinal properties.

Kaylia was just about to lead the sand masters into the nearby forest for further lessons when her legs suddenly gave way and she crumbled to the ground. Weila was instantly at her side.

"Are you ill?" she asked. "Is it your child?"

Kaylia looked up at the old sand master, a broad smile on her face. Without replying, she sprang to her feet and ran at full speed toward the pavilion where Gewey's body lay. The six elf guards protecting the site moved quickly aside when they saw her coming.

She was still at full speed and closing rapidly when the flap opened and Gewey stepped out, shielding his eyes and squinting at the morning sun. Before he even had time to gage his surroundings, Kaylia crashed into him, sending them both tumbling down onto the soft turf. The moment Gewey's back struck the ground she began showering him with innumerable small kisses. This continued for several minutes until Kaylia finally completed her welcome with a single long kiss of deep passion, utter relief, and unending devotion.

Gewey allowed the renewal of their bond to envelop his soul and wash his spirit clean. It was almost painful when their lips parted. He made no move to rise, content merely to gaze into Kaylia's eyes from the flat of his back.

"You have no idea how beautiful you are to me," he whispered, touching her belly. "I love you both."

Kaylia's emotions burst forth, and she embraced Gewey again, weeping for joy. "I knew you would come back to me ... to us."

By the time they finally got to their feet, Lee and Jacob had arrived, while Linis, Dina, Nahali, and Millet could be seen fast approaching. Weila was transfixed, for now, unable to do any more than simply stare in disbelief. Jacob reached out and touched Gewey's arm, just to be sure that he was real. But it was Lee who was the first to embrace him.

"I'm sorry," said Gewey. "I should have never said–"

"Now is not the time for apologies," Lee told him. "Even if they were necessary. That you live is a miracle."

The others took their turn in welcoming Gewey back to the land of the living. Dina did so somberly while still holding the urn containing Maybell's remains.

Gewey knew what they were without being told. He took the urn from Dina, bowing his head with deep respect.

"If you will come with me," he said, "I will tell you all how brave and pure Maybell is. And what she did so that I might live."

"We should call for Lyrial," suggested Kaylia.

Gewey nodded his agreement, then led everyone inside the pavilion and asked them all to sit in a tight circle. When Lyrial arrived she was laughing uncontrollably. That was ... until Kaylia cleared her throat to get her attention.

"Can he be real?" Lyrial asked.

"He is real," said Kayla. "And he has a tale to tell."

"One that I would not miss for every drop of water in the desert," said Weila.

Once they were all settled, Gewey began recounting his experiences in Shagharath, making certain he left out no detail and stopping several times to answer questions. It took the better part of the day, but when he was finished, the group was thoroughly astounded.

"Such things do not even exist in legends," remarked Linis. "And this god Melek that you spoke of—it is hard to imagine that his name could be wiped so completely from memory. Such an evil would be hard to erase."

"And what about Maybell?" added Dina. "It would seem her true destiny was revealed at just the right time. To think she held such knowledge for so many years and never understood why until now."

"Without her, I would still be under the yoke of Melek," Gewey said solemnly. "And there I would have stayed, trapped in Shagharath until the end of time."

"And now that you are free, will you continue to Althetas?" asked Linis.

Gewey shrugged. "I'm not sure yet. But I can tell you that this war will soon be over. Shagharath has given me the peace in my heart I've longed for. I have been fighting a battle ever since the first moment I discovered who and what I am; Kaylia knows this better than anyone. The part of me who is Gewey Stedding and the part of me who is Darshan have been in a constant struggle for control. Now that struggle is over."

"And who won?" asked Millet in his typical, calm yet scrutinizing manner.

Gewey smiled and spread his hands. "I did. That is to say, both parts of me have emerged as one. The Gewey Stedding in me has tempered the steel that is Darshan, and for the first time in what seems like forever, I am whole."

"If your destiny is at hand, should you not seek out your foe?" asked Lyrial.

"I won't need to seek him out," said Gewey. "I intend to draw him away from his stronghold in Angrääl. I want his only hope for victory to be my death. I may not be in turmoil any longer, but that doesn't make me all-powerful. If I march into the jaws of his strength, he *may* be able to defeat me. My experience with the Oracle showed me that his power is not to be underestimated. And my intuition tells me that there is something else hidden. Something I have yet to discover."

He shook his head. "No. I'll be the one to choose the time and place of our battle. But in the meantime, people are still fighting and dying. That needs to be stopped as quickly as possible."

"Isn't that why we go west?" asked Weila. "To aid our kin and allies?

"Yes," said Gewey. "And I think we should still go. But I have an idea, though I need more time to be sure it won't lead us down the wrong path."

"You have friends to help," Lee pointed out. "Friends with experience you don't possess."

Gewey chuckled. "Don't worry. I haven't forgotten that I'm still the student. I promise to consult you later. But first of all, I think Maybell deserves to have her rites performed."

He looked to Dina. "How long will it take to get ready?"

"The ceremony is simple," she replied. "It's the Farewell Song of Ayliazarah. That's usually followed by a celebration, though, I don't see how that will be possible."

Weila slapped her knees. "Not possible? Bah! You clearly still know nothing of the desert elves. We may lack for wine, and our rations will make a meager feast, but we have fire, kinship, and songs enough to last until the light of the sun dims forever."

"Until dawn will do just fine," said Gewey, smiling. He pushed himself to his feet. "And now, much as I have missed you all, I would like to spend some time alone with my wife."

The entire group nodded with understanding, and all grinned as Kaylia stepped beside him and slipped her arm around his waist.

After everyone had departed, Kaylia stepped outside for a moment and returned with a plate of bread and dried meat, along with a jug of wine.

It may not have been a feast, but they ate slowly, savoring every mouthful of their first meal together since being reunited. Once finished, Kaylia poked her head out of the flap and whispered a few words to the guards. A couple of minutes later two elves brought in a large clay pitcher of steaming hot water and sat it in the center of the pavilion. Kaylia retrieved a rag from the corner, which she dipped slowly into the water. Gewey grinned sheepishly.

"Is there a reason that you are still dressed, my love?" she asked playfully.

He reached into the pitcher and took the rag from her hand.

"I was about to ask you the same question," he responded.

CHAPTER 14

Dina performed the rites for Maybell flawlessly. Her clear, strong voice carried out over the entire camp as she sang the Farewell Song of Ayliazarah. At the beginning, Gewey did his best not to weep, but he found himself succumbing to his sorrow long before the song ended. The sight of his tears encouraged at first dozens, then hundreds of the other mourners, to join him in openly sobbing.

With the ceremony completed, Dina held her arms wide and smiled brightly.

"Let us rejoice in the memory of our friend, Sister Maybell," she called out with splendid joy. "For she has earned a place in our hearts and put a song on our lips. May Ayliazarah bless her and keep her forever in the light of heaven."

Though the elves had never witnessed this ritual before, they instinctively knew that it was now time for the celebrations to begin. Their cheers erupted in a symphony of elation.

Weila had been correct about the lack of wine and good food not hindering her kin from merrymaking. Within minutes, the sounds of small wooden flutes and gleeful voices could be heard throughout the encampment.

Gewey and Lee were soon being challenged to wrestling matches and foot races, both of which Gewey respectfully declined. Lee, on the other hand, was in the mood for some sport. He won every match and all but one race. Jacob clearly enjoyed seeing his father having fun and was more than willing to cheer him on. He even took part in one match himself. But unfortunately, this was against Weila, and he was swiftly beaten.

As it neared midnight, Bevaris and Tristan returned. After the initial shock of Gewey's resurrection had worn off a little, they managed to report that scattered units of Angrääl soldiers had been seen, every one of them heading south. None of these units appeared interested in the fact that a large elf army was close at hand, even though their presence would certainly be well known to the enemy by now.

Gewey pulled Lee away from the festivities and, together with Kaylia, led him to an outlying area where a small fire burned. This was surrounded by bedrolls and dishes.

Lee pushed a blanket aside and seated himself close to the fire. "With all these games, it's easy to forget that we are now in the dead of winter." He looked up and smiled. "At least there's no snow. I never did care for that white stuff."

"Not good for a man from Hazrah," joked Gewey, taking a seat beside him.

Kaylia pulled a flask of brandy from a pouch on her belt and passed it to Lee. "A gift from Linis."

Lee eagerly opened the flask and took a large gulp. The sweet scent filled the air, encouraging Gewey to breathe in deeply.

"So, I take it that you want to tell me about this plan of yours," Lee said as he passed the flask over.

Gewey held the flask under his nose. "You know, I never thought I would learn to truly appreciate plum brandy. But after seeing Shagharath..." He paused to take a drink. "I feel there are many things I will never take for granted again."

Lee was still chuckling at this remark when Gewey added: "I think we should take Baltria."

The laughter quickly ceased. Lee sat back, raising an eyebrow. "Do you think we can?"

"I think we must," said Gewey. "King Lousis fights in the west. And I'm sure we can agree that Angrääl is staging its attack from Baltria's port."

Lee nodded. "That would certainly be my guess. It's probably why he moved there first, and why he secured the Goodbranch. But do we have the numbers for this? Even with you leading us, Baltria is well-defended. The approach is made narrow by the swampy terrain, and the city walls are thick and high."

"True," agreed Gewey. "But if we succeed, we take away the Dark Knight's ability to supply his armies in the west. He'll have to pull back and try to re-take the city."

"That, or he'll march overland and concentrate his forces west," countered Lee. "Hoping to win there, where resistance is most fierce."

"Either way, it disrupts his plans," said Gewey. "With Angrääl out of Baltria, we can choke off his supplies, and at the same time create a supply line of our own to the west."

Lee nodded. "This is all true. And if we had three times our numbers, I wouldn't think twice about going through with your plan."

"What about Helenia?" asked Gewey. "Perhaps we could convince them to fight with us."

"I doubt it," said Lee. "The king fears Angrääl, and thinks that the only reason the city remains unconquered is due to his supposed neutrality."

"Then perhaps Darshan can help him understand that neutrality is no longer an option." Gewey grinned wickedly while handing the flask back to Lee. "Surely the name is known there. What would he do if a column of flames erupted in the city square?"

Lee laughed. "I don't know. But I would like to find out."

"I think you should leave the people of Helenia out of the fray," objected Kaylia. "They are *your* people, Gewey, and the Dark Knight has left them in peace for the time being. We should not tempt him to change his mind."

Gewey thought for a moment, then nodded. "I suppose you're right. But so is Lee. Taking Baltria would be much easier with a larger army."

"There is another option," Lee suggested. "I have friends and allies there. Perhaps we could even the odds from within."

"Barty and Randson may still be there as well," added Gewey. "Is there a way we can get into the city unseen?"

"*We* can't," Lee replied. "But *I* can."

Before Gewey could object, Lee held up his hand. "If Vrykol are anywhere in Baltria, they'll sniff you out in a second. I should take Millet with me as well. The two of us know Baltria better than anyone, so it shouldn't be a problem to move about unnoticed. Especially when they have an elf army led by the mighty Darshan bearing down on their city walls. They'll be far too busy worrying about you to care about us."

"Once you're inside, what will you do?" asked Kaylia.

"I suppose I'll have to improvise," replied Lee, giving an elaborate wink.

"Are you sure you should take Millet?" Gewey asked.

Lee chuckled. "I know him well. He won't allow me to go alone. And he is even more familiar with the back streets of Baltria than I." His smile slowly vanished. "Besides, if Millet doesn't go, Jacob will insist that *he* does, and I can't have that. If either Millet or I are caught, we'll likely be killed. Both of us have lived long enough to welcome our end, should it come to that. But Jacob has not. I know I can't keep him out of danger all the time. After all, this is a war. But I'll feel better if my son is under your protection while I'm gone. The thought of something happening to him..."

"You are like a second father to me," said Gewey. "Well ... a third actually, now that I think about it." Lee's smile returned. "That makes Jacob my brother. So, do what you need to do. I will watch over him."

"Thank you," said Lee. With a grunt, he pushed himself to his feet. "I should go speak with Millet. I think I saw him with a bottle in his hand earlier. Hopefully, he's only found one, otherwise, he'll be in a foul mood come morning."

"So you leave tomorrow?" asked Gewey.

Lee nodded. "And I suggest you follow quickly. Speed is your best ally."

Gewey watched as Lee disappeared into the camp. The sounds of the celebration suddenly seemed dull and dreary as he thought of yet another battle to come.

"So you intend to draw the Dark Knight out," said Kaylia.

"Yes," Gewey replied. "Though that's not the only reason I see for taking Baltria. I fear that we may not arrive in time to save King Lousis. But word of Baltria's fall will travel far faster than an army can. And I don't think the Dark Knight will ignore such a bad turn of events to go unchallenged. As we have already discussed, losing Baltria will disrupt his supply line and stop his advance cold."

"Of course, taking the city is one thing," Kaylia pointed out. "But how do you intend to hold it?"

Gewey shrugged. "It doesn't matter if we hold it. The elves will continue west after the assault."

Kaylia cocked her head. "If you don't intend to keep it, why risk the lives?"

A faint smile formed on Gewey's face. "When I was a young boy, my father sent me to Miss Havershan's house in town three days a week to study. She taught most of the children in Sharpstone—at least, those whose parents could spare the extra pair of hands. The first day I went, a boy named Walton Vessty decided he didn't like me. I couldn't tell you why, but he made it clear that he was *not* my friend and made it his mission to make my life difficult. Each day after lessons, he would round up his friends and follow me home, throwing rocks at me the whole way."

"What did you do?" asked Kaylia, clearly bothered by the idea of someone tormenting her *unorem*, even as a child.

Gewey shrugged. "What could I do? I was outnumbered, and they were all bigger and older than me. So I ran.

"Eventually, when my father found out what was happening, he went to talk to Mister Vessty. Well, I can tell you, Mister Vessty was a mean-natured son-of-a-pig farmer. He told my father that if I had a problem with his son, best that I solve it myself."

"And did you?" asked Kaylia.

"In a way," he replied with a smirk. "My father told me that the next time it happened, I should walk right up to Walton and punch him on the nose. Well, sure enough, the next day he and his friends were at it again. So I turned around, ready to do what my father had told me. But for some reason—and I have no idea why—I picked up a rock instead and threw it as hard as I could. It hit Walton right between the eyes and knocked him out cold."

Kaylia gave a loud laugh. "Served him right."

"Yeah," agreed Gewey. "I thought I might have killed him at the time, but luckily, there was no serious harm done. And though we never became friends, he did not bother me again—ever."

"So is that what attacking Baltria is all about?" asked Kaylia.

"In a way," said Gewey. "So far, we've been running and running while our enemy continues to assault us on all sides. He thinks we can't do a thing to stop him and hopes to draw me to his lair where I am at a disadvantage. But if we are successful and deny him Baltria—even for a short time—that could turn the tide in our favor. We will be the aggressor. People need to be shown that the Reborn King is not all-powerful. Then perhaps they will not be so afraid and begin to rise up against him."

"And those same people may be slaughtered in the process," Kaylia told him. "The Dark Knight is not a boy, and he will not be so easily deterred."

Gewey sighed. He couldn't deny that she was speaking the truth. Nonetheless, he also knew that it was the right thing to do. As long as the enemy was allowed to press forward, the Dark Knight would remain in his fortress, unassailable and secure. The only path to victory was to disrupt his plans and force him out.

Baltria was going to burn—Gewey knew that—and he was going to be the one responsible, either in taking the city or defending it. But it was a sacrifice he would have to make. The western kingdoms would not be the only ones to feel the agony of war.

Kaylia hopped up, pulling Gewey with her. "Come. Dance with me. There will be time for war tomorrow. Tonight is for celebrating the memory of Maybell."

Gewey pushed troublesome thoughts to the back of his mind. Soon he and Kaylia were spending the rest of the evening in high-spirited merriment. Luckily, Lee had reached Millet before he'd found a second bottle of wine and they had now retired to a bedroll at the edge of the camp. Gewey spotted them talking in hushed whispers, with Lee drawing lines in the dirt, presumably mapping out their entry into the city.

It was near dawn by the time the elves began to bed down. The music continued on but in contrast to the up-tempo melodies of the early evening, the tunes were now soft and sweet.

Gewey spoke to Lyrial about his intentions. She seemed unconcerned.

"It matters not where we fight," she said. "We will follow you into any fray—and we will be victorious."

Bevaris was less optimistic, though he voiced only a few half-hearted objections. Gewey could tell that the man was still unnerved by his miraculous resurrection. Tristan, on the other hand, was much more accepting of the matter and had no problem telling Gewey the foolishness of his plan.

"You're completely mad," the younger knight said, his mouth twisting in a disapproving scowl. "We'll never take Baltria. I don't care how many fireballs you throw at them. The walls of the city are fifteen feet thick and twice as high. They'll rain down arrows so heavily that they'll blot out the sun."

"You must trust me," Gewey replied. "I promise I can take care of the walls *and* the arrows. The fight will truly begin once we're inside. I can't be in all places at once, and I doubt Angrääl is going to surrender the city easily."

Tristan rubbed his chin thoughtfully. "Get us inside, and *I* can promise that the city will be ours."

Though it was obvious that Bevaris didn't agree, he simply bowed and began gathering the sand masters. Battle plans needed to be made.

Gewey was acutely aware that their success would hinge entirely on his ability to bring down the walls and gate. There was a time when he would have held doubts about this, but ever since returning from Shagharath, he'd had a much greater understanding as to the extent of his powers. He was now confident that he could destroy the wall, regardless of how thick it was.

The sun was breaking the horizon when Kaylia led him back to the pavilion. She insisted that he sleep for at least a few hours. The elves needed only a short time to prepare and seemed unconcerned that they would be marching with very little rest.

Just as Kaylia pulled back the flaps to usher him inside, he glanced over to where he had seen Lee and Millet talking earlier. Their bedrolls were now gone. Jacob was sitting there alone, looking very displeased.

Gewey smiled inwardly. Better angry than dead.

Lee was humming a tune that Millet had taught him when he'd first arrived as a scared yet excited young boy in the home of Dauvis Nal'Thain. The road they were riding along was easy for now, almost entirely because Gewey had frightened the enemy away for at least a hundred miles.

Lee's mind drifted back to those early days. He had been so excited to explore the world around him. And though his escapades then had only ever been in the close vicinity of Hazrah, they had still seemed like a never-ending series of wild adventures to a boy who had spent most of his time before that locked away in a temple.

"You still remember that one," remarked Millet with a lopsided smile. "I sang it to you when you were young."

"It made me feel safe," said Lee. "The manor was so big and imposing. I was crying that night, just before you came into my room."

"I know," said Millet. "You tried to hide it ... but I knew. You may not have missed the temple, but you missed your mother much more than you were willing to admit."

"You always knew me better than I knew myself. And you knew what to say when I was alone and afraid." Lee sighed. "You know, I don't think I'll see the end of this war, old friend." His tone wasn't dark or ominous. Instead, it was accepting ... almost welcoming.

Millet chuckled. "I'm amazed that you've lived *this* long." He then looked at his friend and realized he was not jesting. "Why do you say such things?"

"I don't know." Lee shrugged. "It's a feeling, no more than that. It's like an itch just out of reach. The more I try to ignore it, the more it bothers me."

Millet pretended to scowl. "In that case, I'm glad you asked me to come with you. I assume your intention is that we die together."

Lee laughed merrily. "That was indeed my plan. Why else would we be riding into an enemy stronghold just ahead of an elf army led by an angry god?"

Millet joined in Lee's laughter. "You know, since I became Lord of the House Nal'Thain, it seems as though I've become as big a fool as you."

CHAPTER 15

King Lousis rode beside King Victis at the vanguard of their magnificent army, backs straight and heads held high. Age and weariness had fallen away from both men, leaving only two fierce warrior kings riding boldly to meet their fates.

Mohanisi had chosen to walk at the rear with Lady Bellisia, who, along with the other, more gifted of the elder healers, had continued to work herself far beyond her normal measure of strength. It was only after no small amount of persuasion that she eventually agreed to ride in a wagon rather than continue on foot. Even then, she was reluctant to rest. Most of her time on board was spent with other elders examining the enemy weapon. Mohanisi suggested that perhaps Aaliyah might be able to further the investigation, should they see her again. She was by far the most learned among them and had studied for many years on a myriad of subjects.

The Angrääl army was moving far more swiftly than Lousis would have thought possible. He had managed to close a little on the enemy but remained fearful that he might not be able to catch up with them before they were reinforced. If that happened, the battle would be fierce ... and very short.

On a brighter note, Lord Chiron and his forces were only a few hours away and would be joining them well before nightfall.

"They're giving us quite a chase," remarked Victis, maintaining his optimistic tone.

"They must sense that death is on their heels, my friend," Lousis joked.

Even though a little contrived, the two monarchs' jovial mood as they set off that morning had done much to raise the morale of the soldiers. Combined with a bright cool day, it wasn't long before songs of triumph—of both elf and human composition—were ringing out from the ranks.

They were well into the afternoon when the sound of trumpets calling out from the west was first heard. Lousis scanned the horizon and was soon able to see the column of haggard and war-beaten soldiers led by Lord Chiron coming into view. He immediately ordered a halt, at the same time calling for healers to attend to the newly arriving wounded.

Lord Chiron rode up astride a black mare, his leather armor so beaten and damaged that it looked as if it could fall from his body at any moment. Nonetheless, his familiar, good-natured smile was still very much in evidence. Despite having come straight from a hard-fought battle and a long ride, his eyes sparkled with energy.

"It's good to see you are still amongst the living," called Lousis.

"Am I?" Chiron shouted back, glancing down at the sorry state of his attire. "Until just now, I couldn't tell. I guess the fates still have business with me."

Both Lousis and Victis let out a hearty laugh.

"I'm afraid that may be to meet your end here with us," said Victis.

Chiron positioned his horse alongside the two kings. "Then I could not ask for better company. Tell me what goes on here?"

Lousis told him of their intention to catch the enemy. Chiron approved enthusiastically. But the mood instantly darkened when the subject turned to the death of Theopolou. The news hit Chiron severely, and he remained silent for several minutes.

"How did Bellisia fare?" he finally asked, swallowing back his tears.

Lousis shrugged. "She appears to be managing. Though there is no doubt that she feels the loss keenly."

"As do I," said Chiron. "But there is no time for mourning. We must be swift if we are to catch our prey."

"Can your people march?" asked Victis.

"We are not spent yet," Chiron told him. "Though our ragged appearance may cause you to believe differently."

"We think that we can catch them by tomorrow if we press our pace," said Lousis.

"We can halt long enough to treat your wounded," added Victis. "But no longer."

Chiron nodded sharply. "Then I will tell my captains to make ready." Excusing himself, he set off to find Bellisia.

Lousis couldn't help but feel pity for the elf elder. He had been every bit as close to Theopolou as Bellisia—possibly even closer. From what Lousis had been told, Chiron had been Theopolou's chief supporter when Darshan was first revealed to his people. The two of them had even fought together in the Great War. It boggled the king's mind to imagine losing a friend you had known for five hundred years. He remembered how close to utter despair he had come when Lord Maynard was slain outside his manor. Chiron must be hiding unfathomable pain.

But so are we all, he told himself.

The mood in the camp that night was light and cheerful. Both humans and elves were aware that the next day would likely be their last, but it didn't seem to matter. After having been through so many trials together, they were now happy to meet their destiny among comrades, both old and new. Two widely conflicting peoples had originally entered the crucible, and they had emerged as one, solid in their unity.

At least some good has come of this horror, considered Lousis.

He decided to sleep in the open air that night, much to the chagrin of his guard. The danger of the enemy sending an assassin still existed, and the Vrykol could be as stealthy as they were deadly. But Lousis would not be dissuaded. Soon, Victis, Chiron, and Bellisia elected to join him.

Chiron and Bellisia looked to be in better spirits. Lousis guessed that perhaps their mutual friendships with Theopolou were, in some way, helping them to heal each other. He watched as they sat close, reminiscing with light-hearted tales of Theopolou in days long past. He couldn't help but think the two elders would make a good match. These thoughts quickly brought High Lady Selena back to his mind. Lousis wondered if he would ever see her again. He promised himself immediately that, should he return safely, they would wed as soon as possible. And if she said no, then he would spend the remainder of his days trying to convince her to change her mind.

As dawn broke, the seekers returned. Angrääl had ceased its march and was apparently turning to fight. A mixture of fear and elation swept over King Lousis.

If they could win this day, then perhaps they could push on to the coast and engage the enemy there as well, catching them off-guard. And if not completely off-guard, at least soon enough to prevent them from setting up solid defenses.

"They are three miles to the southwest," reported a young seeker.

"Good," Lousis acknowledged. "Then let's not keep them waiting."

"Indeed," agreed Victis. "We would not want to be discourteous."

The two men shared a short laugh before urging their horses into a slow walk. Trumpets blared as the army advanced—battle cries and songs heralding their approach.

They had only traveled a mile or so when a long series of massive explosions were suddenly heard in the distance. Though unseen, the resulting tide of shock waves that swept into their ranks was powerful—strong enough to have the men wobbling on their feet and the horses rearing with fright. Minutes later, columns of thick, black smoke began rising from beyond the hilltops.

Lousis halted the army immediately.

"We should send scouts," suggested Victis.

Lousis nodded in agreement and began ordering the captain of his guard to locate the elf seekers who had brought him the earlier report.

"Do not trouble yourself, Your Highness," called Chiron, who was already making his way through the ranks. "I sent three of my elves the moment I heard the disturbance."

Bellisia was at his side. Her eyes were now bright, and she no longer had the appearance of someone on the brink of collapse. In one hand, she gripped the staff gifted by Darshan, in the other, a long sword.

"It's good to see you looking better, My Lady," remarked Victis. "It would seem that you're more than ready for battle."

Bellisia smiled and sheathed her sword. "Sometimes the words of a good friend can help where sleep cannot."

It wasn't long before the seekers returned. A tall, dark-haired elf approached, a perplexed look on his face. For a moment, he stood there in silence.

"What's happened?" demanded Lousis.

"I do not know," he admitted, shaking his head. "They're ... they're all dead."

"Who's dead?" asked Victis.

"The Angrääl army," he replied. "Every last one of them. Some burned to ashes, others ripped apart, hundreds piled on top of each other ... but all dead."

Lousis and those around him exchanged looks of utter confusion.

"Show me," the king ordered.

The elf bowed and quickly set off, with Lousis, Victis, Chiron, and Bellisia following close behind. They had only gone a few yards when Mohanisi joined them. The king's guard sprang to life, surrounding the entire group.

"We should use caution," said Mohanisi, troubled by the news.

All nodded in agreement.

The tension was high as the seeker led them to the edge of a large open field. By now, acrid smoke was already burning their eyes and choking their breath, while the stench of burned flesh and charred earth was almost unbearable. Some three hundred yards ahead, a tall hill spanning the entire breadth of the field rose up. The seeker stopped and pointed, but it was unnecessary. The carnage was easy to see.

Beginning at the base of the hill and rising all the way to the top, mutilated and charred bodies were scattered everywhere. At the crest, thousands of corpses had been unceremoniously thrown together and heaped into giant mounds more than twenty feet high. The catapults at the rear of these mounds were still smoldering, causing the air around them to ripple from the heat, giving the horizon an even more disturbing appearance.

"They picked a good spot to fight," was the only thing Lousis could find to say. But his words went unheard.

"What could do this?" gasped Bellisia.

"Only Darshan possesses such power," said Mohanisi.

"Apparently not," corrected Victis.

"We should leave," said one of Lousis's guards. "Whoever—or whatever—did this may still be nearby."

"We are no safer in our camp than we are here," countered Lousis. "It would seem that our army is no protection at all from whatever danger is out there."

"Look!" exclaimed Chiron, pointing to the top of the hill.

At first, only the elves could see what Chiron was pointing at through the ripples of intense heat. Then Lousis and the other humans saw it as well.

From amongst the monstrous piles of bodies, a lone figure emerged. It descended the hill with slow, deliberate steps and headed straight toward them.

As it came closer, the features became clear. It was a young man of no more than twenty years old with shoulder-length, sandy blond hair. He appeared wholly unremarkable in every way: from his medium build and average height, right through to his commonplace attire of a plain white tunic and tan trousers. A small dagger was tucked in his belt, but other than that, he looked to be unarmed. Lousis could see that the man's eyes were fixed firmly on him.

He halted his guard as they moved to intercept the newcomer. "If he is the cause of this devastation, there is nothing you can do. And if not, then I doubt he is any threat."

Though still out of earshot of Lousis's words, the man raised his hand and called out. "I am no threat, my king. Please do not fear me."

Lousis scrutinized the young man closely. There was truly nothing to indicate he was dangerous. In fact, the most remarkable thing about him was that he appeared entirely *un*remarkable. He wasn't ugly, yet not overly attractive—the type of person who could easily pass by completely unnoticed. He stopped a few yards away as if sensing the tension building.

"Who are you?" inquired Lousis firmly. "And what do you know about what happened here?"

The man tilted his head and smiled. "Who am I? I am a friend. And as far as what happened here, I am happy to tell you. But first, do any of you have any food? I have not eaten in..." He burst into laughter. "Well, let us just say that it has been a *very* long time."

Lousis looked over his shoulder and nodded. One of the guards pulled a strip of dried meat from his pouch and tossed it over. The throw fell short, but the man's movements were nimble. He was able to catch the offering well before it hit the ground.

"Thank you," he said, tearing off a piece.

He moaned with satisfaction while slowly chewing the meat, savoring each moment it was in his mouth. At last, he swallowed and sighed. "I hope there is more."

"Indeed," said Lousis. "And you are welcome to as much as you like if you can answer my question."

"Which question is that?"

Lousis glowered. "Do not play games with me, boy. I want to know exactly what happened here."

"You have fed me," said the man, unimpressed by the king's display of anger. "And in return, I will tell you that your enemy was slain by the power of heaven. A power sent by the one you know as Darshan."

The name caused everyone to stir.

"And are you this power?" asked Lousis.

The man nodded. "I am. I am the wrath and the hammer. I am the storm that comes to sweep away those who would destroy you." He bowed low. "My name is Melek. And I am at your command."

"You tell us that you were sent here by Darshan," Lousis said incredulously. "How do we know this to be true?"

Melek glanced over his shoulder at the carnage littering the hillside. "Is that not evidence enough for you? I have defeated your enemy. I have saved the lives of many a brave elf and human who would have undoubtedly died in battle against a superior force. And I will continue to do so—unless you command otherwise."

Lousis thought for a long moment before taking a deep breath. "Will you accompany us back to our camp? There you can be better fed and we can talk further."

Mohanisi stepped forward. His eyes denoted mistrust and apprehension. "If Darshan sent you, why is it he has never mentioned your name to us?"

Melek chuckled. "My dear elf. Darshan was only made aware of me recently. His bravery is the reason I am here, and I am deeply in his debt."

His smile vanished. "And if I was your enemy..." The ground began to tremble, then stopped after a few seconds. "But I am not. And your childish fears are unnecessary."

All the elves stared in wonder.

"Only once have I felt such power," gasped Chiron.

"Then you know that I cannot be false," said Melek. "For I am the same as Darshan."

"How can this be?" asked Mohanisi.

Melek grinned. "If we can obey our king and return to your camp," he suggested, not even trying to disguise a demeaning tone, "perhaps then I can eat and you can hear my tale in full."

Mohanisi stepped back, his face still awash with doubt.

Apart from Melek humming an odd little tune over and over again, the journey back to camp was made in total silence. During the trek, the fact that Lousis's guard made a great show of forming a protective barrier between the two monarchs and their new guest seemed to amuse Melek greatly. Frequently, he waited for a small gap between the guard's horses to appear, then lured them into thinking that he was about to dart through it. As they hurried to close the gap, he would back off and laugh softly. The guards were much less amused.

After arriving back at the camp, Louis ordered his captains to stand down and then led Melek to the southern end of the settlement. Here, he ordered a tent be erected and food prepared for their guest. Melek thanked the king and waited patiently until his accommodation was made ready. A number of curious glances were shot in his direction as he stood there. Rumors were already spreading, and the general mood was changing to one of trepidation and confusion.

Once all was prepared, Lousis showed Melek inside the tent and over to a small table in the corner. On this sat a bowl of beef stew and a plate of fruit and bread. A bottle of wine, together with a small wooden cup, completed the meal.

"I'm afraid that this is the best we can do under the circumstances," said Lousis.

Chairs for the rest of the group had also been brought in and arranged in a semi-circle at the tent's center. Lousis had already instructed his guard and the seekers to keep what they had seen to themselves for the time being. Rumors may be unstoppable within an army, but he did not want to spread the word that a god other than Darshan now walked amongst them. Not until he could be sure of Melek's sincerity and intentions.

Melek ate ravenously, stuffing the food into his mouth and gulping down the wine, as if he was on the brink of starvation. When all was gone, he let out a sad sigh.

"I can have more brought if you wish," offered Lousis.

Melek held up his hand and shook his head. "No thank you, Your Highness. This must all be quite confusing, and I am sure you are anxious to hear answers."

"Indeed," Lousis affirmed. "You can begin by telling us how you know Darshan?"

"The answer to that is not as straightforward as it might seem," Melek replied. "But I will try to tell you as simply as possible." He stood up and carried his chair over to join the others. "As I have already told you, I am the same as Darshan—a god. At least, that is what you call us. I was imprisoned in a place called Shagharath until Darshan freed me. In order to repay this debt, I have pledged to help him vanquish the one you know as the Reborn King. Or the Dark Knight, if you prefer."

"I have heard of Shagharath," said Bellisia.

"As have I," added Chiron. "But only as a legend. I never thought it to be a real place."

Melek's eyes darkened. "It is very real, I can assure you. I languished in that nightmare longer than you can imagine. And there I thought I would spend eternity. That is, until Darshan came. Through his mercy, I have a second chance at life ... now that I am free."

Mohanisi leaned in to meet Melek's eyes. "You say you were a prisoner. How did this happen? How is a god imprisoned? And by whom?"

Melek sniffed. "By those I trusted most. There are many things you do not know. Many tales you have not heard. That the nine gods worshiped in this world were not the first created is one of those tales. *I* was the first and most powerful. And then..."

He paused as if the words would not come. "And then my wife, Ustrea. She came next. Together, *we* gave birth to the nine gods you know today. They are my children and I loved them dearly. And it was my love for them that caused my downfall."

"Are you saying that your children imprisoned you?" Mohanisi pressed. "How could that be accomplished if your power is so great?"

Melek frowned. "Are the gods not imprisoned now? Was this not accomplished by a mere human? I was betrayed; that is the truth. If you do not believe me, I will speak no more of this until Darshan arrives."

"I meant no offense," said Mohanisi, though his tone was unapologetic. "Please continue with your tale."

There was a long pause as the pair locked eyes. Finally, an understanding smile crept over Melek's face. He gave a soft laugh. "You are right to question me, of course. I forget how mortal minds work. I have been alone for such a long time."

He leaned back and folded his hands in his lap. "As I was saying—eventually I was betrayed. In spite of my warnings, and directly against the commands of the Creator, Gerath wished to rule in the mortal realm. He came down from heaven and demanded worship and sacrifice. Those who would not bow to his will were destroyed. My wife and the rest of my children wanted to rise up against him, but I knew they were no match for his power. So I did the unthinkable. I created Shagharath as a place to contain his evil, then forged a weapon known as the Fangs of Yajna that was able to send his spirit there."

A frown formed on Melek's face. "But Gerath was clever. He discovered my plan and set about poisoning the minds of his brothers and sisters. Eventually, they all turned against their mother and me. They stole my weapon, then lured us into a trap. We fought on the shores of what you call the Western Abyss—and in the end, it was not Gerath, but his parents, who were both cast into the hell of Shagharath."

"Is your wife still there?" Mohanisi asked.

Melek shook his head and shut his eyes. "Ustrea could not bear her fate. Before too long, she threw herself into the pit of oblivion. Her light is no more." His words were a lament.

"I am sorry if I have caused you pain with my persistence," said Mohanisi. "But these are things we must know if we are to trust you."

Melek smiled. "I understand. And I would like to tell you the tale in full, but that is far longer than you can ever fathom. You would grow to old age before hearing even the half of it. Darshan was able to know me and trust me because we are kin. As for you, I can only answer your questions and hope that you recognize truth when you hear it."

"I want to believe you," said Lousis. "Another god as an ally would be more than I could dream of. But I must still be cautious. Darshan is not here to corroborate your story."

"That brings me to another question," Bellisia interjected. "*Why* is Darshan not with you?"

"When he released me from Shagharath, his physical body was far away from here," Melek explained. "But I had not yet taken a physical form, so was able to see vast distances in a single instant. When I saw that the friends of my liberator were on the verge of defeat, I chose to take form here so as to aid you in your hour of need."

"And we thank you for that," added Lousis. "But tell me ... how did Darshan know of you? None of us have ever heard the name Melek before. And how did he find a way to release you?"

"I am afraid to say that one of his friends sacrificed her life in order to help him secure my freedom," said Melek. "A human named Maybell had knowledge of my imprisonment, and of how to release me. She was the only human who knew of my plight. She understood that with me at Darshan's side, the war would quickly be over and thousands of lives saved. Unfortunately, it meant that she had to accompany him to Shagharath." He lowered his eyes. "Her body was destroyed in the process."

"I knew Maybell," said Lousis. "She was a good, kind woman. I am saddened to hear of her passing."

Melek stood and surveyed the gathering. "I know you have many reservations. And that your questions are more numerous than the stars. But if you will allow me to prove myself through my actions, by the time Darshan arrives, you will already be calling me friend. Together we can beat back the darkness that threatens to encompass this world and ensure that it never returns."

"How do you propose to prove yourself?" asked Lousis.

Melek flashed a toothy grin. "By rescuing the rest of your army. Those who fight in the south will surely be defeated if no help comes. Let me save them before it is too late."

"You know of their fate?" asked Lousis, anxious to hear news of Nehrutu and Aaliyah.

"Your enemy is clever," Melek replied. "He sent an army to meet them and sank most of their vessels. At this moment, they are attempting to break through to join you." He shook his head. "They will not succeed."

"How do you know this?" asked Chiron.

"Partly because of what I saw when I left Shagharath. And partly because I pried it from the mind of the enemy commander." His grin turned malicious. "He was most helpful."

Lousis rubbed his chin. "Can you give us time to discuss this?"

"As you wish, Your Highness. But know that each minute of delay is another life lost."

Lousis nodded slowly and stood. The others did the same. "Please make yourself comfortable," he said. "My guard will be just outside should you require anything."

"Thank you," said Melek. "If I could have some more to eat..."

"I will see to it at once," said Lousis. He then turned and led the others out.

Melek watched with an artificial smile as they departed. He held his fleshy hands in front of his face and groaned.

"Is this what I am reduced to?" he muttered.

His subtle yet effective use of the *flow* of the spirit had worked. He could have easily used more force while manipulating their minds. But if he had, the elves present might have sensed what he was doing.

Better this way, he thought. To leave Darshan's friends mostly unchanged may be the wiser course. Not that he will need much persuading once he learns the truth about his foe. Then, he will have no choice but to accept my help. And after that, he will give me his in return.

A short time later, a soldier entered with more food. Melek thanked him and began devouring the meal. The body he had used to create his physical form had been nearly starved. But if he'd remained in spirit form any longer than he had, he would have simply blinked out of existence. He'd needed to bind himself to the earth quickly, and this poor creature was the only human close enough to the Angrääl army for him to reach and destroy it before battle commenced.

I should have just used a soldier, he thought. In any event, it was far too late now. This was *his* body in this world until heaven could be unlocked ... unlocked and conquered.

Lousis led the others to the very far edge of the camp. Here, he hoped, they would be beyond the hearing of a god, though he doubted it. He could feel the eyes of the soldiers following him as they passed by. Though the secret of *exactly* what had happened to the enemy army was being well-kept for the time being, there was no hiding the pillars of black smoke rising from their position. Combined with the arrival of a young man who was immediately allowed to speak privately to both himself and King Victis, not to mention all the most senior elves, it was clear to everyone in the camp that something significant must have come about.

Once in a relatively secluded area, Lousis gathered the others close.

"My instincts tell me to believe him," he stated firmly.

Before they even realized what they were doing, everyone but Mohanisi nodded in agreement.

"You have reservations?" asked Chiron.

"I cannot explain why," he replied. "But I feel as if we are being manipulated. Do none of you find his story lacking substance? He explains very little, and yet we are ready to accept it after asking only a few questions."

Lousis shrugged. "Even if you're right, my friend—what can we do? Melek offers to destroy our enemy in our most desperate hour of need. Should he not be who he claims to be, I would still be grateful for that."

"I agree," said Victis. "If not one word of what he says about himself is true, our enemy still lies dead on the field at this very moment. That is a difficult fact to ignore."

"And can we ignore what he tells us of Nehrutu and Aaliyah?" added Lousis. "They may well be in a desperate situation, just as he says. Do we leave their fate to chance?"

His words were met by silent agreement.

"Good," said Lousis. "Then we will accept his help for now. At least until we are able to speak with Darshan."

He paused for any objections. There were none.

Lousis nodded. "So let us inform our new friend."

CHAPTER 16

Aaliyah reached over to give Nehrutu's hand a slight squeeze. She couldn't help notice that his once soft palms were now calloused and rough from the hardships of war. He looked into her eyes and responded through their bond by sending waves of love and strength.

In the distance, the banners of Angrääl fluttered in a gentle breeze. Scouts had told Nehrutu that because of the swift way in which he had moved their army, the enemy was finding it impossible to compensate and consolidate their forces. Even so, they were still greatly outnumbered. It would be a hard-fought victory if they were able to prevail. And afterward, they would be chased north the entire way.

Nehrutu raised his arm and the name Darshan rose like a tide from the ranks. Seconds later, as if in an angry response, the enemy catapults began sending dozens of deadly projectiles hurtling through the air toward them. This was the moment that Nehrutu had been waiting for. He and Aaliyah immediately sent a whirlwind roaring skyward. Their initial combined efforts managed to slow the heavy balls but not completely stop them. The pair of them pressed harder—and then even harder still—until both were at the absolute limit of their power. The missiles gradually slowed more until, with a huge sigh of relief from Nehrutu, they eventually hung motionless in the air. They remained like this for a short time before exploding in a series of mighty booms.

The blasts from these explosions were sufficient to send more than half of their soldiers stumbling to the ground. But it was only a temporary setback. They were back on their feet within moments and charging across the open field toward the enemy ranks. Nehrutu and Aaliyah maintained the *flow* of the air as their soldiers advanced, all the while looking out for the Vrykol they felt sure would be sent to disrupt their power.

"Where are they?" shouted Nehrutu. "Surely our luck cannot be so good?"

Just as his words were spoken, the first sounds of clashing steel tore through the air. Nehrutu smiled over at Aaliyah. She looked supremely confident and powerful. In fact, since she had learned of Darshan's death, it was as if her powers had somehow doubled to match the ferocity of her heart.

She returned his smile. Then, drawing a long knife with one hand and holding the dagger given to her by Darshan in the other, she stormed ahead to join the fray. Nehrutu followed, struggling to keep pace even though the bond he now shared with Aaliyah had given him speed and strength way beyond anything he had ever experienced before.

As he drew closer, Nehrutu could see that their initial charge had already succeeded in pushing Angrääl back at least twenty yards. The humans had taken position on their left and right flanks, allowing the elves to run straight up the middle and wedge the enemy apart. The original plan to send the humans into the center had been set aside following Aaliyah's magnificent motivational performance on the beach. Fueled by her words, such was the fury of the elves they had virtually demanded the new strategy and were confident of winning the day.

Even so, Nehrutu had elected to leave three men bearing trumpets at the rear. In spite of the elves' renewed determination, he knew they would need to be careful. If they penetrated too deeply, there was a danger of finding themselves surrounded. They needed to scatter the enemy's center rather than simply cause it to fall back. If Nehrutu signaled one trumpet blast, they were to halt the advance. Two blasts meant to regroup and fall back slowly.

There was no signal for a full retreat.

By the time Nehrutu approached the front, he found himself being forced to step over dozens of slain Angrääl soldiers. It seemed that the savagery of the elves and the courage of the humans were easily overcoming the handicap of their fewer numbers. What's more, the enemy catapults were becoming much less of a threat; should they fire now they would be destroying their own men as well.

So devastating had their attack been, it was nearly half an hour before he and Aaliyah came face-to-face with an enemy soldier. A fair-haired youth wielding a chipped battle-axe, his helmet and shield battered to the point of uselessness, was the first Nehrutu confronted. Ignoring his enemy's fear, he took the youth's head from his shoulders with one quick stroke.

Aaliyah was faring just as well. Her speed was astonishing. With a single fluid movement, she ducked beneath a lunging spear, plunged her dagger into the heart of its wielder, then gutted a second soldier with her long knife.

The rage he could feel coming from her was not an uncontrollable inferno, but a righteous current of governed passion. Again and again, the enemy fell to her flashing steel. So slow were their reactions to her attacks, that they looked as if frozen in time by comparison.

It was then that Nehrutu felt Vrykol for the first time. Though, to his great relief, there was only one of them. He could sense it approaching from his left, its malice growing by the second. The creature was making no effort to disguise its objective ... Aaliyah.

It wasn't until it was ten yards away that Nehrutu caught sight of its black cloak and wicked steel. Aaliyah also knew it was there, but was heavily occupied with six soldiers who had rushed her position. She was having no trouble avoiding their clumsy attempts to run her through, but they all bore shields. Nehrutu knew it would take her time to overcome them.

With a dozen blinding strokes, he cut his way through the enemy and placed himself directly between the creature and Aaliyah. He heard a hissing laugh escape from beneath its hood.

An elf fighter stepped in and tried to take the beast's head, but it raised its blade and parried the strike. Before the elf could counter, the Vrykol spun. Steel met flesh, ripping through the elf's mid-section until it lodged in his spine. Blood sprayed from his mouth and poured from the wound. In a blur of movement, the Vrykol kicked the elf free from his sword and lurched at Nehrutu.

Sparks flew as the two blades clashed. The Vrykol pushed forward, swinging in tightly controlled arcs that would have cut almost any other opponent to ribbons. While skillfully evading or blocking each new onslaught, Nehrutu was also able to slip his blade through barely perceivable gaps in the Vrykol's defense. He found the creature's flesh at least five times, though none of these strikes slowed it in the slightest. But Nehrutu pressed on, knowing that it was only a matter of time before an opportunity would arise to take the beast's head.

He could feel Aaliyah's concern in the back of his mind but didn't allow this to distract him. She had slain all but two of the soldiers, and both were already badly wounded and falling back. But Nehrutu had every intention of ending his fight with the Vrykol long before she could come to his aid.

Then he saw it—an opening. So focused was he on unleashing the killer blow, he failed to spot the Angrääl swordsman to his right, or hear the anguished cry of Aaliyah as cruel steel pierced his side. The blade pushed deep, causing pain to shoot throughout his entire body. As his legs buckled, the black cloak of the Vrykol closed in.

The last thing Nehrutu heard before fading into oblivion was the beast's foul hissing laugh raking at his ears.

Aaliyah watched in horror as the sword pierced Nehrutu's side. His eyes squeezed tightly shut in the agony of the moment, blood trickling from his mouth. She did not need to be told that the blow was fatal; already she could feel him starting to slip away. Letting out a desperate scream and ignoring all danger to her own people nearby, she released a tremendous blast of fire that instantly consumed her two remaining attackers.

By now, the soldier who had dealt the deadly strike had yanked his sword free and stepped back to allow the Vrykol to finish the job. The sudden eruption of fire startled both of them for a moment. Before they recovered, Aaliyah was already across the distance separating her from the two enemies. Her dagger plunged into the human's heart, meting out instant vengeance. But the Vrykol was undeterred. It raised its sword arm to end Nehrutu.

Without even thinking about her actions, the *flow* of the spirit leaped forth from Aaliyah and ensnared the beast. It struggled desperately to hold on to its life, but her rage would not be denied. In no time at all, the creature's spirit had been torn apart, and its body crumbled to dust.

Dropping her long knife, Aaliyah rushed to her husband's side. His life was all but gone. Drawing every bit of power she could muster, she set to healing the massive wound. Had it been any other case she would have admitted that such an injury was beyond her skill. But such thoughts were never allowed to enter her mind. She *would* save him. Whatever the cost.

Three of her former crewmembers saw her kneeling beside his body and hurried to surround her. The battle still raged yet she was no longer trying to protect herself.

"Let us carry him away," pleaded a tall elder elf.

She did not respond.

"If you allow us to help, we will not leave his side," he pressed. "But we must get his body clear of the battle."

The sense of his remarks finally got through to Aaliyah. She nodded sharply and allowed the elves to carry Nehrutu to the rear. Throughout the withdrawal, her hands never left him as she continued her efforts to save his life.

The battle raged on until the sun disappeared over the horizon, the red sky matching the blood-soaked earth. Finally, a deep clear horn blasted from the Angrääl rear signaling their surviving soldiers into full retreat. With Aaliyah engrossed in attending to her dying husband, several of the commanders took charge and ordered that there be no pursuit. The day was theirs, but the fighting had taken its toll on their lines. The best strategy, they decided, was to regroup and attempt to push north at first light.

Aaliyah was unconcerned with plans and strategies. Nehrutu's life hung by a thread, and she knew that she lacked the strength to save him. But the thought of giving up was not even considered. Her kin from the ships assisted as best they could, but though their ability with the *flow* was strong, their skills at healing were limited. Mostly they helped by simply giving Aaliyah their strength and allowing her to use it in her own way.

This continued without pause until dawn. The army was now ready to move, but Aaliyah showed no sign that she would be joining them. Nehrutu had been stripped of his bloodied clothes and his wound cleaned and dressed, though by now, it was little more than a bright pink line just below his ribcage. Skin was easy to repair. The rest of him was something else.

"My Lady," said one of the senior human commanders. "We must march before Angrääl can recover."

Aaliyah lifted her bloodshot eyes and nodded. "Then go. I will remain here."

"But, My Lady," he protested. "There is no hope. Even your own people say this."

"And they may be right," she affirmed. "But he is my love and the reason I draw breath. However weak he may be, I still feel our bond. He cannot be moved—so *I* cannot be moved."

"But what if the enemy catches you out here alone?" he argued. "You will be killed."

She nodded with acceptance. "Then we shall die together."

"We will stay here with you," offered one of the sailors.

"No," she replied firmly. "You must fight on and find a way to return home." She smiled up at the circle of elves. "And when you arrive back on our shores, speak kindly of us."

It was clear that there would be no debate. The crewmembers bowed reverently in unison, then slowly dispersed.

Hundreds of people came by to pay their respects as the army began to depart, though they all stayed at a discreet distance. After a few hours, the sound of marching boots faded, leaving only the wind, the birds, and Nehrutu's shallow breathing. Aaliyah continued with a slow yet steady stream of healing energy through the thin strand that remained of their bond.

She rested her head on his chest. When the time comes, she thought, I will do as the elves of this land, and allow myself to follow you into death.

Time now held little meaning, and when she next looked up, the sun was once again breaking over the horizon. Nehrutu still lived, but Aaliyah could no longer detect even the slightest thought or emotion. She knew that before the day was over his spirit would finally lose its hold on mortal flesh and their bond would disintegrate.

By midday, the heat of the sun was bearing down. Aaliyah caused a gentle breeze to waft over them and smiled down at her husband as it blew his silken hair away from his face. There were now only minutes remaining. She closed her eyes, continuing to send Nehrutu messages of devotion and undying love while a connection—however slight—still lingered.

All at once, the wind began to rise and swirl around them. Aaliyah huddled closer to Nehrutu's body to shelter it from the flying dust and sand that was stinging her eyes. But then, as suddenly as it had started, the wind was calm again. A bright light was shining only a few feet away—a light so bright and pure that Aaliyah could not bear to look at it directly.

"Why are you sad?" came a voice. It was musical and kind in a way that she had never heard before. It was as if the earth itself had taken pity on her.

From out of the light stepped the lone figure of a young human. His simple dress and youthful features were made beautiful by the heavenly glow that emanated from his earthly flesh.

Aaliyah was overwhelmed by the vision. Tears burst forth. "He dies. My love ... he dies."

In spite of his youth, the human smiled with a father's understanding. "He will not die. Not if you wish him to stay with you." He stepped closer. "*Is* that your wish?"

Unable to speak through her sobs, she nodded her head vigorously.

The man kneeled beside Aaliyah. "Then it shall be so." Placing his hands over Nehrutu's chest, he drew in a deep breath.

Aaliyah gasped as the power of the *flow* sprang to life with an intensity that she never imagined possible. She looked on in spellbound wonder as Nehrutu's eyes fluttered open and a weak smile crept upon his lips.

The man stood. "Now you can find joy again."

Aaliyah reached up and took hold of his hand, kissing it repeatedly and soaking it with tears. "Thank you. Thank you. I ... I can never repay you for this."

"Of course you can," he replied with a soft laugh.

"How?" she asked. "Name the price and it shall be yours."

"My price is your friendship," said the man. "You and your mate will come to Althetas and aid me in cleansing this world of the darkness that so nearly took your love from you."

"I will come," she promised. "But please. Tell me who you are?"

He withdrew his hand. "My name is Melek. Come to me. Do not delay. There is much to be done and time is short. You will find no enemies to hinder you. You are safe now."

Melek moved back into the bright light. In a flash, he was gone.

"Aaliyah..." whispered Nehrutu.

His voice snapped her back. She gazed at her husband, now feeling their bond as strongly as the moment it was formed. She took his face in her hands and kissed him with joy and exaltation.

"That man," said Nehrutu, his voice weak and his eyes heavy, "the one who appeared to me. Where is he? He told me my work was not yet done."

"He saved your life," she said, kissing him again. "His name is Melek, and as soon as you are able, we will go to join him in Althetas."

He sighed and quickly fell into a deep, restful sleep. Aaliyah cradled him in her arms until the evening, then built a small fire. Nehrutu awakened only once—just long enough to tell Aaliyah that he loved her before closing his eyes again.

The next morning, they both awoke refreshed and strong. The knowledge that war was being waged in the direction they must now travel did not concern either of them in the slightest. Melek had said there would be no enemies, and they believed him.

They headed north at a leisurely pace, talking and laughing hand-in-hand as if still in their homeland and never having seen battle or bloodshed. Both were excited at the thought of meeting up with Melek again, hoping they could find a way to repay the miracle he had bestowed upon them.

"He must be the same as Darshan," suggested Nehrutu. "There is no other explanation for such power. As far as I know, only he and the Reborn King are stronger than you in the flow. That is ... unless the enemy holds some secret power. But Melek was most certainly not the enemy."

"Perhaps he was sent by Darshan," she suggested.

"How could that be? Darshan is dead."

Aaliyah squeezed his hand and smiled. "Darshan ... Gewey ... he lives. I felt our bond renew itself during the battle. But I was so distraught by what had happened to you, then so joyful when you were returned to me, I only now have thought of it."

A mixture of unbridled joy and relief washed over Nehrutu's face. "Then perhaps Melek *was* sent to aid us. If so, with two of Darshan's kind fighting against our enemy..." He gave a heartfelt laugh. "I do believe this war may end sooner than we thought."

"And then we can go home," added Aaliyah with a longing sigh. Both of them smiled wistfully at the thought of seeing the shores of their homeland once again.

It was an hour before dusk when they caught sight of a lone elf seeker appearing through the brush. He raised his hand in greeting and broke into a dead run.

He halted a few feet away, his face alight with joy. "Lord Nehrutu. You live! How is this?"

Nehrutu shrugged. "I suppose you could say it was a miracle."

The seeker laughed. "Then the day is replete with miracles. I was sent to tell Lady Aaliyah that the way to Althetas is clear."

"So, you have defeated the enemy?" she asked.

He shook his head. "There was no need. Something else defeated them. Their bodies were burned and strewn about like fall leaves. If you had not already told us of Darshan's death, I would have thought it done by his hand."

Aaliyah smiled knowingly. "Perhaps it was. Come. Walk with us."

"Will we rejoin the army?" the seeker asked.

"No," she replied. "We are going directly to Althetas. There is much to do."

CHAPTER 17

Lee and Millet were at last nearing the end of a slime-coated tunnel that began just beyond the western walls of Baltria and led directly into a ruined warehouse on the fringe of the city. Lee was hoping fervently that the invaders had not yet discovered this ancient smugglers' passage and sealed off the exit. The filth from hundreds of floods was causing the air to reek so badly that Millet had already vomited twice along the way. Lee thought to tease his former servant, but Millet was every bit a lord these days and one stern glance told him that it was a bad idea.

A story for a warm fire and good friends, Lee thought, grinning.

When the pirates had shown him this tunnel many years ago, the warehouse was in the possession of a local merchant who had made most of his fortune by smuggling in goods from the West. It was in a perfect location for such dubious business, being near to the wall and frequently flooded. The repugnant smell alone was enough to keep most people clear, and those few authorities that could not be bribed imagined it to be long abandoned. The hordes of rats and other swamp vermin were also a big help in keeping any unwanted visitors well at bay.

Lee held his breath while pushing up against the steel trapdoor and felt a surge of anxiety when it at first failed to move. He pushed again even harder, and this time it screeched open just enough for him to peer into the gloom. It looked like the place had now been abandoned for real, though not so very long ago. A few broken crates of goods, so molded and deteriorated that they were unrecognizable, still lined the far wall. One thing was for certain. The rats were far fewer in number. Without the pirates and dockworkers providing them with a non-stop source of discarded food, most had undoubtedly found better pickings elsewhere.

With a grunt, Lee pushed hard yet again on the trapdoor, and suddenly there was almost no resistance at all. With an unexpected rush, it flew completely open. The loud crash of metal striking against the stone floor caused him to wince and remain absolutely still until he was certain that no one was reacting to the noise. Millet scowled and shook his head.

Once out of the tunnel, they took a closer look at their surroundings.

"I thought this place could not have gotten worse," remarked Millet. "I was wrong."

"At least the guards won't likely come around," Lee told him.

Millet blew a blast of air from his nose as if this would banish the odor. "Not unless they enjoy smelling like the underside of a sewer."

Lee flashed a playful grin. "Look on the bright side. In our present malodorous condition, no one will want to come near enough to figure out who we are."

"Either that, or they'll know we don't belong in the city," countered Millet. "We should avoid being seen ... or smelled, if we can."

After pulling his hood over his head, Lee led the way across to the exit. Millet groaned several times as his foot sank deep into muck and mire.

A missing board in the old and rotting wooden door had left a sizeable gap. Lee peered through and quickly established that there was no one about. The sun had set an hour ago, though the street lamps had not yet been lit. *All the better,* he thought, easing the door open just enough for them to pass through.

Lord Lanson Brimm's estate was on the other side of the city, so it would take them at least two hours of dodging in and out of alleyways and dark corners to get to the manor district undetected. Lee hoped that his old friend still lived. During their last meeting, Lanson had indicated that he would no longer turn a blind eye to the crimes of Angrääl. Lee now regretted shaming the man into behavior that would most certainly place him at risk and quite possibly get him killed.

As they wound their way through the city, they saw that, although the streets were empty of citizens, Angrääl troops were everywhere. Fortunately, they were far too busy to take much notice of Lee and Millet.

"Word must have arrived that the elves are coming," remarked Lee.

"So it would seem," agreed Millet.

It took them longer than expected to reach their destination. Several times, they were forced to hide while hundreds of soldiers marched from the direction of the docks toward the main gate.

Normally at this time of day, the avenues of the manor district would have been filled with wealthy merchants and nobility on their way out for an evening's entertainment. But as with the rest of the city, no one was about, and only a few lights could be seen in the windows of the lavish homes.

Lanson's estate was as opulent as one might expect for a man of his outward extravagance and charm. The wrought iron gates and fence surrounded lush gardens and a veritable labyrinth of well-manicured paths, fruit trees, and marble fountains. The grand house itself was built in northern fashion—two stories of dark polished granite fronted with imposing columns supporting a broad marble porch. A wide veranda directly above the porch spanned most of the upper floor.

Lee was relieved to see that the gates were unguarded and open. They followed the main drive for a while before turning off onto a red slate path that would take them to the servants' entrance at the rear of the house. Millet, with his hood pulled down as far as it would go, led the way.

The sturdy oak doors that guarded a large kitchen were closed, though the tantalizing scent of freshly baked bread escaped from within. Both men's mouths began to water.

Millet pounded hard and took a step back. Curses could be heard coming from inside. Moments later, the door creaked open.

"We don't give to beggars," snapped a thin, middle-aged woman with dark hair.

"I apologize, miss," said Millet in his humblest voice. "But I have a message for Jansi."

The woman scrutinized the pair. "Give it to me. I'll see that he gets it."

"No ma'am. I was ordered to give it to him in person." Millet could see that the woman was not about to make this easy. "We'll take an awful beating if I don't give it to him. It won't take but a second."

She sniffed the air and curled her lip. "Well, you're certainly not coming inside smelling like that. Wait here. I'll see if I can get him to come down." She turned and slammed the door.

"Well," said Lee. "At least we know he's here."

Millet nodded. "But I don't recall the Brimm house ever turning away hungry people who came calling. This may have been a wasted trip."

Ten minutes passed before the door reopened. There stood Jansi, in a simple brown robe and a dagger in his right hand.

"Speak your message and be gone," he demanded.

Millet pushed back his hood. "You should put that dagger away before you cut yourself, my friend."

Utter astonishment appeared on Jansi's face. He stepped quickly outside and shut the door behind him. "Have you lost your wits? What are you doing here?"

"At this moment," replied Millet, "we are standing at your door, very much hoping that you can help us."

"Is that Lord Starfinder?" he asked.

Lee revealed his face and smiled. "It is indeed."

Jansi regarded him for a moment, then looked back at Millet. "I gave you more credit than your master for common sense. But it seems I was wrong."

"He is no longer my master," corrected Millet. "And I'll thank you to show me a bit of courtesy."

Jansi held up his palm. "Forgive me. But you have no idea the risk you are taking by coming here. If you are caught..."

"Soon, it won't matter," interrupted Millet. "The walls of Baltria are about to fall, and Angrääl will be driven out."

"If you speak of the elves that are on their way here," Jansi shot back, "then you are mistaken. They will be blasted from the field before they fire the first arrow."

Millet and Lee gave each other a knowing smile.

"More than just the elves are coming," said Lee. "Darshan is leading them."

"Are you sure of this?" Jansi asked incredulously. "*Darshan* is coming *here*?"

"I see you have heard the name," said Lee.

Jansi shrugged. "Everyone has heard the name of Darshan. But no one is sure what to believe."

"If you allow us to come inside," said Millet, "and for the love of the gods give us a bath and a change of clothes, we will tell you all that you want to know."

Jansi thought for a moment. "You must wait here until I can dismiss the kitchen staff. Once they're gone, I'll let you in." He opened the door and ran inside, returning a moment later with a loaf of bread. "This will have to do for now."

"Thank you," said Millet, bowing.

Jansi went back inside, smiling at the duo in spite of himself.

Millet and Lee found a spot in the shadows behind a lemon tree where they devoured the bread and settled down to wait. Lee kept a vigilant ear on the comings and goings at the front entrance throughout. Thankfully, no one else came calling.

More than three hours passed before the kitchen staff eventually filed out of the house. Lee's sharp hearing picked up their chatter. Many of them were remarking how odd it was that they had been told to leave through the front entrance that evening.

Jansi returned a short time later.

"Is Lanson at home?" asked Lee.

"My lord is quite ill," Jansi replied. "However, he knows that you are here and wants to see you as soon as you're cleaned and changed."

Lee's face tightened at the news. "How ill is he?" But the man's bleak expression already told him the answer to that.

Jansi ushered them inside and through the kitchen. A stone staircase in the pantry at the far end took them up to the second floor, where bedchambers, the library, and Lanson's personal office were all situated. Lee could hear the remaining maids and cleaning staff downstairs busying about their duties.

Jansi showed them to their separate rooms. Millet and Lee's eyes lit up when they saw that both were equipped with a shower. Clean clothes were in the wardrobes, and to finish things off, Jansi soon returned with a bowl of beef stew and a bottle of wine for each of them.

Once cleaned and dressed, Lee took his meal to Millet's room. Jansi checked in on them just as they were sitting down at a small table close to a window overlooking the southern garden.

"My lord's room is down the hall and the last door on the left," he told them. "Join him there once you're ready." He left with a polite nod.

"He seems greatly worried," said Millet. "I hope that it is only his master's health that occupies his thoughts."

"I sense no deception in him," said Lee. "Only deep concern."

They hurried through their meal, then followed the directions Jansi had given. The polished double doors they came to were slightly ajar, allowing Lee to push them open just far enough to look inside. The room was dimly lit, with only a single lantern on a table in the far corner.

The spacious chamber appeared warm and welcoming. Lee could see immediately that the dark wood furnishings and plush purple rugs had all been imported from the northern towns near Hazrah. Even the immense four-poster bed was not unlike the one that he, himself, used to sleep in back home.

Thick cotton blankets covered a small lump on the bed, with only a head peeking out to show that it was indeed Lanson. But this was not the vigorous man Lee had known. His eyes were sunken deep into his skull and surrounded by black circles. The rest of his face was ghostly pale, and his thin, dry lips bore a grayish color.

"Don't lurk in doorways, Lee Starfinder," Lanson said. His voice was raspy and his breathing labored.

Lee stepped inside. Millet followed close behind.

"I see you've managed to womanize your way into a sickbed," said Lee, using his best lighthearted tone.

"Naturally," he replied, a fragile smile forming. "But it took more than half the women in the city to lay me so low."

Two chairs awaited them beside his bed. Lee took the one nearest to his old friend.

"So, you're still causing trouble, I hear," said Lanson. "When I received news that the *faithful* had been slain in Sharpstone, I knew it had to be you."

"Actually, that was more Millet than me," Lee told him. "I have turned my lands and titles over to him."

Lanson managed a loud laugh, but the effort of this brought on a spasm of coughing. "Best thing you could ever have done," he eventually croaked. "You always were a poor excuse for a noble, Lee. Too idealistic. And too rash." He looked at Millet. "I hope you've finally put him in his proper place, My Lord." There was no sarcasm when he used the title.

Millet smiled and nodded. "I had done that long before I became a noble."

Lee leaned in. "Tell me what afflicts you, old friend?"

Lanson shifted, managing to prop his head up. "Oh, nothing that death won't cure."

Lee and Millet clearly did not find this amusing. Lanson sighed. "I'm afraid I am a casualty of war. After you left the city, I did what I could to hinder the efforts of the Reborn King. I was actually shocked at how many others I was able to enlist to my cause. Apparently, I had underestimated the worth of the Baltrian nobles. We did our best to disrupt things but with only limited success. Most of us are now dead. The lesser nobles were executed—their bodies hung from the city walls. Those who had enough influence to avoid the noose began dying one by one of a mysterious illness. I suppose I fall into that category."

"I should have never talked you into this," said Lee.

Lanson scowled. "You didn't talk me into anything. All you did was point out what I already knew in my heart." He reached over and took hold of Lee's hand. "I will die with no regrets." He chuckled, but this brought on another short fit of coughing. "If we win this war, maybe for once in my life, I'll be called brave. For certain they'll say that Lee Starfinder was brave, but Lord Lanson Brimm ... now *he* was a most courageous fool, if ever there was one."

"You've always been brave," said Lee.

Lanson shook his head with the look of a guilty child. "Only when I was drunk, I'm afraid. But enough about me and my decrepit state. Jansi says Darshan is coming. Is this true?"

"It is," Lee affirmed. "And when he gets here, I'll bring him to you. Perhaps he can heal you of this mystery illness."

"That would be good," said Lanson. "But I don't think I'll make it long enough for him to arrive." Lee started to argue, but Lanson held up his hand. "You must listen to me, Lee. The enemy has a weapon. A terrible weapon. It was shown to us shortly after you escaped from here. Three of the *faithful* who had attempted to flee the city were taken outside the walls. Every noble in Baltria was ordered to bear witness. They tied them to posts and placed a white ball about the size of a man's head at each one's feet. All three balls had a long wick that ran into its center. Another of the *faithful* then lit these wicks, and a few seconds later, the deserters' bodies were blown completely apart."

He shuddered. "I was a hundred feet away, and the force of the fireballs still knocked me over."

"What are they made of?" asked Millet.

"I don't know," he replied. "They keep that secret, and allow no one near them. But they have hundreds stored away—and catapults to launch them too. If your friends assault the gates, they'll be blown apart." His eyes closed as he suppressed a cough. "Some nights you can hear them training in the swamp. The whole city shakes. Darshan had better be as powerful as people say, otherwise his entire elf army is doomed."

"Where do they keep these weapons?" asked Lee.

Lanson chuckled. "I thought you'd ask me that. That's why I told Jansi to speak to a couple of your friends about scouting the area."

Lee looked confused for a moment, then it hit him. "Barty and Randson! They're here?"

"They said they were here to gather information," he replied. "Though they didn't tell me it was Millet, not you, who'd sent them." He gave a lopsided smile. "They have been rather tight-lipped. I didn't trust them at first, but Randson can be quite convincing when he wants to be. Smart lad, too. When this is over, I hope that you will find him something more rewarding than a gardener's position."

"I will indeed," said Millet. "When do you expect them back?"

Lanson shrugged. "It shouldn't take long. The Angrääl soldiers are busy preparing for an assault. They won't bother with two stragglers wandering about."

"And what of the city guard?" asked Lee. "I didn't notice any of them on the way here. Only soldiers."

"Most been inducted into the army," said Lanson. "After the *faithful* wiped out the king and his family, there was no one to stop them."

Millet was shocked. "They killed them all? Then who rules Baltria?"

"Some wretched dog the Reborn King sent from down Angrääl. A man named Lord Ziri." Lanson spoke the name with contempt. "If I could only live long enough to see him dance on the gallows."

"You will, my friend," promised Lee. But he struggled to put any real conviction into his voice. He knew that time was fast running out. The smell of death was thick.

"You never could lie to me, Starfinder," said Lanson. "But still, I thank you. Now stay and talk with me for a while. I miss intelligent company."

They spoke of good times past until Lanson's eyes were no longer able to stay open. Millet and Lee were just rising from their chairs when Jansi entered. He looked at his master with a pained expression before speaking.

"Barty and Randson are waiting for you in the parlor," he whispered.

After leading them through the halls to the opposite end of the house, he showed them into a small room with a fire burning cheerily in the hearth. The walls were lined with paintings of Lanson's family going back at least ten generations, while the floor was covered with a thick Dantory rug woven into hundreds of undulating swirls of color and form. Lee had admired this rug several times in the past and even offered to buy it once.

Sitting on a couch in front of the fire were Barty and Randson. As soon as they caught sight of the arrivals, they leapt to their feet and ran across the room, embracing them both in turn.

Barty had not changed, but Randson seemed older and more careworn. They were clad in black shirts and trousers, and each carried a dagger on his belt.

"It is good to see you both," said Millet.

Barty bowed. "We are grateful to see you still alive, My Lord. There were rumors that you and Lee had been killed."

Millet smiled. "The enemy certainly did try. But now is not the time for tales. We need to know where Angrääl keeps these new weapons that Lord Brimm spoke about."

Everyone took a seat by the fire.

"They had been keeping them all together in a small building near to the main gate," Barty began. "But since they heard about the elves coming, they've spread them around to each catapult along the north and east walls. Mostly on the north. They figure the east approach is too hard for an army of any size, and the west is impossible."

"How well are they guarded?" asked Lee.

Barty shook his head and sighed. "I'm afraid that each machine is guarded by at least ten men, and there are more than twenty machines in all."

"With just the four of us," said Millet, "I don't see what we can do."

"We have a few stout lads," said Barty. "Friends of my son. They'll help if needed."

Lee thought for a moment. "How far apart are the catapults on the east wall?"

"Quite a long way," replied Barty. "Five hundred feet or more. But they are light and easily moved. It only takes one man to use them."

Lee recalled the catapult he had seen atop the barracks in Angrääl. "That leaves nine men to deal with. Tell me more about the weapon itself."

"No one knows very much," said Randson. "I've tried to find out, but they're made in Kratis and then shipped south on the Goodbranch. Whatever they are, they can destroy stone, steel, and wood as if they were parchment."

"If you had one, could you use it?" asked Lee.

Randson thought for a second. "They don't seem complicated. If they were, I doubt these dolts could use them. As far as I can tell, you just need to light the wick. As soon as it burns inside the wrappings—bang—it goes off."

"I think we'll need your friends," said Lee. He stood up. "The elves will be here by midday tomorrow, so we have only until then to prepare."

CHAPTER 18

Lee, Randson, and Barty, together with the seven men Randson had brought along, lay down in a group atop the roof of a small house near the east wall. From this vantage point, they could see the catapult clearly. It was situated about twenty feet back from the wall's base—far enough to give plenty of clearance to launch a bolt over the top, yet near enough to ensure that most incoming arrows would fall well behind them.

Just as Randson had reported, ten men surrounded the device. Beside it lay a neat stack of white balls standing four feet high.

The remainder of Randson's comrades were at the Brimm estate guarding Lanson, as well as a very unhappy Millet. He had argued vehemently that as Lord of the House Nal'Thain, it was his duty to do his part. Nothing Lee could say would sway him. It was Randson who stepped in to remind Millet that he had not yet legally named a successor to his lands and titles, and therefore it was his duty to stay alive until he could do so. Lee could hardly contain his laughter as Millet stood speechless in the face of Randson's irrefutable logic.

More than once had Millet told Lee the very same thing during his younger and far more foolhardy days.

By using his half-man senses, Lee could easily hear the conversation of the Angrääl soldiers. They were apparently unconcerned about the coming siege; their confidence in the new and deadly weapon at their disposal was absolute. In fact, many times they mentioned how they wished they'd been assigned to the north wall, just so they could see the bodies of the elves being blown to bits. Lee felt his blood boiling at such casual callousness.

He calmed his anger. The sun was now high in the sky. It was time for action.

His original plan was to have had Barty and all the others on the roof fire arrows at the soldiers, then he would charge in at ground level and quickly finish off any survivors. But Randson had come up with a better idea and produced two stolen Angrääl uniforms that he and Lee were now wearing.

"Are you ready?" Randson whispered.

Lee nodded. The pair of them slipped down to the rear of the house, where they crept to the corner and waited. A patrol came by this spot every twenty minutes and another one was almost due. Right on schedule, three soldiers passed. They gave the catapult crew a half-hearted salute before continuing along the wall.

Once the patrol was out of sight, Lee and Randson moved out from behind the corner. It took a moment for the soldiers guarding the catapult to notice them, and even then, they only glanced up casually before continuing with their conversations.

They didn't look up again until Lee and Randson were only a few feet away. And by then, even if the soldiers had suspected what was about to happen to them, it was far too late.

In unison, Lee and Randson drew their blades. Randson stepped left and Lee to the right, leaving a clear shot in the center for the others who were now aiming bows from the roof. A series of whizzes and thunks sounded as the missiles found their targets. Those soldiers not hit were quickly cut down before they could make a move or sound the alarm. Lee had to restrain himself from cutting them to pieces. But they needed the uniforms, and too much blood would be hard to hide. Within seconds, all the soldiers lay dead.

By the time Barty and the others joined them, Lee and Randson were already dragging the bodies into the house. The severely dilapidated property had been abandoned some weeks ago; a stroke of luck, Lee considered. And they would need all the luck they could muster that day if they were to succeed.

While they waited for the signal announcing the arrival of the elf army, the regular patrol passed the catapult they were pretending to guard three more times. On none of these occasions did the soldiers notice that the faces of the crew were now different, or that there were bloodstains on most of their uniforms.

Then they heard it. From the north wall, a trumpet sounded, warning the troops that the elves had arrived. An eerie hush settled over the city.

Lee smiled warmly at Randson, Barty, and the others. "Well, this is what we've been waiting for. Let's make the most of it."

Gewey raised his arm, bringing the army grinding to a halt. The walls of Baltria were every bit as impressive as he had been told, and the approach equally as treacherous. He walked forward for another fifty yards, unconcerned that this now brought him within range of the enemy bows.

Kaylia walked beside him, her mind focused and strong. But the mood inside the city was not as Gewey expected.

Normally, an elf army would illicit dread and panic, but the Angrääl soldiers seemed relaxed and eager for the battle. And that *did* concern him.

He'd expected a few arrows to come flying his way, but none did. Instead, he heard a loud creaking and the clank of metal. Moments later, half a dozen white balls flew up from behind the wall, each with a wisp of smoke trailing behind it. Gewey almost laughed. None of these shots were going to hit him; he didn't even need to use the *flow*. All of the missiles struck the ground a few yards ahead of them in a rapid succession of deep thuds.

It was then Gewey noticed a small wick protruding from one of the bolts quickly burning shorter. Something wasn't right. Instinctively, he moved to push Kaylia behind him, but his hand had barely touched her arm when there was a huge flash and a tremendous ball of fire.

Gewey felt as if he'd been rammed by a bull.

And then there was nothing but blackness.

The moment the trumpet sounded, Lee and the others each grabbed two of the catapult bolts and set off speedily to their respective targets.

He arrived at the catapult nearest to the gate just as it was releasing a bolt. Hiding behind a nearby shack, he cursed the fact that he had not got there a few moments sooner.

As soon as the missile had been launched, the operator began rapidly spinning a small crank handle until the launching arm was pulled back into position, ready to fire once again. From a metal tube positioned alongside the cradle, another bolt then dropped into place. Lee couldn't help but admire the skill that had gone into the machine's construction and design.

A series of thunderous explosions sounded, raising loud cheers from the soldiers.

"What were you thinking about?" shouted a laughing soldier atop the wall. "Did you and your woman think we would allow you to march right up to the gates by yourselves? Look at you now, fool." He turned to the men on the ground. "If this army is full of idiots like that, it will be a short day, lads." His mocking words were met by more harsh laughter.

Lee could guess what had just happened and dread gripped his heart. Gewey and Kaylia must have marched ahead of the army to break down the gates.

"Too bad we can't shoot any farther," said another soldier in a thick northern accent. "If we could, this would be over in time for dinner."

Using a flint and steel, Lee quickly lit the wick to one of the bolts he was carrying. It sparked to life and a metallic smell filled the air. He waited until the wick had burned down to less than an inch long, then stepped out from behind the shack and heaved the fizzing ball at the men.

Cries of alarm instantly sprang from the soldiers as the weapon landed right amongst them. Panicked and fearful, they jostled amongst themselves in their efforts to scramble away. But it was too late. The bolt exploded, blowing them apart and their catapult to splinters. The remaining bolts beside the weapon were scattered about over a wide area. Several of them were already beginning to smolder, warning Lee that he needed to get away fast.

He had only made it a few yards when he heard the first of the bolts exploding. He grinned with satisfaction. There was no way he would be able to destroy all the catapults, but he had one more bolt tucked firmly under his arm. And he knew exactly where he was going to put it.

More blasts rocked the city as Randson and his comrades began setting off their own bolts. *Now if only Gewey is not dead, we stand a chance,* Lee thought grimly. But the soldier's mocking words were still echoing in his head. He forced them out of his mind, knowing that he mustn't lose focus.

While winding his way through the streets, he passed hundreds of troops racing in the opposite direction toward the north wall. Not that it mattered. Still in the stolen uniform and looking as if he were hurrying to obey an order, none of these gave him as much as a second glance.

Lee's jaw clenched tight as his target came into view. Three of the *faithful* were standing in front of their so-called "temple", each one carrying a short sword. He had expected soldiers to be guarding the place, but the mayhem he and the others were causing must have drawn them away. The men left in charge looked nervous. Clearly, they were not accustomed to the turmoil of war, and the blades looked awkward in their pale, chubby hands.

Soft, doughy nobles, he thought. So much the better.

The *faithful* looked up at Lee as he approached with long, deliberate strides.

"It's about time too," one of them yelled out. He drew back his hood, revealing pale skin and flat features. His dark brown hair was oiled and pushed back. Without doubt, a noble. He glared at Lee. "You can tell your captain that I'll have him hanged for this. He was told to stay here and..."

The man never got a chance to finish his sentence. In one fluid motion, Lee drew his blade and took the man's head. The two others froze, staring in horror at the still standing body of their fellow *faithful*. Before it even hit the ground, Lee's sword had claimed their heads as well.

At the entrance to the temple, he paused just long enough to light the bolt before smashing the thick oak doors open with his boot. Lee could hear a host of people talking and laughing. He gave a sinister laugh of his own before hurling the deadly ball deep within the building.

"With the compliments of Lord Lanson Brimm," he shouted to those inside.

After waiting just long enough to hear the sounds of laughter abruptly turn to cries of alarm, he turned and ran off in the direction of Lanson's manor. The explosion, when it came seconds later, filled his heart with a sense of righteous justice.

Upon reaching the house, he paused long enough to make sure there were no soldiers about. Happy with the situation, he made his way around to the servants' entrance.

The door was guarded by two of Randson's friends. They nodded a greeting at Lee and gave him a knowing smile.

"Did everyone make it back?" Lee asked.

"You are the last one we've been waiting for," replied a tall lad with short-cropped blond hair. "Randson and his father are upstairs with Millet and Jansi."

"And Lord Lanson?"

"He sleeps," the lad replied solemnly. "Jansi doesn't think he'll last until nightfall."

Lee nodded and went quickly upstairs. Entering the parlor, he saw Millet sitting stone-faced by the fire. He looked up at Lee with obvious relief. The others were talking quietly on the other side of the room.

"It figures that you would be the last to arrive," scolded Millet.

Lee spread his arms and grinned. "I'm sorry, but I had to leave a message with the *faithful* before I returned."

This brought forth smirks and nods of approval from everyone but Millet. Lee sat across from him and snatched up a bottle of wine that was sitting on a small table beside the chair.

"Have you seen Lanson?" he asked.

"About twenty minutes ago," Millet replied. "I'm afraid our visit has over-exerted him."

"Nonsense," said Jansi, crossing the room. "This is the first time my master has smiled in many weeks. Whatever the enemy did to him, it drained his humor and lust for life. It was good to see that return, if even for a moment."

Hearing this made Lee more determined than ever to get Gewey to his friend's bedside as soon as possible.

"Is there more we can do to aid the assault?" asked Millet.

Lee shook his head and took a drink from the bottle. "Not unless we charge the gates ourselves. And I don't think we'd get very far with that. Right now, all we can do is wait until the city has fallen."

"The sooner the better," said Jansi.

Gewey's vision was blurry at first. It took a moment or two before realizing that he was no longer near the vanguard of the army, and had apparently been carried to the rear. As his eyes cleared further, he could see that he was surrounded by dozens of elves, all with looks of deep concern on their faces. On his left kneeled Lyrial.

"Kaylia!" he cried out. He could feel her but knew that she had been injured.

"She is resting," said Lyrial. "She will be fine. But considering her condition, we thought it best to attend her first."

Gewey felt a sudden sense of panic. "Our child?"

"Your child is strong," she replied in a reassuring tone. "Your body took the brunt of the attack and probably saved them both."

Gewey could hear shouts and orders being given. "What's happening? How long was I unconscious?"

Lyrial cocked her head. "Not long. Less than an hour. But my people went mad with rage the moment you fell. They have already begun the assault."

This brought clarity rushing in. He sat up straight, ignoring the throbbing pain in his head. "They must pull back."

"It's too late for that," she responded. "There was a series of explosions just as you were being brought here. Apparently, Lee has been busy. Bevaris didn't think we should wait—not that my kin would have delayed, regardless of his opinion. He ordered trees felled to be used as ladders, guessing that we elves would be excellent climbers. He guessed correctly."

She handed him a cup of water. "Our bows cleared the ramparts, and we were able to scale the wall before the enemy could react. A few of those dreadful weapons came over the top, but nowhere near enough to halt us."

"Lee must have learned of them and destroyed as many as he could," mused Gewey.

"It would seem that way," agreed Lyrial. "Most are now silenced, anyway."

Gewey put down the cup and struggled to his feet. He reached out to Kaylia. She was resting and relieved to touch his thoughts.

I must end this, he said through their bond.

She did not protest, sending him only waves of love and strength in response.

On approaching the north wall, he could see a dozen or more tall trees leaning against it. The elves were scampering up these like squirrels. If not for the occasional body falling after being hit by enemy arrows, it would have been an almost comical sight.

He spotted Bevaris, Tristan, Linis, and Dina standing in a group. Linis waved him over.

"You look well considering," his friend told him. "And Kaylia?"

"She's fine," Gewey replied.

Dina sighed with relief. "Maybe next time you'll be more careful," she chided.

Gewey met her eyes unblinkingly. "If I could convince Kaylia to stay out of danger, I would."

"Then perhaps you should both stay clear of the fray," she shot back. "As you can see, the city will soon be ours."

"I've heard that the elves were unable to take Baltria during the Great War," Bevaris interjected. "That hardly seems possible, from what I am seeing here."

"Baltria was defended from within by fifty thousand soldiers," explained Dina. "As well as another fifty thousand outside the walls."

"And the humans of that era were battle-tested," added Linis. "By the time Baltria was attacked, the war was well into its eighth year. They had learned how to fight us by then."

Gewey ignored everything but the ongoing battle. "They must be defending the gates with all they can muster."

"That's my guess," agreed Tristan. "They know that if the gates open, all is certainly lost."

"Then the gates *will* open," said Gewey.

"There's no need," objected Dina. "The battle will be won without you putting yourself in danger."

Gewey couldn't help but be grateful for her concern. But he knew that lives would be lost needlessly if he did not act.

"I promise that nothing will happen to me," he said.

Before another word could be spoken, he unleashed the *flow* of the air. His body flew skyward and in seconds, he was more than one hundred feet above the battle. Elves were pointing up at him in awe as he drifted closer to the wall.

After crossing over the ramparts, he could see that he and Tristan were correct. Angrääl had set up their defenses around the gates and all along the main avenue toward the docks. There, another large force waited. If the gates were breached, they were obviously hoping to hold off the elves long enough to escape by sea.

Arrows began to streak toward Gewey, but he easily blew them back. The sight of a man flying above their heads was now spreading increasing terror through the Angrääl ranks. Before his time in Shagharath, he might have chosen to engulf them in a blazing inferno. But his spirit no longer raged. His intention was not only to save the lives of the elves but of his enemy as well.

Using the *flow* of the earth, he caused the ground below to shake violently. Very quickly, not a single man was able to remain on his feet.

"I am Darshan!" he called out in an ear-splitting voice. "Throw down your weapons and you will be spared."

Gewey spread his arms wide. A ball of fire shot down and exploded twenty feet above the cowering men. The flames swirled and rose, enveloping Gewey's body.

He descended through the inferno, allowing it to dissipate as his feet touched the ground. He did not need to repeat his command. The clank and clatter of hundreds of swords being dropped echoed off the granite walls. Though the ground no longer shook, the soldiers still did not dare rise to their feet.

Gewey surveyed the scene. The gatehouse had been barricaded and the streets leading from the main avenue blocked with anything they could get their hands on.

He heard the snap of a bowstring and the whiz of an arrow. From the corner of his eye, he saw the deadly missile bearing down. An odd sensation of amusement rushed through him. Just before the arrow found its mark, he sent out a short blast of air that sent it falling harmlessly to the flagstone street.

The ground shook once again. "Do not test the limits of my goodwill." Gewey's voice was like a thunderclap, echoing as if inside a great cavern. "Who is your commander?"

Several moments passed before a man clad in black steel plate, a red plume fixed atop his helmet, stepped forward. Gewey noticed that he still held his sword.

"Do you intend to fight me?" he asked.

"Rather than kneel before someone who will kill me anyway," the man replied. He held his head high and proud. "I will choose to die fighting ... not groveling."

"Surrender to me at once," said Gewey. "And I will not kill you or your men. Nor will any who follow me."

The commander sneered. "Do you expect me to believe that?"

In a blur of speed, Gewey spanned the distance between them. With a quick twist of his wrist, he disarmed the man as easily as swatting a fly. The commander could only stand with his eyes wide and his mouth agape.

Gewey's expression did not change. "I expect you to believe that if I wanted your blood, I could have it now." He reached down and picked up the commander's sword. He examined it for a moment, then offered it back to him. "Have your men lay down their arms and leave the city. Tell them that they may return home, or go back to their master in the north ... it doesn't matter to me. But they are to be out of Baltria by nightfall."

After a brief hesitation, the commander took his blade and saluted. "I am General Leon Kirtzul. The city is yours, Darshan."

Gewey nodded. "Very well. Open the gates and spread word of this to the rest of your troops before more lives are needlessly lost."

General Kirtzul immediately issued the necessary order for the gates. This done, after a final glance at Gewey, he marched away to begin organizing a withdrawal.

As the gates swung wide, Gewey stepped out. The elves came charging headlong toward him but stopped the moment he held up his hand.

"The city is ours," he announced. "None who surrender are to be harmed."

Cheers rose like a flood. Those climbing the walls quickly began descending, many of them jumping from considerable heights in their eagerness to join celebrating comrades on the ground.

Gewey could see Bevaris pushing his way through the ranks, smiling broadly. Tristan, Linis, and Dina were close behind.

"Well done, my lad," shouted Bevaris with a boisterous laugh. "Well done indeed."

"See that once the city is secured, all Angräal soldiers are escorted from the walls," said Gewey.

"So you really intend to let them go?" asked Linis.

"This war is not going to be won with more blood," said Gewey. "Killing these men will accomplish nothing. And I already have enough deaths on my conscience."

"They would not have been so generous if the situation was reversed," countered Tristan. "Nor will they be, should they return."

"I don't care," said Gewey sternly. "If they will lay down their arms and leave, I will allow them to do so. And those who choose to go back to their homes will spread word of the Reborn King's defeat."

"Not to mention the mercy of Darshan," added Linis. "I think it a wise decision."

Gewey smiled. "I'm glad you think so."

He turned back to the gates. Elves were flooding in, nearly all singing songs of the mighty Darshan and their great victory. He could see that Angräal soldiers were already lining the main avenue, defeated but relieved they would be spared.

"Come," he said to the others. "Let us go find Lee."

CHAPTER 19

Basanti squinted up at the noonday sun. Most people found the warmth of the Fire Hills unbearable, but she thoroughly enjoyed it.

It was shortly after the goddess had changed Yanti that they'd first come here. They discovered an ice-cold spring that was so well hidden, only the two of them knew how to find it. They had spent almost a full year together doing little more than talking and resting, though her brother had never much cared for the heat. Still, he endured it for her sake.

Those were the days before his fall. The days before they became reviled and hunted.

The thick turf covering a small hill she was resting on made it feel like a soft bed of goose feathers, while the sweet scent of wildflowers mingling with the earthy aroma of damp tree bark and moss created a fragrance that was uniquely pleasing and wholly unforgettable. A dense jungle surrounding this thirty-mile enclave of green hills, geysers, and hot springs effectively kept most people away, so Basanti had always found it the perfect place to clear her mind and cleanse her heart.

Felsafell had offered to leave her alone here for a time and guard the perimeter, but she merely kissed him and smiled a refusal. They had spent far too long apart already.

She often wished for the ability to bond their spirits in the same way that the elves did. The thought of being so close to Felsafell caused Basanti's heart to ache with longing. But even without the benefits of such unity, she had never been more certain of her love ... or his.

With a howling hiss, a column of steam erupted from the top of a nearby hill. Basanti frowned. The air would soon be filled with the smell of sulfur—the one thing she *didn't* like about the Fire Hills. She sat up and sighed. *I guess nothing is totally perfect*, she thought.

She spotted Felsafell cresting the next hill and smiled, laughing at herself for not yet having grown accustomed to his transformation into his original form. Though he was truly magnificent, she often still saw the odd little hermit who loved her. And the fact that only she could see his true self was a constant source of pride.

"What were you thinking, my love?" Felsafell asked.

"I was thinking of how adorable you were as a little old man," she admitted.

He flashed a smile. "Actually, I miss it myself." He reached down and pulled her to her feet. The strength of his arms was unrelenting, yet tempered with great care. "I could return to that form if it pleases you."

The memory of the pain he'd endured while changing was still fresh in her mind. She shuddered. "No. When this is over, we'll find a place where no one will give you a second look."

He chuckled and kissed her forehead. "I don't know if such a place exists. But it matters not who stares and gawks, just as long as your eyes are among them."

"I always missed the way you speak to me," she said.

"I will still sound like a wild madman when I speak to others," he replied, grinning. "I never could speak their language properly."

"I'll teach you," she offered, taking his hand.

Abruptly, they stiffened, both feeling it in the same instant. The presence they had hoped to escape was now entering the jungle.

"Come," said Felsafell. "If we leave immediately, we can avoid him."

Instant sorrow washed over her. "No. We cannot. He is set to task by his master and will never relent. Even if Darshan is victorious, it will change nothing." She lowered her head and wiped a tear. "This is inevitable."

"I have given you two oaths," said Felsafell. "I cannot ... will not ... break them."

"I know," she replied. "You will not have to."

Basanti kissed his cheek and led him down the hill.

They walked in silence until they came to a small clearing full of thick moss and colorful wildflowers. At the center of this, Felsafell had long ago placed a small wooden bench for the two of them to sit and talk. Wonderful memories had been created in this setting. And now, they would all be overshadowed by tragedy.

Basanti sat down. "Leave me. I will speak to him alone."

Felsafell's eyes narrowed. "I will not allow him to harm you."

"He won't. His orders are to take me with him to Angrääl. I have no intention of that happening."

He leaned in and kissed her with devoted passion. "I will not be far away."

Basanti watched as he disappeared behind the hills, secure in the knowledge that he would protect her, but at the same time fearful of what that protection might mean.

Beads of perspiration formed on her cheeks. She closed her eyes while sending her thoughts out to Yanti. *I know you are coming. Turn back, brother. Please.* But there was no response.

In less than an hour, she heard his muffled footsteps crushing the turf just behind her.

"It is good to see you, sister," Yanti said. "It truly is." He took a seat beside her.

Basanti opened her eyes and looked at him with a woeful gaze. "I had hoped you wouldn't come."

"And I had hoped you would remain hidden," he countered. "You must have known that my master would seek you out."

She nodded. "Yes, I knew. But I also knew he believed Felsafell to be under his power and hoped he would not think it necessary to send you."

"I never believed that," Yanti said with a jeering grin. "Felsafell is far too old and stubborn. But the Reborn King does not listen to me." He scanned the area. "I assume he is not far away?"

She ignored the question. "When I first heard that your master was claiming to be the reincarnation of King Rätsterfel, I hoped that the limit of his ambition was to build on your legend. I prayed he had not found you."

"That is how it began," said Yanti. "He used the stories of King Rätsterfel to inspire and create fear. But then he uncovered an ancient tome revealing where the gods had imprisoned me beneath the Weeping Mountains. It wasn't long before he came to my prison and ... changed me."

"I never wanted you to be imprisoned," said Basanti. "I begged them to..."

"To kill me?" He raised an eyebrow. "Is that what you asked of your *gods*?" He held up his hand before she could answer. "Don't feel guilty, sister. I know you did so out of love. You asked them to give me a gift, and they refused you. Instead, they buried me in the bowels of the earth to rot. Being trapped there all but drove me insane. You can't imagine the never-ending darkness. I watched from within my own mind as hope faded away and I lost all notion of who I was. When my master opened my prison, I thought I was dreaming. But instead, I was thrown into a nightmare."

He paused to take a deep breath. "You cannot defeat him. Not even Darshan has the power to cast him down. He has strength you cannot fathom."

Tears welled in Basanti's eyes, and one by one they began to fall. "I am so sorry that I failed you. And I am sorry that your torment continues. But you're wrong about Darshan. His power grows, and he will defeat your master. And when he does–"

"Your savior has no idea what he will face," Yanti snapped sharply. "My prison was not the only thing my master discovered hidden in the deep of the mountains. Thanks to the lack of wisdom amongst those you serve, he is now far more powerful than any god could be. Darshan has taken Baltria, and he imagines that this will draw the Reborn King out of Angrääl to a battleground of his choosing. He does not understand that the battle is already over."

He looked into Basanti's eyes, his face tense and pale. His mouth twitched. "When at last they meet, Darshan *will* fall."

"What else did he find in the mountains?" asked Basanti.

Yanti's hands trembled. "I cannot say. The power held over me forbids it." He glanced in the direction where he knew Felsafell was waiting. "The old hermit knows. Or at least, he should. And if he slays me, he will tell you."

She reached over to take her brother's hand, but he pulled away. "There is so much I want to say," Basanti told him. "So many things I need you to know."

Yanti managed a smile. "I know you love me, sister. And that is what makes me wish for death. Know that whatever I have become, I have always loved you ... and I am sorry."

He got to his feet. "Come out, old hermit!" he shouted. "It is time for us to settle accounts."

It took only a few seconds for Felsafell to appear.

Yanti smirked. "So, I finally get to see you in your true form. Quite a bit more impressive than before."

Felsafell ignored his words and looked at Basanti. She was openly sobbing.

"I release you from your oath," she whispered. "Do what you must." She stood up on unsteady legs. "But I cannot watch."

Yanti and Felsafell both looked on as she walked away. Then, inevitably, their eyes met.

"Before we end this," said Yanti, his tone sincere and steady. "I would like to thank you for keeping her safe all these long years."

Felsafell nodded. "I love her. And once you are gone, my commitment will remain."

Yanti huffed a laugh. "That is assuming you turn out the victor."

Felsafell's legs parted and his muscles tensed. "For both of your sakes, let us hope that I do."

A hissed curse slipped from Yanti's mouth. He then leapt forward with inhuman speed, a dagger appearing in his hand from seemingly nowhere. Felsafell only just managed to move aside in time as the blade passed less than one inch from his throat.

Before Felsafell could strike back, Yanti ducked low and spun, his left leg extending sharply. It smashed into Felsafell's right ankle, knocking his foot away from the ground. Felsafell stumbled for a moment before quickly regaining balance.

Yanti rolled away, out of reach.

"You have grown stronger," said Felsafell. "It would appear your master has been generous." He pointed to the dagger.

Yanti sneered with contempt. "You didn't think I would challenge you without hope of victory, did you?"

Felsafell did not bother to reply. He spanned the distance between them in the blink of an eye, smashing his fist hard across Yanti's jaw. Yanti grunted as the sheer force of the blow lifted him from his feet. But then, in an amazing display of skill, he tucked his legs in tight and allowed his body to continue spinning. He landed on one knee, the hand still gripping his dagger pressed to the ground. Felsafell was on him before he could rise, but Yanti drove at him low. To escape the lunging blade, Felsafell was forced to jump vertically, so allowing his opponent the space to roll away beneath him.

Yanti rapidly regained his feet. His eyes were twin balls of fire, blazing from the thrill of the battle. In total contrast, Felsafell looked to be calm and in complete control of his emotions.

His appearance unnerved Yanti for a moment. *Perhaps he toys with me*, he thought. The idea was rapidly dismissed. He charged in again, flipping the blade in his hand, then falling to the right. This time, he felt the tip slice through flesh. But Felsafell did not cry out. Instead, Yanti felt a booted foot kick him hard in his ribs. His body flew at least ten feet into the air. He tried to land in an upright position like before, but this time he was too unbalanced. He hit the soft ground on the flat of his back.

He jumped up, slashing in tightly controlled motions. Felsafell loomed above him, seemingly unconcerned when the blade again cut deep, this time into his stomach. With effortless fluid strikes, his ebony fists smashed repeatedly into Yanti's face. Yanti staggered back, dazed and confused. He stepped hard to his right and thrust low in a vain attempt to keep Felsafell away, but this time his steel found only air. The man was already to his left. He caught only a flash of Felsafell's boot before the heel sank hard into his gut.

Yanti winced and was sent sprawling. He tried to raise his dagger, but steely fingers crushed his wrist. The weapon dropped into the soft turf with barely a sound.

Before Yanti could move again, Felsafell was behind him, a sinewy arm wrapped around his neck. He struggled for a moment, but quickly stopped. It was pointless. He was beaten.

"I am truly sorry, Yanti," said Felsafell with genuine remorse.

Yanti gasped out a quiet laugh. "I am not."

Pain suddenly shot through his skull like a piece of hot steel in the center of his brain. He screamed and writhed in Felsafell's grasp as his master bestowed upon him the penalty for failure.

"Do it now!" he pleaded.

With one quick and powerful twist, Felsafell snapped Yanti's neck, then ripped his head from his shoulders. His screams of agony immediately ceased, though for several long moments they continued to echo in Felsafell's mind. He stepped away and allowed the body to fall.

After pausing briefly to utter a quiet prayer, he set off to where he knew Basanti would be waiting. He found her sitting cross-legged on the ground with eyes shut and a tiny smile on her face. He sat beside her, confused by her demeanor.

She took hold of his hand and leaned on his shoulder. "I heard his final thoughts," she said. "They were of gratitude, relief ... and joy. I wasn't sure how his death would affect me. I loved him so much, but now that it is done, I am comforted that he no longer suffers. And I'm happy I was able to see him one final time. In the end, you *saved* him for me. And I thank you, my love."

After dressing Felsafell's wounds, they sat together quietly until the sun began to set. Basanti then stood up, stretched her arms and sighed.

"Are you weary?" asked Felsafell.

"No," she replied. "But I will sleep, nonetheless. Tomorrow, we must leave here and seek out Gewey Stedding. Yanti told me that when the Reborn King uncovered his prison, he also discovered something else hidden within the mountain. He said you would know what it was."

Felsafell nodded slowly, a grave expression appearing on his face. "I heard you speaking to him. It can only be one thing that he found. Four of the god stones were buried within the same mountain as Yanti."

Basanti gasped. "If he has found a way to use their power..."

"Then he may be beyond the strength of Darshan," said Felsafell. "But there is something more that troubles me. While I waited for you, I felt a presence. One that I have felt once before when a great evil plagued the world. One that should not be here. One that could unleash an evil beyond reckoning. And if I am right, then Shagharath has opened."

Basanti stiffened and turned pale. "Then we cannot wait until morning. But where should we go? To Baltria perhaps? Yanti said that Gewey has taken the city."

"No," he replied. "The presence I felt is near Althetas. And if Melek really is free, we must discover what he plans before Darshan confronts him."

There was a long silence. Then, in spite of herself, Basanti began to laugh. "And I imagined that all we had to overcome is a madman with the power of creation at his disposal. But obviously the fates believe this is not challenge enough."

Felsafell joined in with her laughter. "Not for creatures such as us. Our love is so vast that it requires the greatest of obstacles. And it seems the fates intend to oblige us with exactly that."

Basanti wrapped her arms around his neck. "On second thought, perhaps the world can survive until morning." She kissed him passionately.

"I would not dare to argue," he replied, smiling.

CHAPTER 20

Gewey spotted Lee sitting alone on a bench in the rear garden of the Brimm estate. He had been out of sorts ever since the death of his friend, Lanson. Sadly, Gewey had not arrived in time to heal the man. Lee was trying to act unaffected, but it was clear that this particular death had touched him deeply.

Millet had explained earlier that the pair were close friends in their youth. He'd also told Gewey how Lanson, in spite of the danger to himself, had helped Lee and him to flee Baltria only a few months previously.

"I think Lee sees it as a part of his youth passing away," Millet concluded. "Lanson Brimm was vigorous and carefree in the same way that he once was. It's what brought them close all those years ago. And he was a good man to boot."

With no offspring or natural heir, aside from a few personal items to be distributed amongst his friends, Lanson had left everything to Jansi. To Lee he'd bequeathed an ivory handled dagger. Lee wept when he saw this, but said nothing as to why it was so special to him.

He smiled as Gewey approached and invited him to sit. Gewey gladly accepted.

"I hear you are sparing what remains of the *faithful*," Lee said with a hint of displeasure.

"I am," he confirmed. "Though the Baltrian citizens who joined are all exiled from the city. The others can go home. Or wherever else they choose."

Lee nodded but said nothing.

"I know you don't agree," Gewey added.

Lee shrugged. "I know it's the morally right thing to do. But war isn't a moral act. It's savage and brutal. It brings out the hatred and darkness of our nature. To think otherwise is foolish. The men you release will come back to fight you again and again until you are ultimately forced to kill them."

"Perhaps," said Gewey. "But soon the fighting will end. I have to ask myself—how much more blood do I want to spill? I could have slaughtered every Angräal soldier that breathed Baltrian air. But the truth is, even if I killed every single man under the Dark Knight's command, the war would still not be over. It only ends when he dies."

"And then what?" asked Lee. "Have you thought about that? Do you think people can just return to their homes and be welcomed with open arms after having served the enemy?"

"I don't know," admitted Gewey. "Perhaps not. But exterminating them isn't the solution. In the end, it may be that those who fought with Angräal can never return home. But then I wonder, what if my father had chosen such a path? Would I welcome him back?" He hunched forward, his elbows on his knees. "I'm sure I would. That he survived would be enough for me."

"You may be right," said Lee. "But I don't think I can ever forgive what this war has taken from me. After the death of your father, Lanson was the last remaining friend I had from my life as Lord Nal'Thain—apart from Millet, of course. Everything that I once was now seems to be disappearing."

He shook his head and rubbed his face. "I don't know why this has affected me so much. I wasn't even aware of how deeply I cared for the old scoundrel."

He sighed and forced a smile. "But you didn't come here to speak to an old man about his troubles, did you?"

"You're wrong," said Gewey. "I do need to know your troubles. The elves leave Baltria for Althetas in two weeks. Once their ships are ready, I'll have to decide what my next move is to be. When they're gone, there will be nothing to stop Angrääl re-taking the city, and both Bevaris and Tristan are convinced that's exactly what they will do."

"And you?" asked Lee. "Will you go west with them?"

"That's what I'm trying to decide. The point of taking Baltria was to draw out the Dark Knight; to let him know that the only way for him to win this war is to face me directly. I must do everything I can to make him come to me."

"And if he doesn't take the bait?" asked Lee. "What then?"

"Then I'm left with only one choice," Gewey replied somberly. "I will be forced to march an army into the heart of his power."

"And you want me to lead that army, I suppose?" Lee chuckled. "There was no need for you to have wondered my response, or worry that I can no longer fight. My friend is dead, as is my wife..." The mention of his wife made him pause for a moment to clear his throat. "And yes, my heart grows heavier by the day. But I am not yet done. You have my word on that."

Gewey nodded and squeezed Lee's shoulder. "I promise that you will have peace when this is over, my friend. And if I can save your wife, I will."

A pained expression washed over Lee's face. "I fear that she is beyond even your power. I ask only that you release her, so that when my time comes, our spirits can be reunited."

"I swear it," said Gewey earnestly. "But there is also the question of your son. I want him to go to Valshara to be with your mother. He'll be much safer there if Baltria is attacked."

"You'll have to convince him," said Lee. "But I wouldn't object. In fact, I would be grateful."

"I don't intend to leave him with a choice," explained Gewey. "But I wanted to have your permission first. I figured it better for him to hate me rather than you for forcing him to leave."

"He's no fool," said Lee. "He'll know I am aware of it. But the thought is still appreciated." He rose to his feet and stretched his limbs. "I have sat for too long. I noticed The Plank Walker's Café is still open. Come. Let's continue this over the best seafood stew you've ever tasted."

Gewey slapped his knees and hopped up. "An excellent idea."

He followed Lee through the labyrinth of city streets until they reached the Café. Once settled at a table, they spent the next few hours talking on a variety of matters. At first, they went over plans for the city defenses and how to best secure supply lines to the west. Most of the proposals they discussed had originally come from either Jansi or Bevaris, both of who had greater experience than them in such matters. After agreement on Baltria's immediate future, the conversation soon drifted on to more relaxing topics.

That evening, Gewey and Kaylia retired early. Jansi had been more than happy to provide them with a room that came complete with a private shower and a small dining area.

The elves were already voicing a desire to leave for the west; the cold there seemed to bother them far less than the extreme humidity of the deltas. Linis at first objected quite strongly when Gewey told him to go with them to Althetas, but Dina, understanding the danger that Baltria would soon be facing, helped to convince him. Millet, on the other hand, would not be easily moved. Lee planned to use the fact that they were also sending Jacob to persuade him. Gewey hoped this would be effective.

"You know," said Kaylia as they lay in bed. "It may not be any safer in Althetas than it is here."

"That's true," said Gewey. "But with their supply line cut, Angrääl will be hard pressed to hold land that is not their own. And once elf reinforcements arrive, the enemy will be over matched." He pulled her close. "At least, that's my hope. Both Linis and Bevaris agree with me."

There was a soft knock at their door. Grumbling, Kayla grabbed her robe to answer it. She found Millet standing there, a mixture of excitement and confusion on his face. She ushered him inside and turned up the lamp.

"I'm sorry to bother you," Millet told them, "but a fauna bird has just delivered some amazing news." He paused. "Angrääl is defeated in the west."

Gewey leapt from the bed. "Defeated? How?"

"Their commander sent a message to the temple of the *faithful,* not knowing that the city has fallen," Millet explained. He hesitated for a moment, searching for the right words. "They think *you* are responsible."

"Me!" Gewey exclaimed. "How could they think that?"

"It says Darshan has descended upon them and is slaughtering them by the thousands. They say they cannot escape and are begging for help."

Gewey was astonished. "That doesn't make sense. What could have happened?"

"It could be a deception meant to lure you away from Baltria," suggested Kaylia.

"I thought that as well," said Millet. "I sent a message to Althetas just before I came here. If it is a ploy, we may not know for as long as two weeks."

Gewey nodded and rubbed his chin. "I will contact Aaliyah. Perhaps she can shed some light on all of this. Who else knows about the message?"

"Just Lee and Linis," replied Millet. "They were with me when I received the parchment."

"Did *anyone* else read it?" he pressed.

Millet shook his head. "No. Only Jansi, Bevaris and I are permitted to see the *faithful's* correspondence. No need for rumors to spread."

"Good," said Gewey. "Tell as few people as possible for now."

Millet nodded and showed himself out, bowing goodnight as he reached the door.

"There is another possibility," said Kaylia.

Gewey knew exactly what she was thinking. "It couldn't be," he said. "Melek is trapped in Shagharath. There is no way for him to get out. Only Maybell has the power, and she certainly wouldn't allow him to escape."

Kaylia gave Gewey a worried look.

He climbed into bed and pulled her close beside him. "I'll contact Aaliyah. I'm sure there is nothing to worry about. More than likely, it's just as you said before—a ploy."

He closed his eyes to concentrate on the bond. It always felt a little odd whenever he became consciously aware of it; their link existed mostly in the back of his mind. When he reached out this time, however, he was met by a new and strange sensation. It was as if a cloud had settled between them. He could feel Aaliyah's presence, but was unable to capture her form. The veil still remained even when Kaylia added her power to his.

"Are you there?" Gewey called out.

"Come back to Althetas," a distant voice responded. It sounded something like Aaliyah, but different in a way he could not grasp.

"What has happened?" asked Gewey.

"You are needed," the voice told him. "Come back."

Gewey broke the connection. His eyes snapped open. "Something is very wrong. She should not be able to block me like that." He could feel fear rushing through Kaylia and gently took her by the shoulders. "What is it?"

"I felt something," she whispered. "When she spoke, there was a power surrounding her. It reached out for me."

Gewey furrowed his brow in confusion. "I felt nothing. What was it like?"

"I have felt only one thing like it before," she told him. "*You*. Only your spirit can compare."

Gewey's concern deepened. "Then perhaps Melek *did* escape after all," he said. The idea was terrifying. To think that a monster to rival the Reborn King in malice *and* power walked the earth was beyond comprehension. Three warring gods would rip the world apart like wet parchment.

Sensing his sudden fear, Kaylia used her most soothing tone. "What will you do?" she asked.

Gewey shook his head slowly. "I don't know." He closed his eyes and took a deep, cleansing breath. "I can't leave, though. Not until I know for sure."

For the next two weeks, Gewey was on constant edge, spending most of his time either on the Lanson estate grounds or inside his room. Elves relayed regular updates on preparations for their ships' departure, as well as news of any messages received by fauna bird. Though there were none of these birds living in the desert, the elves were most impressed with the ingenuity of using them in such a manner. It wasn't long before there was chatter about using one of their own native species, but no agreement could yet be reached as to which one would be best suited to the task.

The Baltrian citizens were wary of the elves at first, but life under the rule of the Reborn King, which at first seemed like a boon, had turned into a nightmare. This went a long way to easing fears and misgivings. For their part, the elves went to great lengths to reassure the people that they meant them no harm, regularly treating the sick and seeing that food and supplies withheld by Angrääl were distributed to all those in need. Millet had mentioned that people were now even smiling at the newcomers as they passed them in the street.

Lee was equally concerned about the possibility of a mad god rampaging in the west and made a point of taking at least one meal every day with Gewey.

"You can't send the elves to Althetas if this Melek is there," he said during a particularly early breakfast. Kaylia was with Dina exploring the city, so they were alone in the parlor.

"If he *is* there," said Gewey, "then remaining in Baltria is not a refuge. He will come eventually."

This brought about several minutes of unsettling silence, broken only by the rapid footfalls of a young messenger. Finding the door ajar, he entered and bowed. Before Gewey could ask, the boy handed him a folded parchment and ran out.

Gewey read the message with a look of amazement. He gave a short laugh. "Apparently, a Vrykol awaits me at the city gates bearing a banner of truce."

Lee leaned back in his chair and cocked his head. Gewey handed him the note. After reading it for himself, he spread his hands. "What do you want to do?"

Gewey hopped to his feet, smirking. "Let's see what it wants."

As they made their way to the gates, Kaylia appeared from around a corner and fell into step. Gewey took her hand. It never ceased to amaze him how in tune she was to his thoughts.

"A single Vrykol?" she asked with mild amusement.

"You should still be cautious," warned Lee.

"I won't allow him to get near enough to harm us," said Gewey. "I'll rip his spirit to shreds before he can lift a finger."

When they arrived at the gates, they found them shut and barred. The fury of the elves guarding them was obvious, as was the fear of the humans who were scattered amongst them. The gates cracked opened just sufficiently to allow the three of them to slip through.

Standing twenty feet away was a lone figure in the now all too familiar black cloak. It held the truce banner high, and there was no weapon apparent. Gewey reached out and touched its vile mind. It did not resist.

"As far as I can tell, it only wants to talk," he told the others. "And I sense no one else nearby." He took a step forward. "Speak, beast," he commanded.

"My master sends a message to the mighty Darshan," it said in the all too familiar foul hiss. "You have taken what was once his. He now offers that you keep it."

Gewey burst into laughter. "He's very generous. What else that I have taken from him does he offer me?" He could feel the malice bearing down on him from beneath the shadow of the Vrykol's hood.

"My master has an army of one hundred thousand men ready to march from Kratis," the creature continued. "These are not the weak townsfolk and farmers you have battled before. These are barbarians from the frozen wastes of Angrääl. They will burn every city to the ground and slaughter all that breathes air if you do not take his ... kind offer."

Gewey was no longer amused. "So, what does he want in return?"

"My master wishes for you to return to the west," it replied. "A new threat has arisen. One that requires your personal attention."

"And what do you know about this?" Gewey demanded.

"I am but a servant and know nothing. But I have been instructed to tell you that he will not move against you until the matter is resolved. On that, you have his word."

Gewey stared hard at the creature for more than a minute. "And how do I know your master will keep his ... word?"

Thin laughter seeped out of the Vrykol. "You don't. But you *do* know that your beloved home, and every inhabitant of every city, town, and village from here to my master's doorstep, will perish if you ignore him. Your attempt to draw him from his fortress has failed. He will remain in Angrääl until he chooses to do otherwise. He offers you the lives of those you love and a short time of peace so that you can deal with this matter."

Gewey looked to Kaylia and Lee, but they offered nothing. "I will consider it," he said.

"Do not take too long to decide," the creature told him before turning and walking away with slow, even strides.

Gewey shouted after it. "And how will I deliver my answer?"

"There is no need," it hissed without glancing back or pausing. "He will know what you decide." Moments later, it disappeared from view.

"Do you think it's telling the truth?" asked Lee.

Gewey rubbed the back of his neck and shrugged. "I don't know. But if there is really an army of one hundred thousand more soldiers ready to march, I have to take it seriously."

"And if they are truly native Angrääl barbarians," added Lee, "it is a force to be much feared. I've encountered these people before, but only in small groups. Even then, they were formidable. A raiding party of twenty could sack a small city if it was unprepared. Should the Dark Knight have organized them into an army..." He did not need to elaborate any further.

"Tell Millet, Linis, and Bevaris to join me at the manor," Gewey told Lee. "I'll find Lyrial. It looks like Jacob will be staying here after all."

Lee nodded and headed off toward the temple of the *faithful*. At this time of day, Millet was sure to be going through their records, hoping to uncover anything that could give them an advantage. The bolt that Lee had thrown inside, as well as claiming many lives, had also done considerable damage to the temple's main interior. Fortunately, though, the deep vault where all the *faithful's* records were stored had been virtually untouched by the blast and subsequent fire. The thousands of papers discovered there all needed to be thoroughly checked. If there really was anything of great value amongst them, Millet was determined to find it.

Lyrial was at the docks watching the ships being prepared. She spent as much time as possible studying the workings of the strange vessels and had a seemingly endless number of questions for the crews. At the same time, Weila and the other sand masters were working mostly in conjunction with Bevaris, Tristan, and a small human force formed from those former city guards who had chosen not to join the Angrääl army. Only a lucky few of these had escaped being killed following the murder of the royal family.

Lyrial was reluctant to leave the dockside, but the seriousness of Gewey and Kaylia's expressions silenced any complaint that might have been forming.

By the time they reached the manor, everyone apart from Bevaris was gathered in a small study just down the hall from the main dining room. A serving girl brought them each a crystal goblet of sweet wine as they settled down around a mahogany table opposite an elaborately carved marble fireplace.

No one spoke to relieve the somber mood until Bevaris finally arrived. Gewey then told the group of the Reborn King's offer, as well as his suspicions regarding Melek.

Millet was the first to speak after he had finished. "Assuming the Vrykol is telling the truth, I would guess that you intend to return to Althetas."

Gewey nodded. "If the offer is genuine, then I would be a fool to ignore it." He turned to Lyrial. "I know your people are longing to be reunited with your kin in the west, but in light of this, I must ask you to remain here for a time longer."

Lyrial frowned. "You may need us if Melek is as powerful as you say."

"If he really is there," countered Gewey, "then there is nothing you can do to aid me. The fight will be between the two of us. There will be no battles. But if the enemy is being deceptive, you will be needed to hold this city until my return."

"This will not sit well with my people," she said. "But we will do as you ask. However, I would request that you at least allow Weila to go with you as a representative of the desert."

"Agreed," he replied, then looked at Lee. "You and your son will remain here as well."

Lee nodded in compliance but said nothing.

"I hope you do not think I will be left behind too," said Linis. His voice was commanding and serious. "My home is in the west. If a mad god threatens my kin—"

Gewey held up his hand. "That is precisely why I would not suggest you stay. And as for Dina ... I would not dare ask her to stay, either."

He turned to Bevaris. "I would like you here to aid in strengthening the defenses. I will deliver any message you may have for Valshara."

Bevaris simply nodded.

Gewey sighed. "That covers just about everything. I'll leave with the supply ships the moment they're ready to depart."

With that, everyone stood and left. Only Kaylia and Linis lingered.

"Why leave Lee behind?" asked Linis. "Surely he could be of better use where we're going?"

Gewey sat back down and drained the wine left in his glass. "Melek is powerful. How powerful, I'm not sure. But I do know that if he were to somehow ensnare Lee in the same way that the Dark Knight has done to others..."

Linis nodded with understanding. "Yes. He could be used to terrible effect. I can see the wisdom in your decision."

In spite of his words, Linis knew that Gewey's true motives were to keep Lee with his son and as far out of danger as possible. But he was not going to challenge the issue.

"It occurs to me," he added, "that Melek may possibly be more powerful than you—if he is indeed the father of all the gods. Also, if the Dark Knight is aware of this, he may be acting out of fear."

Gewey nodded slowly. "That is certain. But fear of what? Is he afraid that Melek will destroy him, so wishes me to fight what he cannot? Or does he hope Melek will destroy me? Better still, that we destroy each other?"

"The Dark Knight plays a dangerous game," Linis pointed out. "Were Melek to convince you to join with him, it would undoubtedly spell the end for Angrääl."

"If he really is in Althetas, that's exactly what he will try to do," said Gewey. "But at the moment, we still don't know if I'm chasing shadows."

"I would say trust your instincts," Linis remarked. "They've served you well enough so far."

Gewey shrugged. "There are some who might say different."

"And I would be one of them," Kaylia told him with a smirk.

Linis rose. "Dina and I will be ready when all is prepared." He turned and left.

The rest of the day for Kaylia and Gewey was spent walking the gardens and exploring the massive house. They could see that Lanson had been as avid a collector as Lee, though Gewey guessed that most of the treasures on display were purchased from ships importing goods into Baltria rather than from the man's adventuring.

Lyrial reported later that afternoon that the ships would be ready to sail in two days' time.

Just as they were heading for their room to take their meal, Millet arrived.

"There is a message for you," he said. "It arrived by fauna bird a few minutes ago." His shoulders drooped and there were dark circles under his eyes. He handed Gewey a rolled parchment. Just to the left of the unadorned wax seal were scrawled the words: *'For Darshan'.*

Gewey took the parchment and gave Millet a worried glance. "You should get more rest. You look as if you are about to collapse."

"The *faithful* had thousands of letters and journals hidden away," Millet explained. "And my old eyes aren't as sharp as they once were." He bent backward and groaned while stretching his knotted muscles. "My body isn't in much better condition, either."

Kaylia stepped forward, allowing the *flow* to pass into his thin, fatigued frame. He instantly smiled and sighed with relief.

"Now don't start thinking this means you can go straight back to work," she said with false harshness in her tone.

"Ah, my dear lady," said Millet. "I would not dare disobey."

Noticing that Gewey had yet to open the message, he took his leave.

Gewey broke the seal and unrolled the parchment. Kaylia drew close. A sense of dread ran through both of them as they read the brief message.

Darshan,

I forgive you for leaving me behind in Shagharath. Join me in Althetas, where I am a guest of King Lousis. I give you my word that no harm shall befall you, or any in your company.

With warmest regards,
Melek

Gewey crumpled the note in his fist. "Well, I suppose that answers my question."

He could feel Kaylia's heart pounding furiously. He wanted to ease her fears, but his own doubts were on the brink of overcoming him.

For two days after that, Gewey was unable to sleep. By the time the ships were ready to depart, his mind was scattered in a thousand directions. The docks were packed with elves and humans, all there to see the great Darshan sail west and wish him a safe voyage.

Lee, Jacob, Millet, and all the others bid him a solemn goodbye. It was clear that they were acutely aware of the danger he was now facing. In that moment, he wished that he had not told anyone other than Kaylia about Melek. Certainly not the bit about how powerful he thought the father of gods might be.

More than fifty ships were loaded and prepared for the journey. The vessel he would travel on was by far the largest and most seaworthy—or so he had been told. As he boarded, the crowd erupted into cheers and farewells that continued long after the ship had set sail and was moving with the rest of the fleet into open waters.

The trip would take several weeks. That meant several weeks to contemplate what might happen.

In truth, several weeks of apprehension and worry.

Lee had not wanted to appear as somber as he did, but he could not shake off a sense of foreboding and finality about Gewey's departure. Jacob remained at his side for the remainder of the day as he wandered the city, and for that, he was very appreciative. But his dark mood and unintended aloofness soon had his son worrying needlessly.

"I'm fine," Lee lied, forcing a smile. "Just tired, that's all. Being a half-man does not give me infinite strength."

"I can tell that you're lying," Jacob responded. "You're worried that Gewey is quite possibly racing off to his death. As a matter of fact, so am I."

"Yes," Lee admitted. "But there's more. I had hoped that you would go west where you would be safe. Or at least, safer than you are here. But these days it seems there *is* nowhere safe. The world is closing in, and I don't think I have the power to hold it back."

He knew what his son was going to say and held up his hand to silence him. "I know you think it's your duty to stand by my side. And when there is no other way, I would agree. But you are all that survives of me and your mother. I would have you one day worry over your own children, not perish fighting beside an old man who has cheated his fate far too many times."

"The difference between us, Father," began Jacob, "is that I still have hope for us both. You hope only for me and keep none for yourself. You act as if you were already dead. Well, you still live. And until that changes, I will continue holding my hope close to my heart. So if you cannot find any of your own ... share mine."

A tiny smile formed at the corners of Lee's mouth. "Not long ago I would have said that you reminded me of myself as a young man. But now I see you are far wiser than I ever was. For that, you can thank your mother." He slapped his son on the shoulder. "Pay no attention to my foul moods and moping. But for now, I think I need some time to myself. I'll see you in the morning, and then we will banish my melancholy together. Baltria is a large city with many distractions. Tomorrow you can help me remember my youth—just the two of us."

Jacob smiled, hugged his father, and then disappeared into the crowds of people that were now a constant sight on the streets of Baltria.

Lee had remarked on several occasions how the elves had breathed new life into the city. With each passing day, the humans were becoming ever more accommodating. He agreed with Millet that soon it would be as if the elves had always been there.

He wound his way through the streets until arriving at a small tavern close to the western market. The sound of a lute and singing drifted out from the worn front door. He reached into his pocket and jingled the coins he had with him.

"Perhaps some wine and song," he muttered to himself.

The interior was quite shabby and old, but the faces of the patrons were friendly and the musician playing and singing were pleasing enough. The small bar ran along the wall to his right, while two rows of tables were on his left. Here, the musician was perched atop a small stool.

Lee ordered a bottle of wine and found an empty chair beside two drunken sailors. Across from him was a party of elves. He was certain they recognized him, but to his relief, they only nodded and smiled a greeting.

As the night wore on, Lee managed to finish off three bottles of wine and a pitcher of ale. By now, he was well aware that if he didn't eat soon, his head would pay the price in the morning. Unfortunately, the tiny tavern had no kitchen. He drained his final mug and tossed the young serving maid a copper. Not wanting to insult the musician, he leaned back in his chair to wait for the song to end before departing in search of a late meal elsewhere.

As the music stopped and the crowd burst into ale-fueled applause, the maid brought him over another bottle of wine.

"No thank you, my dear," Lee told her.

"I'm sorry, sir," she replied. "But the lady at the bar sent it over." She placed her hand back on the bottle. "Should I take it away?"

Lee looked across the room to the bar. Only one woman was seated there. Though her back was turned to him, her sleek raven hair caused him to struggle for breath. He rose to his feet and slowly made his way toward her. She was wearing a simple blue cotton dress, tied at the waist by a thin white belt. The floral pattern on the cloth was unmistakably northern weave.

Lee's heart began to race with each step. He knew who she was, even without seeing her face. When standing just behind her, he opened his mouth to speak, but the words caught in his throat.

The woman, sensing that he was there, turned around.

Even though he had already known that there could be no mistake, a loud gasp of surprise still shot from Lee's mouth. There, right before his eyes, sat Penelope ... his darling wife.

He reached out with an unsteady hand and touched her bare arm as if to make sure she wasn't simply a specter.

"It *is* me, my love," she said. "I am here."

"How?" was the only word he could manage.

"We must talk," she replied. "Soon, everything will become clear."

CHAPTER 21

They had only just sailed out of sight of Baltria when Gewey spotted Dina storming toward the bow, her face red and her eyes ablaze. Linis followed a short distance behind her, smirking.

Dina spun around to glare at him. "If you think it's funny, you can just leave me alone."

Linis stopped and backed away. After staring hard at him, Dina marched to the rails on the port bow and began screaming curses at the sea.

Linis joined Gewey, who was sitting on an apple barrel near the center mast. "She has just found her mother," the elf explained. He could see Gewey's confusion. "Dina instructed her most firmly not to come. But a few minutes ago, she saw Nahali in the galley helping the cook."

"I can understand why she's upset," said Gewey sympathetically. "I, too, wish I could keep those I love safe. And remember, they are only recently reunited." He laughed softly to himself. "And to think she's off on a quest to challenge a mad god ... *two* mad gods, in fact. And in the company of a third."

Linis grabbed his shoulder and shook it fondly. "Mad? You? Not entirely. A bit moody from time to time, perhaps. But considering you went from being a young farm boy to the hope of the world in such a short span of time, you can be forgiven a little bit of madness."

Gewey recalled the visions he had been shown when visiting the Oracle's hiding place in the forest. Linis had featured in two of these: once as a friend, and once as foe. But in both visions, Gewey had betrayed him.

Since being told of these, Linis had never yet openly questioned whether Gewey would have the strength to remain loyal and true. Even so, Gewey knew that such thoughts must have passed through his friend's mind. Sharply aware of what he might have to face, he'd certainly wondered the same thing himself.

"You know that whatever happens, I'll protect you and Dina with my life," he said.

Linis leaned back and gave him a sideways grin. "You're thinking about those bloody visions again, aren't you? Kaylia told me they still torment you." He lowered his head to meet Gewey at eye level. "I trust you. I do not think you will betray me, my wife, or the people of this world. And if there was ever once a chance of such a thing happening—which I doubt—what you saw has now prevented it."

Gewey was surprised at how easily Linis could tell what he was thinking. It was probably why in both visions Linis was either his friend or, at least, had once been.

"You're right, of course," he said. "And I don't dwell on it as much as I used to." He paused and looked down at the deck planks. "But there are things I can't ignore. In both visions, Kaylia was no longer with me, and that's what keeps it fresh in my thoughts."

Linis waved his hand dismissively. "That means nothing. You said yourself that Ayliazarah told you these things need not be."

"True," he agreed. "But I wish she had told me how to avoid them. My father used to tell me that fate is a trickster. The path you take to avoid it has a way of leading back to where you never wanted to be."

Just then, Dina's angry voice called out. "Linis! Come here now!"

Linis smiled. "Speaking of fate..."

They both laughed as he hurried off to his wife.

Gewey listened to the sounds of the sea and wind, smiling as he did so. The life that emanated from the sea, together with the company of Kaylia and his friends, were going to be his only pleasures during a long journey that would be cramped and uncomfortable. His experience of time on board ships was limited to the elf vessel that had taken Aaliyah and him to the desert. Things this time were very much different—gritty and harsh.

He had heard several tales of the brutal discipline handed out on board human ships, and before the sun had set that first evening, he was to witness it for himself. A young sailor had left a rope unsecured on deck, and apparently, this was not his first offense. The chief mate decided that a lesson was necessary and immediately ordered two other deckhands to rip away the offender's shirt and tie him face-first to the mast. The chief mate then produced a long leather strap, the last few inches of which had been split into six knotted strips.

The first strike cracked loudly across the man's bare back, leaving ugly red marks. He grunted and ground his teeth hard together against the pain. By the fifth lash, blood was oozing from rips in the poor wretch's skin. Gewey could bear it no longer. Using the *flow* of the air, he tore the strap away from the chief mate's grasp.

"Do as you wish when I'm not aboard," Gewey told him sternly. "But while I am here, the beatings will cease." He pointed to a nearby sailor. "You. Untie him."

The sailor stood fear-stricken for a moment, but after a quick glance at the chief mate, obeyed. Gewey snorted with satisfaction and returned to his seat. He could hear murmurs of anxiety and alarm spreading rapidly throughout the ship. Men were asking what might happen if Darshan's anger were to grow beyond control.

A short time later, Kaylia joined him. He could feel her displeasure long before she arrived.

"I hope you do not intend to cause terror among the crew for the entire journey," she scolded.

Gewey shrugged. "I'll not see people tortured. And if it stops from fear of me ... so be it."

The sun was setting as Kaylia grabbed his arm and pulled him to his feet. "Come with me. I want to show you something."

She led him below deck. The interior was not much different from Aaliyah's ship, though with just a few faded paintings of various vessels and bits of old netting hanging along the walls, the décor was not nearly as pleasing to the eye.

The captain had relinquished his cabin to them, in spite of both Gewey and Kaylia's objections. Now, though, he was glad of it. Everyone they passed eyed him with suspicion and fear, and the captain's private quarters was the only place he could escape this.

"Lee told me before we left that human sailors are extremely superstitious," said Kaylia. "Better you not unsettle them if you want us to have a quiet trip."

The cabin was meagerly furnished and designed to serve as the captain's dining room, bedroom, and office all rolled into one. A single bed at the rear of the room was directly beneath a row of small windows overlooking the ocean. Four chairs surrounded a square table in the center, and a desk was pushed into the near left corner. There were no books or items of clothing other than the packs Gewey and Kayla had brought in with them. Most likely, the captain had removed his personal belongings before they boarded.

Kaylia climbed onto the small bed and motioned for Gewey to lie beside her. "Close your eyes," she said in a soothing tone.

Gewey did as she asked. At once, he felt her spirit calling him to her. As they became one, he sensed something he had never felt before. A tiny ball of pure light darted and danced, melding with them both. It was the essence of love and the wind of spirit.

"Our child," said Gewey. "That's my ... my son."

He had felt the baby's life force before, but only as a pulsating beacon—a formless spirit that he instinctively knew was his child. Now, though, it had a substance. And he could feel that his son already knew him to be his father.

"When did this happen?" he asked. His heart was filled to bursting with joy. Even the closed eyes of his resting body were filled with tears.

"When you went to Shagharath," she replied. "His spirit is the strength that kept me from completely losing my mind. He saved us both."

Gewey watched in awe, losing all sense of time. Never had he imagined such powerful emotions were possible. Not even his bond with Kaylia could compare.

"Shagharath helped me to banish my anger," he finally said, more to himself than anyone else. "Now my son has helped me to conquer my fear."

It took a great effort to pull away and open his eyes. By then, many hours had passed, and the sun was rising. He could hear the bustle of the crew going about their duties.

He rose from the bed, his face aglow with happiness. "I think I'll work on deck today. Maybe that will ease the crew's reservations."

Kaylia sat up and gazed out of the windows at the dim morning light. A few lingering stars were still visible in the cloudless sky. "I think that is a good idea. As for me, I would like to rest."

Gewey leaned down to kiss her forehead before leaving the cabin and going up on deck.

Using the knowledge he had gained while aboard the elf vessel, and without bothering to ask, he began helping the sailors with their morning work. Many of the tasks differed from what he had learned, but they were similar enough for him to quickly adjust.

Initially, no one would even look him in the eye, let alone speak. But as the day wore on, the men relaxed and accepted his help without hesitation. In fact, Gewey's tremendous strength had some sailors calling him over to assist them with particularly difficult tasks. This did not sit well with the chief mate, but he was not about to voice his displeasure. Not after Gewey's recent display of power.

Linis joined him about midday. Dina was still mightily displeased with her mother, and it was only after several outbursts at Linis, who simply lowered his head and nodded while trying not to smile, that she eventually calmed herself down. Her mother had insisted on helping the ship's cook, so Dina decided to join her in the galley. By mid-afternoon, an aroma was drifting up on deck that had the men's mouths watering and eager for the evening meal. When the time arrived, they jostled roughly for position in the line forming below deck. Crew manners were usually crude at best, but one firm look from Nahali soon had the desired effect. No one was going to risk upsetting the woman responsible for such delicious new mealtime offerings.

After dinner, Gewey took some time to relax at the stern and watch the sun ease its way to the horizon.

"This is a hard life," said a gruff voice behind him.

Gewey looked over his shoulder to see Captain Carnwell standing there. He was wearing a long brown coat and worn, black trousers. His unruly salt and pepper hair blew wildly in the stiff breeze. His dark eyes were unyielding and told of a man who had lived through many hardships and dangers.

"I'm sorry, Captain," Gewey said unconvincingly. He knew the officer was referring to his intervention with the chief mate. "But beating a man bloody will never inspire him to do better."

"I've been sailing for forty years," he shot back, not in the least intimidated by Gewey's power. "I *do* know how to run my ship ... and my crew. And I would thank you not to interfere."

Gewey couldn't help but respect Carnwell for having the nerve to confront him. "I understand your position, but I refuse to allow senseless violence."

The captain sneered. "After the many men that Saraf has taken to the depths, I find it odd you would be so squeamish about such things."

This sparked a moment of anger in Gewey that he quickly forced back. "I am *not* Saraf. And if I were, I would tell you that I have nothing to do with the death of sailors. The gods are not what you think them to be. They do not choose men's fates."

Carnwell huffed a disdainful chuckle. "Then what good are they?"

Gewey turned, not knowing what to say next. But the captain was already walking away.

What good are they? The words repeated in his mind, again and again.

"Now that's a good question," he said out loud to himself.

Just then, a strong wind blew in from the north, causing the ship to roll and the sails to snap tight. Gewey looked skyward. A thunderhead was looming toward them. On the deck, he could hear orders being shouted and the ship's bell ringing repeatedly. Another gust of wind blew in, this time with even more severe force.

The chief mate bounded up the stairs to the platform where Gewey was now holding on tight to the railing, his expert sea legs unaffected by the ship's increasing instability. "You should get below," he shouted.

"I can help," he called back.

The mate stared at Gewey, then threw up his hands. "Then get to it! Help secure the deck."

Gewey sprang into action, almost knocking the man over as he passed by. From the stories the elves had told him, storms at sea could come up without warning and smash a ship to splinters in mere minutes.

Lightning split the sky, and very soon giant waves were tossing the ship about like a child's toy. Swells broke over the bow, soaking both the deck and the crew. In only a few minutes, the sky was pitch black, the massive storm clouds appearing momentarily like vicious behemoths with each new flash of lightning, then vanishing once more into the blackness.

The captain was on a platform atop the main cabin, hands gripping the wheel tightly while struggling to keep the ship's bow turned into the swells. He spotted Gewey just as he was seizing a rope that had come loose from the mainmast.

"Can't *you* do anything?" the captain yelled, sneering and glancing up at the sky.

Only Gewey's enhanced senses made him able to hear the captain's words over the clamor of the storm. He secured the rope and then stumbled to the port railing.

He could feel Kaylia sending him encouragement and strength. She was below helping Weila, Linis, Dina, and Nahali, all of whom knew nothing of ships or sailing, to secure the cargo and galley.

Several more flashes of lightning revealed the rest of the fleet bobbing in and out of view. They were being scattered further and further apart, and Gewey could feel the dread and anxiety of the men on board as the storm continued to build in strength. The swells were rising ever higher. Some were already half as tall as the ship's mainmast.

He drew in the *flow* of air and water, allowing it to rage through him. He could feel the unrelenting power of the storm surging in all directions. His body rose skyward until he was well above the mainmast. At first, he was uncertain how to proceed. Causing wind to blow or water to move was one thing. This, though, was vast and beyond his comprehension.

At first, he tried to use the *flow* of air to force the storm into retreat, but it was like trying to resist an incoming tide by standing in the surf. Any column of air he created was simply blown back in the direction it had come as the tempest enveloped it. He widened his control to shield the length of the ship, and for a moment, this seemed to be working. The wind lessened. But then a furious blast, so strong that it felt as if it had spawned from the Creator herself, easily overcame his latest efforts. The shield vanished, and the gale blew even harder, as if enraged by Gewey's attempts to control its power.

Join with it. A whisper in the back of his mind eased its way into his consciousness. *Become as one.*

The voice alarmed him for a moment, but the creaking timbers and frightened sailors drew his attention. His vision penetrated the darkness, and he could see that one of the other vessels had already capsized. Those that were not trapped within the ship were clinging desperately to its hull. He knew that the ship would be lost and all aboard would likely perish if he didn't act quickly.

In one great effort, he combined air and water to right the vessel. The ship heaved and rolled, and slowly the edge of the deck became visible again. The sailors clinging to the hull scrambled to grab at the railing, but most were thrown into the sea long before they could reach it. Gewey could see them desperately thrashing about in the waves.

As soon as the ship was fully righted, he drew away the water on board and then, one by one, lifted the drowning crewmen back onto the deck.

A feeling of satisfaction and pride took hold of him. But this was short-lived. Four other ships were also in serious trouble. He needed to find a way to deal with the storm quickly, or hundreds of people would die.

Become one. The voice echoed in Gewey's mind again, and this time he knew who it was and it filled him with dread.

"Melek," he muttered.

Your flesh is unimportant. Only your spirit matters.

Melek or not, he had to do something. Summoning all of his concentration, Gewey allowed his spirit to drift out into the tempest. The complexity of nature's raw power was unfathomable. The *flow* that saturated it was disobedient and wild. He pushed with all his power, yet even now his efforts were achieving nothing.

Become the storm. Do not contain your spirit. Allow it to grow.

All at once, Gewey understood. The "body" he saw himself in when his spirit traveled was not real. It was a creation of his mind. Jubilation washed over him as he let go, allowing himself to spread out in all directions at the same time. Instantly, *he* was larger than the storm. At first, it was alarming. His vision expanded to encompass mile upon mile of ocean and sky. The entire fleet was laid out before him. He was below the clouds, and yet at the same time, above them.

Calming his nerves, he concentrated on the storm. Suddenly, its complexity was diminished and he could grasp its every movement. He wrapped himself around it and drew its power within his own. And, just as Melek had told him, he *became* the storm. It was not the mindless rage he would have imagined. Instead, it was a flawless power, devoid of passion and yet full of intent. It existed simply to exist. There was no malice toward those who were unfortunate enough to be in its path. But neither was there love or benevolence.

It was simple to assert his will because there was now nothing to oppose him. Gradually, the wind died, and the seas calmed. He dispersed the clouds until they were an invisible mist.

As Gewey's spirit withdrew and condensed, he heard a cacophony of cheers rising from the deck of his ship, as well as cries of relief and praises to the gods from the rest of the fleet.

During the moments his body drifted back onto the deck, he could feel the presence of Melek ever more keenly.

There is so much more, Darshan. Wonders such as you have never dreamed.

And then ... he was gone.

Linis, Dina, and Kaylia were standing a few feet behind him. Linis had the look of approval splashed across his face. Dina and Kaylia ... worry.

"That was magnificent," Linis cried joyously. "I had never imagined such a thing possible."

Gewey glanced at Kaylia. He was uncertain how to feel. He had saved lives, but only with the help of a bitter enemy. He forced a thin smile. "Neither had I," he told Linis.

The crew were still shouting their praises and thanks. The name Darshan rose like the storm he had just banished. In the midst of all this, a sudden fatigue shot through him; he stumbled with the sway of the ship. Kaylia rushed to his side and caught his arm.

"It seems that took rather a lot out of me," he said with a chuckle.

"I don't doubt it," said Dina, her eyes narrow and unblinking.

Linis grabbed her playfully around her waist and pulled her to him. "Come, my love. Let us stroll to the bow and bask in the air of this clear night."

Dina looked at him sideways, at first resistant to his hold on her. But then she relaxed and allowed him to lead her away.

"She worries whether you can control such power," said Kaylia. Pulling Gewey's arm over her shoulder, she walked him toward the main cabin door.

Gewey looked back. Linis was holding Dina in his arms and whispering into her ear. Her eyes softened and a sweet smile crept its way to the corners of her mouth.

"Should I speak to her?" asked Gewey.

"No," Kaylia replied. "Her fears will fade in due course. Don't forget that she is a historian. If history tells us anything, it is that power corrupts, and that those who wield it cannot be trusted. It will take time for her to know that you are different."

Just before they stepped inside, the captain called down from above. Gewey stepped back until he could see the man. His hands were draped over the wheel pegs. His clothes and hair were still drenched from the storm.

"I asked you what the gods are good for," he shouted, letting out a good-natured laugh. "And my word, you showed me well enough."

Gewey smiled and gave him an appreciative nod, but other than that, he felt uncertain of how to respond.

"All praise Darshan," shouted a crewman. "God of the wind and skies."

Together, the rest of the crew repeated this chant, as if saying a prayer. Gewey glanced at the bow. Dina's worried look had returned. Linis was rubbing the bridge of his nose and shaking his head.

"Let's get inside," said Kaylia.

Gewey allowed himself to be led on. Once back in their quarters, Kaylia helped him to undress and get into bed.

"And what do *you* think?" he asked. "Can I wield such power and not be corrupted?"

Kaylia thought for a moment and then nodded. "It was wondrous. And yet it was startling. As you spread your spirit out, I could feel a fire within you come to life—a fire that I have not felt before. It was at the same time both beautiful and terrible. But I did not fear it."

"I wouldn't have been able to accomplish it without Melek's help," Gewey told her.

She cocked her head and her eyes narrowed. "I did not feel his presence. How did he help?"

Gewey recounted the experience.

She sat on the edge of the bed. "Do you think perhaps Melek caused the storm to test you?"

Gewey considered this. "It's possible. And if so, his power is far greater than mine. To do such a thing from Althetas..."

His vision blurred and he could feel fatigue pressing in.

"There is no use worrying," said Kaylia. "Rest now. I will join you shortly."

With that, she got up and left the cabin.

Sleep found Gewey quickly. And this time it was restful and pleasant. Somehow he knew that Melek, whatever his plans and schemes, would wait until he arrived in Althetas before unleashing any more mischief. The storm *had* been of his making. Of that, Gewey was now certain.

He also felt certain that Melek was still hoping they would join together in his cause.

CHAPTER 22

L ee sat in the upstairs parlor of the manor, gazing through tear-filled eyes at his wife. She had been silent on the way there, and he had not pressed her to speak. That she was walking beside him was a miracle in itself, and far more than he could have hoped for. Yet he knew that if it *was* a miracle, it was not a miracle from the gods. This miracle came from a different, far more treacherous source. But at that very moment, he didn't care.

"Don't weep, my love," said Penelope. Her voice was soft music on a spring wind. Her tender smile was a jewel sparkling in the darkness.

Lee wiped at his tears, at the same time swallowing away the lump in his throat that was choking off his words. "Why— why has he sent you to me?"

"To give you a message," she replied. Her smile remained in place, yet bore a hint of the pain she felt at seeing her husband so conflicted. "And to give us both a gift."

A chill gripped Lee's heart. He knew the game that was being played. And yet he cared only that she was close to him.

"Please, my love. I know you are his servant. You must keep his message and his gift. I cannot bow to his will."

"He does not wish for that," she said, reaching over and taking hold of his hand. The warmth of her touch brought fresh tears spilling down Lee's face. "He asks only that you withdraw. He wants you to take Jacob and me to the desert, where we can live in peace. Once settled, we should stay there until the war is over."

She could see the doubt in his eyes. "Yes, I *am* his servant," she continued. "I cannot change that. And I cannot say anything other than what I have been told. This you knew already. But make no mistake of my intent. I was granted this gift in spite of my disloyalty."

Lee squeezed her hand and kneeled before her. "Don't you see? He only wishes for me to no longer aid his enemy. He sees me as a threat and wishes to weaken Gewey. He cares nothing for our happiness."

Penelope laughed, though it was kind rather than mocking. "Of course, he doesn't. But he does want allies once this war is done."

"You can't think that I would—"

Penelope put her finger to his lips to silence him. "Gewey Stedding will die and this world will burn. When that happens, I would have you alive and with me. I would see our son given the chance for a family of his own one day."

"As would I," agreed Lee. "But I think you underestimate Gewey." He tried to sound resolved, but even though he knew this to be a ploy, he could feel weakness and doubt creeping into his heart. The Dark Knight had made this offer before, and it had taken all of his strength to refuse. He had already watched Penelope die once and didn't think he could go through the terrible pain of that again. This time, the enemy had the upper hand.

"The Reborn King has more power than you or Gewey Stedding realize," she countered. "The Sword of Truth is not his only source. Please believe it when I say that it is *me* telling you this. Not him. I cannot say more, but I swear I speak the truth."

Lee noticed a small twitch of pain in her cheek. "I do believe you. And I won't ask you to tell me things you are forbidden to say. But even if it's true that Gewey is doomed, what's to stop your master from killing us once the war is over?"

Penelope let out a soft laugh. "Nothing. But that is a risk I'm prepared to take if it will reunite us—even if only for a short while."

The words were barely out of her mouth when the door burst open. A broadly grinning Jacob appeared in the doorway. "I was told you were home. And in the company of a woma..."

His voice trailed off, and the smile vanished. "Mother?"

Penelope slowly stood up, her hands covering her mouth to hold back the sobs. She cleared her throat, wiped her eyes, and opened her arms wide, but he showed no signs of coming to her. Eventually, she sat back down again.

Her voice was quiet. "Won't you join us, Jacob? Please."

He remained where he was for several more seconds before making his way across the room with tentative steps and sitting on the couch beside her.

She reached out to embrace him, but he leaned away.

"I understand," she said, her voice now barely above a whisper.

Lee quickly explained to his son what had been said. Once he was finished, Penelope placed her hand on top of Jacob's. This time, he permitted her touch.

"Am I to take it that you are considering this offer?" Jacob asked.

"I don't know what to do, son," admitted Lee. "I truly don't."

"So you really are considering abandoning all of your friends, and the cause they've been fighting and dying for?"

Jacob's tone was accusing. He pulled his hand free, deliberately avoiding looking at his mother while doing so. "You said yourself that she is dead. And even if she did live, it would only be as a slave to our enemy."

Lee nodded. "I know. But it's one thing to say such things, and another to actually believe them. Especially when she is here ... alive and warm." His eyes turned to Penelope. She looked back at him, smiling through a veil of sorrow and longing.

There was a long silence, at first simply because all three of them were unsure what to say next. Later, it became more the fear of where an unwise remark might lead.

"Nothing needs to be decided tonight," Penelope eventually said.

"And just how long has your *master* given you?" asked Jacob, not hiding his scorn.

Penelope did not appear hurt and only shrugged. "A few days at least, I think. And I would see Millet before I depart. Even if I am to travel on alone."

Her words stung Lee. "So you intend to leave us, regardless of what we decide?"

"I must," she replied. "My destination is the only choice I am left with. I will not be permitted to stay. I will go into the desert—alone, if it comes to that."

There was another long pause.

"Then we shall enjoy our time together for now," said Lee.

Jacob forced himself to look into his mother's eyes. His expression slowly softened, and this time, he did not resist when she embraced him.

They talked for a short time longer, though both Lee and Jacob were careful not to speak of anything that might compromise their plans.

"I am so very tired," Penelope eventually told them. She smiled lovingly at Lee.

Jacob, understanding her meaning, embraced his mother once more and excused himself.

"He has become quite a man since last I saw him," she said approvingly, once he'd departed.

Lee nodded in agreement. "He is stronger than I could have ever hoped for. And far wiser than I was at his age. He has made me very proud."

"You should have seen him as a boy. He was just like you. Rash and ruled by his heart."

Lee chuckled. "Thankfully, it didn't take him nearly as long to gain some maturity. A character flaw I still struggle with."

"I don't know," Penelope said playfully. "I've always enjoyed the childish side of your nature." She rose to her feet, pulling him up with her. "But if you would forgive me, I think we have *talked* enough."

Lee's heart began to beat rapidly. Only with a great effort was he able to keep his breathing steady. He led Penelope from the parlor and upstairs to his bedchamber.

He could only watch silently as she dimmed the lanterns and approached him with graceful, seductive steps. He had dreamed of her so often—the curves of her hips, the softness of her touches—and now that she was actually with him again, he felt like a newlywed youth. But of course, the truth was that she'd always had this effect on him.

Lee felt the heat of her body even before she was within arm's length. He reached out for her, his breaths coming in short, excited gasps. The moment he touched her, she melted into his arms. They kissed with complete abandon. For an instant, he worried that he might hurt her with the strength of his passion, but a long moan of pleasure quickly dispelled this concern.

He lifted her with his powerful arms and carried her over to the bed, their lips never parting for a second. As he lay her gently down, he took a moment to bask in her beauty.

The moonlight shining in through the window cast a blue aura around her entire form. Her eyes twinkled like a pair of flawless sapphires.

"I have waited so long for this," she whispered.

"As have I," he replied. "And I have made my decision."

The next morning, Lee awoke late. Later, in fact, than he had done since his youthful days. All the years of loneliness and hardship had been washed away. He looked beside him to where Penelope had fallen asleep and felt a sudden chill of panic—she was no longer there. He was just about to call out when the door opened. She entered the room wearing a red cotton dress and a pair of black silk slippers. Her hair had been combed to a beautiful sheen and was tied back into a ponytail by a strip of red cloth.

"I needed to find a change of clothing," she explained with a mischievous grin. "My dress is ... well, let's just say I can no longer wear it." She spun in a rapid circle, the cloth swishing around her curves. Once again, Lee's heart began to race. "Luckily, it seems that the lord of this manor was not unaccustomed to having female guests. I found this."

"It looks as if it were made for you," remarked Lee. "The lord was a friend of mine. I would introduce you, but sadly, he passed away."

Penelope frowned. "I am sorry. But soon death will be something neither of us will have to worry about for some time." She paused and cocked her head. "Assuming that your mind is still set?"

Lee nodded. "It is. But you must allow me to tell Millet and Jacob of our intentions."

She crossed the room as though her feet were not touching the floor and kissed him softly on his cheek. "I heard them downstairs. Should I wait for you?"

"No need," he replied. "Jacob will have told Millet everything by now. I'm sure he's impatient to see you."

She gave him a playful peck on the nose and danced gracefully out of the room. Lee lay back in the bed for a minute, yet again turning over in his mind what had happened. His decision was indeed made, but he was far from comfortable with it.

He washed and dressed, then made his way downstairs to a glass-enclosed patio at the rear of the house. The warmth of the midday sun was making the air muggy, but it also brought forth the sweet scent of honeysuckle and lavender from the garden. He could hear his wife's laughter long before he reached them.

Millet Jacob and Penelope were all sitting around a small round table in the center of the patio, smiling and talking. Millet looked happy to see Penelope, but Lee had known him long enough to detect that his cheer was disguising a deep concern.

"You look rested," said Millet as Lee sat down.

The table was filled with fruits, breads, and a large pitcher of cool peach cider. Lee listened as Millet regaled his wife with tales of their adventures, in true form, never forgetting to tell of the many times when he saved the day after Lee had leaped before he looked.

Jacob pretended to listen, but his eyes kept darting between his mother and father. Lee could feel his suspicion and see his unease in the way he constantly shifted in his chair.

They talked for an hour and ate at a leisurely pace. Eventually, Millet passed a comment about the beads of sweat forming on Penelope's brow.

"I'm unaccustomed to the heat," she explained.

Of course, Lee thought, reflecting on what he knew Millet was thinking. *Angrääl is cold.*

They adjourned to the downstairs parlor and took seats: Lee beside his wife on a sofa, with Millet and Jacob across from them in a pair of matching armchairs. It was clear that the time for more serious talk had arrived.

Lee poured everyone a glass of plum brandy.

"You have no idea how happy I am to see you, My Lady," said Millet. He leaned forward. "But I am aware of who you are forced to serve, as well as why you are here."

Penelope sighed and laughed kindly. "I am so very glad that Lee has had your wisdom to guide him all these years. And you are right to be suspicious. Should I be told of your plans, I would not be able to keep the information secret. Which is why I am grateful that you have guarded your tongue. But know this—I am only here to be with my family. The Reborn King may have other designs for us, but I am not aware of them, nor am I conspiring against my son and husband. At least, not knowingly. He wants Lee out of the way. That much doesn't take a great mind to see. And though it hurts to know that I am the enemy, I am still the woman you knew. That has not changed, and never will."

She drew in a deep breath. "I have lived for years without my family. Difficult as that was to bear, I have always told myself that it was for the greater good, and that the gods had set my husband to an important task." The hint of a smile appeared. "Well, the time has now come for that task to be set aside. I cannot be free of my king. But nor can I pretend I am not filled with joy that his schemes are finally bringing my family back together."

"And what do you say?" Millet asked Lee.

Lee lowered his head and steadied his nerves. The tension was palpable as both Millet and Jacob awaited his answer. He looked up, his eyes going from Millet to Jacob, then back again.

"The war is over for me," he announced. "My heart will not allow me to continue." He could see both men sit back in unison. "I know you will object, but I will not be dissuaded."

"And what do you expect me to do?" snapped Jacob, his face red with fury. "Go with you? After all we've been through, do you really expect me to serve Angrääl? It was the Reborn King who deceived me in the first place. He has invaded our land, enslaved and murdered our people, and as far as I can see..." His top lip curled in disgust. "He has killed my mother."

Penelope grabbed hold of Lee's hand, desperate for reassurance. He looked at her and could see that her heart was breaking. This was the part of his choice he had not told her about.

"I thought you would say this," Lee said to Jacob. He pulled his wife's hand into his lap. "I did not think you would come. Nor do I want you to."

"What?" exclaimed Penelope, jerking her hand free. "I thought—"

"I will come with you, my love," said Lee. "But I will not allow Jacob to follow. I do not believe your master will honor his promise. And if I am right about this, I do not want our son anywhere near me when his true plan is revealed. Though Jacob is in danger if he remains in Baltria, here, at least, he has a chance to live. In spite of anything you may say, I believe in Gewey Stedding. I believe he will defeat the Dark Knight and restore peace to the world. If you are truly the woman I love, you will understand."

Penelope closed her eyes and wiped away the tears that were spilling down her cheeks. It took her a few moments to steady herself sufficiently to speak. "You are right. I know it. And I will trust in your wisdom."

"Then we must leave at once," Lee told her. "My choice has made me a danger to Baltria." He looked at Jacob. "Honor my decision and quell your anger. I simply could not bear the pain of losing her again ... not for a third time. I beg your forgiveness."

Jacob glared at Lee, but slowly his posture relaxed. He nodded his head. "I can't say that I understand. My heart tells me you are making a terrible mistake, and a part of it believes you are simply seeking the death you have spoken of so many times."

He looked directly at his mother. "And I don't think I could ever forgive *you* for that."

Penelope's eyes dropped, unable to meet his condemning gaze. "How I wish I could be as I was," she said. "And how I wish I could say that all will be well in the end. But I can't. All I can say is that I love you both, and would gladly meet my end to save you."

Lee put an arm around his wife's shoulders. "Son. You must trust me when I tell you that this is the only way either of us will ever have a chance to be free."

He got to his feet. "Now I must speak to Millet alone. And if we are on our way to meet our fate, you should take this time to talk to your mother."

Jacob glanced sideways at her, but said nothing as Lee continued. "A piece inside of me died every time I thought of what I'd left unsaid to both of you when you were a child. Please Jacob, do not suffer as I did. She is here with you now, and you may never have another chance."

He nodded to Millet, and the two of them moved off to leave Jacob and Penelope alone.

They wandered around the back garden for a while until settling on a bench beside a small marble fountain.

"Are you sure you know what you're doing?" Millet asked. His head was bowed and his shoulders slumped, as if carrying a great weight.

Lee was grateful that his old friend was not trying to dissuade him. He gave a crooked smile. "To be honest, no. But the moment I saw her again, I knew I couldn't bear for us to be parted. And to keep her here would mean—"

"To keep her here would mean us having to imprison her." Millet completed for him. He sighed. "I would not wish to be responsible for that, either." Leaning back, he met Lee's eyes with understanding and forgiveness. "Where will you go?"

"The desert," he replied. "She can do no harm there. And neither can I, should the Dark Knight break my will further." He squeezed Millet's shoulder fondly. "Take care of my son. If given the chance, he'll be a great man. Far greater than I ever hoped to be."

Millet could not find the words to express the deep sorrow and boundless respect he was feeling at that moment. But Lee understood anyway. Between the two friends, such words were unnecessary. They sat listening to the sounds of the city until the afternoon threatened to turn into evening.

When the sun fully set, Lee would leave Baltria. He would leave Millet. And he would leave his son ... for the final time.

CHAPTER 23

It was many mortal lifetimes since Felsafell had been so close to a city while in his true form. The last time didn't go well, he recalled. The elves became fearful and tried to capture him. *Would it have made any difference*, he wondered, *had they had known how closely they were related?* He doubted it. The elves of that era were a brutish lot—confused and full of rage.

From outside the Althetas city walls, he could easily hear the bustle of people within working, seeking entertainment, and spending time with friends and family. All the things that brought mortals together. And all the things that he missed about having living kin.

For a while, he listened beyond these common sounds but could hear nothing unusual. If Melek was close by, then he was certainly not drawing attention to himself.

The army returning from the south had been divided in two. One half had marched east for twenty miles and was currently awaiting orders. The other half had been set to work repairing damage to the city. The all too familiar smell of recent battle was still hanging in the air.

The king had returned three days ago amid tremendous fanfare, but from Felsafell's vantage point of more than a mile away, he could not tell if the mad god was accompanying him. Word of how Melek destroyed the invading armies of Angrääl had spread like wildfire, and the mood inside Althetas was one of hope and joy. The enemy was all but defeated—or so everyone imagined. Felsafell pitied the humans and elves. To be given such hope only to have it stripped away was a miserable thing. And he was certain this was exactly what Melek intended to do.

Within a day of the king's return, there was a subtle change. The people began speaking about *"The Messenger of Darshan"* rather than of Melek directly. It appeared as if he was doing all he could to win Gewey's support and favor. But to what end, Felsafell wondered?

He could still see the once proud cities of his people crumbling before the wrath of the mad god. The screams of those who would not bow before him still haunted Felsafell's dreams. Just once had he seen Melek up close, and for this he had barely escaped being consumed by flames. It was Melek who had shown his people destruction and pain for the first time—a concept they later used to cause themselves immeasurable harm. Though his name and deeds were erased from all records and never spoken aloud, his people never forgot. To them, he was always Melek: The Bringer of True Death.

Felsafell had circled the city walls many times in the hope that listening to talk amongst the inhabitants would lead him to a course of action. But Melek was not behaving as he once had by marching boldly through the streets and imposing his evil will. In fact, after the second day, it was the name of Darshan—and not Melek—that was being spoken of as the savior of the battle.

Avoiding detection by humans and elves had, so far, been simple. Even when they thought they'd seen something, Felsafell's incredible speed allowed him to disappear before they could be sure he was actually there. He marveled at how much trust had been built between the races in so short a time. All the patrols were now integrated, and they had found ways to complement their inherent strengths. Though physically weaker and unable to use the flow, humans showed an uncanny sense of knowing when something was not quite as it should be. Many times it was the humans who had spotted him in the shadows, even if only for a split second. And when the elves could find no one there, they did not ridicule their new comrades for being wrong. Rather, they respected the human's instincts and became ever more cautious as they patrolled.

It was well past midnight when he began his search for the best spot along the wall to enter Althetas. There was nothing more he could learn from eavesdropping outside. Now he would have to risk the city itself. He smiled at the fact that, had he remained in the form of a doddering old fool, he could have simply walked in through the main gates unnoticed. But the transformation would take too long. Last time it was three days, and rushing it was painful beyond imagining.

He made his way toward a section of wall where there was a large warehouse on the other side. From there, he would be able to make his way to the king's manor with less chance of encounters. What he would do after arriving was still uncertain at this stage.

He paused at the base of the wall and listened carefully. All was quiet at present. He was about to leap up and over—a feat that would certainly cause a stir if witnessed—when he caught a foul yet familiar scent. Six Vrykol were approaching from the southeast. He backed away and raced toward the tree line two hundred yards away. A few people were still about, but his immense speed made him seem like a blur to their eyes—gone before they could be even sure something was there.

Just seconds after taking up position behind a thick oak, he saw the Vrykol change their course and move in his direction. He was clearly their target. But who had sent them? The Reborn King or Melek? They were spread in a wide semi-circle that gradually tightened as they drew closer. Felsafell knew he could still evade them, but if he did, he would risk having to abandon his objective. That was unthinkable, so he would have to deal with the beasts quickly.

Only six should be easy enough. They may be deadly to mortals, but they were in no way a threat to him. He decided to go to their right and take them one at a time. However, the second he moved they began falling back at a speed he had never seen from a Vrykol before.

This may be more challenging than I suspected, he thought.

He changed direction and headed straight at their center, knowing they would surround him. But it didn't matter. He certainly wasn't going to be defeated by this small group of abominations. He stopped just as the first Vrykol came into view.

The thwack of two bowstrings simultaneously being loosed brought a sinister grin to his lips. The creatures on either far side were hoping to catch him off guard. But he was *never* off his guard. He stepped back, allowing the missiles to whiz by him and disappear into the darkness of the dense forest. The Vrykol halted.

"Ah! The last of the *firstborn*," came a voice that echoed from seemingly everywhere at once. "Are you still as fierce and defiant as I remember? The way your kind would scream ... it was like sweet music. I so loved burning your cities ... and your people. Their suffering and pain warmed my spirit."

Felsafell snarled. "Show yourself, Melek. I have no patience for your mad games."

The disembodied sound of childlike laughter echoed tauntingly. "You *will* play my game. You will indeed. Then you will tell me where the creature you travel with is hiding. But first, a small test."

All six Vrykol burst forth, unsheathing cruel steel. Felsafell suspected that these would be far more dangerous than those he'd previously encountered. This suspicion was quickly confirmed.

He moved left and leapt forward, high enough to pass over the advancing foe. But before he'd even landed, the Vrykol had spun around and was bearing down on him. Though not as fast as Yanti, it was considerably faster than the creatures he and Gewey had faced in the Spirit Hills. His feet had barely touched the ground when he was forced to duck and roll beneath the Vrykol's steel. His fist smashed into the back of its head, sending it stumbling forward.

Another Vrykol closed in. Felsafell crouched, and with his massive strength, struck it in the mid-section. The force of the blow would have sent the beast flying, but Felsafell caught its sword arm and ripped it from its shoulder. An ear-rending shriek pierced the air.

The detached arm was still gripping the sword as Felsafell swung it around, and with a growl, took the head of another foe. Before the injured Vrykol could gain its bearings, he reached over and tore its head off, too.

"Enough!" thundered Melek. The remaining Vrykol stopped and backed away.

Felsafell watched closely as they all turned and headed south. To his right, he then heard soft footfalls deftly navigating the weeds and roots of the forest floor. A young, fair-haired human male appeared from the darkness, as if stepping from behind a curtain.

"You are different from what I remember," remarked Felsafell. "More ... mundane."

Melek smiled. "Being inconspicuous has advantages. Though I must admit, I wish I'd had more time to choose a form. I would have preferred to appear a bit older."

"No doubt it is easier to deceive your human prey in this form," said Felsafell, not disguising his contempt. "But you do not fool me. You are the same monster you have always been."

Melek's eyes darkened. "Mind your insults. I am not Darshan, and I do not look at you in awe. To me, you are just another mistake of the Creator. One that I will correct here and now if you are not careful."

"I do not fear you, Melek," Felsafell growled. "Do what you must."

Melek cocked his head and smirked. "In due time. But for now, I am wondering where your companion is? You know, the one who is behind the love I see in your eyes." He took a menacing step forward. "If you tell me, I may allow you to go free."

Felsafell clenched his fists and glared. "You will not find her."

"You think not?" Melek chuckled and shrugged. "Perhaps you're right. Perhaps she can stay hidden. And perhaps you can resist what I have in store for you." He moved a bit closer. "Or perhaps I will forget about her altogether and allow you to help me in other ways."

"If you think to coerce me," said Felsafell. "You are wasting your time."

"Time?" scoffed Melek. "What could time possibly mean to either of us?"

"It should mean something to *you*," he countered. "Once Darshan arrives, he will see through your masquerade. Then your time will be up."

Melek threw back his head in laughter. "Darshan? He is a child, easily manipulated. And once he discovers that he is truly no match for his enemy, he will have no choice but to accept an alliance with me. Which brings me to my next question. Where are the remaining god stones?"

Felsafell met his question with silence.

Melek sighed. "So you wish to test your endurance? Very well." He took another step. "If you would like to experience the exquisite ways I know of how to inflict suffering, I will oblige."

Felsafell could see the tiny changes in Melek's expression and knew that he had to act quickly. Melek had moved close enough for him to almost reach out and touch him. Close enough to strike. His fist shot out so fast that even a god would struggle to see it. But instead of flesh, his blow passed right through Melek's form as if through a mist.

"You are a fool, *firstborn*," Melek said. His tone was calm and unemotional. "I am not unaware of my power, as is the child Darshan. You can no more defeat me than you could your own kin."

The dim light from the stars and moon suddenly went black and Felsafell was struck blind. But he knew the area well and could recall every tree and bush that surrounded him. The sinews of his legs burst into life as he made a desperate dash to escape.

"To where do you run?" taunted Melek, his voice carrying on the wind into Felsafell's ears. "Do you run to your love? Do you run to Darshan? Give in, *firstborn*. Nothing can save you from me."

Felsafell knew that he had passed the tree line and was now out in the open; he could hear a few wagons plodding down the nearby road. The main gate to the city was to the north. In the opposite direction, the road split to lead both east and south. His keen hearing could help him navigate even the densest wooded areas, but it would be easy for Melek to ambush him.

The angry realization then settled. Why would he even bother doing that? He can likely take me at any time he wishes.

"Do you really think you can run blindly forever?" asked Melek.

Felsafell skidded to a halt. "Then face me!" he shouted.

Almost at once, the veil of darkness lifted. He was no more than a few dozen yards away from the road. The tall grass surrounding him was still for a few moments, then bent low as a stiff breeze blew in from the north.

"So you wish to fight me?"

Felsafell spun around. There was Melek, still smiling broadly and holding a dagger in each hand. "You didn't use a weapon with the Vrykol," he remarked. "I would be happy to lend you one of mine." He held out his left hand, offering the blade. When Felsafell did not respond, Melek shrugged. In a blinding flash, the two daggers vanished. "You're right. It's better this way."

Felsafell seized the initiative and charged. But Melek had anticipated his move and stepped aside, at the same time driving a foot hard into his gut. Such was the force of the impact that Felsafell was sent flying. Even so, he landed on his feet with uncanny agility, eyes fixed on his opponent.

"Predictable and clumsy," remarked Melek. "Unbefitting for one of your kind." He held out a hand and waved him in with the tips of his fingers. "Come, try again."

Felsafell would not be goaded. He squared his shoulders and waited for his opponent to come to him. Not that this helped. Despite his readiness, the blow still struck his jaw before he realized that Melek had moved. He tried to step back, but was struck three more times and sent sprawling.

He looked up and pushed himself to his feet. Melek was standing in the same spot he had been before, smirking. "Did you really hope to win?" he asked. "I mastered the power that Darshan now wields like a lumbering oaf thousands of years before your people were even created."

Felsafell spat blood on the ground and wiped his mouth with his sleeve. "If you are so powerful, why do you need him? Why enlist the aid of a lumbering oaf if you are so mighty?"

"I have my own reasons," Melek replied. A hint of anger had seeped into his voice. "For now, all you need to know is one thing. Should you continue your defiance, what little time that remains of your life will be spent in agonizing pain, the like of which you have never imagined."

Felsafell knew that attacking would only result in further injury, and that running was equally useless. "Then do what you will," he challenged. "For I will tell you nothing."

Melek's smile took on a sinister quality. "We shall see."

Felsafell lowered his eyes. The first blow that struck his temple was massive and very nearly sent him straight into unconsciousness. He fell to one knee. He knew that one more would be all Melek needed. He thought of Basanti and hoped she would heed his request to stay where she was. If she did, Melek might not find her—and perhaps Gewey would.

For the first time in many thousands of years, despair crept into his heart. Would Gewey be able to triumph over such power? Before he could answer his own thoughts, the second blow sent him into darkness.

CHAPTER 24

Gewey looked out from their small landing craft as it headed for the shores of the Tarvansia Peninsula. Ahead of them, the wreckage of the ruined ships protruding from the water was a depressing sight.

On drawing closer, his heart seized when he recognized the familiar curved bow of an elf vessel. It must have been caught unaware and assaulted with the strange new weapon they had seen in Baltria. His only consolation was that he knew Aaliyah still lived. There was a short time when he'd felt unfathomable anguish from her and he feared that she had lost Nehrutu. Her anguish, though, was very soon replaced by immeasurable joy. But there was no explanation for this sudden change. Whatever had happened, she was still keeping her thoughts closely hidden.

Linis and Dina had decided to join him in going ashore, and it was only after a very long argument that Dina was able to prevent her mother from coming along, too. It helped that Kaylia had intervened and agreed to stay on board with Nahali. She would know what was going on through Gewey, and he had sensed no enemies—only a small group of elves.

As the landing boat slid onto the sands, they saw an elder elf woman approaching from atop a low dune. Linis raised his hand in greeting. The woman returned the gesture, though without a great show of enthusiasm.

Linis introduced himself and the others, taking care to use the name of Gewey rather than Darshan.

"I am Aquilia," she said, giving a slight bow. "What brings you ashore?"

"We spotted the wrecks as we were passing and wondered what had happened," Linis replied.

The woman sighed. "I was not here at the time. But I have spoken with many who were."

She went on to describe the destruction of the ships as related to her by wounded survivors of the battle. "It was as if our enemy had acquired the wrath of heaven as its ally," she concluded. "The dead and wounded were beyond counting."

Linis and Gewey exchanged glances.

"You don't have the look of a warrior or seeker," said Linis. "So what is your purpose here?"

"We came to heal the wounded who could not travel," she explained. "Once we had done all we could, a few of us remained to keep watch, lest more enemies approach. In fact, had you not landed, we would have sent word ahead to have your fleet intercepted before you reach the next port." She smiled and sighed. "But the name Linis is well known among all the elf clans, and your ships will now pass unmolested. Even though I do not recognize the rest of your companions."

"They are friends," said Linis. "But not known widely among our people." He lied convincingly, though it was against his nature to do so and chaffed his morals.

"Then they are most welcome," she replied

"Do you have need of supplies?" asked Linis.

Aquilia nodded. "If you could spare any, we would be most grateful. Game is scarce and there is little vegetation this close to the ocean. We have been forced to venture further and further from our camp to find what we need."

"You shall have it," said Linis. "But you will only require enough for your journey home. Angrääl has been defeated in Baltria."

Her face brightened. "That is good news indeed. These old bones long for my soft bed. Come, let us tell the others."

The camp had been set up a few hundred yards back on the far side of the dunes, where the sand gave way to firmer grassland and sparse pines. Gewey offered to return to the ship and make arrangements for supplies to be brought ashore. Meanwhile, Linis set about gathering any information that might be useful.

The elves still there were mostly elders and healers who had come from their lands in the east to aid their kin as best they could. All of them were delighted to hear the news of Angrääl's defeat and now appeared as anxious as Aquilia to return home. They informed Linis that most of the wounded who were unable to travel under their own power after being treated had already been moved back to their homeland by wagon. This included both elves *and* humans.

"They will be the first humans to set foot within elf borders since the Great War," remarked Linis approvingly.

The others shrugged indifferently.

"The world changes," said Aquilia. "Old elves like us can only watch and hope. Our fighting days are far behind us, and most of us who remember the Great War will be gone soon enough."

Linis quickly realized that there was little of practical value to be learned from this group and so allowed Dina to guide the conversation. An elf named Froemis was from her mother's village and knew of Nahali, but said that those living there had thought her dead for many years. He appeared very pleased to hear that she was, in fact, still alive and returning home.

Linis could see the fatigue in everyone's eyes and posture, but this disappeared as soon as he mentioned the elves of the desert.

"It was they who captured Baltria," he explained. "And they still hold it at this very moment. One of their kin travels with us now—a woman sent as an emissary for her people."

"To think that those legends of a lost tribe really were true," remarked Aquilia. "If only we could meet her."

"You will meet many of her people very soon, I suspect," said Linis. He went on to tell them what he knew of the desert elves, and about his time among them. They were amazed to hear of their long life and rejection of the *flow*.

By the time Gewey returned, everyone was laughing and talking as if they had not a care in the world. While Linis and Dina were happy to talk for a while longer with their new friends, Gewey ventured off to scout the area. The lessons learned from turning back the storm had been well remembered, and he soon discovered that they could be applied in other useful ways. By allowing his spirit to drift free and spread wide, he was able to see over vast distances quite easily. He made certain that the elf elders would be traveling back home unmolested, at least for the first day.

Eventually, they all said farewell and returned to the ship. While Gewey was making his way across the deck, he noticed that a carved figure had been fixed to the rail surrounding the main wheel. He groaned as he realized what it was and pointed it out to Kaylia.

"A few of the sailors have even made pendants with your likeness engraved upon them," she told him.

"Yes," remarked Dina. "You appear to have gained quite a following." She paused to look closely at Gewey before adding: "I wonder where it will all end?"

The remainder of the journey was without incident. Gewey ensured that the wind was in their favor, but spent most of his time in the cabin. Kaylia told him that the crew had built a small shrine to Darshan in their quarters and that his name could be regularly heard throughout the ship in quiet prayers. Gewey tried telling them to stop, but each time they simply looked at him with stricken expressions and begged forgiveness. Eventually, he could do nothing more and was forced to accept the situation.

After some thought, he decided to disembark just west of Valshara to see Lady Selena. Weila, Linis, Dina, and Nahali would all accompany him and they would determine their next move from there. When the time came for them to board the small landing boat, the entire crew lined the deck to bid the group farewell. Rugged sailors wept as they descended the rope ladder, many of them shouting out desperate pleas for a blessing. Gewey waved in response, then, using the *flow* of wind and water caused the boat to speed away.

The sun was just setting when they reached the shore, though Gewey was in no hurry to arrive at his destination. After selecting a suitable spot on the beach to make camp, he watched the fleet disappear slowly into the distance.

While sleeping, he could feel Melek's presence, albeit distant and unfocused. He knew that Melek was aware of him too, though he seemed content to leave Gewey alone for now. This in itself was unsettling. Melek was powerful, true—but thousands of years in captivity had allowed his madness to fester. In his mind, the people around him were inconsequential. He would not hesitate to burn them all if he thought it would gain him an advantage.

During the next few days, Gewey set a leisurely pace and kept all conversations light and friendly. By the time they arrived at the gates of Valshara, he was feeling much more at ease. Dina was treating him with far less suspicion and doubt now. In fact, she and Kaylia had begun having almost girlish conversations about where to live once the war was over. Kaylia had practically begged her and Linis to choose Sharpstone, stating that she had no desire to be the only elf living in the village.

It was heartening to see that the gates of Valshara were now fully repaired and that soldiers were standing at regular intervals along the ramparts. Six elves in polished leather armor and carrying long spears guarded the entrance. They recognized Gewey instantly and snapped to attention. As the gates swung open, a trumpet blared a greeting, its shrill blast echoing off the cliffs and temple walls.

After stepping through, Gewey immediately noticed that the pathways and buildings were cleaned as new. The lawn was meticulously manicured and flowers had been planted in little round gardens all along the covered walkways. The sword in the center was polished so brightly that a person could see their reflection in its blade. Even the roof tiles on the main temple had been replaced. Humans and elves were scattered everywhere—talking, reading, and walking about— giving Valshara renewed life. This was a complete contrast to the first time Gewey had set eyes on the place. Back then, it had been all but abandoned, housing only a handful of priests, priestesses, and knights.

"They *have* been busy," remarked Linis, also taking note of the changes.

While approaching the main temple, Gewey noticed that two of the guards had filed in behind them and that pass- ers-by were looking at them with open suspicion.

The doors swung wide to reveal Ertik, a welcoming smile on his face. He was wearing a casual brown shirt and pants, together with soft suede boots. Gewey recalled him not so very long ago clad in the ill-fitting leather armor. He grinned. "I see you've discarded your battledress," he teased.

"And I see you have once again come to our door in dire need of grooming," replied Ertik, with a good-natured laugh.

Gewey chuckled while brushing some of the dirt from his trousers. "Sadly, life on the long road takes its toll on grooming and clothing." He touched his hair. It was indeed becoming long. "And I have no attendants to keep me neatly clipped and shaved."

"I'm certain that we can arrange something for you," said Ertik. He bowed low to the others, settling his gaze on Dina. "The High Lady will want to see you at once, I suspect."

"I will go to her as soon as I am presentable. There is much she should know."

Ertik noticed Linis holding Dina's hand and smiled. "I see. As for the rest of you, I'm sure you are all hungry and tired." He nodded to a young boy standing just inside the door, who quickly stepped up. "This young man will show you to your rooms while I arrange food and bath water." He bowed once more and disappeared down the hall.

Inside, the temple was far busier than Gewey remembered. Hundreds of people scurried about, though he noted that very few of them were wearing the robes of the order. Most were clad in simple attire that could be seen in almost any city or town.

The boy showed them to their rooms, and soon after that, food and bath water were brought. Ertik stopped by to let them know that High Lady Selena would send for them before the evening meal, which was still a few hours away. In the meantime, they could do as they wished.

Once Dina was ready, she immediately set off to see the High Lady. Linis accompanied her. As for the rest of them, Weila and Nahali decided to explore the temple and grounds, while Gewey and Kaylia chose to remain in their room and rest for a while.

Dina knocked on their door sometime later to escort them to Selena's private chambers. Linis, however, had the slightly more difficult task of tracking down Weila and

Nahali, who by now had disappeared deep into the labyrinth of the temple.

As they walked, Gewey could see that Dina's expression bore deep concern and even a touch of fear. Kaylia noticed it as well. Gewey guessed that her meeting with the High Lady had not gone well.

Selena greeted them at her door and gave them both a fond embrace. "Come and sit," she said, offering them chairs placed around a glass-topped table near an arched window.

The woman was largely unchanged, though perhaps slightly more careworn. She wore a simple, white cotton dress and soft satin shoes. Her hair was tied loosely away from her face.

She poured everyone a cup of wine and took her seat across from Gewey.

"Dina tells me that you are expecting," she said. Her smile was genuine, but something in her eyes was trying to hide her true feelings.

Kaylia nodded in affirmation. "A fact we would not have spread about until things are dealt with in Althetas."

Selena clasped her hands together. "And we must speak of that soon. But first, there is something you need to know." She took a deep breath. "Lord Theopolou is dead."

Waves of pain and sorrow shot through Kaylia and Gewey simultaneously. Kaylia gasped loudly, and tears filled both of their eyes. The words they'd just heard seemed unreal—as if they hadn't been spoken at all.

Kaylia swallowed hard. "How? How did it happen?"

Selena recounted the story as Mohanisi had told it. When she was finished, Kaylia instantly got to her feet and walked to the door. Gewey started after her, but she held up her hand.

"I need some time," she said, choking back her sobs. "Time alone."

Gewey was in anguish. He was feeling the loss of Theopolou keenly. But the whole experience was being made even more torturous when combined with the utter misery that flowed into him from Kaylia. He knew how much Theopolou had meant to her. Other than himself and their child, she had loved no one more.

"If you need time," started Selena, but Gewey shook his head and wiped his face.

"Time is fast running out," he said, sitting back down. "And our enemies know it."

"And what enemies do you speak of?" asked Selena. "Your … emissary has told us that the war will soon be over."

"So you have seen Melek?"

The sudden sharpness in Gewey's voice caused Selena to lean back and scrutinize him for a moment. "I have," she said. "He came to see me as the armies were returning from the south. He claimed that you had sent him to destroy our enemies. Even so, his attempt to manipulate my spirit and alter my perception told me that there was something more to it than that."

"What exactly did he say?" asked Gewey.

"No more than what I've already told you. He merely introduced himself as your emissary and said that the enemy would soon be defeated. Once he was convinced that I was accepting of this, he left." She gave a thin smile. "I would guess he thought I was already under his influence and needed no further conversation. But I have resisted the full onslaught of your powers when you unleashed the *flow* of the spirit. I am not so easily overcome."

"And the king?" asked Gewey.

"Before we go on, I must ask…"

Gewey looked straight into her eyes. "He was *not* sent by me. He is *not* my emissary. And if you fear him, your fears are justified."

"Then perhaps you should tell me who he really is." Her request was actually a demand, though her tone never changed.

Gewey told her of his experience in Shagharath, and of his escape. Selena was greatly saddened to hear of Maybell's death but accepting of her choice.

She sat in silent contemplation for several minutes after Gewey had finished. "Then Lousis is undeniably under Melek's control," she said finally. "As is King Victis, though to what extent I can't tell. I lack the talent of the elves. But I am guessing that he has given them only a slight push in the direction he requires. I've sent spies to the city, but so far, they have been unable to discover anything useful."

"And what of Aaliyah and Nehrutu?" Gewey asked.

Selena shrugged. "I have not seen or heard from either of them. Nor Mohanisi, for that matter. I shudder to think what he might have done to them."

Gewey closed his eyes and reached out to Aaliyah. But just like every time before, a thin fog obscured his vision and dulled their bond. She was alive. But that was all he could tell without forcing his way through. And if Aaliyah resisted him in this, there was a danger that he might do her great harm, so he dared not try.

"What will you do?" Selena asked.

"There is only one thing I can do," Gewey replied. "I must go to Althetas and face Melek."

Selena nodded and gave a tight smile. He knew that she was holding something back. But what? He didn't think she was lying, but there was definitely something she was not telling him.

At that moment Linis entered, along with Weila and Nahali. Linis's eyes were red from tears.

"I saw Kaylia on our way here," he said. "She told me about Theopolou."

There was a moment of silence. Linis then cleared his throat and set about introducing Weila and Nahali.

Selena gave them a formal bow. "You are both most welcome here."

Gewey stood and excused himself. The pain he was feeling from Kaylia was relentless and clearly reflected on his face. In spite of her insistence for solitude, he needed to find her.

"We will speak again before you leave," said Selena understandingly. "But for now, I'm sure I can learn all that I need from those here."

Gewey found Kaylia walking the halls with her arms folded tightly across her chest. Her eyes were now dry, but the pain was obviously still raw. For a long while, he did nothing but walk silently beside her. Eventually, she took his arm and rested her head on his shoulder.

"So many have died," she whispered. "But Theopolou was like a father to me. I feel his loss so very deeply."

"I feel it too. And I wish I could take away your pain."

Kaylia stopped and looked at him sharply. "Do not wish that. Theopolou was my uncle and loved by many. He deserves to be mourned. And I will give him what he is due. To take away my pain would be to take away my love, and I would not want that." Her features then softened, and she kissed his cheek. "For now, allow me to hurt and just walk beside me."

Gewey smiled and took her hand. Knowing it was fully dark, they made their way outside and took in the crisp night air. It was then he noticed a small bump beneath Kaylia's shirt for the first time. Without thinking, he reached out and touched it.

"Do you know when?" he asked.

Kaylia squeezed his hand. "An elf carries a bit longer than a human. I would say we have six months yet."

Six months, he thought. Not much time to defeat the two greatest threats to all life on earth in the history of creation.

"You will triumph," she said, hearing his thoughts. "I have faith in you."

Linis sat back in his chair, scowling. "I do not feel right keeping things from him."

"Nor do I," added Weila.

"We must," argued Dina. "Everything depends on it."

"If Gewey discovers our plan," said Selena, "we risk failure. And then we'll be at the mercy of Melek. From what I have learned thus far, that is not a position I want to be in."

"How do you plan to succeed without his knowledge?" asked Linis. "Timing will be everything. If he is ignorant to our actions..."

"All that can be done will be done," interrupted Selena. "There is no way to include him. We must follow the plan and pray for good fortune."

There was a long silence. Linis stood up and began pacing back and forth, at the same time shooting disapproving glances at both Selena and Dina. Weila looked to be no more pleased with the situation than he. Nahali was conspicuously quiet.

"There are many things that could go wrong," Weila eventually said. "But if Melek truly is more powerful than Darshan, then we must even the odds. He has spoken of his trust for the people here, and you, in particular, High Lady. And though I dislike deceiving a friend, I will do what it takes to save him. Please say what you wish of me."

Everyone's eyes fell on Linis, who was continuing with his pacing.

"We only await you," Selena told him. "Are you with us?"

Linis grumbled with dissatisfaction before answering. "Very well. I will do what you ask."

Selena's features relaxed, and she unfolded her hands. "Then let us go over the details."

CHAPTER 25

Awagon might not have been the quickest way to travel, but it was considerably more comfortable than horseback. And for Lee, comfort was now the priority—though the cold weather would most likely have a say in the matter as well. Still, with no reason for him to hide his presence from the enemy any longer, he intended to make full use of the inns they came across along the way.

Penelope was in high spirits, spending most days telling him of the day-to-day life in Hazrah and of Jacob growing up. He never tired of her stories, even when *she* grew weary of talking.

Once they were beyond the borders of Baltria, he steered the wagon northeast onto some of the lesser traveled roads and trails. Though not hiding, he had no desire to see Sharpstone again, and that's where a direct road north would take them. The village would only serve to remind him of the life he had left behind and the friends he'd abandoned.

News of Angrääl's defeat at Baltria was already spreading, though none of the people thought for a moment that the war was now over. But seeing as how the Reborn King had recalled all soldiers from Eastland outposts, including the smaller ports along the southern borders, they were quick to take advantage of this respite from occupation and conflict. Trade was resuming, albeit slowly and on a limited basis.

The road east was crowded most days with refugees from the west, mostly the elderly, mothers with their children, and those either unwilling or unable to fight. Camps were beginning to spring up close to the larger cities, straining their already diminished supplies. But thus far, the kings and queens had not turned anyone away. Likely, they would soon be looking to Baltria for aid, and Lee was certain that Millet would ensure they received whatever was needed.

So far, the four weeks of their journey had passed completely without incident. However, Lee had become increasingly aware that Penelope's demeanor was changing. She seemed anxious and distracted. He had suggested that they find a trade caravan that was going to Dantory, or at least a borderland town, but Penelope rejected the idea outright.

"I just don't feel like being around so many people," she explained. Her expression was strained, but it relaxed as soon as she saw the look of concern in Lee's eyes. "You are enough for me. I would rather it was just the two of us."

Lee smiled and pulled her close.

As the east road curved south, the snow began to disappear, and the days grew warmer. Most nights, they were able to find accommodation easily enough, but every now and then the towns were spread too far apart or the inns were full. At such times, they were forced to camp under the stars, and it was on these nights that Lee became aware they were being followed. Whoever it was, they were just at the limit of his senses and would fall back the moment he moved toward them. He knew it must be an agent of the Dark Knight, but whether they were there simply to ensure his compliance or had some other more sinister purpose, there was no way of knowing. He had decided not to mention it to Penelope. It was likely that she knew anyway, and as she had not said anything, there was no point pressing the issue. He was committed, and whatever was going to happen would happen, regardless.

They had just turned south toward a small trading post on a narrow, seldom-used trail when Penelope asked to stop.

"I think I would prefer not to spend any more nights in a smelly hovel," she said, injecting a tinge of humor in her voice. "At least here we'll have a fire to keep us warm, and the fresh air is far better than the stench of unwashed brutes."

Lee was happy to comply and soon found a small clearing not far from the road. The thin forests on either side provided little cover for anyone with ill intent—not that he had anything to fear from the riff-raff that roamed the eastern highways. The few they'd encountered had taken one look at Lee and decided it would be best to wait for easier prey.

He built a small fire and began heating some stew and roast lamb they'd purchased at an inn the day before. Though the days were considerably warmer of late, the nights still carried a chill. Soon Penelope was huddled close. He draped his arm around her shoulders and wrapped a wool blanket around both of them.

He had put away their dishes and was just laying out their bedrolls when he felt the foul presence of five Vrykol approaching from the west. Penelope looked at him in alarm as he retrieved his sword from the wagon, but he placed a finger to her lips before she could speak.

When about one hundred yards away, the Vrykol began to spread out to surround them. Lee pointed to the wagon and signaled for her to hide, but she remained motionless.

"Get under the wagon," he pleaded. "I can't protect you if you're in the open."

It was then that he felt another presence approaching. But this was not a Vrykol—it was a human. He walked casually toward them without drawing steel. *If he thinks being unarmed will save him, he is sorely mistaken,* Lee thought with cold resolve.

He gripped his sword, ready to attack.

The man drew closer and with a rush. Lee recognized the face of Captain Lanmore. His strides were confident, his countenance like stone. He halted ten yards away from their fire and surveyed the small campsite.

"Lord Starfinder," he said. "I hoped we would see each other again." His icy gaze fell on Penelope crouching low beside the wagon. "And you ... you have failed, Lady Penelope."

Penelope rose up on unsteady legs. "I have brought my husband, as I was told. The master has nothing more to fear from him."

Lanmore shook his head and clicked his tongue. "And where is your son?"

"You will leave my son alone, snake!" roared Lee. "He is no concern of yours—or of your bloody master."

Lanmore chuckled. "The Reborn King decides what is or is not his concern. The end is nearly upon us, and all the pieces must be in place." He turned to Penelope. "Your task was simple. Bring your husband and your son to the desert and await the arrival of our lord."

"Your *lord* has me," said Lee, his fury rising. "And that is all he shall have."

Lanmore cocked his head. "Does your wife's betrayal not bother you? She journeyed to Baltria solely with the intent of delivering you into the hands of your enemy, yet you seem unmoved by this."

Lee glanced across at Penelope, but she was unable to look him in the eye.

"I knew," he replied. "I knew from the moment she arrived. There was no way for her to hide her allegiance, nor did she attempt to do so. I had hoped that I would be enough to satisfy your master, but I was not fooled as to his intent." He reached over and took his wife's hand.

"I'm sorry," she whispered.

He tightened his grip slightly. "There is no need. I knew this would come. I just hoped for a little more time."

"Then you know what comes next," said Lanmore darkly. He stepped back just as the snap of a bowstring cut through the air.

Time slowed as Lee instantly focused, bringing all his years of training and experience to the fore. He could see the arrow streaking toward him from just over Lanmore's shoulder. After pushing Penelope to the ground as roughly as he dared, he twisted hard to his left. The steel tip of the deadly missile flew past where his heart had been only a fraction of a second before, ripping through his shirt and slicing across his chest.

All the Vrykol, apart from one, began moving in. The creature holding the bow was notching another arrow. The sight of this sent a chill running through Lee. Unable to leave his wife unprotected, he would be forced to avoid both arrows and blades simultaneously.

Lanmore backed farther away. It was clear that he intended for the Vrykol to do the fighting. The creatures paused just long enough for a second arrow to be loosed. This one was aimed, not at Lee, but at Penelope. With a swipe of his blade, he cut the arrow in half just before it reached her. The tip spun and buried itself in the ground, only inches away from her leg.

But there was no time to ponder on this near miss. Lee brought up his sword just in time to deflect the first Vrykol blade. He tried to counter, but the rest were already upon him. Steel found the flesh of his arm and shoulder. Only Lee's half-man reflexes allowed him to step back in time to avoid another two swords sinking in. Parrying furiously to fend off the continuous stream of attacks, he sought desperately to hold ground. But all the time he was being forced farther and farther away from where Penelope still lay.

Growling with anger, he made an immense effort to fight his way back toward his wife, but this only resulted in him receiving two more deep gashes in his chest. He was left with no other choice but to spin right and then to the rear in order to gain a better position. This took him several feet farther away from Penelope, but at least caused the Vrykol to bunch up and slow their attack.

Lee roared as he took his first head. His rage burned, but his heart was desperate, knowing that enough time had passed for the Vrykol archer to notch another arrow.

Ignoring all peril, he drove forward again. Blood soaked his clothing and sprayed his enemy as he ducked and pushed his sword into the gullet of the nearest Vrykol. Tearing the blade free, he slashed into yet another. Such wounds weren't fatal to the foul beasts, but they were enough to slow them down a bit.

"Drop your weapon, Starfinder!" shouted the voice of Lanmore.

Lee looked in horror at the captain. He was standing over Penelope. Beside him was the Vrykol archer, its bow pointed at her head.

Lee froze, and the other Vrykol backed away from him. After only a moment of hesitation, he allowed his sword to slip from his grasp onto the ground. Tears were streaming down Penelope's face, though she did not make a sound.

Lanmore went over to their wagon and found a coil of rope. He looked to the Vrykol standing a few feet away from Lee and tossed it over. "Bind his hands," he instructed.

Lee's skin crawled at the touch of the creature's dead flesh as it followed Lanmore's order. The binding was tight and expertly knotted. There would be no way to escape. He looked at Penelope with an apology in his eyes before turning back to Lanmore.

"I ask only that you kill me first," he said. His tone, though pleading, remained steady and proud. "I beg you not to make me watch her die again."

Lanmore smirked and shook his head. "If I wanted you dead, why would I bother to tie you?" He reached into his belt pouch and retrieved a small piece of folded cloth.

"Don't do this," begged Penelope, struggling to her knees.

"You brought this on yourself," Lanmore snapped. "Now you will suffer the consequences." He unfolded the cloth. Inside was a thin piece of gleaming metal that resembled a small nail.

He turned his attention back to Lee. "Hold him tight," he ordered.

The Vrykol tightened their grip on Lee. As Lanmore drew closer, Lee could see more clearly what it was he carried. His heart raced. He had seen something nearly identical when they had encountered the corrupted half-man in the Xenex Valley.

"So you intend to turn me into a monster," he snarled.

"That depends on you," replied Lanmore. "And your loving wife." He held the tip of the shard just above Lee's heart. "Brace yourself, Starfinder. I've never seen this done before, but the stories I've heard..."

Lee glared defiantly. "Get it over with."

With a sharp nod, Lanmore pushed firmly. A wave of searing pain instantly shot through Lee's entire body. The muscles in his arms and legs convulsed so violently that the Vrykol lost their hold on him completely. He jerked and rolled, sucking in gasping breaths through clenched teeth. He could feel himself losing consciousness ... and for that, at least he was grateful.

Just as his eyes closed, he saw Penelope running toward him. She was screaming out his name.

Lee woke with a dull pain throbbing in his chest. The sun was well over the horizon, blinding him for a moment.

He shielded his eyes and saw Penelope sitting on the ground a few feet away, staring at a small medallion that was now hanging around her neck. She had cleaned and dressed his wounds, and placed a blanket under his head. He touched his chest above his heart. His fingers immediately came into contact with the small round head of the metal spike that was now invading his body.

He gave a groan and sat up, the movement sending pain from his injuries shooting through his body. Penelope didn't take her eyes off the medallion, nor even appear to notice him after he'd crawled over to sit beside her.

"Are you hurt?" he asked. His tongue was dry and swollen.

Her gaze still did not shift and her reply was almost inaudible. "How can you speak to me after what I have done? I have ruined us."

Lee took her by the shoulders, forcing her to meet his eyes. "You did not choose this. The Dark Knight did it to you. I knew what could happen when I left Baltria, and that's why I could not allow Jacob to come with us—even if he had chosen to do so."

"I was ordered to persuade you both to come," she confessed. "But I swear I was promised that neither of you would be harmed."

Lee smiled. "Had it been any other way, he knew you would not agree to go through with it. Even with the hold he has on your spirit, your love was still able to fight back." He pulled her into a firm embrace, ignoring the pain it caused him. She resisted at first, but after a moment, allowed herself to melt into his arms.

They stayed like this for several minutes. Reluctantly, Lee then he eased her away. "You must leave me. This thing Lanmore has put into my chest will turn me into a monster." He touched the round head with the tip of his finger. "And I doubt I can simply remove it."

Penelope held up the medallion she was wearing for Lee to inspect closer. It looked as if it had been crafted from silver—the broken scales sigil was engraved on both sides. "This will hold the change at bay," she told him. "Lanmore put it on me while you were unconscious. He said that as long as you remain near to me, it will keep you as you are. But should we be parted, you will become a mad, feral beast."

Lee examined the medallion carefully. "Can you take it off?"

Penelope shook her head. "If I do, I will perish and the medallion will lose its power. You will then change."

Lee thought on this for a time before struggling to his feet. He offered Penelope his hand to help her up. "It would seem that the Reborn King has plans for us." She looked at him with confusion, but he smiled and shrugged. "If he wanted me dead, I would be already. If he wanted me dragged before him so he could enslave my spirit, he could have done that, too."

Penelope looked even more confused. "What could he want? Why do all this? What purpose does it serve?"

"I don't know his ultimate design," admitted Lee. "But for now, he is aware of exactly where I am and knows that I can only travel as quickly as you are able."

"Then how did Jacob fit in?" she wondered.

"I'm not sure," Lee replied. "But I hope whatever it was, he remains far removed from it."

Seeing that their wagon and horses had been left undisturbed, Lee began preparing to depart.

"Where are we going?" asked Penelope.

"There is only one place I can think to go," he answered. "We should continue to the desert. There is somewhere I know of where we might be safe." He walked up to Penelope and took her hand. "It will take many weeks to get there, so we first need to head to Dantory for supplies."

"So you know a way that we can be free?" she asked, hope springing into her voice.

"Perhaps—perhaps not," he said. "But I certainly can't think of anything better."

Captain Lanmore approached the camp where his men were waiting. The handful of trusted soldiers he had selected to accompany him were not happy about the presence of the Vrykol. The beasts may well have been the creation of the king, but in the past, they had been known to be unpredictable and volatile. They also carried the foul stench of death and decay—a smell that every soldier knew only too well.

But now that their mission was over, the Vrykol would be departing their company. Lanmore was to return to Angrääl and make ready for an invasion by the enemy. The thought still bewildered his mind. Word had reached Kratis that the Western armies were annihilated and that Baltria had been lost.

Despite all of this, the Reborn King seemed unconcerned. He'd made no move to retake the city, or to reinforce the west. Talk of losing the war had begun to spring up among the ranks. And though the officers would never dare to say such things themselves, it was obvious that the idea was taking hold with them as well. Lanmore reviled such cowardice and made no secret of this when among his peers. On several occasions, he had openly berated his own commanders for questioning the wisdom and power of the king.

Not so long ago, such behavior would have got him demoted ... or worse. But since the escape of Lee Starfinder, Lanmore had been afforded a certain amount of trust among the upper echelon. His master must have recognized his talents because those closest to the king had begun to call upon him quite frequently. He was even allowed to take part in high-level councils to give his opinion on strategy. This was completely unexpected. He had thought that his failure to recognize Starfinder as a spy would have doomed him, but instead of punishment, he seemed to be receiving one reward after another.

Even if he had never been brought before the king to have his spirit altered, he would still remain loyal. His master was not worried, so he wasn't either. And should the king be wrong and Angrääl were to fall, he would defend it to the last. If Darshan and his army dared to march on Kratis, they would be marching to their end.

No matter what happened, he would see that Kratis endured.

CHAPTER 26

Gewey was surprised at how easy it had been to convince Linis, Dina, and Nahali to stay behind in Valshara. Kaylia suggested that perhaps Dina was concerned for her mother's safety, but neither of them really believed this. High Lady Selena had also been acting in a most peculiar way, and even Weila wasn't quite herself—though there was never any question of her not traveling with them to Althetas.

Weila had spent their few days at Valshara getting to know the elves who dwelled in the temple. News of a desert elf's arrival had quickly spread, and she found herself with no lack of company. However, the resident's first reaction to her was one of confusion. Their desert kin's rejection of the flow made it seem to them as if Weila wasn't really there—at least, not in the way that elves sense one another. But their trepidation quickly vanished. Only a few short months ago, they would have been unable to imagine living among humans, but these days they were growing accustomed to new experiences.

On the morning of their departure, Gewey, Kaylia, and Weila joined Linis and High Lady Selena for breakfast. Dina and her mother also made a brief appearance but quickly excused themselves. Nahali had discovered a small group of elves within the temple who came from her home village. She had promised to meet with them in the main library to tell tales and renew ties.

Conversation was light and friendly, but still, Gewey couldn't help but notice that no one would look at him directly.

"Is there something I should know?" he asked, exasperated. "If so, now is the time to tell me."

Selena forced a smile. "We are just worried about you. You go to face an enemy like no other, and we are powerless to help."

Gewey looked closely at the High Lady. She was lying, and her lie was reflected in the eyes of everyone else there. He surveyed each of his friends in turn with a probing stare.

Finally, he shook his head and stood up. "In that case, I should be leaving." He tried not to appear angry, but his brusque movements and hard tone betrayed his feelings. "If I return, I hope you will then be able to tell me what you are hiding from me. And perhaps explain why I have not earned your trust."

"We trust you," said Linis. "Never think we do not."

Gewey paused. The sincerity in Linis's voice, together with the expression on his face, went far to calm his frustration. He chuckled and held up his hand in a gesture of acceptance.

"Forgive my irritation," he said. "If you have secrets, then I am sure you have good reasons to keep them."

He sat back down and finished his breakfast. This done, Selena bid the trio farewell. Linis walked with them to the gates where three horses awaited.

Weila's face twisted in displeasure. "I prefer to walk," she grumbled. "I do not enjoy riding on the back of these beasts."

"Nor do I," said Kaylia. "But if we are set upon, we will need their speed."

"What fool would attack Darshan on the open road?" scoffed Weila.

"Never underestimate a person's capacity for stupidity," Kaylia replied, smirking.

They had just mounted when Dina and Nahali arrived to see them off. Nahali was glowing with sheer joy. The reunion with her kin had clearly gone well.

It was moments such as this that reminded Gewey of how far the people of this world had come in so short a time. These days, any mention of the Great War was rare, and always spoken of with regret. Human and elf acted as if they had lived as one for many years rather than just months. Even the older elves, who were still uncomfortable with the way things had changed, were no longer protesting, content simply to grumble and glare. War, it seemed, however terrible, could produce something far more than just death and hardship.

As they rode through the gates and on along the narrow canyon, Gewey could feel eyes following him. They were watching from above, just out of reach. From precisely where he couldn't tell, but he knew exactly who it was.

"Melek," he muttered.

After the first day, Weila refused to continue riding her horse, instead choosing to walk beside it. There were few travelers on the road at first, and those that were took little notice of them. Gewey's face was not yet easily recognizable—a fact for which he was truly grateful.

He continued to feel Melek's watchful gaze and knew that Kaylia was feeling it as well. He tried several times to reach Aaliyah, but as before, she refused to make contact.

Though this caused his concern to deepen, there was nothing that could be done about it for now. He had to trust in her friendship and loyalty.

When they were but a few hours away from Althetas' city gates, the traffic along the road suddenly increased sharply in both volume and urgency. A seemingly never-ending stream of wagons loaded with men and building materials jostled along in both directions, while everywhere they looked there appeared to be yet more construction sites for half-completed homes and markets. The thudding of hammers and clinking of picks, together with the raucous shouts of workmen, became a constant assault on their ears.

"It looks like King Lousis is taking advantage of victory," remarked Kaylia.

"If this is indeed the king's doing," countered Gewey. "They are building as though the war was already over and the threat of invasion gone for good."

"Perhaps it is," suggested Weila. "If this god Melek has completely destroyed the armies of your enemy, who can say differently?"

Gewey frowned. "The Dark Knight was dealt a devastating blow. But I don't believe his entire force has been destroyed. The danger remains and Althetas should be prepared."

When the city walls finally came into view, Gewey could not fail to miss a gigantic streamer flying high above the towers; it bore a silver sword set against the full moon—the sigil of Darshan.

Barely had this sight registered when he spotted half a dozen soldiers on horseback racing toward him. Two of these were carrying tall banners, also bearing his sigil. Gewey groaned with despair, and then again when he noticed it splashed across their breastplates as well.

They halted a few yards away and saluted in unison. A soldier with a lieutenant's red chevron on his arm dismounted and bowed low. He removed his helmet, revealing a youthful face and a mane of shimmering blond hair.

"Greetings, Darshan," he said. "Your arrival has been highly anticipated. King Lousis has sent us to lead you and your companions through the city to his manor, where a feast is being prepared in your honor." After another sharp bow, he remounted his horse.

Gewey looked down at Weila. "You should ride from here onward."

He thought back to the first time he had been within the walls of a big city, not long after Lee had spirited him away from his farm. He smiled inwardly at the experience the desert elf was about to have and hoped it wouldn't be too jarring for her.

Weila huffed but mounted her horse.

"If you become unsettled," said Kaylia sympathetically. "Try to keep your eyes focused straight ahead."

Weila straightened her back and steadied her nerves. "I am not a child. There is no need to worry." She then saw the kindness in Kaylia's eyes and her tight expression gave way to an appreciative smile. "But thank you for the advice. I'll remember it."

The two standard bearers rode ahead while the rest fell back. The gates to the city were flung wide, and even before they entered Gewey could see that the streets were lined with thousands of people, many waving tiny sword and moon flags. Atop the ramparts, twenty men with golden trumpets let out a mighty blast.

The crowd erupted with deafening cheers the instant they passed inside, causing their horses to stomp and rear nervously. Weila looked as if she was ready to leap off, but Kaylia calmed her own mount and then quickly reached over to grab hold of the other woman's reins. It took a few seconds, but Weila gradually regained her composure. She nodded to Kaylia in appreciation.

Flowers and silks were being thrown from windows, and the name *Darshan* was on everyone's lips. Guards lined the edge of the avenues to keep the crowd at bay.

"I suppose we should wave," said Gewey jokingly.

Kaylia frowned. "I think not."

Gewey glanced over his shoulder. Weila was staring straight ahead, her hands gripping the reins so tightly that her knuckles were white. Kaylia noticed this too and eased her horse close enough to reach out and take hold of Weila's hand. She did not resist the touch and mouthed a silent 'thank you'.

When they arrived at the king's manor, more trumpets rang out and the gates ceremoniously swung open. Lousis was standing immediately in front of the large, double oak doors. He was dressed in a white silk shirt with gold stitching, matching pants, and a resplendent purple cape fastened at the neck by a thick gold chain.

The king smiled broadly and held his arms wide apart in greeting.

To his left stood Nehrutu, and to his right, Aaliyah. Nehrutu was clad in a black satin shirt with matching pants. A long, thin sword with a jewel-encrusted hilt hung loosely at his side. Aaliyah wore a blood-red dress with a white sash tied around her thin waist. Their smiles were bright and friendly, but their eyes told Gewey a different story. Melek's influence was apparent, and he could feel anxiety slipping through the bond that Aaliyah had so closely guarded. She leaned over to Lousis and whispered something in his ear.

The trio dismounted and strode along the newly cobbled walkway to their waiting friends.

"At last!" exclaimed Louis, laughing boisterously. "The mighty Darshan, savior of the twelve kingdoms has arrived." He wrapped his arms around Gewey in a welcoming embrace. "And the beautiful Kaylia. Your light warms my heart and brightens my fair city." He kissed her hand. "Aaliyah has just informed me that you have brought a very special guest to my home. An elf of the desert." He turned to Weila. "Welcome. Word of your arrival will cause quite a stir among the elves in Althetas."

"I am Weila, Your Highness," she told him, bowing low. "I have been sent as an emissary until the rest of my people can join me."

"Yes," said Lousis. "We were surprised to see supply ships so soon after the fall of Baltria. But they were a welcome sight, to be sure."

Aaliyah took a step toward Gewey. "It is good to see you, my friend. We have much to talk about—after you have rested from your journey, of course."

Gewey nodded and forced a smile. "Indeed, we do."

Aaliyah embraced Kaylia, then looked at her belly and grinned. Next, she introduced Weila to Nehrutu.

Nehrutu looked at her with an odd, twisted expression. "You were correct. No flow at all."

"My people have rejected it," Weila explained proudly.

Nehrutu held up his hand apologetically. "Forgive my rudeness. Aaliyah told me, but I was unprepared for how it would feel. In any event, I am pleased to meet you. Our people reuniting from the desert and from across the sea can only be the design of fate. I look forward to knowing you better."

"As do I," agreed Weila. "And I pray that our reunion will give us the strength to defeat our enemy."

Lousis let out another hearty laugh. "Enemy? Thanks to Darshan, the enemy will soon be crushed throughout the whole of the world. We will see peace quite soon I think." He stepped back, allowing his guests to pass inside. "But we can talk of war after the feast. All of Althetas is celebrating your arrival. Such joy has not been seen among my people in quite some time."

"And what of Melek?" asked Gewey. Speaking his name caused his skin to crawl. "Will he be at the feast as well?"

"Of course," replied Lousis. "It was Melek who arranged it all, and he certainly wouldn't miss his master's banquet."

"I see," said Gewey. He didn't want to reveal what he knew until he had a better knowledge of the situation in Althetas. He also needed to know why Aaliyah had refused contact. "Where is Mohanisi?" he asked.

Lousis stopped with a jerk. There was an awkward silence.

"I'm afraid Mohanisi will not be joining us," the king eventually said. He spoke as if searching for each word. "A few unfortunate things have transpired in your absence."

"He is ill," Aaliyah cut in. "But you can see him after you have been shown to your rooms if you wish."

"Yes," said Gewey apprehensively. "If he's ill, perhaps I can help him." He wondered what illness could possibly have afflicted Mohanisi. His suspicions immediately turned to Melek.

Aaliyah sighed. "I doubt it. All that can be done has been done. He suffers from a malady of the spirit. It is rare among my people ... and incurable. Melek has already attended him and failed. But still, you are welcome to try."

Hearing Melek's name spoken so casually was disquieting. None of them knew the depths of the evil they were openly welcoming into their lives. The horrors Melek had unleashed upon the *firstborn*, the slaying of his own wife ... and his desire to kill the Creator *herself*. Gewey shuddered at the thought of what he might have in store for the world now that he was finally free from Shagharath.

"I will indeed try," he told Aaliyah. "And I would also like to speak with you privately *before* the feast."

Aaliyah nodded. "Of course. I will join you in your quarters in one hour."

Two young serving maids approached and beckoned for Gewey, Kaylia, and Weila to follow.

"Until tonight then," said Lousis.

Gewey and the others had only walked a few yards when the king called after them. "I forgot to ask. Why are Linis and Dina not with you?"

"They decided to remain in Valshara for a time," replied Gewey.

Lousis grinned roguishly. "I can understand why. I would much rather be in the company of High Lady Selena than in the beehive that has become Althetas." He sighed. "But alas, rebuilding what war has torn down requires my presence for the time being." He shrugged and waved his hand dismissively.

The serving maids led them upstairs and down a long corridor lined with a series of polished oak doors. Weila was given a spacious, beautifully furnished room, fully equipped with a shower. The sand master stared for a moment in awe at the sheer scope of it. She had stayed at a small inn near the docks while in Baltria, and even the rooms in Valshara, though far from uncomfortable, could not compare to the luxury that was now before her.

"I—I can't stay here," she stammered.

"Of course you can," assured Kaylia. "Don't worry. I'll help you settle in."

She turned to the nearest maid. "Is our room nearby?"

"It's the next one down," the girl replied.

"Well, that's most convenient," Kaylia said. She ushered a still uncertain Weila into her room, at the same time looking over her shoulder to flash Gewey an amused smile.

Gewey smiled back and moved down the corridor to their room. Once inside, he immediately stripped off his dusty clothes and turned on the shower, moaning with pleasure the moment the hot water struck him.

A selection of new clothes had been provided for both him and Kaylia in the massive wardrobe. After picking out a pair of tan pants and a white cotton shirt, he was just about to pull on a pair of suede boots when Kaylia entered.

"It's all a bit much for her," she said. "I do believe she would rather be in her desert hut."

Gewey laughed. "She'll get used to it."

Kaylia kissed his cheek. "You did."

She showered and picked out a pair of black pants, together with a red linen shirt that clung nicely to her athletic form. She was still searching for a pair of shoes when there was a soft knock on the door. Gewey answered. Aaliyah was standing in the hall, a sweet smile on her face.

"Where is Nehrutu?" he asked.

"Helping King Lousis to prepare for the feast," she replied.

They took seats around a breakfast table set just across from the enormous canopy bed. Silence hung heavily. Only the muffled sounds of the city making ready to celebrate could be heard through the closed window. Aaliyah looked first to Gewey, then to Kaylia, her smile never fading.

"He is not your enemy," she finally said. "He wants you to know this. He also wants you to know that he remains your servant, in spite of the lies you may have been told and your anger toward him."

Her words caused the hair on the back of Gewey's neck to stand up.

"And what lies might that be?" he asked.

"He didn't say. Only that there was a possibility you have been misled."

"And do you believe him?" asked Gewey, trying to maintain an even tone.

"I do," she affirmed. "He is here to help us. He has destroyed our enemy and saved my love. There is no evil in his heart."

"How did he save your love?" asked Kaylia.

Aaliyah told them of the battle, Nehrutu's wounds, and of Melek saving his life.

"I see," mused Gewey thoughtfully. "And what has he had you doing for him since then?"

"He told us to help the people of Althetas," she replied. Her voice was filled with contentment and pride. "We have aided as best we could by healing the sick and bringing comfort to those who have been displaced. He said that once the Reborn King has been destroyed, you and he will usher in a new age of peace and prosperity."

"I have tried to reach out to you," said Gewey. "Why have you kept me away?"

Aaliyah laughed almost girlishly, her usual reserved manner giving way to an inner bliss that was apparent even without their bond bleeding out her feelings. "Melek asked me to wait until you arrived."

"And you did as he asked without question?" Gewey's tone was hard and critical.

Aaliyah looked at him in confusion. "Why should I question him? His grace is why I still live ... why Nehrutu still lives. Why would he save us if he has ill intent?"

Gewey reached out through their bond. This time, she did not resist. Instantly, he knew that Melek had altered her spirit. It was slight and subtle, but it was there. It took him a few moments longer to understand exactly what Melek had done. When he did, he broke contact at once.

"You see," said Aaliyah. "I am as I have always been."

Gewey forced a smile and nodded. "You are indeed. But from here on, I would have you allow contact should I reach out. I may need you."

"I will be there," she replied earnestly.

Gewey pushed back his chair and stood. "Now, I would like to see Mohanisi."

Aaliyah rose. "I will take you to him. But I must warn you, his mind is not as it was."

She led them from the room and down the corridor. Mohanisi was being kept in a small room at the far east end of the manor. The door was guarded by two elves who clicked smartly to attention when they saw the trio approaching. Aaliyah gave them a nod, and they moved aside.

"I'll see him alone," said Gewey.

"Then be prepared," Aaliyah warned. "He may become violent."

Gewey nodded and opened the door. The interior of the room was barren, containing only a small wooden table, two chairs, a cot, and a few elf glow globes hanging from the ceiling. Mohanisi was sitting cross-legged in the center of the room, his eyes closed and his hands clutched together. His usual clothing had been replaced by a simple rough tunic and trousers. His hair was matted and clumped.

Gewey closed the door behind him and took a seat at the table. Mohanisi displayed no indication that he was even aware of Gewey's entry. He watched the elf for more than five minutes in complete silence. Finally, Mohanisi's eyes fluttered open, and he turned to Gewey.

"You cannot help me," he said. His voice was thin and raspy. "I am corrupted."

"How did this happen?" asked Gewey.

"When I brought Malstisos from the foul nightmare, the enemy had cursed him with, I brought the taint of it with me."

Gewey had been told of Mohanisi curing Malstisos from the Dark Knight's curse, but the details were sketchy at best. "And where is Malstisos now?" he asked.

"Dead," the elf replied flatly. "And better off for it. The darkness that claimed him would not be expelled. He took his own life to prevent himself from harming those he loves."

This news was a blow to Gewey. He had great affection for Malstisos and had always held him in high regard. "When did this happen?"

"Three days ago. He remained behind when I marched south to aid the king. His body was too weak to go to war..."

His voice trailed off and the muscles in his cheeks began to twitch.

Gewey could see that Mohanisi was fighting some terrible inner battle. The pain and madness in his eyes came and went from moment to moment. Gewey reached out to touch his spirit. At once, he felt the sickness that now ravaged his soul. It was as if thorny vines were working their way into the very essence of his being, slowly tearing him apart. Gewey shuddered to think of the agony the once powerful elf must be experiencing.

Mohanisi leapt to his feet, snarling and forcing Gewey to break contact. "If you wish to kill me, you will find I am not easy prey."

Gewey held his palm up in a calming gesture. "I only want to help you. Will you let me try?"

"Lies!" he shouted. "You are just like the others. Kind words and foul deeds. Stay away if you value your life."

Gewey eased out of his chair. "I cannot stay away. But you must believe me when I say that my only wish is to help you."

But Mohanisi wasn't listening. Letting out an ear-piercing cry, he rushed forward, fingers curled into savage claws. Gewey caught his wrists and twisted his body, allowing Mohanisi's momentum to throw him off balance. Normally, he would be a formidable opponent, but the rage caused by his sickness made him clumsy and undisciplined. Gewey kicked his feet from beneath him and threw him hard down onto his back. Before the elf could react, Gewey slammed his fist into his jaw. Mohanisi grunted, then fell into unconsciousness.

The door burst open and both Kaylia and Aaliyah rushed in.

"I'm fine," said Gewey. "I need more time."

Kaylia looked at him doubtfully. She had felt what was ailing Mohanisi through their bond and it had clearly horrified her. Aaliyah merely regarded the scene with quiet pity. After a brief hesitation, they retreated from the room.

Gewey closed his eyes and took a deep breath. Reaching into Mohanisi's spirit without encountering resistance showed him the true extent of the damage. The corruption was wrapped around his spirit, squeezing its way in to his very core and choking out the light of life. The more Gewey looked, the more he came to realize the horrible truth. This was no illness. This had been *done to him.* Melek's evil hand had been at work here.

He tried to cleanse Mohanisi's spirit, but the foulness fought him as if it was a living thing. He needed guidance. Gewey's mind raced back to the time when his soul was being revealed to him, recalling in detail the vision that had shown him extracting the last remnants of purity from Kaylia's tortured spirit. By focusing firmly on this memory, he was now able, little by little, to destroy the corruption within Mohanisi. For two hours, he meticulously removed every last remnant. Kaylia came in after the first hour and sat beside him. Feeling that the level of exertion was draining his strength, she gave him hers. When it was finally done, Gewey slumped over and rubbed the back of his neck.

Kaylia, although equally exhausted, managed to help Gewey to a chair. Mohanisi was still unconscious, but the strain on his face had vanished, and Gewey could feel that he was no longer in pain.

A few minutes later, Mohanisi's eyes opened. He struggled up into a sitting position to look at Gewey and nod his appreciation. "You have undone Melek's evil. I thought I was without hope. Thank you."

"Why did he do this to you?" asked Gewey.

"I don't know. But I was never convinced of his good intentions. Perhaps he knew this."

"And what of Malstisos? No one mentioned anything about him when we arrived."

"I cannot say. Melek told me that he had taken his own life. But I do not know if that's true."

Mohanisi went on to tell Gewey the details of what had happened on the Steppes. The retelling of Theopolou's death stung at his and Kaylia's heart, but she was glad to hear the story from a first-hand account.

"I'll find out the truth of what happened to Malstisos," Gewey promised. "But for now, I need you to remain here. I'll tell everyone you are still ill, and that I wasn't able to help you. If Melek discovers you are healed, he may try to hurt you again."

"Should I not tell Aaliyah and Nehrutu that I am well?" he asked.

"For now, no," Gewey replied. "I'm not certain about Nehrutu, but Aaliyah has been tampered with and I'm not sure that she can be trusted."

Mohanisi nodded his head and frowned. "Then good luck to you." He reached out and seized Gewey's arm as he was rising. "And if Melek *has* ensnared them, free my kin."

"I'll try."

Gewey opened the door and, together with Kaylia, stepped into the hall where Aaliyah was patiently waiting.

"I'm sorry," he said, feigning frustration. "There's nothing I can do."

Aaliyah placed her hand on his shoulder. "Thank you for trying. But I knew Melek was right. He is beyond hope."

"Yes," said Gewey. "Melek. I'm really looking forward to seeing him again."

CHAPTER 27

The banquet was due to begin just after sundown, though Gewey and Kaylia arrived early to take up the places especially set for them on a dais at the front of the hall. Weila, after finding the turmoil of their arrival a bit too much, had decided not to join the festivities. Instead, she was gratefully settled down in her room reading some books of elf tales that Kaylia had found for her.

To Gewey's disappointment, Melek was conspicuously absent so far; he had been hoping to see him before the celebration got under way. He cast his eyes around again. Banners bearing the sigil of Darshan were hanging everywhere, and a band of musicians were already filling the massive hall with their lively tunes, even though many of the guests were still to arrive.

By arriving first, Gewey had hoped to avoid fanfare. But as each new guest entered, they made a point of passing by his table and bowing low, praising his name in every imaginable way. This continued until King Lousis arrived and the hall was finally full.

The king was accompanied by Aaliyah and Nehrutu—also a young man Gewey had never seen before. His tousled blond hair, simple tan-colored clothing and boyish smile made him appear an unassuming figure when alongside the majesty of the king and the splendor of the elves. But Gewey knew exactly who he was the moment their eyes met.

The four of them stopped in front of Gewey and Kaylia to bow before taking their seats. Gewey's eyes never left Melek.

The corners of Melek's mouth turned up in the slightest of smiles. He spread his arms in a low, exaggerated bow. "It is so good to see you again, Darshan." His voice dripped with false cheer. "Your absence has pained me, as well as the entire city of Althetas."

Gewey forced a smile in return. "I am happy to be back."

"I told Melek that you were anxious to see him," said Lousis. "But the dear fellow insisted there were still preparations to be made."

Melek's seat was just on the far side of the king. He leaned forward and looked at Gewey with a humble expression. "I wanted things to be perfect for your arrival. Do you approve?"

"It is very nice," Gewey replied. He was simmering inside but somehow managed to keep his tone civil.

"Nice?" cried Lousis. "Why, this city has not seen such a celebration since the end of the Great War. People have come from many miles to celebrate your return and the defeat of the Reborn King."

"The Reborn King is not yet defeated, Your Highness," corrected Gewey. "He is merely halted for the time being. The war is far from over."

"My lord is too modest," countered Melek. "There is no army that can stand against him. And no mere mortal claiming kingship or godhood who can oppose his will. The Reborn King will soon fall and fade from memory. And it will be Darshan who is the instrument of his doom."

"Hear, hear," bellowed Lousis. "But let us not speak of war and hardship. Tonight we feast!" He raised his glass and drank deeply. Aaliyah and Nehrutu did the same, and though their smiles were friendly, their eyes remained guarded.

Lousis rose to his feet, the wineglass still in his hand. Trumpets instantly sounded from the four corners of the hall, silencing the crowd.

The king's voice boomed and reverberated from the stone walls. "We have gathered here on this joyous occasion to honor he who has delivered us from the foul grip of the evil that seeks to envelop the world. And though there is no way to truly express our gratitude for the strength of his spirit and generosity of his heart, I can say to all of you that I pledge my life, my honor, my kingdom—indeed all of the twelve western kingdoms—to his service."

Lousis raised his glass high. "To Darshan!"

Suddenly, everyone in the hall was on their feet, cheering and calling out Darshan's name. Wave after wave of unrestrained love and admiration washed over Gewey. It felt as though it was never going to stop. The king motioned for him to stand. He could see Melek's amused grin. His voice sounded in Gewey's head. *This is what you really want, isn't it? See how they love you ... how they worship you?*

"I would like to thank King Lousis for this honor," announced Gewey. "But in my heart, I know that there can be no victory without the courage you all have shown. And though we still have far to go, I know that the free people of this world, both human and elf, will see it through to the end. And it is I who is, and will ever be, at *your* service ... come what may."

"Praise Darshan!" shouted a single voice, prompting the crowd to explode into a renewed fervor of cheers and adulation.

With Gewey seated once more, the king held up his hands to call for quiet. "And now I would like to recognize

Melek, the emissary of Darshan. He has risen from the depths where he was cast after a foul betrayal—newly liberated to help deliver us from certain destruction."

Melek rose, hands folded in front of him, an embarrassed smile on his face. "You honor me, Your Highness. But I have only been the instrument of Darshan's will. When he bravely entered Shagharath to release me from bondage, I knew that a great and benevolent power walked the earth that would not, *could not*, be denied. Once, long ago, I lived in heaven as a god, but through my own weakness I failed to protect the people whom I cared for so very deeply. And for that, I paid a price beyond imagining. But now, what I left undone will be made possible. And it is all because of the strength and courage of my lord and master." His eyes drifted to Gewey. "All hail the mighty Darshan!"

Yet again, the crowd erupted. Gewey could feel the smug satisfaction coming from Melek. *What do you hope to accomplish with all this?* he asked.

Surprised at having his own thoughts invaded, Melek stiffened and shot him a bewildered glance, though he quickly relaxed before this was noticed by anyone else.

As the evening wore on, Gewey felt his anxiety continuing to grow. Melek made regular small talk with King Lousis and would occasionally whisper in Aaliyah's ear, but he made no effort whatsoever to talk to Gewey himself. When midnight arrived and the celebration was still showing no signs of ending, Gewey's patience was finally exhausted. He was on the point of getting up and demanding to speak with Melek privately when he heard a whisper from close behind him.

"Come, my friend."

The warmth of Melek's breath on his neck gave Gewey chills. Kaylia began to rise, but Gewey shook his head. "I must speak to him alone." She nodded her acceptance of this, even though he could feel her concern.

Melek made their excuses to King Lousis and led Gewey from the hall. Cheers and offerings of praise followed them out. Gewey remained silent as they headed to the main entrance, with everyone they passed on the way, either staring in dumb wonder or falling to their knees. This was not altogether surprising. Gewey could feel that Melek was allowing the *flow* of the spirit to form an aura around them.

When they exited the manor, the lights and sounds of the city celebrating momentarily stunned Gewey. The bliss felt by the whole population was overwhelming.

"Do you see?" said Melek, after they had walked through the manor gates. "You have made them so very happy."

"I have done nothing," countered Gewey irritably. "Your deceit has given them a false sense of security. And if you think to deceive me..."

"I intend to *educate* you," he cut in. "I forgive you for leaving me in Shagharath. You were misled by that ... human. She showed you false images and lies. Had I been aware of human power in Shagharath, I would have taken precautions."

"I do not need your forgiveness," snapped Gewey. "And what I was shown was the truth. Maybell did not, and would not, lie to me."

Melek stopped short to face Gewey, his eyes burning with suppressed anger. "Maybell is a mortal fool who thought she could be my master. What she showed you was distorted to fit her own designs. She could not fathom the depths of who I am—and neither can you."

Gewey met his gaze with equal fury. "Perhaps not. But I know evil when I see it. And I also know the malaise of madness."

"You think me mad?" Melek chuckled. "If I am, then it was caused by the same beings who trapped you in *this* miserable world. I still need your help, Darshan. And now that I am free, I know that you need mine as well."

"I need nothing from you," Gewey shot back. "You seek domination and death, and I will not be a part of that."

"You think you can defeat your enemy without me?" scoffed Melek. "You have no idea what you will be facing. We most certainly *do* need each other."

"I would never accept even the smallest aid from you, Melek." Gewey's rage was building.

Melek shook his head and smiled. "This argument is pointless. I must show you." A blast of wind lifted him off the ground. "Come."

Gewey watched for a moment as Melek disappeared into the night sky. Then, clenching his jaw, he used the *flow* of air to follow. He could hear Melek calling to him as he flew south at astonishing speed. He did his best to keep up, but was soon trailing many miles behind.

"You see?" said Melek's voice. It sounded as if he were right beside him, yet Gewey could sense his presence far to the south. "You have no idea how to use your abilities. Without my help, the storm you encountered would have destroyed your ship. And look at you now. Unable to even keep pace. I can change that. I can teach you all you need to know. I can show you powers that you never have dreamed of."

Gewey wanted to answer, but could find no words. He knew that Melek was right. Though he was now forcing the air to move him as high and fast as possible, he was still unable to catch up, even by a little. The wind roared in his ears and blasted cold across his face.

Guided only by the directions called out to him by Melek, he traveled on over a vast distance for more than two hours. Finally, he sensed that Melek had landed in a small clearing just a mile or so away from the shores of the Western Abyss. All along the beach, several thousand soldiers were camped. The stench of sweat and decay wafted on the breeze. He knew at once that they were from Angrääl; their fear carried on the *flow* like a cry for help. Something had terrified them, and Gewey thought he knew what.

He set down a few feet away from Melek, who was staring up at the night sky. A few clouds passed in front of the stars, briefly winking them out of existence before allowing them to reappear as bright and magnificent as ever.

"Do you know what they are?" asked Melek. "I do." His voice was distant. "I speak of the stars. I was there when they were created." He glanced down at Gewey and sighed. "There is so much I know. So many wonders. And I can share it all with you."

Before Gewey could respond, he felt the *flow* spring forth from Melek. But this time it was in a way he had never known before. It wasn't quite earth or air, nor water or spirit—but a strange and wonderful combination of all four. The ground trembled for a brief moment, then two pillars of earth pushed themselves up about two feet above the ground. They twisted, swirled and expanded, slowly taking the form of two chairs. Gewey gawked in amazement.

"Even such simple things are beyond you," said Melek. He sat down, motioning for Gewey to do the same. "But they don't need to be."

Gewey approached the chair and brushed his finger across the arm. It was as solid as granite, yet warm to the touch. When he sat, the seat gave way as if he were settling onto a soft pillow. He looked up at Melek, trying to mask a sudden feeling of inferiority.

"You have tremendous power, Darshan," he continued. "And considering your teachers, you have come far. But it is time for you to leave mortals behind you."

"I am as much a human as a god," Gewey contended. "And I am bound to this world. If you think I can simply turn my back..."

Melek held up his hand. "I don't expect that. Why do you think I have seen to it that you are to rule here once I am gone? If you want this world—take it. I have never desired this place, or its people. If you want to amuse yourself with humans and elves, I will not stop you."

"I have never wanted to rule. And the people of this world are not playthings put here for amusement." Gewey calmed himself and leveled his gaze. "I can't allow you to carry out your plans. The gods didn't wrong you, and war on the Creator is insanity. Can't you see this?"

Melek was unmoved. "The gods wronged us both. The *real* insanity is that you fail to understand this. As for the Creator ... *she* will fall, even if I have to tear down heaven to make it happen." His fists clenched tightly together, and for a moment, his eyes became wild. Then it was gone. He regained his composure and leaned forward. "You are not accepting the inevitability of your situation. You *cannot* win without me. And even if you could, what do you imagine is going to happen once heaven is free?"

Gewey thought, but quickly realized that he had no real idea.

"When they learn that you have freed me from my prison," Melek continued. "Do you really believe they will be forgiving?"

"I didn't free you," Gewey contended. "You escaped."

Melek laughed sardonically. "That won't matter. They'll hold you responsible, anyway. Then war with the gods will come in spite of all your efforts. And like me, you will fall." He sat back and folded his hands. "That is, unless you help me. Then we can both have what we desire."

Gewey couldn't help but see his logic. But the glimmer of a lie hiding behind his boyish smile was something he could not ignore. "Before we go any further, there is something I would ask."

Melek gave him a friendly grin. "That we are going further is encouraging. Ask your question."

"What did you do to Malstisos?"

Melek chuckled and scratched his chin. "He proved to be an entertaining distraction. Your enemy—the one you call the Dark Knight—had corrupted his spirit. Mohanisi healed him, but only to a point. His spirit was still weak and tormented. It was simplicity itself to wrench the information I needed from him." His expression was distant, as if recalling something amusing. "He screamed and begged for death, swearing to me that he knew nothing. Which, of course, he didn't. At least, not consciously. The funny thing is that he had no idea of what he really knew. The healing process had wiped most of the knowledge from his awareness. But I found it. It was still there, buried deep in the dark recesses of his mind."

"So you killed him?"

"Of course," replied Melek, waving a hand dismissively. "He had served his purpose. And I needed to know the extent of his kind's tolerances. He was a stubborn one, to be sure. I was amazed as to how much pain he could endure before madness took him. But don't worry. Everyone believes he has gone east." He cocked his head and shrugged. "Everyone but Mohanisi, that is. He knew what I had done, so I was forced to deal with him as well."

Gewey fumed and very nearly leapt from his seat. But he needed to know more. He took a deep breath to steady himself. "And what of Aaliyah and Nehrutu?"

This time, Melek burst into laughter. "Those two fools have actually sworn fealty to me. As if I would desire such service from those wretched mongrels. I saved the male after he had been injured in battle, and the female thought me her savior for doing so. I knew her to be your friend, so I used her to ease any fears of those I was unable to influence directly. I had planned on killing them both later. That is, unless you have some other use for them."

"You will not touch them," commanded Gewey hotly. "Or anyone else."

Melek scrutinized him for a long moment. "Before I agree not to harm your pets, I would show you something." He pushed himself up from his chair and rose skyward. "Follow me."

Before Gewey could object, Melek was racing away. Grumbling, he set off after him. A few minutes later, he found him hovering a few hundred feet above the Angrääl soldiers.

Melek waved his arm in a grand sweeping gesture. "Can you see them? Can you feel their weakness and fear? Are you not appalled that they would dare to challenge you? These festering boils on the face of the Creator actually had the audacity to count themselves your equal. But look at them now, huddled together, devoid of hope, groveling in the mud and slime like the worms they are. The mortals you care for are no different, and soon you will understand this."

Gewey knew what was about to happen. He flew forward to prevent it, but just as he was within reach of Melek, he stopped short. It was as if he had struck a wall. He dropped like a stone for several feet, only to be caught and held fast by invisible hands.

Melek looked down and shook his head. "Why are you fighting me? They are your enemies and not deserving of mercy."

Gewey struggled to respond, but his voice was muffled. Melek turned him over so that he could see the soldiers below. A massive blast of fire was slowly descending upon them. It extended for a mile across, turning the night into day. The terrified cries of the men below raked at Gewey's ears as the flames continued to fall. Then, when the blazing inferno was a mere twenty feet above the ground, it suddenly vanished.

Melek pointed to the vast mass of men running aimlessly around, trying to save themselves. "Do you see how they tremble? How they run?" He began to laugh like a child with a new toy. "I could burn them all if I wished. But then, what would that teach you? You are perfectly capable of doing the same thing yourself. No. What I have to teach requires a different method."

Gewey looked on in horror as Melek reached inside the soldiers ... thousands of them, all at the very same time. Almost as one, they fell to the ground screaming while he crushed them from the inside. Blood spewed from every orifice as they spent their last agonizing moments writhing and squirming, pleading for mercy. Then all was still.

"Impressive, yes?" asked Melek. He surveyed the carnage, clearly pleased with himself. "And that is just the beginning."

Gewey felt himself being released. He drifted to the ground well beyond the dead soldiers. The fury that he thought was banished in Shagharath had now returned tenfold.

Melek landed a few yards away. "I know you are angry," he said. "I can feel it. Though I confess, I don't understand why. But I will give you time to quell your rage before we go on."

Gewey glared at him. "You're a monster."

"And you still look at me with mortal eyes," countered Melek. "But I am no more a monster than the Creator who allows such pain to exist." He shook his head, grinning. "I can see in your eyes that you think you can challenge me. And if you had knowledge of your power, perhaps you could. But as it stands, you have no hope. In your heart, you know that to be true. Even if you could find a way, you would still fall in the end. Your enemy has in his possession four of the god stones. He has stolen their power, just as he did with the Sword of Truth. You *cannot* defeat him without my help." He rose up and spread his arms wide. "You can have all that you desire if only you join me. I give you until tomorrow to decide."

Gewey watched as he disappeared into the night, his mind filled with impossible choices. What if Melek *was* telling the truth? What if the Dark Knight *was* as strong as he said? What if the only way to save the world *was* to join with a creature equally as evil?

The journey back seemed to take an eternity, though, in truth, there were still several hours before the sun would break the horizon. Althetas was still glowing as he approached, the celebrating and mirth yet to cease. He landed just outside the king's manor, where he knew he wouldn't be seen. But just as he was passing through the main gates, he felt a sudden spasm of fear shooting through his bond with Kaylia.

Melek was with her!

He broke into a dead run.

The doors to the manor were closed, but that was never going to slow him down. He sent a blast of air ahead that had them flying open with such force that they almost came away from their hinges. The guards nearby were thrown from their feet, landing in the flower bushes that surrounded the base of the manor. Not that Gewey gave them even a glance. He navigated the halls with such speed that he was nothing more than a blur to passers-by. As he threw open the door to his room and reached for his sword, he realized that he did not have it with him.

Kaylia was sitting at the edge of the bed, staring intensely into the far corner of the room where Melek was leaning casually against the wall. He was staring right back at her with a look of deep contemplation in his eyes. Gewey quickly placed himself between them, poised to attack.

He reached back and touched Kaylia's arm. "Are you all right?"

"I am unhurt," she replied.

Gewey returned his attention to Melek. "What the hell are you doing here?"

"Trying to understand you," he replied calmly. "You have mated with this creature. You care for her. I am trying to understand why."

"Get out!" he shouted. "Now!"

"I mean her no harm," said Melek. "But tell me, do you care for her because she bears your offspring? If so, why are you allowing her to continue carrying it inside her? Why not simply speed up the process and be done with her?" He took a step forward and used the *flow* of the spirit to penetrate Kaylia's body and enter her womb.

She gasped and fell back, clutching at her stomach.

Gewey's rage exploded. He leapt at Melek with enormous speed, landing a fist solidly on his jaw. Melek's head twisted with a loud crack. He stumbled back, slamming against the wall. Gewey tried to land another blow, but this time Melek caught his wrist and spun him around.

Melek's physical strength rivaled his own, and his speed was far greater. Melek landed three solid punches to the abdomen that took Gewey's breath away. This should have been enough to cripple him, or at least slow him down, but the thought of what Melek might be doing to Kaylia and their child was enough to overcome the pain and drive him on.

Gewey's fist crushed into Melek's nose. Blood splattered, covering them both. Another blow landed on Melek's temple, this one hard enough to send him tumbling to the floor. The *flow* he was directing at Kaylia had ceased, but Gewey's fury was far from over. Seizing hold of Melek's collar, he continued to rain punches down on him.

"Enough!" shouted Melek. A massive burst of air sent Gewey reeling back. The room darkened and Melek slowly rose to his feet. "It is clear you cannot be reasoned with. Perhaps I have been looking to the wrong source for an ally. Perhaps your enemy will see my wisdom."

Gewey regained his footing, his temper still boiling. He wanted to continue with the thrashing, but couldn't risk Melek unleashing the flow once again. Not with Kaylia so close by. He glanced over his shoulder and panic gripped his heart. She was writhing in pain, her arms still wrapped tightly around her stomach.

"What did you do to her?" he demanded.

Melek was busy healing his own wounds, the blood already fading from his flesh and clothing. His angry expression turned to disgust and contempt. "Spend what time you have left contemplating your folly. Come sundown tomorrow, you will join me. If not, I will kill every living soul within the walls of this pathetic city."

"What did you do?" Gewey cried desperately.

Melek simply sneered and strolled casually from the room. Gewey gave chase, but Kaylia's cry of agony stopped him short and he rushed back to her side.

He reached within her, trying to see what Melek had done, and immediately felt his unborn child. The light of his spirit was pulsating rapidly. Little by little, he was growing larger. But something was aiding this growth—something unnatural. He could feel that his son was aware of this ... aware and afraid.

'Help me!' he cried out to Aaliyah. He was doing his best to calm Kaylia, but her breathing was rapid and he knew that she was terrified.

Barely a minute had passed when the door flew open, and Aaliyah sprinted into the room. Without hesitation, she pushed Gewey aside and set about examining Kaylia. Each second seemed like an eternity to him as she tried to determine the reason for Kaylia's pain and the sudden growth of their child.

"The baby will come soon," she said finally, taking a long, deep breath.

"Will he live?" gasped Kaylia, her face soaked in tears.

Aaliyah pursed her lips tight. "I don't know. As far as I can tell, he is healthy, but his growth has accelerated beyond anything I have ever seen."

"And what about Kaylia?" asked Gewey. He was afraid to hear the answer. He could feel the baby sending waves of panic through his mother as the growth stretched her to the limits of endurance.

"That will depend on how strong she is," Aaliyah replied, grim faced.

Kaylia reached out and clutched hold of Gewey's hand. "Protect him," she pleaded. "Whatever happens to me, protect our son."

"Nothing is going to happen to you," said Gewey, desperation bleeding through his tone. "I swear it. You and our child will both live." He looked at Aaliyah. "Watch over her."

Aaliyah nodded. "Where are you going?" she asked.

"To find Melek," he replied, a deep and menacing tone now in his voice.

Kaylia squeezed his hand. She gave a fragile smile. "I'll be here when you return."

Gewey leaned down and kissed her. He wanted to believe it. He truly did. Fear gripped him, but he forced it back.

Now was not the time for weakness.

CHAPTER 28

Gewey stretched out with his spirit, furiously searching for Melek but finding only a void staring back at him. He left the manor and scoured the city for a time, but to no avail. His heart sank. Melek could literally be anywhere, and he had no idea where to start.

The celebrations had finally withered to a halt, though the streets were still filled with streamers, trash, and drunken men incapable of making it back to their homes. Gewey had considered taking to the air to expand his search, but at present was unwilling to put too much distance between himself and Kaylia. Through their bond, he could feel her pain but took comfort that her life force remained strong. Aaliyah was still watching over her, even though there was little she could do other than share her own strength. Whatever Melek had done, it was unstoppable.

As he entered the temple district, he saw that a new temple was in the process of being built. Muttered curses slipped from his mouth when he realized that this latest addition was dedicated to Darshan. The other temples were as yet undamaged, which was mildly surprising considering Melek's all-consuming hatred of the nine gods.

By mid-afternoon, Gewey was forced to accept that Melek would only reappear at a time of his own choosing—at sundown if he meant to keep his word, though the place of their meeting was unclear. Gewey thought that it should be away from the city. Far enough away so that, should they do battle, others would not be hurt.

He returned to their room. Kaylia was sleeping, though not restfully. Aaliyah was sitting dutifully by her bed, holding her hand.

"The king was here earlier," said Aaliyah. "He wanted to say that Kaylia is in his prayers."

Gewey sighed. "Considering the entire city is praying to me, I don't think that will do much good."

Aaliyah gave no reaction. "So you go to face him?"

Gewey nodded. "I must."

"He will kill you," she stated flatly. "Unless you join him."

Gewey could still feel the touch of Melek's influence within her. "And would you mourn me if he did?"

"Of course," she replied, though without conviction. "But this is all unnecessary. He has already told you that the Reborn King possesses four of the god stones. How can you hope to win without his help? All he wants is to return to heaven. He will leave the earth to you."

"And that is where he and I are truly different," said Gewey. He looked down at his suffering wife. "I want only a small piece of the world. Not the whole thing." He leaned down and kissed Kaylia's forehead. Through the blankets, he could see that her belly had now tripled in size. "Regardless of where your allegiance lies, I hope that you will continue to watch over her until this is done."

Aaliyah bowed her head. "You have my word."

Gewey glanced at the window. The sun would be going down very soon; he should leave the confines of the city immediately. With a final loving look at Kaylia, he hurried from the room.

Once outside the city gates, he walked for a few miles along the road heading south, then entered the forest to the east. After a short time, he came to a small clearing where he sat on the soft turf and waited.

As the sun sank over the horizon, a few stars penetrated the twilight. Gewey remembered what Melek had said about knowing what the stars really were. *I should have asked him*, he thought.

Barely had this passed through his mind when the wind picked up and he could hear soft footfalls approaching from the south. A minute later, Melek appeared from the brush. His countenance was grim and his posture aggressive.

"So, have you made your choice?"

"I have," Gewey affirmed. He rose to his feet. "I cannot allow you to spread your evil here *or* in heaven. And I will not join you in destroying the gods ... or the Creator. I have to stop you, whatever the cost to myself."

Melek shook his head and scowled. "You will only succeed in dying. I really did not want to turn to your mortal foe for aid, but it would seem you are leaving me with little choice."

Gewey drew his sword. The steel sang its deadly song.

A look of vast amusement showed on Melek's face. "You think *this* is the battle you have come to fight? One with clumsy mortal weapons and brute strength?"

The world gradually turned darker until only the figures of the two gods were visible. Gewey could sense the strength of Melek's spirit growing to unimaginable heights. A ghostly mist rose from his opponent's back, rising and expanding until it was seven feet tall and twice the width of a man. Light flashed within the mist and began to solidify into the form of a massive warrior. Its armor gleamed with an unnatural light, while in each hand was a massive blade. The warrior's long, ghostly hair blew carelessly about, as if facing an ocean wind. Its face looked somewhat like Melek's human form, but was far more intimidating and powerful.

"Now do you see?" Melek's voice thundered in Gewey's ears. "You cannot win."

Gewey allowed his own spirit to rise up, but he was without armor or weapon. Looking down, he was no longer able to see his own body.

"You can't even find a way to fight me," Melek scoffed. "I think I will enjoy killing the son of Gerath."

He leapt forward with both swords raised to strike. Gewey jumped left, narrowly avoiding the blades splitting him in two. Melek laughed wickedly and gave chase. Again and again, Gewey was forced to dodge Melek's attacks. He thought to counter with his bare hands, but could see no openings that would not expose him to almost certain death.

Gewey sent a ball of fire at his adversary, but this passed through him as if he was without substance. Melek smiled and charged in again, now with even greater speed. A sword grazed Gewey's shoulder, sending him flying back. Though the ground was nothing but blackness, it jarred him to the bone as he landed. He touched the wound. No blood, but the spot where the blade had struck looked distorted and pain burned from deep inside.

Melek didn't give Gewey time to recover his feet, coming at him once again with both blades held high. All Gewey could do was raise an arm defensively, while at the same time bracing himself for the deadly impact. But just as the blows were falling, from seemingly nowhere, a shield appeared on his forearm. The swords crashed into this with dull thumps. With shock waves of pain shooting through his arm, Gewey scampered to his feet.

"You learn quickly," remarked Melek with approval. "A pity it will be your final lesson."

Gewey concentrated on envisioning a weapon, but was disrupted by yet another attack. Again and again, both blades collided into the shield. He could feel it weakening, and knew that in moments it would splinter.

One final blow exploded the shield into a million shards of sparkling light, throwing Gewey hard onto the ground once more. Melek moved in for the kill. As Gewey desperately rolled away from the fatal strike, the sword in Melek's right hand buried itself deep into the ground a mere inch away from his head. He sought to regain his footing, but Melek kicked him in the chest.

Snarling, Melek ripped his sword free from the earth. The tiny clumps of soil that came up with it were set aflame as they scattered. In this briefest of breathing spaces, Gewey managed to scramble to his feet. As he did so, he once again tried to manifest a weapon. This time, a sword appeared in his hand.

"Good," said Melek. "I was beginning to think this would be no challenge at all." Tauntingly, he waved Gewey in.

He was a fearsome sight. Confronted with such obvious power, the sword in Gewey's hand suddenly felt small and useless. Forcing this notion aside and steeling his nerves, he gripped the handle tightly and moved forward. In response, Melek relaxed his stance, lowered his weapons, and shot Gewey a knowing smirk.

Gewey hesitated, momentarily confused, but then recovered to swing his blade at Melek's neck with astonishing speed and precision. There was a blinding flash of light and a ring of clashing steel. As the light faded and vision returned, Gewey's heart chilled at the sight of his own blade now firmly in the grip of Melek's gauntlet.

"Farewell, Darshan," Melek hissed.

He tossed the captured sword into the air, where it immediately exploded into a million tiny sparks. An instant later, Melek's own sword reappeared back in his hand. The hilt of this crashed into Gewey's jaw. His second sword swung at Gewey's chest, its blade digging two inches into his spiritual flesh. Searing pain screamed its way through every fiber of his being as he fell to the ground yet again.

Clutching at his chest, Gewey let out a blood-curdling cry. But through all the agony, a single thought still prevailed. Now there was nothing to stop Melek—or the Reborn King.

The world around him became visible once again as his spirit receded back into his body. Melek, in his earthly form, was only a few feet away, laughing triumphantly, a small dagger in his hand. Gewey wanted to move but was completely paralyzed.

"You are beaten," Melek chided. "There is nothing left for you but death. Continuing to struggle is useless and embarrassing." He strolled up beside Gewey as if he hadn't a care, kneeled beside him, and held the dagger above his throat. "I could shred your spirit while it is still clinging to this disgusting mortal form if I so chose. But as I am merciful, I will end your earthly life first. It is less ... distressing that way."

Gewey glared at Melek with unfathomable contempt and defiance. He wanted to speak, but his voice had abandoned him. He closed his eyes and sent Kaylia a final wave of love through their bond.

The words *I'm sorry* would be the last thing she would hear from him.

Basanti crept through the forest with as much speed as she dared. She prayed that her information was accurate. Everything depended on it.

The open air felt good on her face—the scent of grass and trees was a refreshing change. She was now only a few hundred yards away from the clearing. If she ran, she could be there in an instant, but that would risk showing herself prematurely. She listened carefully for the others. They were there and in position. Melek had arrived too and was speaking to Gewey, so all she could do was wait and hope.

Her wait was soon over as the two gods clashed. Basanti immediately picked up her pace, striving to time her arrival as planned. But the suspicion that Melek was aware of her presence refused to go away. It was only with a tremendous effort that she was able to push aside her fear. Melek could easily end her life in an instant.

She arrived at the clearing just as Gewey's body crumpled to the ground. He had lost, but was thankfully still alive. For how much longer, though? Melek was kneeling over him with a dagger at his throat, about to finish matters.

At that critical moment, twenty Vrykol rushed in from the cover of the trees. Unconcerned, Melek merely glanced over his shoulder, a knowing smirk on his lips. Before the Vrykol had taken even half a dozen paces, he'd raised his hand and simultaneously ripped out the spirit from each and every one of them.

Basanti had already drawn her dagger and was running headlong at Melek from the opposite direction. He spun around and was about to tear her spirit out too when an arrow whizzed through the air, striking the Oracle in the right thigh. She stumbled and fell to her knees just in front of Melek's feet.

Shaking his head, he sneered at her. "Did you really think you could surprise me?"

From the tree line strode Aaliyah, bow in hand. Melek nodded in her direction. "Your help was unnecessary. I knew they were coming."

"I apologize," she said, bowing low. She walked up and stood beside Melek. "But when I learned of the plot, I had to act."

Ignoring Aaliyah, Melek turned his attention to Basanti. "You are different from the others. Created by one of my children. Though which one, I can't tell." He bent down and jerked the arrow from her leg. Basanti cried out in pain. "A pity they didn't make you stronger. Killing you is no challenge."

"Felsafell," whispered Basanti. "What did you do to him?"

"Ah, yes." Melek smiled broadly. "The *firstborn*. He is unharmed as of yet. Though I will not be able to tell him the same of you. For now, he is locked safely away in the cellar of the king's manor. But rest assured, I will attend to him soon enough." He cocked his head and laughed softly. "I must admit that the use of your enemy's creatures in an attempt to distract me was ... creative. For that, I think I will let you die without your lovely head on your shoulders."

"Demon," she spat. "Shagharath was too kind a sentence."

Anger flashed across Melek's face. He nodded to Aaliyah. "Kill her."

Aaliyah dropped her bow and unsheathed a long, thin sword that hung at her side. She looked down at the Oracle with stone determination and unyielding resolve. Basanti closed her eyes and prepared to die.

Then, everything changed. In the blink of an eye, Aaliyah spun around—her blade, instead of delivering death to Basanti, cut through the air directly at Melek's throat. But fast as she was, Melek would not be taken off-guard. Swiftly ducking beneath the sword, he struck her savagely on the temple with the hilt of his dagger. Aaliyah stumbled back, clinging desperately to consciousness.

"I thought you might betray me," Melek told her. His voice was cold and emotionless. "I should have altered your spirit completely." He shrugged. "Little matter. I'm tired of these games. It's time to end this."

Even as he spoke, a tall figure rushed from out of the trees and leapt at his back. Basanti knew instantly that it was Felsafell. Melek jumped forward, easily avoiding the attack. He spun around to face Felsafell and gave a mocking laugh.

"Did you imagine I would not sense your approach, *firstborn?* You are no more of a threat to me than the rest of these fools."

He was still laughing when his body abruptly went rigid, as if struck by a thunderbolt. His eyes flew wide apart in a macabre mixture of stunned surprise and horrific realization of the fate about to befall him. For a long moment, he remained locked in this position.

"*Now* it ends," said Weila. She was standing directly behind Melek, in her hand the Fangs of Yajna that she had just jabbed into his back.

All at once, Melek's limbs collapsed. His body crumpled lifelessly to the ground, only the grotesque expression mirroring his final living thoughts still frozen on his face.

Weila regarded him briefly with a satisfied smile, then leapt over the body to kneel beside Gewey. Aaliyah quickly joined her and began examining the damage to Gewey's spirit. He was still in extreme pain and unable to move or speak, but her reassuring glance helped to calm him.

"There is no permanent damage," Aaliyah said, brushing back his hair.

Gewey mouthed Kaylia's name.

"Nehrutu, Linis and Dina are watching over her."

Gewey smiled weakly and nodded.

Aaliyah looked back at Basanti. Felsafell was tending to the arrow wound in her leg. "I'm sorry," she said. "But if I hadn't shot you…"

Basanti laughed, then winced as Felsafell tightened the bandage. "Yes, I know. I would be dead. You did the right thing. And don't worry, I'll heal in no time at all. But I am curious about how you were able to be freed from Melek's influence."

Aaliyah looked at the dead god's body and scowled. "Melek was unable to understand how the bond between Gewey and myself works. Such things were unknown to him. They didn't come into existence until after the elves became a race. By then, he was already locked in Shagharath. Gewey merely allowed me to hear their conversation on the night of the banquet. The moment I learned of Melek's intent, his influence was broken." She pursed her lips. "I am fortunate that he did not alter me beyond my ability to resist."

"And praise the Creator for that," Weila added. "The plan would have never worked without you."

Aaliyah cocked her head. "Me? It was you who held the key to it all. Your rejection of the flow made you invisible to him and allowed the distractions to work."

Weila paused, her expression reflective. "It makes me wonder if this is not all a part of the Creator's design."

"Yes, I wonder that too," agreed Aaliyah.

Felsafell finished treating Basanti and kissed her on the cheek.

"Can Gewey be moved?" she asked.

"He can," said Aaliyah.

After helping Basanti to her feet, Felsafell went over to Gewey and lifted him in his arms.

"I must go on ahead," said Aaliyah. "I need to be with Kaylia." She smiled at Gewey. "She will give birth very soon. But you needn't worry. Her body is strong and her will to live even stronger. All will be well."

"A good day," remarked Weila. "Your baby comes, your wife will survive, and one of your enemies has fallen."

Gewey managed a smile.

"We should keep what has happened to ourselves until after Gewey has healed," Aaliyah warned. "Melek has influenced many, including the king. For now, we should simply say that we do not know of Melek's whereabouts."

"But how will we explain Felsafell?" asked Weila. "It was hard enough for *me* to accept what he is. And he won't exactly blend in."

"We will remain hidden," said Basanti. "Once we near the gates, you must attend to Gewey."

Gewey groaned. "I—I think. I—I think..." His voice was muffled, as if he were speaking with his mouth covered.

Weila laughed. "If that sentence ends with 'I can walk', then Melek must have bashed the sense from your head. I may not have the strength of a god, but I can manage your weight long enough to get you home."

Aaliyah took her leave and raced toward the city.

Basanti and Felsafell departed when a quarter mile away from the gates, leaving Weila to heft Gewey over her shoulder. On seeing them approach, the guards quickly procured a wagon to carry him. They eyed Gewey with confusion, but Weila commanded them to remain quiet about what they had seen, and had them accompany her to ensure that they did.

By the time they reached the manor, though still unable to walk, Gewey was capable of speaking a few words. He ordered the guards to stay at the entrance, reaffirming to them that they should remain silent about his condition. As they moved on inside, Weila was beading with sweat and grunting from the exertion of bearing his not inconsiderable weight. Much to her relief, two soldiers quickly came to their aid and took over in helping Gewey to his chambers.

Kaylia was still sleeping, though more peacefully than before, with Aaliyah seated beside the bed holding her hand. Linis and Dina helped Weila to strip Gewey of his clothing, then laid him beside Kaylia.

"It's good to see that you live," said Linis with a friendly smile. "I am beginning to believe that fate is your ally, my friend." Wrapping his arm around Dina, they stood there together watching as Gewey drifted off to sleep huddled up close to Kaylia.

Gewey awoke slowly. The light shining through the window told him that it was late in the afternoon. Kaylia was still beside him, though now awake and smiling sweetly. Her belly was full and round and ready to birth their son.

She leaned over and kissed him. "Aaliyah says that whatever Melek did, it has not injured our son ... or me. But I will give birth within the next day and cannot leave this bed until then."

Gewey was relieved beyond measure. "How long have I been asleep?"

"Only a day," she replied. "Aaliyah has tended us both, aided considerably by Mohanisi and Nehrutu. They say that the damage to your spirit has already healed—also that Melek's influence over the people is slowly fading now that he is gone."

"That's good to hear."

The door opened and Linis stepped inside. He took one look at Gewey and laughed exuberantly. "I see you are feeling better now."

Smiling, Gewey slipped from out of the bed. His legs were unsteady at first, causing him to grab hold of the bedpost until able to gain his balance. Once stable, he embraced his friend tightly. "Thank you."

Linis raised an eyebrow. "Why thank me? It was not I who faced a mad god and lived to tell the tale."

"No," said Gewey. "But it was you who saved me. You and the others. I assume that was the secret you were all keeping."

Linis held out his hands and shrugged his shoulders. "What else could we do? Both the Oracle and High Lady Selena feared that if you were unable to keep our plan from Melek, we would be undone."

"She may have been right," Gewey admitted. "I still have a hard time imagining his power. It was far beyond anything I expected. But what about Aaliyah? I had hoped by allowing her to hear Melek's plans that she would be able to overcome his influence, but I was never entirely sure if this had been successful."

Linis chuckled. "Oh, your plan worked well enough. Once she was free of him, she searched the manor and found Felsafell locked away in the basement. I was supposed to break in and rescue him, but she beat me to it. Without her, I don't think we would have succeeded."

Gewey nodded approvingly. "That leaves me with only one question. The Vrykol?"

Linis's smile vanished. "I'm afraid you have the Reborn King to thank for that. Apparently, he had no more desire to have Melek walking the earth than we do. He sent word that he would deliver us with enough Vrykol to provide a distraction."

"And you accepted?" exclaimed Gewey.

"We were left with little choice," explained Linis. "They arrived in Valshara, and well ... they insisted. They said if they were killed, more would come. They knew of a place within the temple where they could hide from Melek's sight. As it happened, the Oracle was able to hide there as well. Though I did pity her being forced to stay in such foul company. As it turned out, the room was entirely unknown to the High Lady. A fact that she was none too happy about."

Gewey considered this information. The Dark Knight had once been a member of the Order of Amon Dähl, so it was likely that he'd gained this knowledge during that time. He smiled inwardly at the sheer absurdity of the situation.

"Still," he said. "It's amazing that you were able to beat Melek. And fortunate that Weila was among you to strike with the Fangs of Yajna."

Linis nodded. "Yes. Without her, I am sure we would have failed."

"Gewey!" cried Kaylia.

Gewey spun around. Kaylia was smiling, but only doing so through a wave of pain.

"Aaliyah was wrong," she said, straining through each word. "It won't be one more day."

It took a moment for Gewey to grasp her meaning; his eyes shot wide and his heart began to pound with panic. Before he could think of what to do, the door flew open and Aaliyah raced to the bedside. Her manner was relaxed and her face glowed with joy as she took Gewey's hand and kissed his cheek. She then turned her attention to Kaylia.

Linis touched his shoulder. "Come, my friend. We should not be here." Seeing Gewey hesitating, he added: "She is well tended. Elf men are not welcome during the birthing."

"I am no elf," Gewey pointed out, moving to take up position beside Aaliyah. "And I will not leave her."

Kaylia looked at him, her eyes filled with love. Her lips turned up into a sweet smile. "Yes. I want you here."

Aaliyah looked over her shoulder at Linis. "You, on the other hand, can go."

Linis bowed and gave Gewey's shoulder a squeeze. "I will be just outside if I am needed."

Gewey didn't hear Linis's words. His attention was on Kaylia and the life she was about to bring into the world. A life they had created together.

A life that he would do anything to protect.

CHAPTER 29

Though the room was filled with his friends, Gewey could neither see nor hear them. He was transfixed. The whole of his world rested inside a soft cotton blanket he held in his arms.

His full head of hair was raven, just like Gewey's, but his skin held the deep bronze tint of his mother. Sleepy ice-blue eyes opened and closed as they gazed at his father.

Only Kaylia's touch was able to tear Gewey's attention away. She looked both exhausted and blissful. Gewey carefully handed their son over and wrapped his arm around her shoulders.

"Do you have a name?" asked Dina.

Gewey looked up, suddenly aware that Aaliyah, Nehrutu, Mohanisi, Linis, Dina, King Lousis, Weila, and Nahali were all surrounding the bed. Their faces beamed. With a rush, he wished that Lee and Millet were also there.

Kaylia brushed a finger across the baby's cheek. "Jayden." She looked up at Gewey. "It means the light of heaven."

"Jayden," Gewey repeated softly.

"A fine name," said Linis.

"Fit for a god," added King Lousis.

Dina stepped close. Tears fell down her cheeks as she gazed at the dozing infant. "He's perfect," she whispered. "Just perfect."

There was a long silence as everyone watched Gewey and Kaylia holding the baby, Jayden. Eventually, Aaliyah stepped forward and demanded the gathering's attention.

"Kaylia needs rest," she stated firmly. "And so do I."

Everyone took their turn to congratulate the proud parents, then reluctantly filed out of the room. Aaliyah was the last to leave, pausing to examine both mother and child one final time before departing.

"You realize this changes things," said Gewey.

"I know," Kaylia replied. "And though I swore that I would never leave your side, I feel I must break my oath. To take Jayden into the jaws of death is beyond comprehension. And that is where you must now go."

"I will leave you both well-guarded," he promised. "I sense that Melek's hold on King Lousis has nearly disappeared. Mohanisi may have had a hand in that, I suspect—or perhaps Aaliyah. But I can leave you in his charge without fear."

"Once you go east, I will not remain in Althetas."

"Where then?"

"I will go to the home of Theopolou," she said firmly, though recalling the loss of her uncle caused his name to stick for a moment in her throat. "It is well hidden and easily defended. There are those among the elves in Althetas who still serve his house, and they will serve me faithfully, too."

Gewey thought on this for a time before nodding his agreement. "Very well, but I would want to send more than just Theopolou's elves. And no one can know where you have gone."

"Lord Chiron and Lady Bellisia should be returning from Skalhalis soon," said Kaylia. "They can provide me with any additional help I may need."

The idea of being parted brought a huge sadness to Gewey. All of a sudden he wanted to take his wife and child and run, though to where he didn't know. Only with great effort was he able to push unhappy thoughts from his mind. "That is something we can discuss later," he said. "For now, let's just pretend that this moment will last forever."

Kaylia tilted her head and smiled. "Yes, let's do that."

Gewey entered the council chambers. Though sad to be parted even for a moment from Kaylia and Jayden, he knew that he must discuss plans.

Kaylia was not interested in joining him. Her focus was completely on caring for their child, at least for the time being. Talk of war and darkness could wait for a bit longer.

Gewey could feel that his bond with Kaylia had now extended to Jayden, though in a different way. It was just as powerful, yet in some respects more distant. He remembered what his father had once told him on one of the anniversaries of his mother's death. Gewey was only five, and couldn't understand why his father was sitting in his chair staring at her picture.

"Did you love her more than me?" Gewey had asked. A silly thing to say—that is, unless you're a five-year-old boy who wants nothing more than his father's love. And though Harman never withheld his love, on that night every year, he was distant and inconsolable.

"No, son," he had said, wiping the tears from his face. "But my love for her was different. You are my son and I love you beyond your understanding. From the first moment I saw you, I knew you were mine, and that nothing could ever change that. But your mother…"

He cleared the lump from his throat. "She was not mine. I was *hers*. From the very first time she looked at me, I was helpless against her power. She chose me above all others, and for that, I have always felt unworthy." His father's smile was sad, yet it had still comforted Gewey. "Son. One day, you will meet someone who captures your heart in ways you never thought possible. You'll love her beyond reason. And when you are blessed with a child, you'll do anything to protect it. You would face a horde of demons, and your wife is the one person who would stand by your side while you did it. This bond you will share is stronger than any other. It is a mutual love, joined in a way only parents can understand."

Harman's words had never made much sense to him before. Now it was clear. Their love for Jayden strengthened their love for each other. That she would give her life—as well as sacrifice his—to protect their son was the greatest love imaginable. He pictured her cradling Jayden in her arms and felt the warm rush of happiness filling his spirit.

The sound of the chamber door closing behind him snapped Gewey back to reality. King Lousis, Aaliyah, Nehrutu, Mohanisi, Weila, Linis, and Dina were already sitting around the table.

He took a seat directly across from King Lousis. "Is there any word from Lord Chiron and Lady Bellisia?"

"Not yet," replied Lousis. "They're not due back for another few days."

The door opened and a nervous-looking guard hurried over to whisper something into the king's ear. The king nodded, and the guard scurried away. A moment later, the door opened again, this time for Felsafell and Basanti to enter. Felsafell wore a long purple robe with undulating gold patterns stitched down the front and around the cuffs. His silver hair flowed carelessly down his back, shimmering in the warm lamplight. Basanti was dressed to match, though, with tiny white flowers decorating her hair.

Neither Dina nor the king had ever seen Felsafell before, and the sight of him clearly made an impact. Dina gasped audibly, while Lousis simply stared in wide-eyed wonder.

They took seats alongside Gewey. The chairs were not designed for someone of Felsafell's unusual height, so it took a moment for him to settle himself.

"I can see that ... my appearance has ... upset you," Felsafell said. His words came out slowly, as if each syllable was an effort. "Please pardon ... my ... speech. Your language is ... difficult for me ... as you speak it. And I ... did not wish the voice ... of the old hermit to utter forth ... from the lips of my true form. Basanti knows my thoughts ... and will speak for me."

Lousis cleared his throat and shook his head. "Do not be concerned. I was told of your coming. And that you would be ... different. And your manner of speech is perfectly fine. I have heard your name spoken of many times over the years and the fact that you always talked in riddles. I am pleased that you will be plain."

"Felsafell speaks the language of his kin," explained Basanti. "Gewey understands him, as does Kaylia. But when he tries to speak in your common tongue, the metaphors and symbolisms sound odd to your ears. A fact he has used to great advantage for countless generations in the guise of a crazy old man."

"You're beautiful," was all Dina could manage to say.

Felsafell smiled and lowered his head in a slight bow.

"As you already know," Basanti continued, "I am the Oracle of Manisalia. Felsafell and I are here to aid you in your hour of need."

Lousis leaned back in his chair and clasped his hands in front of him. "Fables and myths come to life under my very roof. It is said you are a thousand years old, Oracle."

"I am far older," she asserted. "Only Felsafell is my elder in this world. It was he who spun the legend around my name back in a time when humankind had barely left the sands of the East and the elves were still a savage race. But now is not the time to hear our story. Melek is gone, and Angrääl will soon move against you. His armies are driven back, but the king remains on his throne."

"What would you suggest we do?" asked Lousis.

"There can only be one ending to this war," said Gewey. "I must face the Dark Knight and destroy him."

Basanti nodded in agreement. "That much is certain. But as Melek told you, the Dark Knight has found four of the nine god stones. If he has learned to use their power, you may be no match for him. Melek knew this and tried to use it as leverage against you."

"But can Melek's word be trusted?" asked Linis.

"In this case, I believe so," Basanti replied. "Melek hoped to force Felsafell into telling him where the other stones were hidden. And if he had succeeded, he would have killed every one of you. He would have had enough power to accomplish all of his goals without Darshan's aid."

"Then why enlist my help to begin with?" asked Gewey. "Why not simply find the stones and be done with it?"

"He couldn't be certain they are still intact," she replied. "Nor could he be certain that Felsafell knew of their location—not until he'd had enough time to break him. He suspected that Felsafell knew, but if it turned out he was wrong and the stones really were lost, he would be without an ally other than the Dark Knight himself. And seeing as how Melek detested mortals, he would only do that as a very last resort."

"He certainly did enjoy playing with our lives and minds," spat Lousis.

"Yes," agreed Basanti. "But the thought of joining with a mortal in a common cause seemed to be more than his palate could endure. Which is why he sought to persuade Gewey. Only when he was convinced that Gewey would not join his campaign did he try to destroy him."

"And do you know where the rest of the stones are?" Dina asked Felsafell.

Felsafell nodded. "I do. But they will ... not be easy ... to retrieve."

Basanti touched Felsafell's hand while passing a few words to him in the ancient tongue.

"Felsafell will guide Gewey to their locations," she said, turning back to the others. "But should the Dark Knight learn of this, he will move to stop them."

"What do you suggest?" asked Linis.

There was a long silence.

King Lousis began to laugh quietly to himself until he had the attention of the entire group. "There is only one way to distract him." He waited for a moment. All but Basanti and Felsafell looked perplexed. The king heaved a sigh. "We will march on Angrääl. To the very gates of Kratis."

"You can't be serious," said Dina.

"It's the only way," Basanti told her. "And many will perish. But unless Gewey finds a way to defeat the Dark Knight, the numbers will be far greater. And he will not stop here." She looked at Aaliyah and Nehrutu. "Eventually, he will cross the Abyss and raze your cities to the ground."

"I don't understand," Dina interjected. "If the Dark Knight is so powerful, why doesn't he seek Gewey out now? Why not just kill him and be done with it?"

Basanti shook her head and held out her hands. "I wish I knew. Perhaps he has the same motive as did Melek and intends to turn Gewey to his cause. There is no way to know; I truly wish I did. But for whatever reason, he has chosen to remain hidden and locked away in his fortress. And for that, I am glad. It gives us precious time."

"And who will go with you?" asked Linis. He saw Dina's jaw tighten and her fists clench.

"Gewey and I ... will go ... alone," said Felsafell.

Dina was visibly relieved.

"And what of Kaylia and your son?" asked Aaliyah.

"She will go to a location known only to those who accompany her," answered Gewey. "There can be no risk of discovery."

"Then you can tell *me* later," she shot back. "For I will be with her ... and Jayden."

Gewey was both pleased and relieved to hear this. He had hoped for as much. He would send an army if he could. The thought of Kaylia and Jayden being so far from his protection was becoming ever more unnerving.

"It will take some time before I can muster an army for such a march," said Lousis. "At least a month or two."

"Then I intend to spend what time I have left with those I love most," announced Gewey. He pushed back his chair and stood up. "You will forgive me if I leave the rest of the details to you for now."

"Of course," said Lousis. "I would do the same. Go be with your wife and child."

"I will check on Kaylia and Jayden later," said Aaliyah. "We can speak about her plans then."

Gewey nodded and left the hall. One month, perhaps two, to spend with his wife and child. That was all. After that, there was no guarantee he would ever see them again and he would not waste a moment of the time he'd been granted.

Kaylia was sleeping soundly while holding Jayden to her chest. He was cooing to the rhythm of his mother's breathing. At the sound of Gewey's entry, Kaylia's eyes cracked open, and a smile crept upon her face.

"Two months," said Gewey. "Then I must leave."

He recounted the details of their plan. Kaylia nodded approvingly.

"I must say I am happy that Aaliyah will be with us," she said. "And that Felsafell is to be with you."

Gewey removed his boots and slid into bed. Whatever may happen in the future, and however this war might end, at least they would have this time together. And though the Dark Knight may have stolen vast power from the gods and heaven, he would never have enough power to make Gewey give in. Not when he had so much to protect. He wrapped his arms around his family and closed his eyes. Their spirits combined with his.

"If this is all we get," Gewey whispered, while kissing Kaylia's ear, "it is still more than I could have hoped for."

"This is not all," she promised. "Soon, the vision you saw of us living in your home in Sharpstone will become reality. I know it."

Gewey looked down at Jayden. His tiny fingers were clenching and relaxing, his eyes tightly closed. Determination swelled in Gewey's heart. He would make this world safe for his son.

Even if it cost him his life, the Dark Knight would fall.

End Book Five

BOOK CLUB QUESTIONS

1. Who is your favorite character? Why? And what about them make them enjoyable to read about? Has your favorite character changed since the last book?

2. How well does the author follow the formula of the hero's journey while making the story unique in its own right? Has the journey held true from book to book?

3. How well developed do you feel the character arcs are? And how do you think they develop throughout the book and series?

4. Do you feel Gewey will be the savior he is prophesied to be or will he succumb to the temptations of power? Have your feelings on this changed since the last book?

ACKNOWLEDGMENTS

Jonathan and Eleni Anderson, George Panagos, Vincentine Williams, Gerald and Donna Anderson, Hunter and Sarah Anderson, Bobby and Bobbie Anderson, George Stratford, The Ramos family, the DiBatista family, Helen Paton and "K", Cassidy Webb, Tom Riddell, Jen Frith-Couch, Alex Harris, Chris and (Fancy) Nancy Jones, Jacob and Elizabeth Bunton, Jenny Bunton, Kitty Bullard, and everyone who has supported me.

I love you all!

ABOUT THE AUTHORS

Brian D. Anderson was born in 1971 and grew up in the small town of Spanish Fort, AL. He attended Fairhope High, then later Springhill College, where his love for fantasy grew into a lifelong obsession. His hobbies include chess, history, and spending time with his son.

Jonathan Anderson was born in March 2003. His creative spirit became evident by the age of three when he told his first original story. In 2010, he came up with the concept for The Godling Chronicles. It grew into an exciting collaboration between father and son. Jonathan enjoys sports, chess, music, games, and, of course, telling stories.

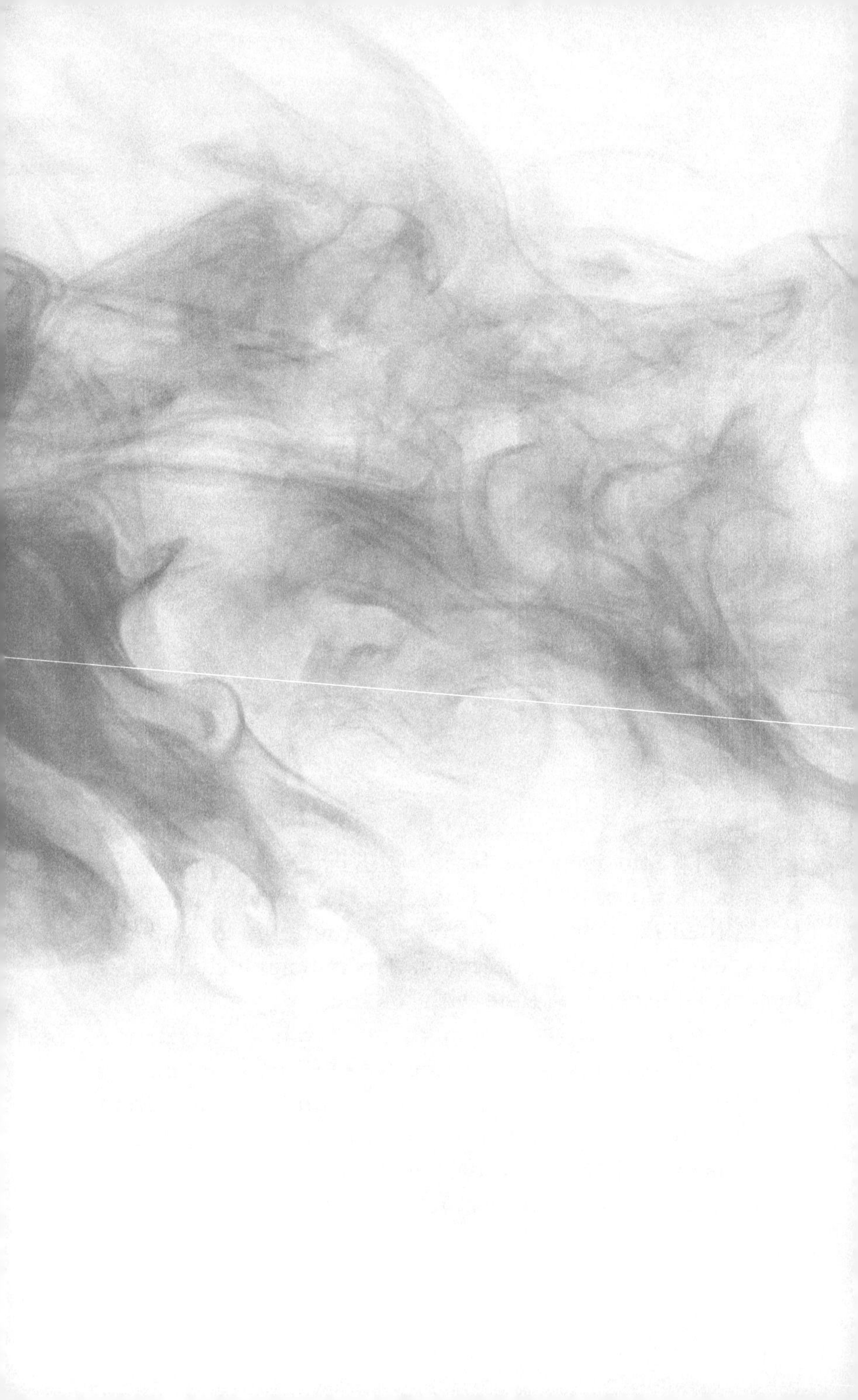

Discover more at
4HorsemenPublications.com

10% off using HORSEMEN10